To Professor, with Love

Linda Kage

To Professor, With Love

Contact Information : linda@lindakage.com

Publishing History
Linda Kage, May 2014
Print ISBN: 978-1497518094

Credits
Cover Artist: Kage Covers©
Editor: Stephanie Parent
Proofreader: Brynna Curry at Sizzling PR

Published in the United States of America

*D*EDICATION

For all the English teachers who taught me to love
literature:

Mrs. Coltrane, Mrs. Harris, Mrs. Sand,
Mrs. Lomshek, Mrs. Hefley, Mrs. Elrod,
Mr. Cooper, Mrs. Tilley, Mr. Parsons, Mrs. Lee,
Ms. Halloran, Dr. Spitzer, Ms. Washburn,
Dr. DeGrave, Dr. Carlson, Dr. Hermansson,
Dr. McCallum, and Dr. Teller.

Thank You.

CHAPTER ONE

"Begin at the beginning," the King said, very gravely, "and go on till you come to the end: then stop." - Lewis Carroll, Alice's Adventures in Wonderland

~NOEL~

A SICK NAUSEA SWIRLED through me as I stared at the paper in my suddenly clammy hand.

She'd given me another D. I'd actually tried, too. I had planted my ass in a chair, focused all my attention on the assignment, and typed out the complete required five pages of crap. There hadn't been a single plagiarized line in the entire essay either.

And it had all been for another fucking D?

"Unbelievable," I gritted out under my breath.

"Did you say something, Mr. Gamble?"

I lifted my face from the big red D on my paper to find dark eyebrows arched in smug supremacy. A shrewd green gaze penetrated me, daring me to question my score.

Jaw locked, I shook my head, my neck so stiff from the lie I barely got it to move. "Nope," I said, my voice low enough it was barely audible. "Didn't say a thing." *Not one damn thing.*

Dr. Kavanagh eyed me a second longer, her expression gloating. I knew my narrow-eyed glare and clenched teeth only fed her ego, but I couldn't help it. I also couldn't help the way my stupid, betraying man-whore eyes sought her ass when she turned and continued up the row between desks to hand out the rest of her graded papers. Fortunately, the hem of her frumpy suit jacket dipped down to cover the back of her skirt, hiding any feminine curves she might have, because I'm not sure I could've fully appreciated a nice ass at the moment.

But being rejected from the view only pissed me off more. It figured she would give a guy a sucky grade and then deny him the pleasure of ogling some tight, rounded goodness. Didn't matter how ridiculous she looked in that getup either—kind of like a little girl invading her grandparents' closet to play dress up—an ass was an ass, and I wanted a glimpse. Blame my Y chromosome.

Eyeing her huge shoulder pads and her sleeves rolled up to her elbows, I was tempted to tell her the eighties had called, wanting their blazer back. It'd probably coax a derisive laugh from the class. I'd maybe even get her to blush or some shit, which would sure as hell make me feel better for the way she'd just humiliated me. Tit for tat and all that. But my jaw refused to unclench enough to form actual words.

Seriously, how dare she give me another D after all the work I'd put into her stupid assignment? Did she realize how hard I'd tried, how much I needed a decent score?

"Psst. Hey, Gam." Oren Tenning, my favorite

first-string receiver and roommate, leaned across the aisle to get my attention. "How'd you do?"

I rolled my eyes in the irritated universal symbol for *don't ask*. "You?"

"Another C. I swear Kavanagh is afraid of handing out an A."

"I got an A." Sidney Chin, the ultimate teacher's pet, twisted in her seat to wave her paper merrily in our faces.

As the scarlet letter at the top of her essay flashed by, I noticed there was also a plus sign attached to it. There had been no such positive mark beside my D.

Tenning snorted. "That's because you have tits, honey. I swear to God, Kavanagh must be a dyke. She doesn't give an A to anyone with a dick, especially if he's on the football team."

I winced at his offensive retort, wondering how long it'd take before one of his stupid-ass comments got him into trouble, even as I silently agreed about the football part of what he'd said. Kavanagh had treated me like a dumb jock from the moment she'd discovered I was the university's starting quarterback. It was completely beside the point that I *was* a jock and not at all academically inclined. But I *tried*, damn it. Wasn't like I blew off the work for better things; I'd actually put a lot of fucking effort into making a good grade.

Did she have to so gleefully rub my shortcomings in my face?

"If anyone has questions about your grade, feel free to see me after class." Her voice rose above the hushed conversations echoing around the room, making me roll my eyes.

Yeah, right. I bet I could go see her about my score. She'd probably turn my D into an F if I questioned her hallowed opinion.

But Jesus Christ, what the hell was I supposed to do now?

Rubbing the center of my forehead as a headache started, I tried to calm myself because this wasn't the end of the world just yet. It was barely March. I still had time to repair my grade, but holy freaking hell. With each paper I'd written in this class, I'd put in twice the effort, only to get half the score. I was going to lose my scholarship if I didn't pull at least a C in Modern American Literature. And I needed this scholarship. More than I needed anything.

"Since *The Great Gatsby* is now out of the way, we're going to begin Steinbeck's *The Grapes of Wrath* next. I want everyone to read the first hundred pages and make a few notes about how the theme of changing your dreams is important in the text. We'll discuss our discoveries the next time we meet."

As she blathered on about symbolism and some other writerly crap I didn't get, I flipped open the book to the back where biographies were kept so I could scan Steinbeck's details. When I realized good ol' John had been born in 1902, I snorted. What part of over a century old made this *modern* literature? Jesus.

"...and with that, I hope everyone has a great weekend." Dr, Kavanagh's chipper voice grated against my already pounding temples. "See you guys next Tuesday."

Oh, I was sure *she'd* have a grand weekend. She was about to ruin the life of her least favorite student. All was roses on her end of the spectrum.

As people around me gathered their things, I shoved my worthless essay into the depths of my bag along with my English book, wondering why I'd even bothered to try. Who was I kidding? I wasn't cut out to graduate from college. I was already defying fate by making it this far.

You're a nobody. The voices of all my grade school and high school teachers echoed through me. *You'll never amount to anything, just like your trailer park trash whore of a mama.*

"Hey, Noel baby." The silky, feminine voice that startled me out of my rising panic made me jerk my head up as I approached the exit.

I couldn't say I was disappointed to find a pair of football groupies closing in on me, though, hmm, I hadn't realized I shared this class with these two ladies. In fact, I wondered if they even took Modern American Literature or if they were here merely to see me. It wouldn't be the first time random girls had followed me into a class they didn't take. It kind of came with my image.

"You look all depressed." Tianna Moore ran her hand soothingly up my arm as she pressed against my side. "What's wrong, handsome?"

Tianna was an experienced groupie, and I'd hooked up with her a few times. Leaning into her, I welcomed all the sympathy I could get. "I didn't make the grade I was hoping to get on my paper."

"Oh, you poor thing, you." Her fingers tickled my elbow, then my shoulder. When they landed at the base of my neck where she cupped the back of my head, she swayed closer. "Want me to kiss it all better for you?"

Exhaling a sad sigh, I shrugged. "You could try, I guess."

She touched her lips to mine, and I let her. I loved the warm, wet feel of anything feminine. When she opened up and pressed her tongue into my mouth, I obligingly tangled it with my own. My dick stirred with a pleasant hum and I cupped the side of her face to continue the contact before another pair of hands grabbed me and tugged me away.

"I want to kiss it all better too, Noel."

Not one to disappoint a lady begging to kiss me, I broke away from Tianna to glance at the second girl. I knew her face but couldn't remember her name. A vague, blurry image of her at some wild after-game celebration told me I might've hooked up with her too, but I couldn't be positive about this one.

Curious if I remembered her kiss, since I was kind of a connoisseur of kisses and could always recall a notable mouth, I bent toward the redhead and let her wrap her arms around my neck before she stuck *her* tongue in.

No fond memories rose, but she was a little more enthusiastic than Tianna had been, making me think maybe I hadn't bagged her yet, but she wanted me to, hence the reason she was so avidly giving me a resume of her oral accomplishments.

And she would *not* be getting a D.

A sharp clearing of the throat shot a bolt of pure testosterone down my dick, making every nerve ending I possessed crackle like a live wire. I pulled away from hottie number two, blinking myself back to reality, curious to discover the source of that strangely rousing sound...until I glanced toward the instructor's podium.

Dr. Kavanagh watched the three of us making out in her room with narrowed eyes and a mouth puckered in prim disapproval. The sight should've shriveled up my budding arousal like a bucket of ice-cold water straight to my junk, but alarmingly, seeing her watch me suck on some other girl's tongue only juiced me up more.

Not for the first time, I wondered how old she was. Vinegar and piss must really preserve a body, because there was no way she could be as young as she looked. I definitely would've carded her if she'd been a stranger who'd come into the bar where I worked. Without a wrinkle in sight, her lips had that fresh, inexperienced plush look about them, making them young...and incredibly kissable.

Which was an unexpected, disturbing thought I wanted to scrub from my brain with acid and a wire brush. What freak thought about their most detested teacher that way? Still, that mouth lacked age lines that would cup an older woman. She had to be in her early twenties, even though that couldn't be possible.

"Excuse us." I smirked as I curled my arms around both Tianna and her friend and escorted them from the lecture hall.

Kavanagh might be like every other educator in my life who'd told me I was shit, but here, in this world, I was a king, and I needed my groupies to help remind me of that. The girls giggled and snuggled in around me, more than willing to oblige.

"Want to come to lunch with us, Noel?" Tianna asked, rubbing my back, while her friend smoothed a palm over my chest. "We have something especially tasty for you up in our room."

Her companion snickered at the not-so-hidden double meaning. "You're into *sandwiches* aren't you?"

Oh, hot damn. A threesome. I was tempted. I mean, what guy wouldn't be? A couple hours between the sheets with a pair of no-strings-attached beauties *would* ease my nerves, a lot, but...

I winced. "I really shouldn't. I have another class I can't miss." I couldn't afford to flunk one course, let alone two.

"Are you sure?" the redhead asked, her fingers trailing downward now. "We'd make it worth your while."

I caught her hand so she couldn't tempt me into changing my mind just as my cell phone vibrated in my jeans pocket. Offering her another apologetic cringe, I shrugged. "I'm sorry, sweetheart, but...rain check?" *Please.*

Her wide smile was instant. "Of course."

"All right, then. I look forward to it." Grinning, I swatted her on the ass, nudging her along. Tianna hooked her arm through the redhead's, and the two girls strolled away.

With a wistful sigh, I stole a moment to enjoy

their firm backsides sheathed in tight denim as I blindly dug my phone free. I answered, unable to take my gaze from the snack I'd just turned down.

"What's up?" Even as I spoke, my eyes tracked those swaying hips. Maybe I could meet up with them later today because seriously...a threesome.

"Noel?" The girl on the other end of the line sniffed. "Colton's sick. He won't eat or get out of bed. I don't know what to do."

Alarm, thick and instant, roared through me, immediately ripping my thoughts away from sex. "What's wrong?"

I plugged one ear with my finger and turned my back to the sprawling campus to move away from the sidewalk. The shadow of a small tree growing by a row of perfectly trimmed hedge didn't provide the privacy I would've liked, but it would have to do.

"I don't know. He has a fever of a hundred and four and says his throat hurts."

I closed my eyes and rubbed my face. Fuck. "Have you called the doctor? Is he drinking enough fluids? Where's Mom?"

"*I don't know.*" Caroline exploded into a round of sobs. "She hasn't been home all week. Colton begged to stay back from school yesterday and since he hadn't missed yet this year, I thought it'd be okay. But he's worse today and—"

"Okay, okay." Out of habit, I lifted my hand to stop her, even though I knew she couldn't see me. "It's going to be fine. Just calm down. He probably has strep throat or something like that. See if you can get him to take some Tylenol and water. Get that fever down. I'll contact the doctor's office and find out if they can see him today. Call you back in a few."

I hung up on my sister before she could pile any more shit on me. Caroline had been forced to shoulder a lot of responsibility after I'd left home, but I was doing the whole college bit and gunning for a pick on the NFL draft for *them*, so I could take care of her and our two younger brothers.

Because our mother sure as hell didn't give a shit.

Relieved I had saved the number of Colton's pediatrician in my phone after last year when he'd gotten chicken pox, I dialed the receptionist and was grateful they could fit him in for a late afternoon checkup.

When I called my sister back, she sounded calmer. "Thanks, Noel. I'm sorry I freaked on you. I just—"

"Hey, no apologies. I know what it's like, remember? And that's what I'm here for. Just let me know what the doctor says. Oh, and wait, do you have any money for the appointment or medicine they'll prescribe?"

She sighed. "Yeah. I have...a little tucked away."

I winced. From her reluctant tone, I knew she'd have to take from her private stash she'd probably been hiding from Mom. That was what I'd always had to do.

"What were you saving for?"

"Nothing," she mumbled.

"Caroline." The warning in my voice made her sigh again.

"I just...there's a sweetheart dance coming up at school. And Sander Scotini asked me go. I was hoping I could afford a new dress—"

"Wait, wait, wait." I shook my hand to stop her. "Hold up. Sander *who*? Do I know this kid? Why have I never heard of him before? Is he your boyfriend or just a date for this dance?"

"Noel." I could practically hear her rolling her eyes, but I didn't care. It pissed me off that this was the first I was hearing of her and some *guy*. I didn't like the idea of any horny dick sniffing around my pure, innocent little sister.

"And did you say Scotini? As in *Terrance* Scotini,

the tire king?" A visual of the commercials I'd watched on TV when I was growing up flashed through my head. Terrance Scotini liked to stroll through his store, wearing a dorky cape and crown, telling his audience to shop at his place for all their automotive needs.

"His son," Caroline quietly admitted.

The hairs on the back of my neck spiked with concern. I knew my sister was nearly eighteen and almost legally an adult, but she was still my little sister. Always would be. I didn't want some rich prick's son thinking she handed things out for free just because she was Daisy Gamble's daughter.

"Is he—?"

"He's nice," she stressed. "And he likes me for me, okay. I know what you're thinking."

"What? That no piece of slime ball shit bag will ever be good enough for my little sister?"

She laughed. "Yeah. Something like that."

"What about his parents?" I pressed, still not liking the idea in the least. "Are they okay with all this?" Because if they treated her with anything less that absolute respect, I'd snap. I'd just...snap.

After a quiet pause, Caroline admitted, "I don't think they know."

I groaned. "Car—" Her situation already had trouble written all over it.

"Don't," she pleaded. "Please. It's just one dance. He's nice, and fun, and I know we'd have a good time together. That's all."

That wasn't even close to being all. I hadn't been born yesterday. I knew if some punk, high school douche was defying his parents to take the poor, trailer park girl to a dance, there had to be a hell of a lot more going on. I was ready to borrow my roommate's truck and drive the eleven and a half hours back home so I could kick some rich Scotini ass.

But I didn't want a miserable sister. I wanted her

to have as much fun in her worn-down, hopeless life as possible. Forbidding her from attending a dance wouldn't put a smile on her face. Besides, she'd probably go anyway, and since I was seven hundred miles away, I couldn't exactly stop her.

Rubbing one side of my aching temples, I forced myself to cool it. It was better to play friend than asshole big brother; that way, she'd come to me if she did get herself into trouble. "Okay. All right. But you'll let me know if *anything* happens, right?" Damn, I was such a pushover.

"Of course." I could tell she was smiling, which helped loosen the knot in my chest.

I nodded and turned back toward the campus, not ready to face the obstacles in my own life but determined to do so anyway. "Let me know how much you have to spend today too. I'll make sure you're reimbursed before the dance. All right?"

"Okay. Thank you. You're the best big brother ever, Noel."

Chuckling, I moved toward the sidewalk. "And don't forget it. Take care of Colton for me."

I smiled as I hung up, even though a heavy ache pierced my chest. Talking to one of my siblings always made me miss home.

Okay, I didn't exactly miss the hole-in-the-floor single-wide trailer where I used to sleep each night, always worried what kind of trouble my mother might bring home—if she even bothered to come home—but I sure as hell did miss the three underage kids still stuck there. My smile faltered.

Shoving down the gnawing guilt and not-for-the-first-time feeling that I'd abandoned them, I realized I'd forgotten to ask about Brandt. In her previous what-do-I-do phone call, Caroline had been freaked about a couple ruffians who'd been hanging around the thirteen-year-old. The last thing we needed was for our middle brother to get caught up in drugs or a

11

gang. Or both. Jesus. That would be my luck.

"Hey, Gamble. Wait up."

At the call, I cringed, wondering what catastrophe was going to strike now. My bad-shit karma usually came in threes, and since I needed something else to even up the score, I braced myself for the last item to get in line with my D essay and worrisome siblings.

When I turned, however, I only found Quinn Hamilton, a freshman tight end, jogging to catch up. I relaxed. "Hey, man. What's up?"

"I was wondering if you were going to the training session tonight or in the morning."

During off-season, the football team had mandatory sessions to train in the weight room. Since I worked every evening I was available, I usually opted for the early morning workouts before class. It only afforded me three or four hours of sleep on the nights I worked, but to keep my athletic scholarship, sleep was overrated. I had three very special people relying on me to keep it together.

"I'm a morning bird, didn't you know?" I playfully shoulder checked the freshman as I lied. I'd never been a morning bird. I hated mornings. I'd sleep in every day if I could.

"Cool. That's what I'm doing too." Quinn scratched the back of his neck and glanced away, letting me know he had something more important to ask. "And I was hoping you could —if you wanted to— um, show me a couple throwing techniques."

I lifted my eyebrows. Shit. Was this bad karma number three? "What? You looking to steal my position?"

Though a small fissure of dread and panic caught me unaware, I grinned and threw my arm around Quinn's shoulder to let him know I was teasing, though honestly, I didn't want competition. I already had a second and third-string QB foaming at the mouth for my spot. What was worse, Hamilton had fucking talent, and I could see him making a better quarterback than the spot he held now. He had never quite fit as a tight end.

As long as he wasn't better than me, I could handle this.

Quinn blushed and ducked his head. "I played quarterback in high school," he admitted.

"Hey, that's cool." I squeezed his shoulder in reassurance. "You need to do what's best for you. Who knows? If Dr. Kavanagh has anything to say about it, I'm well on my way to being academically dismissed. We'd definitely need another QB then."

The freshman blinked until he realized I was joking...or, at least, half joking. Then he grinned. "You have a class with Kavanagh, too? Man, she's harsh."

"Yeah," I agreed wholeheartedly, "a total, raging bitch." Not that I actually considered her a bitch per say. She was just tough and stuck by her guns in a classroom, which I kind of respected. But it was so much easier to blame her for my sucky grades than admit I just wasn't smart enough. So, yeah. Let's call her a bitch.

From nearby, someone let out a shocked, sputtering cough.

Fuck. For some reason, I knew I wouldn't need three guesses to figure out who'd just heard me. Enter karma number three. Already fearing what I would discover, I glanced around to focus on Kavanagh herself walking along the path directly behind us.

I could actually see my D dwindle to an F even as her green-eyed glare latched onto me.

Well, shit. Whatever happened next, I refused to let her see how crappy I felt for letting her overhear what I'd just said.

CHAPTER TWO

"She looked at nice young men as if she could smell their stupidity." - Flannery O'Connor, *Good Country People*

~*A*SPEN~

I CAN'T SAY I WAS surprised to hear Noel Gamble call me a bitch. I would've been shocked if he'd actually defended me.

No, really, she's an amazing teacher; I've learned so much from her. I feel as if her impact on my life has helped improve the quality of who I am as a person.

Yeah, that was never going to happen.

Still. His insult—even expected as it was—stung. The sound I made was unplanned. It just sort of tore through my chest and gurgled from my throat in a pained choke.

When Gamble and his little disciple swung around, I felt caught in the act, even though I'd done nothing wrong. An embarrassing heat flooded my limbs. Wanting to die before I let him see me hurt, I schooled my features as tightly as possible, reining in my expression as I arched a silent eyebrow.

"Let me guess," I murmured coolly, or at least in a tone I hoped sounded glacially chilled, as if I didn't care about his opinion, because the last thing I wanted him to think was that I cared...about him. "You're a little put out about the grade you received on your paper today."

His powder blue, almost periwinkle, eyes went flint hard as they narrowed. "You know, it's like you can read my mind, Dr. Kavanagh."

He didn't look apologetic for being caught bashing me. He didn't sound embarrassed. He didn't even pretend to feel an iota of remorse. He merely looked pissed. I wondered if he'd known all along I'd been walking behind him and he'd *wanted* me to hear his insult.

Next to him, the football player who took Introduction to Literature from me jerked a step away, disassociating himself from his beloved quarterback. Smart boy.

Faking a gracious smile, I nodded to my nemesis. "Well, maybe when you receive *your* PhD, you'll obtain the fine art of telepathy too, Mr. Hot Shot Quarterback."

His baby blues sizzled with loathing as his jaw shifted when he clenched his teeth. We both knew his academic achievements would never climb so high; he was only here because of football. In fact, I bet if I checked his records, I'd find something like basket weaving as his major. But Gamble was a fighter. He refused to lie down and take my verbal punches.

"If getting a doctorate turned me into a raging bitch who flunked undeserving underclassmen for no reason whatsoever, then I'd just as soon pass. Thanks."

Notching my chin high, I scowled right back. "Like I said in class, if you have any questions about your score, you can always discuss it with me. I'm in my office every day from three to five, available to speak with any *serious*-minded pupil."

From the distaste in his gaze, I knew he'd never go anywhere near my office. Thank God. Being closed inside my cramped little workspace alone with him would send me into a panic—literally, as in short-of-breath, need a paper bag to breathe into, full-scale panic attack. He reminded me way too much of Zach.

What was worse, he even affected me the same way Zach initially had. I loathed the way his gorgeous eyes made my body heat with all kinds of inappropriate responses, just as much as I hated how the curve of his lips made me want to touch my own mouth, wondering what the two would feel like straining together. Most of all, I detested how I'd never gotten over my high school obsession of fixating myself on the lead jock.

It must be some internal, natural selection thing I couldn't control. Survival of the fittest lured me into gravitating toward the strongest, healthiest, most attractive male in the pack who seemed most appropriate for reproduction of the species. After watching those two sluts maul him after class a few minutes ago, I knew he had to be good for some scintillating reproductive activities.

"Maybe I will," he murmured.

And Lord above, even his voice affected me. It caused something low in my abdomen to clench and then buzz. Like the silent vibration of a doorbell. *Ding dong, anyone home? Want to come out and play?*

God, why did my body want to play with this asshole in any way, shape, or form? Hadn't my first disaster with a star football player during my senior year of high school taught me anything? He was exactly the kind of person I needed to stay as far away from as possible.

And why was I attracted to a student, anyway? A *student*!

It didn't matter that we were practically the same age, he was still an undergrad. The entire attraction was completely unethical. And I had always been ethical. Professional. Hell, I'd come out of the womb proficient at calm, sensible, and orderly. I had followed every rule and policy to a T. No one, and I mean no one, knocked my world askew the way those freaking football hotties did.

This was exactly why boys who sent my insides haywire pissed me off. Big time.

"Then I guess I'll see you in my office later today," I challenged and immediately veered off the sidewalk to march away from him. I was going in the wrong direction now, but I didn't care. I had to escape.

Gamble's derisive snort followed me, telling me he knew I was running scared. The arrogant douche thought he was all that just because he was an athlete, a treasured football star. Okay, so everyone on campus treated him that way, from students to teachers and even the president of the university. To them, Noel Gamble could do no wrong. To me, he still couldn't write a decent English essay to save his life.

But I didn't want to think about him anymore. Blocking all things blue eyed and cretin from my brain, I marched on. After growing up with my parents, I'd mastered the small talent of shoving away unsettling thoughts. And I was particularly grateful for the technique now.

Thinking of the book I'd begun this morning, I focused on where I was going. Since I was headed in the direction of the student union and had an hour to spare before my next class, I decided not to head out to my car to fetch my jacket as I'd originally planned because I'd been chilled in the classroom, where it felt as if I'd been standing directly under the air handlers. I popped into the union and bought a sandwich and cappuccino from the food court.

It was an unseasonably sunny day, so I ate on a bench, warming myself under an oak tree where the spring air was coaxing a wealth of green buds to sprout among its branches. I liked how pockets of sunshine stole through the limbs and splashed warm puddles of color in the grass around me.

Comforted by the cozy umbrella of shadow and light, I pulled out my Kindle and took up reading the story I'd started before leaving for work today. A hopeless romantic, I was currently devouring everything Jennifer L. Armentrout.

Two chapters and half of my ham and cheese sandwich later, just when I'd decided Alex had to hook up with Aiden soon, my cell phone buzzed from my briefcase I was using as a makeshift table. It took me a few seconds to sweep it clean of food, crumbs and ereader before I could snap the lid open and check my caller ID. When I saw my parents' names on the screen, my stomach clenched.

I cleared my throat and took a deep breath before answering. I could do this. I could do this. I could do this. "Hello?"

"Hello, Aspen." Just hearing my mother's voice, frigid and businesslike as always, made my heart thump hard in my chest with a combination of hope and intimidation. "As you know, your father had his last treatment this morning."

Swallowing the suddenly dry piece of bread I'd been chewing, I nodded. "Yes, I...I was going to call after my last class today. How did it go?"

In the past two years, my father had needed to get three toes amputated. His diabetes had progressed so badly he'd just finished a six-week stint of oxygen therapy, visiting a hyperbaric chamber twice a day, to heal from a nasty gash he'd gotten on his calf. If the sore hadn't healed after his last treatment this morning, his doctor wanted to take his leg next, from the knee joint down.

Holding my breath for the prognosis, I waited tensely for my mother to answer. "They want to extend his therapy another two weeks."

I exhaled a lungful of air. "Well, that's...that's good." *Right*? At least they weren't ready to pull out the ol' saw and start chopping off limbs yet.

"Really?" My mother's tone suggested she was frowning with her usual pinched-eyebrow expression.

Oh, shit. Maybe that wasn't so good.

"And how is this *good*, Aspen? Your father's health is still at risk, and you're...rejoicing?"

I flushed. Even at twenty-three and living eight hundred miles from home, teaching at a top-notch university, I still gave her the power to render me into a blubbering moron with a single question.

"I..." Fumbling blindly, I used my napkin to pat my face free of stray crumbs. My palms began to sweat, so I rubbed them dry too. "I just meant—"

"Stop being facetious. Your attempt at humor is completely uncouth and disrespectful. This is nothing to jest about."

"But I didn't mean..." Biting my lip, I hung my head, wishing my hair were down so I could conceal the tears glistening in my eyes. God, why did words to defend myself always fail me when Dr. Mallory Kavanagh attacked? "Yes, you're right," I murmured. "I apologize."

She sniffed in irritation. Not quite a pardon. "I just knew studying that rubbish *literature* would transform you into some kind of vulgar imbecile. You should've listened to us when we tried to steer you toward theoretical physics. Something sensible and worthwhile."

Studying literature *had* been my one great rebellion, and neither of my parents had ever forgiven me for it. Briefly, I'd been tempted to appease them by going into the sciences, but I'd never been able to betray my devotion to the written word. And the one thing I hadn't acquiesced to had led to their eternal scorn.

If it had been up to me, I would've been satisfied with a bachelor's degree in English. I would've been fine sharing my love of stories with first graders. But I'd gone all the way through a doctorate program to mollify Richard and Mallory.

It didn't seem to matter what I did, though. Neither of my parents had ever been "proud" of my accomplishments. They had never shown approval. They had always pushed for something bigger and better.

But their constant disapproval was becoming tiresome. For once, I wished I could simply be *good enough* in their eyes.

Sadly, today obviously wasn't going to be that day.

"One would think with your *degree*, you'd be able to master what words come from your mouth with a little more respect and decorum."

"Again, I'm sorry. I—"

"Apologies are for the flawed, Aspen. Stop highlighting your imperfections." She let out a disgusted breath. "I'll update you on your father's prognosis again when I deem it necessary."

She disconnected the line before I could get in another word.

"Crap," I muttered. Who knew how long it would be before she stooped to call me again. I knew she wouldn't answer if I tried to patch back through to her with an eloquent apology that didn't actually sound like the apology of a "flawed, imbecile" daughter.

I just hoped she'd be merciful enough to keep me updated about my father.

This time when I lifted my napkin, I dabbed the

base of my lashes instead of my mouth. I had another class to teach in fifteen minutes; I didn't want to show up with wet, swollen eyes or a runny nose. If my parents had taught me anything, it was that a dignified image meant everything.

But damn it, I wished I knew why I always let my mother's words get to me. I should *expect* her chilly, impersonal and condescending treatment by now. Yet I still ached for a little nugget of affection from both of my parents. Ninety percent of everything I did was to win their love. I couldn't give up trying. Because honestly, if a girl couldn't get her own family to care about her, who would?

After putting my cell phone and ereader away, I clasped my briefcase closed and brushed stray crumbs off my lap. Acting as if nothing whatsoever was bothering me, I tossed the rest of my lunch and returned to the English department to finish my last two classes for the day.

The afternoon dragged by, and more than once, I had to bite the inside of my lip to keep from thinking about the conversation I'd had with my mother. Good news was it diverted my mind from a certain blue-eyed cretin I wanted to hate.

Except I should've known he'd find a way to steal back into my day. After all, blue-eyed cretins had a way of doing that.

By three ten, I entered the sanctuary of my office. Pausing in the doorway, I breathed in the scent of old books lining the walls, which immediately helped loosen my tight muscles. My briefcase slid neatly into the nook between my desk and the wall where I always kept it, and my rump sank into the cushion of my chair. Then and only then did I let out a small moan of delight.

Home.

Some might consider it sad and pathetic that one of the two places I felt at home was tucked away in my cramped office at the university, but I didn't care. At least I finally *had* a place that felt welcoming. So I embraced it.

Booting up my computer, I chewed on a fingernail as I waited for my welcome screen to pop up and ask for my password.

Just as it did, a knock came at the opened door of my office. For the briefest moment, my heart leapt into my throat. But dear God, if Noel Gamble had actually accepted my invitation to talk about his essay this afternoon, I was going to have heart failure. He couldn't invade my safe haven. My home. He just couldn't.

I almost passed out from relief when I saw the dean of the English department framed in the doorway instead. Thank God.

"Dr. Frenetti." I sprang to my feet, brushing my bangs out of my eyes. "Please come in."

He stepped into the room. "Dr. Kavanagh," he greeted with a tight nod before he got straight to his point. "I hear you're giving Noel Gamble a hard time?"

Oh, good God, you had to be kidding me.

I'm not sure what was worse; Noel Gamble visiting my office, or someone *concerned* about Noel Gamble visiting my office. I just wanted to escape everything that was Noel Gamble.

Shaking my head, I offered Dr. Frenetti a tense, confused smile. "Where did you hear that?"

"His coach contacted me today."

My teeth ground together. What do you know; the arrogant douche had whined to someone about me. Why was I not surprised?

Dr. Frenetti's face showed some serious disapproval, and unfortunately, he already had one of those faces that looked condemning without any help. With a large, flat nose, permanent frown wrinkles marring his forehead, and fleshy jowls that sagged with outright censure, he looked positively reproachful as he scowled.

Ignoring the urge to slink back into my seat and start apologizing for my failures, I forced a stiff nod. This was about Noel Gamble's shortcomings, not mine. Still, it felt as if I was confessing a sin when I answered, "He's not doing well, no."

Without waiting for my invitation, Dr. Frenetti seated himself in the chair opposite mine and left me standing uneasily in front of him. I shifted a step, uncertain if I should sit too. It was a good thing I finally did because what he said next left me too weak-kneed to remain upright.

"I had my doubts when the board hired you, Aspen. Someone so young and inexperienced..." He shook his head and sighed. "I *knew* it would cause problems. But the reference your old professor gave us was impeccable. She spoke so highly of you I hoped it would all work out. Except I'm not sure you quite understand the gravity that flunking this student would have. We were undefeated this season until the playoffs. And you might not see it yet, but football is the backbone of this university."

Oh, I saw it all right. I just didn't see how that should affect my grading.

"The sooner everyone in the entire English department realizes it, the better. If the team gets the divisional championship next year, our recruiting power goes through the roof, which means more students taking more English courses and more money coming in, hence a better chance for pay raises...bonuses. In essence, you're helping yourself and *everyone* on campus if you help this boy. He's the key to a better university, Aspen. His passing grades are the only thing keeping him here. He absolutely cannot lose his scholarship."

I had to pinch my leg to keep myself from rolling my eyes. But seriously? One guy—who wrote really sucky essays—was the key to everything? Drama much, old man?

Overdramatic speech or not, my poor little ears rang with shock. I had realized from the very day I'd come here that sports on campus trumped everything else, but to hear the English department *Dean* speak so candidly about it disappointed me. What about an honest grade? Integrity? Education?

I silently counted to ten before speaking. "So, you're telling me to pass him no matter how badly he's *truly* failing?"

"Of course not." With an irritated huff, the dean frowned and pinched his flabby lips together. They looked like two pink pancakes, one stacked on top of the other. "But I'm certain there's something you can do to make him *not* fail. You're a teacher. For God's sake, *teach the boy.*"

Oh, no, he did not. No one questioned my teaching abilities. "I *am*! Dr. Frenetti, I—"

"Well, obviously you're not doing it well enough if he isn't picking up the curriculum. Yours is the only class he's failing. Why *is* that?"

Probably because every other lemming professor on campus was passing him, no matter how awful he was actually doing. Maybe they'd already received the same lecture I was currently getting.

"I..." I shook my head, and my face heated to a scorching degree.

How dare he? How dare he make this *my* fault? I couldn't even defend myself. Being the newest faculty member on campus, I couldn't exactly go complaining to anyone about him, either, without risking my job. Besides, who the hell would I know to complain to that didn't share his skewed opinions?

God, I hated that I could never defend myself against anyone.

"Aspen, I'm concerned about you."

I wanted to slap him. The jerk wasn't concerned about me. And I didn't appreciate his phony tactic to get through to me. Questioning my abilities as a teacher had pissed me off enough.

Folding his hands together, he leaned forward. "I don't want anyone to hold anything against you if it's your fault Gamble loses his scholarship and has to drop out. After a few years here, when you try to get tenured—which is something I know you want since you've already mentioned it to me—you'll need the other faculty members to go to bat for you. They won't if you single-handedly ruin our first real chance in *twenty* years to win a divisional football championship."

Ice ran through my veins. And here came the threatening tactics. Wow, he wasn't going to pull a single punch, was he?

Rubbing my forehead, I nodded my humble compliance. "I understand."

"Good. I hoped you would. Now I'd like you to—"

A knock on the door interrupted us.

Great. I wondered who it could be now. My guess was the Grim Reaper coming to take my damn soul away. When I glanced toward the doorway, though, I wished it *had* been the Grim Reaper, because he could've at least put me out of my misery.

Noel Gamble's presence only added to it.

"Well." Managing to look surprised, Frenetti popped to his feet and grinned engagingly at the new arrival. "Hey there, Noel. What a pleasant surprise."

I rolled my eyes and then flushed when Noel glanced my way and caught my immature response to Frenetti's brown-noser greeting.

"I really enjoyed that last showdown against South Central," Frenetti was telling him. "The pass you threw at the end and won the game was amazing. I swear you were going to get sacked."

Noel gazed at the older man a second. Then he flashed a quick glance my way before turning back to the dean. "Well...I did get sacked as soon as the ball

25

left my hand."

"But you still got it into the end zone and into your receiver's hands. That's all that mattered. And what was that, anyway. A thirty-yard pass?"

"Forty-two yards."

Frenetti whistled. "Quite an arm you have there, son."

Noel nodded respectfully. "Thank you, sir." He glanced at me again. "Is this a bad time?"

"No, no." Frenetti—the ass—answered for me. "Come on in. I'm sure you and Dr. Kavanagh have plenty to discuss. So I'll leave you to it."

Wait? What? We did?

The dean sent me a speaking glance before shutting me inside my office...alone...with Noel Gamble. The walls instantly closed in around us and my chest followed suit, squeezing in around my lungs until I was sure I'd asphyxiate any second. I could almost feel phantom hands holding me down and covering my mouth as a strong body pinned me to the backseat of his car.

"Who was that guy?" Noel asked, turning away from the closed door to send me a perplexed glance.

He in no way acted as if he was about to attack, so I forced oxygen through my clenched teeth, calming my racing nerves. Then I narrowed my eyes, wondering if he really had no idea who Frenetti was or if he was trying to play me. Finally, I shrugged, figuring it didn't matter if he was acting out a role or if he was honestly here under his own steam. Either way, I was going to have to "work with him" as Frenetti had put it.

"That was Dr. Frenetti," I said. "He's the dean of the English department." When Noel only blinked, his expression blank of understanding, I sighed impatiently. "He's my boss."

"Oh. So, how'd he know who *I* was?"

I think it was the fury igniting in me that kept me

from exploding into a ball of mushy panic, because suddenly, I no longer cared about being alone in a small room with this man. And I no longer worried about how I was going to catch my next breath. I only wondered how hard it would be to sneak a dead body out of here and dispose of it for good.

"Who *doesn't* know who you are, Mr. Gamble?"

His nostrils flared as he drew in a breath. I could actually see him rein in his temper as he worked his jaw and focused on the keyboard on the top of my desk. His calming process must've worked, because the only thing he said to me was, "Right." Then he glanced at the chair Frenetti had abandoned but didn't sit down. "So, uh...I came to talk to you about my last paper if you have a minute." He cocked me a smirk. "Like you said I should."

I nodded, not making eye contact. "Well, apparently, I better make a minute for you since my boss just threatened my job if you were put on academic probation because of me."

"He did?" Noel looked genuinely shocked as he glanced toward the doorway where Dr. Frenetti had been standing. Squinting in confusion, he swung back. "Why would he do that?"

I closed my eyes briefly. "Why do you think, Mr. Forty-Two Yards?"

His face reddened. It was hard to tell if the color came from anger, shock, humiliation, guilt, embarrassment, or what. Clenching his teeth, he bit out, "I didn't go to anyone to complain if that's what you're implying."

It really didn't matter if he had or hadn't. I'd gotten my warning regardless. Now I had to behave by *the Man's* stupid, unfair rules.

But no one said I couldn't take my anger out on the student I was being forced to pass.

"You know, I find it ironic that *you're* the one writing subpar assignments and *I'm* the one getting a slap on the hand for it."

If Noel Gamble had feathers, I swear they would've ruffled. He looked so affronted I actually wanted to cheer on my ability to piss him off. "Look, I'm not asking for special treatment just because your *boss* happens to like the way I play ball."

"And yet you'll be getting it anyway, despite *both* our wishes."

"You know what? Fuck you. You told me to come here if I needed help. So here I am. But you obviously don't want to help me. So, thanks so much for your worthless time."

When he turned away, I panicked. Pissing off the dean of the English department during my first semester as a professor would not bode well for my future. I had to soothe Noel Gamble's ruffled feathers. Now.

Clenching my teeth, I surged to my feet and muttered, "Gamble, sit down."

"Hell no." Without pausing, he yanked open the door and lifted a hand to send me a jerky, middle-finger wave of dismissal over his shoulder. "Excuse me for *bothering* you, Professor."

Damn it, he and I would both be screwed if he walked out that door.

"Do you want to pass my class or not?"

Finally, he paused and glanced back. When I caught the glint of vulnerability and stubborn pride in his tense expression, I melted. Shit, why'd he have to go and do something human like that? Strong, obstinate people who slipped up and showed a weakness always melted me like sugar in warm water.

"Sit down," I murmured in a quiet, apologetic voice. Motioning toward the chair, I more calmly added, "Please."

Jaw knitted hard, he closed his eyes and muttered something unintelligible under his breath before he re-shut the door and slouched low into the chair with a petulant glare. Drumming his fingers impatiently on his jean-clad knee, he lifted an eyebrow, silently saying, *Well? Teach me already.*

I had no idea how I was going to accomplish this, but I was determined to make Noel Gamble *earn* the passing grade I was being forced to give him.

CHAPTER THREE

"Everybody is a genius. But, if you judge a fish by its ability to climb a tree, it'll spend its whole life believing that it is stupid." - Albert Einstein

~NOEL~

THROAT BONE DRY WHILE the acid in my stomach did somersaults, I stared through narrowed eyes across an eerily clean desk at my English teacher and her delectable mouth, which had driven me crazy since the first day of class when she'd taken her place behind the instructor's podium.

That skeeved me out more than anything. Nothing about Dr. Kavanagh was my type. I preferred blondes with gorgeous long, flowing hair. My Literature professor kept her dark mass scraped back and hidden away in a tight holy-roller bun secured at the base of her neck.

I was a lover of long lean bodies that liked to show off their impressive curves with fashionable, revealing clothes. Kavanagh was tiny, and probably too rounded for my taste. Or at least I figured she had chub rolls she wanted to hide. Why else would she wear clothes three sizes too large for her?

And I liked confident sensuality in a female, someone who knew she had it and moved as if she wanted every guy in a fifty-mile radius to stop whatever he was doing just to gawk at her whenever she sauntered by. Kavanagh didn't have a single saunter in her repertoire. She had the sensuality of a nun, and she didn't seem to like guys at all. Not that I believed she was a dyke as Tenning had suggested. I just viewed her as an anti-sexual being. Genderless. At least, I wanted to.

Which was another reason I hated being so aware of her as a woman whenever she was around. While I was imagining how her sweet, plush lips would feel wrapped around my favorite body part, I knew she had nothing but freaking literature on the brain.

"I actually tried, you know," I said, attempting to focus on her green eyes and not her mouth. "That was probably the best damn paper I ever wrote. And I didn't cheat like I'm sure half the class did. I read the book, the Cliff Notes, sample essays. I even watched the weird-ass movie. I did *all* the fucking work."

Silently seating herself in the chair opposite the desk from me, Dr. Kavanagh gave me a tight smile. "And yet you completely missed the entire point of the assignment."

Well, shit, you think? I jerked my hands into the air. "Maybe because I didn't *understand* the goddamn point. I mean, what the hell did you want me to say?"

I knew I should've toned down the language, but she had me turned inside-out. And I'd only been in her office for two minutes. How this one tiny little person could get me so instantly and completely riled, I didn't know. But here I was, mad, turned-on, ashamed, alarmed and frankly disturbed by my attraction, while I was equally pissed at her for knowing exactly how much I didn't deserve to step foot on this campus because I was too freaking stupid.

And, fuck, had she put on lip gloss or something since I'd seen her this morning in class? Her mouth looked shinier than ever. I caught myself looking at it again and jerked my gaze away. Damn it, bitchy teachers should not have lips like that.

She sighed and interlaced her hands before resting them on top of her desk. "It wasn't about what I wanted you to say; it was about what you *needed* to say."

And there went all my composure. Again.

"What I *needed* to say?" I surged to my feet and clutched my hair as I began to pace the five feet of room I had in her snug office. "*What I needed to say? What the fuck does that even mean?*"

Dr. Kavanagh remained cool and collected, damn her, seated in her chair as she calmly watched me unravel into a hot pile of anxiety. "It means you didn't do what you were asked to do. I wanted you to make a correlation between a character in the story and *yourself.* You made no such connection. In fact, you didn't talk about you at all."

I snorted. "Maybe I didn't *feel* a connection with a bunch of rich-ass idiots from the *twenties*, whining about lost love while they spread around adultery like it was some kind of candy. How am I supposed to correlate anything when there is *nothing* to correlate?"

She fell back in her chair and sent me a frustrated frown. "Mr. Gamble..." With another sigh, she shook her head and ran her hands wearily over her face, which unfortunately made me focus on her lips.

God damn, that mouth should not be legal. I could picture it pursed so perfectly around my cock, could almost feel the wet slide of her tongue running up my entire length as she sucked me in deep.

Shit, now I had wood.

Fortunately oblivious to my crude, unwanted thoughts, she stiffened her shoulders, sat forward again and looked me straight in the eye. "Truly talented literature is truly talented for a reason. It always—always—finds a way to reach every person who reads it. It takes a theme about the human condition and makes it its little bitch."

My eyebrows shot up into my hairline. What the hell? Shaking my head, I blinked. "Did you just say—"

"Yes!" she snapped. "I did. Because it's true. Take one word about feelings or emotions and you'll be able to find a theme for it in *The Great Gatsby*. I promise you." When I did nothing but gape at her, she arched a curious brow. "You do have emotions, don't you?"

"I'm having some right now." And they were totally freaking me out, but fuck, I really liked watching her perfect, too-pure mouth forming dirty words. It was like some awful, humiliating sickness. I wanted her to do it again.

Say bitch again. Please. Just one more time.

But she didn't.

"Good." Her stare was direct. Knowing. "Let me guess. You're feeling frustration. Anger. Hate."

"Uh..." I lifted an eyebrow. *Close, but not quite.*

"That's perfectly fine. You can use those. Make them bond with someone in this book and tell me all about it."

As her words sank in, I frowned. Something hot and seeking inside me melted. Defeat. "How?" I asked quietly, feeling like a complete idiot because I still didn't understand, would probably *never* understand.

She blinked. "What do you mean how? If you're really frustrated, mad, and full of hatred for me right now, write about it, explain why, then explain where someone in the story shares these same sentiments and why they experienced them. Make the two one and the same. Bash me all you want on paper, just

33

show me that correlation I want to see, and I will give you a better score."

I snorted and shook my head. No way. No effing way. "I just don't get *why* I have to write about my fucking feelings?"

She let out a frustrated growl, which only turned me on more. "So I know you understand the story and what happened."

"Well, I didn't understand the story. Goddamn it. I told you. I have nothing in common with—"

"Yes, you do!" she roared back, smacking both her palms on top of her desk before pushing to her feet to glare at me. "Everyone on the planet has at least one thing in common with at least one character in that story. Now go prove it!"

Seething, I just glared at her.

She closed her eyes and rubbed at the center of her head. "Okay," she mumbled as if giving up the fight.

When she licked her lips, I almost lost it. Christ, this was getting embarrassing. Her mouth was going to be my downfall. If she asked me, I would probably take her on her nice, clean desk right then and there. I could so clearly see myself tossing her down, gathering up her frumpy skirt, wedging myself between her thighs and just hammering it home.

I also wanted to wrap my hands around her throat and strangle her for making me feel like such an idiot.

It probably wasn't healthy to have two such drastic emotions roaring through me at the same moment, but there they were. Absolutely roaring.

The good professor sank back into her chair. "How about this? I'll make your paper as easy as I can on you."

Yeah, just cater to the idiot. I glanced away, my jaw knitting with mutiny. "I don't need—" Damn it. Yes, I did. It's why I was here, because I needed help.

34

"I'll give you a theme to use. So...let's pick a theme. Any theme." Her eyes opened, the lines in her skin around them deeper than before. "Greed? Power?" She lifted her hands as she shrugged. "I don't know. What do you feel whenever you play football?"

My face heated with outrage. "Oh, thanks a lot. I like how you mentioned my football right after saying greed and power." Leaning ominously over the desk to glare, I poked my index finger into my own chest. "You think my entire reason for being on this campus is just some greedy, selfish *power trip*? Well, you don't know shit, lady. You don't know me at all."

She pulled back in her chair, her green eyes huge as they blinked rapidly. Finally, she glanced away and her tongue darted out to wet her lips. Yeah, yeah, the move made my dick pulse with gluttonous need, but I was too pissed to care. At the moment, I hated what she was doing to my ego more.

In a much calmer voice, she murmured, "I'm sorry if I offended you," which totally shocked the shit out of me and made me back up a step to sink into my chair and gawk back. "But I honestly have no idea what football is to you. So, why don't you tell me? One word. What is football...to you?"

My breathing came hard as I glanced down at my fisted hand in my lap. "Desperation," I said without meaning to.

Shit. Why had I said that? It was the honest-to-God truth. But why would I confess it? *To her?*

When I dared to glance up, I was surprised to find she looked equally startled. Her mouth had fallen open. "I..." She blinked, her eyes wide with shock. "I wasn't expecting you to say that."

Turning my gaze away, I ripped my hand through my hair and cursed silently. "Yeah, well, I didn't mean to."

Amusement lined her voice. "And yet I have a feeling it's the most honest thing you've said since you stepped inside my office."

My glower swerved back to her, but she merely lifted that damn challenging eyebrow of hers, daring me to contradict her.

Hissing out a breath, I slumped deeper into my seat. "So, what do I do with the theme of desperation then?"

Seemingly eager all the sudden, Dr. Kavanagh sat forward, her eyes lighting with an excited gleam. "Well, now is the easy part. You find a part in the story where someone feels desperate, on edge, as if nothing is under his or her own control. Explain why, then tell me how you understand this emotion and how you can relate to it by listing all the reasons *you* feel or have felt desperate, on edge, and like nothing is under your control."

That should be easy. I felt that way most every day. About everything. Hell, I was feeling that way right now, about her. But still...

Closing my eyes, I whispered, "Christ." The woman might as well ask me to bare my soul to her. Opening my lashes, I shot her a frown. "And you don't have any qualms over the fact this assignment is utterly intrusive and infringes on a person's privacy?"

She beamed. "None whatsoever." Her bright smile threw me off guard. It was...lovely.

Hmm. Strange. Dr. Kavanagh had a lovely smile. It took my breath away and left me reeling.

I didn't mean for it to happen, but my lips quirked in reluctant admiration. "You're kind of evil, Professor."

That seemed to please her. She straightened her back and preened. "Hey, I bet I just nudged you into writing the best damn paper you've ever written."

Damn, I loved the way she said *damn*.

This time, I chuckled. I liked how she kept shocking me today. She acted so prim and proper in class, as if a curse word had never left her saintly lips.

36

"Maybe," I murmured, looking at her in a new light. "We'll see. How soon do you need it?"

"As soon as possible."

I rolled my eyes. "No pressure or anything." With a sigh, I pushed to my feet. "Okay, Dr. Kavanagh. I will have the best *damn* paper I've ever written in your hands as soon as possible."

"Excellent." She stood as well. "That's all I ask."

Jesus. She was a snarky little thing. I didn't want to dig that. But I totally dug that.

I hesitated, and an awkward impasse passed between us. If she had been a man, I probably would've held out my hand to shake and thanked her for the second chance she'd just given me. Hell, if she'd been an older woman, or maybe just any *other* woman, I might've done the same thing. But with her, right then, it felt...forbidden. Naughty.

Hard-ass, straight-laced teacher or not, there was something about the soft curve of her porcelain pale face with an almost invisible splash of freckles dusting her cheeks and nose to go with her succulent lips that stirred me. I instinctively knew I should never touch her.

She must've sensed my unease because she shifted and cleared her throat, not making eye contact. "Well, then. I assume that's all you need."

"Yeah." With a single bob of the head, I murmured, "Thanks." I turned, but just before I left the small room crammed with shelves of books, I paused and glanced back. "And I'm, you know, sorry...about calling you a bitch earlier."

This time, both of her trim, dark eyebrows lifted. She pressed a hand against the center of her chest. "What? You're rescinding what might possibly be the nicest compliment I've received from a student all semester?"

I snorted out a laugh but nodded. "Yeah, I am. It was rude and undeserving. And I apologize."

Her lashes responded by beating in overtime against the tops of her cheeks. When moisture glistened like a fine sheen over her green eyes, I panicked. Shit, I didn't want to make her cry.

But wow. Who knew I could actually make the hard-ass, expressionless Dr. Kavanagh cry? She must not be nearly as tough as she put herself out there to be. It made me wonder just how soft she could get.

Which was wrong. Wrong, wrong, wrong.

She held it together, thank God, and nodded. "Apology accepted," she murmured as she motioned toward the door to let me know I was excused.

Wavering another second, I studied her delicate features, still amazed she was old enough to be a college professor. If she didn't act so hoity-toity and wore such frumpy clothes, I probably would've mistaken her for an underclassman and hit on her by now. I wouldn't have stopped my pursuit either, not until she gave in and let me have a piece of her, because my type or not, there was something about her that drew me in.

"How old are you?" I blurted out before I could stop myself.

Shit. Why had I just asked that? It made no difference what age my teacher was.

Lifting her eyebrows with what was either irritation or amusement—I couldn't quite tell—she murmured, "None of your business," in a low voice packed with heated sensuality.

It stirred every hormone inside me, even though I knew she hadn't meant it to.

I shook myself free of the generating lust and muttered, "Right." It was time to get out of here. Now.

***

"Quotable quotes are coins rubbed smooth by circulation." - Louis Menand

***

~*A*SPEN~

Noel Gamble turned away and was about out of the door of my office when he paused and glanced at my quote board. A pincushion of cork for all my thumbtacks to hold up Post-it notes and scraps of paper, my quote board was full of sayings from books I had collected over the years.

Slowing to a stop, he studied some of the quotes I had accumulated. "What's this?"

No one had ever asked me that before.

I ducked my hot face, feeling suddenly shy. But it felt like he was scanning a piece of my soul. Still unsettled by how he'd asked how old I was, I mumbled, "It's nothing. Just my quote board."

He glanced back, and the curiosity in his blue eyes sizzled my insides.

I cleared my throat. "When I read a line from a story I like, I tack it up there." It was kind of my thing.

"Hmm." He lifted his hand to slip aside one of the newer quotes to read one of the older ones hidden behind it. When he gave a low chuckle, my hormones jackknifed into immediate awareness. God, his laugh was stirring. "That's a good one."

Since I had no idea which one he was referring to, I didn't respond. Then again, I considered all of them good since I'd taken the time to put them there, so I probably couldn't help but agree.

He glanced back. "'Sometimes the questions are complicated but the answers are simple.'"

That had to be the deepest thing anyone had ever said to me. But what did he mean? Was he referring to my assignment? Did he think I'd made it too convoluted? Should I work on my teaching approach?

I cleared my throat. "Excuse me?"

He flushed slightly and turned back to the quote board to tap the Post-its. "It's Dr. Seuss. Another quote you could add."

"O-oh. Thanks. That...that's actually an excellent one." And it was. It really was. Strange.

Noel gifted me with the hint of a smile. Then he ducked his face and headed from the room.

Once he was gone, I felt bereft. Setting my hand over my heart, I sank back into my chair and blew out a long, shaky breath. Okay, so my crush on a student had just grown to epic proportions. Wonder what my flawless, judgmental mother would have to say about that?

CHAPTER FOUR

"When you're in jail, a good friend will be trying to bail you out. A best friend will be in the cell next to you saying, 'Damn, that was fun.'" -Groucho Marx

~NOEL~

TENNING WAS LOITERING in the kitchen when I came through the front door of our apartment. As I kicked it shut behind me, he appeared in the opening next to the breakfast bar, barefoot and shirtless with his track pants hanging low around his hips. He only had to look at my face to know something was up.

A smug leer spread across his features. "So...how'd your meeting with *Kavanagh* go?"

I sent him my best *fuck you* glare and dropped my bag heavily on the floor before slumping spine-first onto the couch. "Feels like I just had an hour-long session with a head shrink. I swear to God, who knew literature was all about *feelings* and *emotions*? God damn."

Tenning chuckled. "So, is she going to let you rewrite a new paper or what?"

"Actually, yeah. Freaky, huh? But only because her boss has a hard-on for me or something and forced her to give me a second chance."

"Really? Did you have to go down on him to make that happen?" Tenning leaned against the wall and waggled his eyebrows suggestively.

"*What*?" Swiping up a throw pillow that had been lumped behind my head, I threw it at him as hard as I could. "Jesus, Ten. You're such a crude asshole, and you completely annoy me."

Catching the cushion to his chest, he snickered. "Damn, I love you too, babe. Hey, I bet if you offered to teach the dyke to bat for the right team, she'd change your grade to an A without you having to worry about writing another paper for the rest of the semester."

I sighed and decided to ignore him or he'd only get worse. But the douche had hit a nerve. If he ever realized I actually thought about her in that way, he'd never let me live it down. Talk about utter humiliation.

Focusing my attention on the ceiling, I noticed a new water stain growing in the corner. Swell. The worst part was I couldn't mention the leak to our landlord or he'd just raise our rent again, as he had this winter when we'd asked him to fix the central heating system. *Repairs aren't free*, he'd said.

"Hey, quit daydreaming about banging your teacher, dickwad." Ten kicked my feet off the end of the couch as he passed, making his way toward the hallway that led down to our separate rooms. "It's ladies' night. We got work to do. I call dibs on the shower first."

I groaned, completely having forgotten what day it was. Every Thursday was ladies' night at Forbidden, the bar where both Ten and I worked. That meant only the male employees had to clock in, and since all five of us guys were bartenders, some of us had to switch over and play waiter for the evening.

My tips went through the roof when I waited tables on ladies' night, but damn, drunk women could get freaking frisky. Not that I didn't mind a little grab-ass from a table full of cute co-eds. But after a couple hours of it, my butt cheeks grew chaffed.

And that was only from the women who went for the back door. I'd taken to wearing a cup a couple months back due to all the hungry hands grabbing my junk.

Yeah, it was that insane.

An hour later, I was following Ten out the door, decked out in a tight black T-shirt and blue jeans, which was the regulation uniform for the men of Forbidden. Since I didn't own my own set of wheels, I climbed into the passenger seat of Ten's truck as he slid behind the wheel.

Five minutes later, we parked across the street from the nightclub and took a minute to stare at the quiet building before slipping out of the truck. In an hour, the place would be banging, and the peace we had now would be no more. But...it paid the bills and helped me send home some extra funds to Caroline so she could pay those bills too.

"You ready for this?" I asked, pushing open my door.

Ten snickered. "I was born ready, mother-fucker." As he followed me to the front door, I shook my head, wondering if he'd ever not been able to come up with some politically incorrect answer to any question a person asked him.

After unlocking the door and slipping inside, I glanced around the interior for the other three guys who were supposed to work tonight.

"Where is everyone?" Ten and I were rarely the first to arrive, and we weren't even running early.

"Well, Pick's always late," Ten said, taking a chair off the first table he saw and tucking it upright underneath. "And the twins are..." He glanced around and scratched his head. "Huh. The twins are never late. Where the fuck are the twins?"

As if answering his question, the door to the manager's office opened, and the owner of Forbidden's oldest daughter, Jessie, strolled out followed by a stranger—a dark-haired guy, my age, about the same height and size...which could mean only one thing.

New employee. One of my coworkers must've quit.

"Fuck," Ten growled, mirroring my thoughts, before he lifted his voice and called across the empty bar. "Yo, Jess. Where's Huey and Louie?" The twins were actually named Heath and Landon, but Ten tended to assign everyone his own nickname.

Jess had never been an Oren Tenning fan, so she narrowed him a harsh glower. "Where do you *think*? They quit. Probably didn't want to work with your punk ass anymore. Here's his replacement. Someone show him what to do."

With that, she turned away and started back into the office.

"Hey," Ten called after her. "What about the other one?"

Jessie paused and glanced back to arch one intimidating eyebrow. "Other one what?"

"This place is going to be overrun within an hour, woman. We *need* at least five guys working tonight, not three and some clueless newbie. Are you seriously just going to replace *both* the twins with this one douche?"

The clueless newbie douche in question sent him a sidelong look that seemed more amused than insulted by the remark while Jess hissed with aggravation.

"Yeah, I am. So show him what to do." With that, she slammed back into her office, leaving the three of us alone in the bar.

"She totally wants me." Ten sniffed knowingly at the closed door, while I sighed and set my hands on my hips, taking in the new guy.

God, I couldn't wait until Jess's dad returned to work. He'd recently had open-heart surgery, and she'd taken over while he was down. But if he didn't hurry his ass up and recover soon, his precious baby girl was going to run his nightclub into the ground.

Tipping my head up in greeting, I said, "Hey. What's your name?"

The new guy shoved his hands into his back pockets and tore his attention away from Ten to glance my way. "Mason," he said. "Mason Lowe."

I nodded. "Nice to meet you. You ever bartend before?"

When Lowe shook his head, Ten snorted and slapped me in the stomach. "He's all yours, baby." Dismissing us both, he returned to his job of taking the chairs off the tables.

"Fine," I called. "We get the bar then; you wait tables."

"What the fuck ever. Make the new guy wait tables."

"Shit, you want him to quit on his first night?"

Ten paused to study Lowe from head to foot. Then he nodded. "Yeah, with a pretty face like his, he'd be molested beyond repair within the first five minutes. I'll take the tables. But just for tonight." He pointed threateningly at Lowe. "You got that, newbie?"

Lowe was beginning to look a little alarmed. "What's he talking about? I thought this was just a regular bar."

Humph. There was nothing regular about Forbidden. But to reassure him, I said, "It is." With a friendly pat on his back, I shrugged. "Don't listen to Ten. He's just sore because his vagina got ridden too hard last night."

"Fucker," Ten called from across the room.

I ignored him, focusing on Lowe. "But every Thursday *is* ladies' night. So it'll probably get a little crazy. Drinks are fifty percent off for every woman who comes in, which means a lot of drunk, handsy chicks are going to try to get a piece of you...all night long."

A green tinge immediately coated Lowe's face. "Great," he muttered weakly.

With a laugh, I slugged my elbow into his arm. "Trust me. It is. Your tips will triple. But seriously. You might want to protect the boys. I recommend wearing a cup every Thursday from here on out."

"Sure." With a gulp and longing glance toward the exit, Lowe nodded.

"Your accent's different," I noted as I led him toward the bar. "Where're you from?"

"Florida. Just moved here a couple months ago."

"Dude." Appearing out of nowhere, Ten plopped down on a stool and rested his elbows on the bar while he frowned at Lowe. "Why the hell would you leave *Florida* for fucking Ellamore, Illinois?"

Mason shrugged as if it was no big deal. "My girlfriend's from here. She wanted to come home."

Ten snorted. "Wait, wait, wait. You traveled halfway across the country for some pussy? Damn, that's lame."

I thought Lowe was going to leap across the bar and strangle my pathetic excuse for a roommate, so I beat him to the punch. "Ignore him," I said, slinging my hand out to smack Ten on the side of the head. "Like I said; sore vagina."

Glaring at me, Ten sniffed. "At least I'm not banging my teacher for a good grade."

Oh, that did it.

"Go away." I pointed at his face and sent him the stare of death until he rolled his eyes and pushed from the bar to saunter off. Once his back was turned, I couldn't help but slice a worried glance toward Lowe. "I'm not—"

Lowe lifted his hands and waved me quiet, telling me I didn't have to explain myself. "Hey, cougars aren't my thing. But if you—"

"She's not a cougar," I hissed in defense before I could stop myself. "I mean...shit." I stabbed my fingers through my hair, my mind skipping to figure out how to talk my way out of this because now it totally sounded like I was banging my teacher. "I'm not sleeping with any of my teachers, okay. Butt Licker over there is just harassing me because I somehow miraculously sweet-talked my hard-ass English professor into letting me rewrite a paper. *That's it.*"

Fuck, I sounded too defensive, didn't I?

"Kavanagh and Gamble sitting in a tree," Ten—the five-year-old trapped in a horny twenty-one-year old's body—sang from across the room. "K.I.S.S.I.N.G."

I shut him up at that point by grabbing a football from a shelf behind the bar and winding back my arm to take aim. When I hit him square in the back, he grunted and went sprawling forward to the floor.

Lowe whistled, clearly impressed by my skill. "Lucky shot."

"*Lucky?*" I cranked my head around to gape at the new guy. "Obviously you have no idea who I am."

"Uh..." His eyebrows wrinkled as he shook his head. "No. Who are you?"

"Son, you are in the presence of a local legend." With a sweeping bow, I introduced myself. "Noel Gamble, beloved quarterback for the university's football team."

"Oh, okay." Lowe nodded as recognition sparked

in his gaze. "I didn't transfer over until this semester, but I heard how well the team did this year. And I'm pretty sure I've heard your name float around campus."

With a hoot of pride, I called toward my roommate. "Hear that, Ten? Even the newbie's heard of me."

Ten snorted. "You're only popular because *we* make you look good."

I laughed and turned back to Lowe. "That's Asswipe, otherwise known as Oren Tenning. But most everyone calls him Ten. If you ask me, though, he's more like a Zero. He's a third-string receiver for the team."

"Third string my ass. I played more than you did this season."

True. But I didn't admit it aloud. Ignoring him, I asked Lowe, "So how much do you know about mixing drinks?"

The rueful grin and lifting of his eyebrows told me he knew absolutely nothing. I sighed, already ready for this night to be over. "Awesome. Let's get started learning then, shall we?"

I was giving him the lay of the land, showing him how to mix up the most basic of drinks and run the cash register when Pick slipped in right before opening, pissing me off with his usual tardiness. Personality-wise, the guy was my favorite coworker, but damn, sometimes he didn't make it in until after we opened.

"Nice of you to finally join us," I called, tossing him a waist apron so it hit him square in the face. "You got the floor with Ten tonight. The twins quit. This is the new guy, Mason Lowe. Now get to work."

My abrupt little speech, getting him up to speed, only made him smile. The silver studs in his eyebrow twitched. "Damn, your bossy little mouth never fails to turn me on, Gamble."

I snorted because Pick Ryan was more of a man-whore than Ten and I put together. I guess women totally went for the tatted-up, metal-faced, bad-boy image. But if you asked me, I'd say he was the furthest thing from a true bad boy as a guy could get.

He worked his ass off with two jobs to support himself, plus he respected women more than anyone I knew. He was always the first to jump in and kick ass if some drunk idiot was harassing a female, and he knew exactly what to say to make them happy. He just loved everything there was about the ladies, and they loved everything there was about him.

"Pick! My *man*!" Ten bounded forward, practically tackling the new arrival. "Thank God you didn't quit too. Looks like we have the floor tonight, fucker. You got your cup on?"

When he balled his hand into a fist and went to roshambo Pick in the junk, Pick slapped his hand down. "Hey, hey. That's not a toy, princess. Some lucky lady may need to use it later on."

Ten snorted. "Whatever, douche. You know you're saving yourself for me." He really mauled the other guy then, dry humping his leg.

"Not tonight, sweetheart." His voice mild, Pick shoved Ten back by the forehead. "I've got a headache."

"What the fuck ever. You totally want me."

As they moved off still bantering back and forth to unlock the front doors, Mason glanced my way. "You weren't kidding about the cup thing, were you?"

I chuckled and shook my head. "No. No, I wasn't."

He paled. "That's what I was afraid of."

***

Half an hour later, we were already overcrowded with chicks slurping down their fifty-percent frou-frou

49

drinks and horny dicks hoping to reap the benefits. I watched the new guy make a sale, smiling uneasily at a girl who handed him her phone number along with her cash payment. Once she turned her back, he tossed the slip of paper discretely into the trash.

Easing up to his side when he reached for the wrong nozzle to make a Tom Collins for the next girl who was unable to take her eyes off him, I silently corrected him, physically taking his hand to reach for the right lever. "Jesus, you're popular tonight. *I'm* supposed to be the big deal around here, but every single woman who comes up to the bar passes right over me to check *you* out." *Must be a fresh meat thing.*

With a roll of his eyes, he muttered, "Have at 'em. I'm not interested."

I snorted. "Yeah, I could tell."

About to inform him he could field them my way the next time some randy girl wanted to hand out her number, I caught sight of a familiar face approaching the bar. Relieved to know someone was here to see me, not Lowe, I leapt forward with a ready smile. "There's my favorite groupie." Reaching across the bar to catch Tianna by the back of the neck and haul her halfway across the counter for a quick but deliciously dirty kiss, I smiled appreciatively at her.

"Hey, Noel baby," she said, distracted, immediately pulling away from me so she could crane her head and peer around me to get a look at Lowe. "Who's the new guy?"

When her eyes glittered with straight-up lust, I gritted my teeth and seared Lowe with a lethal glance. He only smirked as if amused by my jealousy. His loose-shouldered shrug seemed to say, *Hey, what do you want me to do about it?*

No way was I letting go of my favorite football groupie. So I turned back to Tianna and lied through my teeth. "That's Milo. Just got out of the pen. He's married with three kids."

But the lie didn't seem to deter her in the least. She kept staring and even tossed her hair before wiggling her fingers at him in a cutesy wave before introducing herself.

Fuck. I didn't think the guy was that good-looking, but apparently he was some kind of freaking catnip for women. The bastard.

Tianna's stalkerish stare seemed to skeeve him out though, because he helpfully added, "Four kids. We have another one on the way."

I grinned, deciding he might be okay after all.

"Where's your friend tonight?" I asked Tianna, taking her hand to play with her fingers and coax her attention back to me. "You guys still keeping my rain check on that threesome you offered me?"

Tianna finally tore her gaze away from Lowe. "Oh, sorry. Marci had dance class tonight. So we'll have to do it another time. But yeah, don't worry. She's still good for it. I swear that girl's panties have been wet for you for months. Ever since I introduced you two during that party after the last football game, she will not stop talking about you. It's actually annoying."

"So, she talks about me, huh?" A slow grin spread across my face, my ego suitably fed, knowing *someone* still preferred me over freaking Mason Lowe. And her name was Marci. Cute.

"Well, I hate to make a girl suffer. What say you hook us up sometime? Soon."

"Sure." Her gaze returned to Lowe as she kept talking to me. "You going to that frat party next weekend?"

"Next weekend?" I groaned. "You're killing me here, Tianna. I need something before next weekend."

She let out a harassed sigh and sent me a scowl. "Okay, fine. I'll see what I can do."

"You're the best." I hauled her in for another

quick kiss. "Thanks."

"Yeah, yeah. Just make sure to bring your new friend there to the party too, and I'll pay you back...big time." She ran a fingernail down my cheek as her face lit with a devious smile.

I was about to tell her not to even try with Lowe, he seemed attached to his girlfriend, but Ten appeared behind her. "Tianna!" He gave her a loud slap on the ass. "You ready to give me another go yet?"

Snorting, Tianna spun around to cross her arms over her chest and glare. "I haven't lost my mind yet, so...hell no. Touch me again, and I'll kick your nuts up into your throat."

As she stormed away, I let out a low whistle and winced at the mere thought. Ten had some kind of talent. He was the only guy I knew who could piss off the queen of casual sex. Tianna never got mad at any guy, for anything. Made me wonder what the hell he'd done to offend her. Then again, he *was* Ten. The possibilities were endless.

After watching her march away, he turned to grin at me. "She totally wants me. She was asking about me, wasn't she?"

I laughed. "Between kissing me, staring at Lowe, and setting me up with one of her friends, no, your name didn't come up once."

"A setup, huh? Who's her friend? *Dr. Kavanagh?*"

Narrowing my eyes, I pointed at him threateningly. "I swear to God, if you don't shut up about that, *I'll* kick your nuts up into your throat."

"Whatever, man. You know you want your teacher." Then he put in his order to Mason and started flirting with a pair of ladies sitting at the bar.

The sad thing was, Ten was only teasing me about her because he was sure I didn't want her, while, Jesus, even the mention of her stirred something inside me.

I should've gotten Marci's number from Tianna. I needed something—anything—to flush thoughts of a certain dowdy teacher from my head. Because if this kept up, I'd no doubt find myself in a shit bowl full of trouble.

***

When closing time came, I put Lowe on cleaning duty. While he was wiping down the back counter, his cell phone rang. He fished it out of his pocket and, I swear, as soon as he saw the I.D. on his screen, his face lit up like a kid on Christmas morning.

"Hey, sweet pea," he answered, his voice going all husky and private, letting me know he must be talking to his girl. Tucking the phone between his shoulder and ear so he could continue his work, he chuckled in response to something she said. "It's been... interesting. I'll tell you all about it when I get home. Oh yeah?" His eyebrows shot up, and I could only imagine what else his girl was suggesting they do when he got home, because all kinds of horny lit up across his face.

I couldn't seem to look away as I watched him talk to her, though. It was just so...strange. The guys on the football team who had steady girlfriends never looked happy when their old ladies called to *check in.* They were rarely faithful to their girls, always hooking up with one-night-stands whenever we had out-of-town games. It made me wonder why they even bothered to stick with one girl.

Now that I thought of it, I hadn't grown up around *any* monogamous couples in my life. My mom had rarely brought home the same guy more than twice, and all the marriages in our neighborhood ended in divorce or widowhood. So, okay, it really was rare for me to see a guy talking to his girl as if he wanted to talk to no one else in the world. And he looked so damn happy about it, too. It was kind of...sweet.

When he hung up with her, still grinning, Lowe pocketed his phone and went back to work, looking as if he'd just won the national championships or something.

"Who the hell was that?" Ten wanted to know as he neared the bar with a handful of glasses that needed to be cleaned. "You just win the lottery, newbie?"

"Hmm?" Lowe turned and glanced at him. "Oh. My girlfriend. She just wanted to know how my first night went."

Again with the sweetness. It was a little endearing to watch such a pure, open emotion light his face when he talked about her. I was suddenly very curious about girlfriends and monogamy. Maybe they weren't as awful as some of the guys on the team made them seem. Maybe it wouldn't be the end of the world to settle down with one person.

I mean, no one had ever called me just to see how my day had gone. No one had cared. I knew my brothers and sister loved me, but they'd never checked in just to reassure me whenever I was nervous as hell before a big game, or huge test, or even asked me how something had gone. Not that I bothered them with that kind of shit; they had their own problems to worry about.

But maybe, I don't know, maybe it'd be nice if—

"God, newbie, you are so whipped." Ten snorted and was off again, wiping down tables as Pick swept the floor.

I turned away and finished counting the cash register, slightly mortified by my own thoughts. I had no problem getting female companionship in this town. Most of my teammates complained about how lucky I was. Why the hell was I daydreaming about something else?

Another quick glance at Lowe, who was cheerfully humming—yes, *humming*—under his breath, told me exactly why though. He had something good and dependable, something that made him happy and brightened his entire day. He didn't have to meet a new girl each night and try to learn her in a couple minutes so he'd know how to charm her into a bed. He already had someone he probably knew inside and out, and who no doubt understood him in return. He didn't have to pretend to like her stories just to get her shirt off or act like some badass quarterback to keep up an image. He could just be himself with her, and enjoy life.

For the first time in my life, I was jealous of someone in a committed relationship. It felt really uncomfortable, but I just couldn't seem to help myself. Lowe looked so damn content. And I wanted something like that for myself.

CHAPTER FIVE

"All I ever wanted was to reach out and touch another human being, not just with my hands but with my heart." - Tahereh Mafi, *Shatter Me*

~ASPEN~

I LOVED THE SMELL OF popcorn. It was the forbidden scent of a youth I'd never been allowed to taste. Carbonated sodas had also been taboo in my home growing up.

As soon as I paid for my Pepsi and popcorn combo at the concession stand, I had to take a quick suck from my straw and scoop up a handful of buttery deliciousness straight off the top of the tub. A couple kernels tumbled off the overfilled sides and fell to the concrete floor to mix with fallen popcorn from all the purchases past. I loved it. It was so messy and carefree, something that would've given my parents a coronary.

"Thanks," I muffled out my appreciation to the

girl who'd just handed me my snack. My parents would've scolded me for talking with my mouth full, but here, no one cared. Delighting in my shameful deviousness, I turned and nearly plowed into two girls waiting in line behind me.

"I have an algebra class with him, and oh my God, he is so fine," one of them was saying, not even realizing I needed to get by.

"True that." The second girl fanned herself. "I'd have Noel Gamble's babies in a heartbeat."

Oh, brother. Rolling my eyes, I muttered a harsh, "excuse me," and turned sideways to slip between them. But this was bad. I was lusting after the same guy as a pair of airheaded teenie-bopper skanks. What the hell was wrong with me? And why the hell was I making my obsession worse by attending the spring scrimmage...where he would obviously be playing?

Maybe because I actually loved football, despite how much all the other professors I worked with senselessly thought it should come before a good education. Or maybe I just wanted to watch Noel Gamble in tight pants throw a ball around all afternoon long. I shivered from the thought and entered the football stadium through the first gate I found. My seat was two sections over, but I didn't mind the walk. It helped clear my head for what I was about to watch.

A couple players were on the field, warming up, but I didn't know who anyone was by their number or with their helmets on, so I focused on finding my seat. It had been taken by a pair of squatters, but I ran them off with a meaningful glance to my ticket before sending them my arched-eyebrow teacher stare.

Once settled in with my popcorn in my lap, I pulled my ball cap lower on my head, hoping I'd disguised myself well enough. Going incognito was also part of the fun. Since I'd never dared to do anything my parents had disapproved of when I'd lived at home, I'd never had the thrill of sneaking out.

Here, where it was perfectly fine for me to attend a game that would appall Mallory and Richard Kavanagh, I didn't really have to sneak. But it was still fun to pretend. Besides, I didn't want to be recognized as *Dr.* Kavanagh just now. Students always approached with some kind of assignment question, and right now, I just wanted to be Aspen, spectator of hot men in tight pants—er, I mean, of football. People didn't tend to recognize me when I was wearing jeans and a long-sleeved T-shirt with the campus mascot of a Viking on it. So I went with it.

Lifting my hip just enough to pull the roster I'd purchased and rolled up from my back pocket, I unfolded it and immediately checked for you-know-who's name. He was number twelve.

Twelve became my new favorite number.

The only off-season game, this scrimmage was an exhibition. And boy, was I ready for a show. Delving into my popcorn, I ate handfuls at a time and sucked on my drink, feeling surprisingly young and lighthearted. Mmm, refreshing.

Raised by two university professors who'd had me in their forties, I sometimes felt as if I'd never been allowed a childhood. I'd been expected to rise above the rest; and I usually had. When I'd started school, I'd immediately been stuck in gifted classes. I'd always been younger than all my classmates and yet expected to act as mature as they were, if not more mature because of my IQ. And since no one ever wanted to associate with the freak, genius girl, I'd never had any friends who might've taught me how to be a normal kid.

Today seemed like it might be one of those days where I could feel as blithe as I wanted to.

This end of the stadium was shaded perfectly from the afternoon sun, so when a gentle wind blew across my face, it actually chilled me a little. I cuddled deeper into my shirt, curling my shoulders forward to keep in as much body heat as possible, only to jump when a rowdy group of guys in the next section over burst out laughing amongst themselves.

I glanced their way and smiled slightly at how much fun they were having. The perplexing dynamics of friendships had always eluded me, but in a curious way. Just because no one had ever befriended me didn't mean I hadn't observed the social cliques over the years, or yearned to be welcomed into one. I watched, and wondered, and envied.

But as I watched them, the shine on my euphoria dimmed, and my shoulders slumped while the loneliness crept in. The rowdy group grew louder as the guys jostled each other and passed friendly insults back and forth, setting up a pecking order of sorts. Honestly, how could friends be so mean to each other and call each other names I wouldn't pin on my worst enemy, only to smile and laugh as if they'd handed out the ultimate compliment?

God, I wanted someone to call me a dirty name and then sling an arm around me, squeezing me with genuine companionship.

With my next glance at the loud boys, my brow wrinkled with jealous irritation. Did they have to rub in their happiness like that? I knew good and well I was all alone over here without a single—

"Getting to you too, aren't they?" the man next to me asked as he glanced over and took in my expression.

I blinked and turned my attention to him, startled to find him smiling at me. He appeared to be in his early to mid-thirties with light brown hair and tea-colored eyes to match. Wearing loose blue jeans and a T-shirt supporting the college, he could be anyone.

Rolling his eyes to exaggeration, he tipped his head toward the rowdy crowd. "Seems like it's always my luck; I get stuck by the unruliest group of immature idiots in the entire stadium." Just as he said that, every guy in the rowdy bunch stood up as a trio of pretty girls passed. Whistling and catcalling at them, they lifted their shirts to show off their painted bellies, which spelled out the word "Viking" with each letter on a different chest. The impressed girls laughed and shouted back compliments but kept walking.

"See what I mean?" My companion set his elbow on the back of the empty seat between us, which made him seem suddenly very close. "Idiots."

I sent him a small smile, not about to confess I'd been craving to be an idiot right along with them. "At least they excel in school spirit," I answered diplomatically.

Throwing back his head to reveal a strong tanned neck, the man laughed. "That's probably the only thing they excel at. I swear I've flunked at least half of that crowd."

Sitting up straighter, I perked to attention. "You're a teacher at Ellamore?"

With a regal kind of nod, he held out a hand. "Philip Chaplain. I'm a professor for the history department."

"Then we're neighbors." Brightening, I took his hand. I knew the history department building was located next to Morella Hall, my building, but I'd never met any faculty from there. "I just started this semester, teaching literature."

Surprise reigned on his features before he gave an uncertain smile. "You're a graduate assistant?"

I shook my head. "No. I'm straight up faculty. Like you."

It usually annoyed me when someone mistook me for a student or a mere teacher's assistant. But Philip was being so nice, I forgave him without a thought.

Again, he looked surprised and confused before his face cleared. "*Oh,*" he drew out the word as recognition lit his eyes. "You're the—" Gaze traveling over my face and down my body until his eyes paused on my chest, he nodded. "Yes, of course you are."

Those four murmured words confused me. Of course I was *what*? Had even *he* heard I was the only professor on campus willing to flunk Noel Gamble? Maybe Frenetti had been right; I was going to get a bad reputation if I didn't—

"Your reputation precedes you, Dr. Kavanagh," Philip cut into my thoughts, his smile flashing with genuine warmth. "We've all heard about the youngest faculty member to ever teach for Ellamore, but no one from my department has actually met you yet. We were beginning to think you were a myth the English people had created, because you know, they do like their fiction."

I refrained from rolling my eyes at his corny pun. "Yes, we do. But I can assure you I'm quite real. Please, call me Aspen."

"Aspen," he repeated, his eyes taking on a husky kind of glow and his voice lowering. "A lovely name for a lovely woman."

I flushed from head to toe, not sure how to take such a compliment. I kind of liked it, but I wasn't sure if I was allowed to.

Before I could stumble out some halfhearted thank you, the game's announcer broke in over the speaker system, kicking the day's events into gear.

Philip and I turned our attention to the end zone where a gigantic Jumbotron sat. A series of two-second clips from various players flashed across the screen, creating an inspiring monologue from the team as a whole. When they showed Noel wearing a number twelve jersey with a ball cradled in his large hands, my insides jumped with restless energy.

"It's about that moment when everything comes

down to nothing but the drive and determination to succeed," he said to the crowd before a new player's face lit up the entire screen.

Still picturing number twelve though, I pursed my lips, remembering another "D" word he'd used to describe the game he played. It hadn't been drive or determination, but desperation.

I still wondered why he'd said that and what he'd meant. It'd been two days since our meeting in my office and he'd yet to turn in his revision paper, but I was curious to learn why he'd chosen that one word.

"So, you like football, huh?" Philip's voice broke into my thoughts and I literally jumped, making him chuckle and reach out to set a hand on my shoulder, steadying me. "Sorry about that."

I waved my hand, instantly forgiving him. "No, it's fine. I was...woolgathering. But, yes, I've always enjoyed watching. It's almost like a chessboard, but more...physical." Rolling my eyes, because I probably sounded like an idiot, I sent him a bashful smile. "There's not a lot of contact in my vocation, so I've always been curious and somewhat stimulated by it."

Glancing up to catch his reaction, I abruptly decided *physical, contact* and *stimulated* might not have been the ideal word choices. That glimmer in his eyes he'd gotten when he'd said my name returned.

His lips twitched with an amused smile. "I love it when a woman is stimulated by football," was all he said before the people in the crowd around us flew out of their seats and began cheering. I ripped my attention away from Philip and turned to the field to see all the players making their big entrance. Immediately, I stood up with everyone else.

It didn't take me long to find player number twelve. He was jogging near the front of the line, wearing a maroon jersey, while half the team wore white. With his helmet on and his pads making his shoulders impossibly wide, he epitomized the perfect football star. I held my breath and brought my knuckles to my mouth, stretching up onto my tiptoes so I could keep a constant visual of him.

"With Gamble as a senior next year, I think we'll take national championships, no problem," Philip said, leaning in toward me.

I jumped, already having forgotten he was there. But seriously? How had he known to mention Noel Gamble just when I was thinking about him? Ugh, probably because I was always thinking about Noel Gamble.

I sent the history professor a weak smile. "So, he's that good, huh?"

Philip's grin was knowing and kind of flirtatious. "Just watch. He's the best QB we've probably ever had."

"Hmm." I tried not to appear too intrigued. But there was no way to mask my anticipation twenty minutes later when Noel's side took the offensive and he jogged onto the field. On his first play, he wound back his arm as soon as the center snapped the ball into his hands. With perfect precision, he zipped it toward another player racing down the field. His receiver didn't have to slow down or speed up. He didn't even have to stretch for the catch. He merely cupped his fingers and the pigskin landed within the gloved cradle of his waiting palms.

"Oh, my God," I murmured, astounded. "He could be the next Aaron Rodgers."

Next to me, Philip moaned and then laughed as he set his hand over his heart, wincing. "God, please don't tell me you're a Packers fan."

With an arch of my eyebrows, I turned to him, ready to defend my team loyally. "Of course. Why, which pro team do you support?"

"Hello. We're in Illinois. I'm Bears, all the way." I wrinkled my nose, but he was quick to add, "But my favorite quarterback in the league is Tom Brady."

Nodding, I let him have that one. Brady wasn't bad. Not bad at all. But... "I'm pretty partial to Alex Smith myself."

This time, it was Philip's turn to nod as if allowing me that concession before he added, "At least you didn't say Manning."

I grinned. "Which one?"

He pointed at me, a big grin spreading across his face. "Hell, you do know your quarterbacks. Very nice, Dr. Kavanagh." He never did tell me whether he was talking about Eli or Peyton, but he seemed so impressed by my sports knowledge, I guess it didn't matter.

Pleased I'd been able to impress him, I smiled back and reminded him, "It's just Aspen."

"Right. Aspen." As his gaze heated in that interested-male way of his, I bit the inside of my lip, not sure what to do with all his attention.

Around us, the stadium went crazy. I wrenched my attention to the field just in time to see number twelve dodge a hulking defender and leap into the end zone, scoring a touchdown.

"Hey, what're you doing next Saturday?" Phillip asked, distracting me again, and shocking the ever-loving crap out of me. "Because I'd love to take you out."

My mouth fell open. "Umm..." I couldn't believe this. I'd come here to ogle another man, and ended up getting asked out by a coworker. Shaking my head because I was still confounded by the fact that this was actually happening, I sputtered. "Doesn't the administration look down on that type of thing? Coworkers...mingling?"

Philip shrugged. "I wouldn't exactly call us coworkers. We work in totally different departments. Besides, there're a couple faculty members on campus who're actually married to each other. The only policy I'm certain they have about mingling is between teachers and students."

I glanced toward number twelve on the field, who was currently getting mauled by his teammates as they congratulated him. The twinge in my chest told me I was disappointed to hear the teacher/student policy spoken aloud, though I already knew it existed. I was even more boggled about my reaction because even if we'd been free to date, Noel Gamble would never give me the time of day, and the last thing I needed was a man-whore like him. So why was I upset?

Turning back to Philip, I took a deep breath. My heart thudded fast in my chest, unable to believe I was actually going to do this. "Okay then," I said. "Yes. I think I'd like that."

He grinned back. "Really?" When I nodded, he drew in a deep breath and sent me a huge, relieved grin. "Great. It's a date then."

Wow. A date.

A cheer from the crowd had me jerking my attention to the field just as the defense intercepted the ball, and Gamble's offense trotted back onto the field.

I shook my head in bewilderment. I couldn't help but wonder what number twelve would do if he knew he'd just assisted me in setting up my first date in eighteen months. Since he hated me, I'm sure it'd annoy him, so I smiled even wider. Good. It served the guy right for making me think about him as inappropriately as I did.

CHAPTER SIX

"Men go to far greater lengths to avoid what they fear than to obtain what they desire." - Dan Brown, *The Da Vinci Code*

~NOEL~

TUESDAY MORNING, I entered Literature class cantankerous and on edge. After coming straight from the nearest print lab where I'd printed out an eight-page remake paper for Dr. Kavanagh, I felt cracked open and raw.

She had demanded I talk about my feelings. So I'd talked. I'd poured my soul into the dumb assignment. I had dug inside myself and laid it all on the line, uncovering things I hadn't realized I'd even felt.

Without a word to the woman already seated behind the desk as she dug through an opened briefcase, I slapped the stapled pages onto a bare spot, facedown.

Her head jerked up, wide green eyes making her look way too young to have a PhD.

Narrowing my gaze, I spent a second to glare before I turned away and found a seat.

After settling into my chair, I glanced her way to see her eyeing the essay curiously. Then, without turning it over to read it, she slipped it gingerly off the desk and tucked it into the mesh pocket inside the lid of her briefcase. After clicking the latch shut, she lifted her attention and began class...as if nothing earth shattering had just happened.

I blew out a breath. There. It was finished. Done. I didn't have to stress about that stupid, ridiculous thing again.

Though a couple of my fingers were taped together because I'd banged them up in the scrimmage this weekend, I drummed them ceaselessly on my thigh. I couldn't take my gaze off that closed briefcase. With blood rushing through my veins like a speeding train, I just couldn't brush off this crazy, antsy, panicked feeling flooding me.

Halfway through class it suddenly struck me what I'd done. I'd let a woman I totally disliked into my innermost thoughts. Jesus, I'd spilled everything to her, all my fears and insecurities, my deepest wishes and dreams, my fucked-up childhood and all my siblings' problems, too. And my biggest secret ever.

Now she'd know how many times I'd had to stay home to babysit while my mother had left us to get drunk and stoned before she came home to fuck some stranger as loudly as possible on our couch. She'd know how many times I'd gotten the shit beat out of me in school for being a member of the Gamble family. She'd know exactly how poorly everyone in my hometown really thought of me. She'd know...she'd know...

Holy shit, she could break me with all the fodder I'd just stapled neatly together and hand-delivered to her. What the hell had I done? What had I been thinking to write all that shit? As soon as I'd started typing, though, purposely going overboard on my thoughts and feeling and home life, I just kept on, unable to stop. The words had bled out of me.

But now... Now...

A cold sweat leaked down the center of my back. I didn't hear a word of the discussion going on around me. I could only stare in bleak doom at that closed black briefcase.

As soon as she dismissed class an hour and a half later, I shot out of my seat, determined to rectify this. Darting past other students to catch her before she left, I found her still at her desk. She'd barely re-opened her case to set her notes inside when I reached her.

"Dr. Kavanagh?" Totally out of breath, my voice caused her to start. She looked up, and I held out my hand impatiently. "I just remembered something I forgot to put on that paper. Can I have it back?"

With a lift of her eyebrows, she taunted, "I don't know. *Can* you?"

I barely refrained from rolling my eyes. The woman unknowingly had the power to crush me into nothing sitting innocuously in her briefcase, and she wanted to stand around, correcting my fucking grammar? It figured.

"*May* I?" I ground out obligingly. I'd play her way as long as I got that paper back.

"I'm sorry, but no." Sending me a tight smile, she slapped her briefcase closed, the sound echoing through my chest and tightening my muscles with dread.

No? What did she mean by no?

As she grasped the handle and pulled the case off her desk to leave the room, I dogged her steps. But she didn't seem to notice, so I dodged around her to block the exit. "But I forgot to proofread it. Give me another few hours, and I'll have it right back to you. I swear."

She shook her head. "It's too late, Mr. Gamble. I already gave you more opportunity to fix your grade than anyone else in the class. This is the last time I'll accept anything for this assignment." She began to walk around me.

"Then I'll take the original D," I burst out, beyond frantic. Shit, what was I saying? I couldn't accept the original D. But that had to be better than her reading my paper.

Dr. Kavanagh slowed to a stop. When she lifted her face to arch that damn eyebrow of hers again, I caved, ready to get down on both knees, begging.

"I was angry, okay." The rasp in my voice revealed my desperation, and I hated that. But I kept pleading, needing her to give up my paper more than I needed my next breath. "You dared me, and I responded out of some kind of knee-jerk reaction. I didn't mean to write all that shit. So..." I held out my hand cautiously, as if approaching a cornered and wounded, wild animal. "Just let me redo it. One last time. Please."

She gaped at me, her green eyes wide with shock. Glancing at my seeking palm, she said, "Now I really feel compelled to keep this essay, just to see what you've written."

"Damn it," I growled. "Give me back the fucking paper. It's *mine!*"

Without thinking, I reached for her briefcase. She skipped away, jerking it out of my reach. "*Mr. Gamble!* What do you think you're doing?"

Realizing what I'd just done, I pulled back, only to lift my trembling fingers to my mouth and pinch my lips together, keeping in the instinctive urge to apologize.

But, Jesus. What the hell was I thinking? To tackle her just outside a classroom while hundreds of students—*witnesses*—streamed past?

I shook my head and closed my eyes, pulling my scattered wits back in around me. *Get it together, Gamble.*

When I opened my lashes, she still stared at me with wide, wary eyes. A hint of fear stirred in those green depths, and I experienced a profound regret I couldn't even name. I opened my mouth to apologize, but once again, I stopped myself.

"Whatever," I murmured, sliding a step away.

It was just words. Words were nothing. If she tried to make something of this, I'd just shrug it off and say I'd made it up. Only sticks and stones could break me, right? I'd make her meaningless response to my words slide right off my back.

Except an innate fear had already soaked in. I spun away before I could embarrass myself further.

But holy shit, this was probably going to break me. Not only had I given her the power to crush my spirit on a personal level, but I'd also handed her a very valid reason to get me kicked out of her university permanently.

***

"You never really understand a person until you consider things from his point of view... Until you climb inside of his skin and walk around in it."
- Harper Lee, *To Kill a Mockingbird*

***

~*A*SPEN~

I messed up. I opened Noel Gamble's essay at work and read it in my office.

I just couldn't help myself. The way he'd

confronted me to get it back, to keep me from seeing what he'd written, had gotten me curious and left me a little too shaken. For the briefest moment, I had thought he was going to wrestle me down in order to retrieve it. He'd looked desperate enough.

Then his face had cleared, and he'd seemed so shocked and appalled by his actions, I'd been worried he was going to burst into tears. What was worse, if he had, I would've done something equally horrifying, like hug him. Or give him his paper back.

Thank God I'd done neither.

Because once I started reading his essay, I couldn't stop. It was like witnessing a fatal car accident, watching his awful life unfold, one tear-jerking sentence at a time.

My chest ached as I finished the last line of the essay. Damn it. Noel Gamble wasn't supposed to be like this. He wasn't supposed to have such a tough childhood, or possess redeemable qualities, or make me feel any kind of compassion for him. He wasn't supposed to reach into my soul and get a handhold of my heart or squeeze these feelings out of me, exactly as he'd just done. No one should be able to do that in eight double-spaced pages. But he had.

My cheeks were still wet from the tears that had fallen. From reading his stupid, amazing, well-written paper.

It's possible he could've lied. He could've made everything up just to get the work done. But from the way he'd reacted after class earlier, I knew he hadn't. These were his true thoughts. His true feelings. His true actions.

He'd broken rules, done things I normally would've been appalled about, but he'd done it for the noblest, sweetest, most amazing reason. His desperate love for his siblings had given him the determination to get where he was today.

I shivered, hugging his essay to my chest as the

last of my tears dried on my face. If only someone had loved me the way he loved his brothers and sister.

Well, one thing was certain. Noel Gamble had achieved the impossible; he'd managed to completely revise my point of view of him.

Oh, hell.

CHAPTER SEVEN

"Your emotions are the slaves to your thoughts, and you are the slave to your emotions." - Elizabeth Gilbert, *Eat, Pray, Love*

~NOEL~

"SO, WHAT DO YOU think I should do?"

Groaning, I closed my eyes and let the back of my head clunk against the weight lifting bench underneath me. Above me, the bar I'd just bench-pressed rested solidly in the chrome uprights.

"I don't know, Caroline." It was too early for this. I'd worked late last night, and I had ladies' night to look forward to again this evening with still only four of us to man the entire bar. "How bad's the bruise?"

"What do you mean, how bad is it?" My sister's voice screeched through the phone. "It's a freaking bruise...around his *eye*. You know that little thug gang of bullies gave it to him."

I blew out an exhausted breath. We really needed

a fifth bartender at Forbidden. Immediately. I loved the money working overtime brought, but this was going to kill me. "Yeah, probably," I said halfheartedly, only to yawn.

"Oh, my God," Caroline chastised. "Don't pretend to care about us or anything. Our middle brother's getting jumped by a gang. But poor Noel is tired so—"

"Christ!" I sat up, scowling across the training room as I cut my sister off. "I'm sorry if I'm not completely with it. I've been working my ass off to help support you, you know. Which reminds me, did you get the last check I sent on Monday?" *Or had our mother intercepted it again and bought more drugs?*

"Yeah, it arrived yesterday, but that doesn't help—"

"What do you expect me to do? Drive twelve hours to come home to kick the little punks' asses? I don't even own a car."

"I *wanted* you to talk to him."

"Fine." I rubbed my aching temples. "Put him on the phone."

"He's sleeping right now."

With a sigh, I closed my eyes. "Okay, then. I'll call later today after classes and before I head into work. Now, what about Colt? Is he still feeling better?"

His fever had persisted for a few days after his episode with strep throat. Caroline had called me in tears on Saturday, just before my scrimmage game, to wonder if he'd ever get better again, but then yesterday, she'd finally reported he'd returned to school.

"Oh, he's fine. You can't even tell he was ever sick. I'm not sure why I was so worried."

I smiled fondly. "Because you're a born worrier. You're probably worrying as we speak about that dance you have this weekend."

"Am not," she argued, but I could hear the grin in her voice.

I chuckled, only to fall sober as I asked, "Mom ever come home?"

It was a question I rarely bothered to voice any longer, but my sister seemed more stressed than usual. She needed some relief. And horrible parent that our mother was, her presence had to be better than nothing.

"She dropped in for a few hours on Tuesday night. Ate half the groceries in the fridge, then took a shower, and was gone again."

I rolled my eyes. "Sounds about right." At least she hadn't brought some loser in with her to harass my siblings this time.

When a sigh came through the other end of the line, I felt the urge to make Caroline smile. She didn't smile enough anymore. I could tell by listening to the sound of her voice.

"So, you got that new dress for the dance yet?" I asked, totally not caring about dresses, but loving my sister unconditionally.

"Yeah. My friends and I went shopping after school on Tuesday."

I nodded. "What color is it?" When a right tackle on the butterfly press a couple feet away paused to send me an odd look for asking that question, I flipped him off. He could think whatever he wanted about me. I knew talking about dresses would cheer Caroline up.

And it seemed to. "Blue," she answered, her voice brightening noticeably. "Well, teal, technically."

I didn't have a clue what color teal was, but that didn't matter. Caroline kept rambling, describing its length and type of cloth and amount of ruffles.

"Sander even came over last night so he could see it and find a corsage to match."

My eyebrows lifted. "He came over, huh?"

"Oh, my God. Nothing happened. I swear, you are the most overprotective brother ever. Colton was here the entire time. And he followed Sander around everywhere he went."

"Just Colt? Where was Brandt?"

"I told you, he was out getting beaten up by that freaking gang."

"Oh, right. I forgot." Wondering what exactly I was going to say to Brandt to help him stay out of trouble, I yawned again. Damn, I needed more sleep. My brain had gone fuzzy. Closing my eyes, I envisioned my mattress at the apartment and wondered how long it would be before I could rest my head on my pillow again, curl up under the sheets, and just—

Unbidden, an image of my English professor popped into the scene. Her hair was all plucked up in its bun and her baggie blazer was tossed crumbled to the foot of my bed. When soft, phantom hands slid up my bare chest, I jumped and snapped my eyes open.

Jesus, it'd definitely been too long since I'd gotten laid.

Still sweaty and shirtless, lifting weights in the university's training room, I noticed Quinn Hamilton approaching, probably wanting more throwing tips. I gave an internal sigh.

"I gotta go, Care. But I'll check in with Brandt later today, find out what's going on with him. Okay?"

She grumbled something I didn't catch but finally consented and told me she loved me before hanging up.

The next half hour passed with more grueling exercise, running through different plays and scenarios with Hamilton, teaching him how to be a better player than I was. God, I hoped he didn't turn out to be better than me. All this wasn't worth it if I ended up losing my spot on the team and not even garnering the attention of NFL scouts.

Some days, I just wanted to give up, and sleep in, or skip work, or just totally blow off weight training and not even attend classes. But I had a sinking feeling that slipping, even once, would come back to haunt me. So I kept plowing forward with everything I had, hoping it would all come out okay.

But, God, I was so tired. Felt like there was a fifty-pound weight on my chest. If I could just unload all my crap onto someone else, talk to someone...

Caroline had me to listen to her problems, but I told no one about all my worries and concerns. Not even Ten. He had no idea what my life was like outside Ellamore.

Still half out of it after my sleepless night, I tromped to class. I was so far gone, I'd completely forgotten about my dreaded make-up assignment I'd turned in to Kavanagh on Tuesday. I didn't think a thing of it as I entered the room on autopilot...until she called my name.

Damn, but her voice always did something to me.

I paused, my foot lifted to step up the first set of stairs to head toward the back of the class where I saw Ten lounging. Turning my gaze, I glanced her way, but she wasn't looking at me. With her attention on a paper she was examining on her desk, she reached over and lifted another stapled pile off the top of her briefcase and held it out for me to come fetch.

My stomach dropped into my knees. Shit. She'd already read it?

I froze, unable to move an inch. She continued to read over the sheet on her desk for another ten seconds before she finally lifted her face and arched me a dry look. As she wiggled my paper in an invitation to come take it, I just stared at her, my entire life flashing before my eyes.

She'd read my paper, and now she knew. And, huh, I guess I'd unloaded all my problems on someone after all, hadn't I? Shit, why did it have to be her? I studied her face cautiously, fearing the worst. But she gave away nothing except a half-annoyed expression because I wasn't moving.

She just had to be one of those people who had a freaking good poker face, didn't she? I couldn't decipher a single thing she was thinking.

More concerned with what she must think of me now than I was worried about my actual grade, I took a step toward her, only to pause. God, I didn't want to take it back. It had to be littered with red, telling me exactly what she was going to do with all her newfound knowledge about me.

Lowering my gaze to my paper in her raised hand, I strode the last few steps and slipped it free, only to roll it into a tube so I couldn't see the score or all her comments in the margins.

My heart banged in my chest as I walked sightlessly to my desk. She'd read it. She knew. So what the hell did she think of me now? And what was she going to do about everything she'd learned?

"What'd you get?" Ten demanded as soon as I sat down. I glanced at him but I didn't see him. Fear and anxiety completely fuzzed my vision; I could only feel the loss of my paper when he ripped the essay out of my hand.

"Hey! Fucker." I snagged it back before he could unroll it. "Hands off, asshole."

"Well, what're you waiting for? The grade fairy to come along and magically transform it into an A?"

I set my jaw and sent him a look. When he merely stared back, waiting, I sighed and rolled my eyes. Trying to act as if it wasn't the end of the world, I slowly unrolled the pages, hoping to God he didn't notice the slight tremor in my hand.

When I saw an A staring up at me, my mouth fell open. I blinked, thinking my eyes were still fucked up. But the A didn't go away.

"Holy shit.,"

"What?" Ten ripped it out of my hand again, but I was too shocked to yank it back. "Holy shit," he echoed. His mouth fell open too as he lifted his eyebrows my way. Then he leaned in to grin. "And you said you didn't fuck her, you freaking liar."

"Excuse me?" Instantly irritated, I jerked the paper back and cradled it to my chest. "I earned this score, thank you very much."

He lifted his hands. "Hey, I'm all for fixing your grade with a make-up paper. But from a D to an A?" He glanced around before leaning in closer. "Man, that's suspicious. What'd you have to do to get it?"

"Nothing," I growled, scowling at him hard. "I had to *re-write* the paper."

Ten lifted his eyebrows in disbelief. "Really? That's it?"

"Yes." Eyes snapping, I glared him down until he lifted his hands again and backed off.

"Okay, man," he said, but his expression crinkled with mirth as if he knew better. "If you say so...teacher's pet."

"I do, goddamn it."

When Dr. Kavanagh stood up and started class, Ten turned around to face the front of the room, but I continued to glare at the back of his head. I wanted to keep arguing with him, telling him how much it had taken to earn this grade. I'd damn well earned it too.

But like him, I also found it impossible to believe.

At the front, my teacher acted as cool and collected as always, as if she didn't know everything about me I kept hidden from this town. Though I tried to keep inconspicuous about it, I watched her, waiting for the moment she'd look my way and reveal what she really thought of me now and what she was going to do about my turpitudes. But for the entire hour, she didn't even glance in my direction.

I didn't want to admit it, but that kind of stung. I'd shared something personal with her, and it hadn't even seemed to hit her radar. Nothing about her had changed. Gritting my teeth, I glanced at the top of my desk, disappointed she didn't seem as completely altered as I felt.

After class, I filed out with everyone else, refraining from glancing her way. I waited until I had a moment alone, away from people, before I ducked into a bathroom and trapped myself in a stall. Just to make sure it still had an A on it, I dug my paper back out of my bag. It didn't have a plus sign next to it the way Sidney Chin's essay had, but it still had that beautiful scarlet letter slashed across the top.

I glanced down to make sure it was the same paper I'd turned in, and I finally saw little grammar marks she'd made, correcting commas and misspelled words. No notes were scribbled in the margins until I flipped to the last page. After my final, closing paragraph, she'd penned in the line, *Much better. I knew you could grasp the concept of the assignment.*

I blinked. Was that it? I had told her about the time one of my mother's men had beat the shit out of me when he'd gotten high in our living room. I'd told her about all the hiding places I'd found for my brothers and sister whenever my mother had drank too much and was pissed off. But the mack daddy of all, I'd told her how I'd saved up all my money to pay off some geek from high school to fix my GPA in the school's computer system so I had a better chance at receiving a scholarship.

I was a fake and a liar who didn't belong here. And now she knew it. If she wanted, she could make everyone else know it, too. She could ruin me.

I had no idea why I'd incriminated myself like that. She could've gone to the administration and turned me in. But my transgressions had eerily reminded me of that fucking Gatsby character in her book and how he'd cheated and lied to get everything for the woman he loved. I'd done just that for the three people I loved most in the world.

And all Kavanagh had to say about it was *much*

better?

Jesus. What did that mean? Was she going to keep my secret? Was she going to use it as blackmail against me? Was she even going to mention it to me at all?

I flipped back to the front page and stared at the letter she'd given me. I had a feeling she wouldn't have written in an A if she'd had any plans of getting me kicked out of Ellamore. She could've taken the paper straight to her sour-faced boss. But she *had* given me an A. And she'd handed the evidence back to me.

I blew out a breath, and finally, the muscles in my stomach relaxed.

Shit. She was giving me another chance. I was back in the game and actually felt good for the first time all semester about the possibility I just might succeed in all this.

***

I was still floating from the high of that amazing score the next morning when I saw Coach Jacobi in the training room.

"Hey, Gam!" he called in his booming coach's voice. "How'd you do on that make-up paper you wrote for your literature class?"

I paused and tilted my head to the side. How the hell did he know I'd managed to talk Kavanagh into letting me redo a paper? "I got an A," I murmured, curiously. "How'd you know about that?" Oh, hell. Maybe Kavanagh *had* gone to him after all and told him I'd cheated on my high school grade point average.

My coach merely grinned. "What? You think I don't keep tabs on my star player? Jesus, Gamble, I've been watching your score slip all semester in that class. Thought it was time to have a word with

Frenetti, the dean of the English department. Glad to see they're finally snapping themselves back into shape."

My mouth fell open. I couldn't fucking believe this. I knew Kavanagh had been forced to give me another chance by her dean, but I hadn't known... Fuck, my own coach? *Et tu*, Jacobi?

And here, I thought I'd actually earned that A. It had taken enough out of me to deserve an A. But...

Maybe she really *had* tried to tell someone how I'd cheated to get my scholarship. Maybe no one had listened to her. Maybe...

Feeling suddenly sick, I half-assed my way through the rest of my weights. If she'd been forced to give me a good score, then what had I really earned on my paper? Had it just been another D?

Since I'd stepped foot on this campus, I'd played it straight. I'd worked my ass off to be a good player, a good, honest student, and a good employee at Forbidden. But if others were lying and cheating for me, did that mean I was incapable of improving, doomed to be a fraud for the rest of my life? Was I still a great big nothing who just happened to have a good throwing arm.

CHAPTER EIGHT

"Be who you are and say what you feel, because those who mind don't matter, and those who matter, don't mind." - Bernard M. Baruch

~ASPEN~

FRIDAY MORNING, I arrived early to work. I liked reading in my office before class. It settled my nerves more than anything else could.

My big date with Philip was scheduled for tomorrow, making me as antsy as hell, and I'd broken down and tried to call my mother this morning. She'd refused to answer the phone, so I had no idea about my father's prognosis, if he still had two legs, or what.

After glancing over the curriculum I wanted to go through in each class, I let out a little sigh of relief and opened my ereader, eager to escape into some juicy fiction. But a tap on my doorframe had me gritting my teeth.

I needed some alone time here, people. Why

did—

All thought process stalled in my head when I saw Noel Gamble.

"Wha...?" I didn't know what to say. I simply gaped. His hair was wet and face gleamed as if he'd just stepped out of the shower or he'd been sweating profusely. Skimming my gaze down his athletic body, I noticed he was wearing gray sweats, running shoes with no socks, and a wrinkled, maroon Ellamore Vikings shirt that hugged his defined chest.

He stepped into my office, his jaw hard and eyes heated with anger. "Look, I don't want you to give me a grade I don't deserve. I fought for an A, damn it. And I want to actually *earn* one."

My mouth fell open. "Wha..." I said again, then shook my head. *Decorum, Aspen.* After a deep breath, I tried again. "What makes you think you *didn't* earn it?"

"Because I just came from fucking weight training where my coach told me he went to your dean person and complained. And I remember that guy being in your office when I came to talk to you last week. I thought I told you I didn't want any special treatment just because I'm—"

"And I didn't give you any." I glowered as my senses crashed back into me. Of course, he'd come back to argue with me about an A. Only Noel Gamble would do such a thing. "I'm sorry, Mr. Gamble, but if anything, I judged you more harshly because of that. Believe me, you *earned* your score."

He gave a harsh laugh and spun away to wipe his hand through his hair. "Why do I have such a hard time believing that?"

"I have no idea." Pushing to my feet, I set my hands on my hips and kept scowling. "Maybe because you're a stubborn, untrusting, relentless individual." He whirled back to send me a surprised glance.

I arched an eyebrow. "And for your information, I

didn't exactly enjoy getting bitched out by my boss for the fair and just grades I provide. It made me want to give you an even worse score than before. But then you went and wrote what you wrote, and suddenly, I didn't have to worry about what Frenetti told me to do anymore, because I could just take your essay to the board and get you permanently expelled. There was no reason to give you an A at all, except you shocked the shit out of me when you actually wrote a decent paper. You showed me how much you're willing to put forth to reach your goals, and I decided not to take that away from you. So you're just going to have to accept the fact that I am such an amazing, kickass teacher I actually got through your thick skull in that one meeting we had and miraculously taught you the meaning of literature analysis. Got it?"

He blinked. When I didn't change my expression, he blinked a couple more times until his face finally softened. After blowing out a breath, he shook his head and took a step back. Eyes filling with questions, he murmured, "You really think you taught me that well, huh?"

I lifted my chin stubbornly. "Oh, I _know_ I did."

A grin tugged at his mouth. Then he huffed out a quick laugh. "Well, okay then. If you say it was honestly an A, then I won't argue."

"You mean, like you've been doing for the past five minutes?"

"Right." This time, his smile was a full-fledged beam.

It did things to me I would be too mortified to admit to anyone aloud. But my body kept responding despite how much I commanded it to cool down.

"Okay, then." He nodded and turned away to leave.

Startled he was going to vanish just as abruptly as he'd appeared, I panicked. I didn't want to see him go yet. My brain scrambled for something. There were so many things I knew I should say, but instead I blurted out, "And for future reference, you might want to look up the meaning to TMI."

When he whirled back, I lurched a little in reverse. I wasn't expecting that to stop him in his tracks, but I was perversely pleased it had.

"If you'll remember," he murmured, sauntering back to my desk and setting his hands on top so he could lean over and stare me right in the eyes. "I did try to get it back from you."

With a small nod, I managed to meet his gaze with what I hoped was a cool expression. "And I should've given it back. But I'm glad I didn't."

I sank back into my seat, trying to turn my attention to the screen saver on my computer. But all I could focus on was the man on the other side of my desk.

He alarmed me when he sat down on the chair in the seat across from me, his eyes alert and seeking. I sat up straighter, my gaze darting from the chair to his face as he demanded, "What does that mean?"

Shit, I'd exposed too much by saying that, hadn't I? "I...I...Nothing. I'm sorry I said anything. I shouldn't have."

"But you did. Now spill it." His hand curled into a fist and slid off the desk so he could press it to his mouth. Over his whitened knuckles, he stared at me with...what was that, *worry*?

No. He couldn't be worried about my opinion. Surely not. I'd already told him I wasn't going to rat him out.

"I assure you, there's nothing to spill." My voice was soft as if it wanted to reassure him. But I didn't want to reassure him. Did I?

His throat worked as he swallowed. Then he dropped his hand, and his tongue gave a quick nervous lick over his lips.

"You—" Cutting himself off, he glanced down at

his fingers clenching and unclenching in his lap. With a soft, self-conscious laugh, he lifted his face only to glance to the side at one of my bookshelves. "You're really not going to expose me? That's just—" He turned back to me, his expression confused and yet hopeful. "You could've gotten rid of me for good."

"Yes," I said. "But I didn't."

He leaned toward me, his eyes seeking. "Why not?"

"I...I just told you why."

His brows furrowed. "Because you were impressed by how well I'd fixed my essay? *That's all?*"

Clearing my throat discreetly, I glanced away, wishing I didn't feel like a bug pinned under a microscope. "Well...mostly," I hedged my answer.

"Then why else?" His voice was compelling. I had to turn the tables on him before I blurted out something embarrassing.

"Why did you tell me something like that?" I charged right back, but I could see on his face exactly why. I'd read enough books about serial killers to know sometimes people just needed to confess what they'd done, to get all their secrets off their chest.

But why had Noel Gamble cleared his conscience to *me*?

Shaking his head, he sent me a look that told me clearly he wasn't sure why he'd chosen me. "I don't..." He closed his eyes. "You challenged me. You told me to find a correlation with someone in that book. And I did."

I nodded, my head heavy from what was happening here, between us. "Yes, you most certainly did. And you handed me written proof that you cheated your way into this university."

"And you gave that written proof back to me," he countered, his voice low and blue eyes alert.

I had. I'd given it back without telling another soul what he'd written. "How much did you have your

GPA doctored?"

He blew out a quick breath. "Four tenths of a percent. Just enough to get the scholarship."

I believed him. I'd looked up his records to see he'd made it the minimum possible GPA to get a scholarship. He could've given himself a straight 4.0, but he'd kept it humbly low. For a cheater, he'd remained surprisingly honest.

That had been another small but insignificant reason I hadn't said anything to anyone.

His blue eyes watched me, reminding me of the other, biggest reason I'd kept silent.

He shook his head. "I haven't...I swear to you, I haven't done anything like that since I've come here. Everything at Ellamore has been all me. One hundred percent." His grin was self-derisive. "Even those D essays."

I placed my hands into my lap because they'd begun to shake. They wanted to reach for him and soothe and reassure him I'd never do anything to harm his education here. I could never hurt him. I wanted him to succeed as much as he wanted to. I wanted him to be able to escape his old life and help pull his siblings from it as well.

"I believe you," I said. "That's why I haven't said anything."

He blew out a breath. "Thanks. You have no idea how much this means to me. I'm not...I'm not used to second chances."

"I know. I read your paper, remember?" I meant it as a lighthearted tease, but he winced.

"Yeah, you did, didn't you? Jesus, you probably think I'm a poor, stupid piece of shit right now."

Glad he wasn't looking at me, I blinked repeatedly as the threat of tears stung my eyes. God, I wanted to hug him, so hard. What had happened to the ego-inflated football star I'd always seen in him? And aside from keeping my mouth shut about his cheating, why was he so worried about what *I* thought about him as a person? Aside from being his bitchy literature professor, I was no one to him.

He obviously didn't let many people know these things about him. The insistent way he'd tried to retrieve his paper before I'd even read it was proof of that. And yet, he'd let me in. He'd shown me the real Noel Gamble, something he didn't show just anyone.

Flattered I had received such a gift and yet scared to death about handling the fragility of it, I breathed in a deep breath before murmuring, "That's the very last thing I thought. In fact, it didn't even make the list of things I thought."

His gaze veered to me, and I felt electrocuted. Dear God, but the hope glittering in his eyes sucked me into this bubble where there was nothing but him and me.

"Then what did you think?"

My cheeks heated. No way could I tell him what I'd really thought. No matter what, he could not find out I had a huge, embarrassing crush on him. So I blurted out something just as awful. "I thought I was an idiot."

Noel blinked. "Huh?"

Damn it. Now I had to look away and address the bookshelves as I reluctantly admitted, "I judged you too harshly at the beginning of the semester and made biased, preconceived notions I shouldn't have, based on my own past. Reading your paper told me I was utterly and completely wrong. I don't blame you at all for what you had to do to save yourself and your brothers and sister. All this time, I thought you were the careless, arrogant, self-centered type who thought the world did and should revolve around you. I thought you would be a braggart, a show-off, and...and cruel."

He tipped his head to the side. "Cruel?"

Scratching behind my ear and not even touching

that one, all the while thinking about the cruel quarterback from my high school years, I cleared my throat. "The point is you completely astounded me. You had the courage to risk everything for the people you love. You came from an incredibly...difficult childhood, all the while taking on the responsibilities of your younger siblings, and still, you managed to accomplish so much. The whole paper was completely heartbreaking and inspirational. It was brilliant, and I needed an entire box of tissues to read it."

I set my hand against the desk, hoping to brace myself and somehow stop the word vomit. To my complete horror, it kept gushing.

"I keep thinking about it and hoping the amazing man I read about accomplishes all his goals and finds a measure of satisfaction in his life. Plus I really hope he gets his family out of that awful place. And I really need to shut up now because this is truly embarrassing, and I've never said anything so unprofessional to a student before in my life. And if you knew what was good for you, you'd stand up and—"

Noel reached out and set his hand on the desk next to mine. He didn't even touch me—a good three inches of space separated us—but it felt as if he'd just covered my fingers with his and squeezed pure life into me.

It effectively stopped my flow of words.

"Thank you," he said. That's all. One simple *thank you* and I almost started bawling. My lashes beat madly and my entire face was enflamed; I'm surprised I didn't set off the smoke detectors.

When he leaned in toward me, I swayed closer too until we were both straining across the desk to meet in the middle.

He paused less than a foot away. "What am I doing?" he whispered aloud to himself.

I was kind of asking myself the same question. And why had I leaned in to meet him? Answering in my own covert whisper, I said, "I don't know. What *are* you doing?"

He jerked back, ripping his hand off my desk. Balling his fingers into a fist, he brought them to his mouth, his expression full of frozen shock and dread as he gaped at me. Then he blinked, shook his head and quickly said, "Sorry."

Since I was in total denial over the fact he'd even been entertaining the idea of kissing me, I arched my eyebrows. "For what?"

"Nothing," he said immediately. He clutched the sides of his chair, still gawking at me with that petrified stare. "I'm going to go now."

Shooting up to his feet, he whirled around and fled. But then he paused at my quote board. After digging into his pocket, he pulled free a sheet of folded paper. Without opening it, he plucked one of my tacks from the cork and stabbed his note into the center. Then he was gone, and the doorway where he'd disappeared looked extra empty.

A nanosecond later, I scrambled from my chair and snagged the note off my board. Whipping it open, I gaped slack-jawed at the words he'd written in a sloppy, bold scrawl.

"The greatest scholars are not usually the wisest people." - Geoffrey Chaucer.

A second later, I shook my head and grinned. "*Touché*, Mr. Gamble. *Touché*."

Literary scholar or not, I'd just made a huge mistake; I had let Noel Gamble know how much he affected me.

I was still rattled by the time I eased back into my chair. I stared at my ereader but couldn't make myself reopen the story I'd been reading. All I could think about was—

My desk phone rang.

I answered without paying attention to what I was doing.

"Hey," an upbeat male voice entered my ear. "Are we still on for tomorrow night?"

"What?" I shook my head. "Who is this?"

"It's, uh...It's Philip. Philip Chaplain...from the—"

"Oh, my God. I'm sorry. Of course." Who else would it be? Wasn't like I had an active social life. "I wasn't thinking. Please excuse me. I have my Friday brain on."

He gave an uncertain chuckle. "It's fine. Been a long week."

Boy, hadn't it. "Yes, it has."

"Look, about tomorrow..." When he paused, I knew he was going to cancel. Damn. This had to be a record; I'd bombed my date before even going on it.

"Something came up..." Yep, I knew it. *Something came up...unavoidable...maybe some other time...blah, blah, blah. We can still be friends. Don't call me, I'll call you.* "So do you think we could just meet there at, say, seven thirty?"

It took me a moment to realize what he was asking. I'd been expecting the usual brush-off. *Meeting there* totally threw me for a loop.

"Oh! Uh...sure. Wait, where exactly are we meeting?"

"The Forbidden Nightclub. It's on Second between Grand and Admiral. Huge place. Amazing drinks. I think you'll like it."

I'd never been there before, hadn't even heard of it, and clubs were definitely not my thing. But I agreed because I'd already bought a dress for the occasion and I wanted—no, I *needed*—a reason to get my mind off a certain student of mine. "That sounds great. I'll see you there."

CHAPTER NINE

"Few people dare now to say that two beings have fallen in love because they have looked at each other. Yet it is in this way that love begins, and in this way only." - Victor Hugo, *Les Misérables*

~NOEL~

THE CLUB WAS MORE crowded than usual. I swiped a white towel across the beading sweat on my brow as I glanced at the swarming bodies swamping the other side of the bar.

When a waitress appeared with a round tray full of empty bottles, I lifted my chin to her in greeting. "Tips any good tonight?"

"Oh yeah." She wiggled her eyebrows before tossing the empties into the nearby trash. The familiar clink and shattering glass almost comforted me because it had become so common. But that was the only comfort I felt this evening.

I should've had the night off, yet in the past nine

days since the twins had quit, I'd been stuck behind the bar of Forbidden all fucking nine of those days. I'd had plans to meet up with Tianna and her friend, Marci, at the frat party for my long-overdue threesome tonight. It'd been almost six weeks since I'd been inside a woman. That was a dry spell for me.

It was probably what had me thinking dirty thoughts about my English professor too. Lately, I thought about her just before I went to sleep. When my head was nestled deep in a pillow and my eyes had just fluttered closed, there she'd come, wavering into my subconscious until I'd officially had way-more-than-one wet dream about her.

I still couldn't believe I'd almost kissed her in her office yesterday morning. It had to be the most embarrassing, horrifying thing I'd ever done.

It was impossible to tell whether she'd played dumb afterward, or if she honestly hadn't had a clue how close I'd come to leaning in and devouring her mouth. I was just grateful she hadn't made an issue of it.

But it heaped on one more reason why I really, really, *really* needed to find a woman for a nice, satisfying release. And soon. Except, Jessie, damn her, just had to call me into work. With Ten out of town visiting his family and the new guy, Lowe, doing something or other with his girlfriend, that left me and Pick unwillingly dragged in on our nights off.

"What can we get you, sweetheart?" Pick asked the waitress as she rested her elbows against the bar and drew in a deep, bracing breath as if she needed a day off too.

"Need a double rum and Coke with two Coors in a bottle. And I'll take some valium if you have any."

"Aww, it can't be that bad," Pick reached across the counter to massage her temples for her while I snagged a tumbler to make her order.

I chuckled. "Yeah, you should try working ladies'

night for us sometime. *Then* I'll listen to you talk about a bad shift."

She cocked me a dirty look only to close her eyes and moan when Pick hit a sensitive area. Shaking my head over how effortlessly he always made the girls sigh, I set the rum and Coke on a cocktail napkin and fished the beers out of the cooler.

Holding the neck of the two bottles in one hand as I flipped off the lids with an opener, I glanced toward Pick and the waitress just as a woman crossed my line of sight between people directly behind them. I barely caught a glimpse of her profile, but it was enough for me to crane my neck some more and try to catch another.

She'd been wearing a dark, backless dress that flared out from her tiny waist and ended just above her knees. Her slim, delicate shoulders had looked creamy pale and inviting. And her hair...wow, her hair had been dark, but not black. Maybe a deep red-brown mahogany. She'd swept one side up and pinned it in a loose roll, while she'd let the other side tumble down her back.

I loved it when women did that, leaving one side all mysterious and hidden away under a bounty of rich curls, while the other half tempted me with an open view of bare flesh. I always wanted to stroll up behind them and bend my head to kiss the exposed shoulder while I tunneled my fingers through the free-flowing part to caress what was hidden beneath. Best of both worlds.

And with this lady wearing a backless dress, my mind was already digging up visuals of how I could just keep kissing my way down to those twin dimples at the top of her ass.

I shuddered from the sudden weight tightening my pants and blindly set the two bottles on the waiting tray beside Pick.

"Thanks, Noel," the waitress called as I wandered

off. I didn't even acknowledge her as I leaned a little over the bar to squint into the crowd.

Damn. Where had she gone?

"Hey, can we get a screaming orgasm over here?"

Gnashing my teeth, I turned toward three girls motioning me over. They were all scantily dressed and smoking hot, but I was still tempted to keep searching for the lady in the black backless number.

Controlling myself, I shook my head free of little black dresses and returned to my duties. Grinning obligingly at the three, I lowered the timbre of my voice. "Why, yes. Yes, you can. Who wants to scream first?"

They giggled and drew in closer, leaning on the bar to give me a glimpse down all three tops. One wasn't wearing a bra. Nice.

Braless giggled. "We meant the drink."

"Oh, *oh*." I pressed my hand to my brow, feigning embarrassment. "Silly me. Of course you did. Well, you can have some of those, too." I winked at her. "Be right back."

Pick sidled up beside me as I was whipping up the first concoction for them. "Sure you can handle all three of those lovely honeys over there, partner?" he asked, spelling out his double meaning when he wiggled his eyebrows, making the silver stud in one glint under the dim overhead lights.

I snorted. "Trust me. I got this."

He chuckled but stepped back to help some guy who approached for an order. I returned to the girls and passed out their drinks. They paid in cash, and when they stuffed a couple extra bills into my tip jar, I smiled a little wider. "Thanks."

"Hey, aren't you Noel Gamble, the quarterback for ESU?" the tallest of the group finally gained the courage to ask.

"Yep. That's me." Always thrilled when someone recognized my face for something good, I propped my elbows onto the bar as I leaned in toward them. "Have you ladies seen me play?"

Two shook their heads while a third said not-so-successfully under her breath, "I'd sure *like* to see you play."

The grin I sent her pretty much said, *anytime, sweetheart*, though honestly, my mind was still on Black Dress. But flirting made me more money, so I kept flirting.

"When do you get off work?" another asked.

I opened my mouth to dish out another impish response that would hopefully drag more tip money from them when I saw someone approach the bar and sit at a stool at the other end. I glanced over and nearly swallowed my tongue when I saw her. Gorgeous dark hair tumbled over one shoulder, and that elusive black dress glimmered slightly in the overhead lights.

"Excuse me," I murmured and deserted the three co-eds to approach my mystery lady. Nothing was going to keep me from at least securing her digits.

But Pick was beating me to her. I grabbed his arm and jerked him back, unsettling his balance.

"What the fuck?" he said, stumbling into me.

"I changed my mind. You can have those three. I want her instead."

He snickered and glanced back at the woman who was busy with her head bent, searching for something in her clutch purse that matched the fabric of her dress. When he looked back toward the flirty girls, a slow grin spread across his face.

"Well, hell, Gamble. I think this is the first time you've preferred quality over quantity. I'm impressed."

"Just go take care of the airheads." I pushed him toward the three who were still lingering by the bar.

He laughed at my obvious fixation with the lone woman, but complied, strolling toward the trio.

I took a deep breath, a little anxious about the first impression I was going to give, and stepped toward her. She didn't notice my approach, which gave me a moment to plan my strategy.

In the end, I decided to go simple.

"What can I get you?" I asked, setting my hands on the edge of the bar and bracing my arms wide because I knew damn well how doing that made my muscles strain through my shirt. I let my slow smile start to spread as she lifted her face. Chicks always claimed to dig my smile as much as they did my biceps.

She looked up, and I held my breath, waiting for the moment our eyes connected. A jolt tore through me. I'd been hoping for a pretty face, and fuck, I wasn't disappointed. But the crushed emotion I saw in a pair of green, green eyes caught me off guard. They were wide and lined with some dark, smoky eye makeup that made her look all sexy and edible. But so very, very sad. My protective instincts kicked into gear, ready to rip apart whoever had hurt her.

Then I glanced at her mouth. Her lips were ripe and edible and shaped divinely, just like...wait a second. I knew those lips. They were way too familiar, even as they parted in surprise.

"Holy shit." I pulled back, zipping my gaze back up to her eyes and then all around her face, to take in the entire picture.

The fucking hot woman was my fucking hot English professor.

Jaw dropping, I couldn't have contained my shock if I tried.

"Dr. *Kavanagh*?"

What. The. Hell? This wouldn't do. It wouldn't do at all. I'd been craving some woman to help me take my mind off my teacher. And the universe had sent me her wearing a hot black dress instead? Un-fucking-believable.

I was immediately pissed for two reasons. This was totally not helping me get over my fixation on her. And the mystery woman who might've actually helped me do that turned out to be just as forbidden as she was, because they were one and the same. I narrowed my eyes and clenched my teeth. Well, this was just peachy.

***

"I wondered if he realized that the way he looked at me was far more intimate than copping a feel could ever be." - Maggie Stiefvater, *Shiver*

***

~*Aspen*~

I'd been stood up. I hadn't talked to Philip since the day before when we'd revised our plans, but I figured we were still on.

Oh, how wrong I was.

But I was already here, so I stayed and kept looking for him. I didn't want to become a lame loser and go home alone in the nicest, sexiest dress I owned to sulk on the couch as I ate bon-bons and watched reruns of my one true love, Damon, on *The Vampire Diaries*. I wanted my damn date to show.

So, here I wandered through clusters of partying friends, feeling alone and abandoned. Uncomfortable to find myself surrounded by so many college students, I wondered why Philip had even chosen this place. Wouldn't he want a break from this crowd?

Thank God, no one had recognized me as their English professor yet, but I'd certainly recognized a few of them. Or maybe I should say no one recognized me until I finally approached the bar after searching the place for Philip for the past forty-five minutes.

But as one of my student's eyes widened in shock and he uttered, "Dr. *Kavanagh*?" I gaped back at the football star, deciding Joseph Conrad had been a genius when he'd written *Heart of Darkness* and coined the phrase, *The horror, the horror!* Because that was exactly how I felt. Absolutely horrified.

Number one way to make my night a living hell: toss Noel Gamble into the mix while I was being stood up on a date.

I moaned out a little whimper under my breath, wondering what I'd ever done to karma to make it kick me in the tits like this. If Philip showed up now, I'd never be able to concentrate on him because Noel looked incredible in that tight black shirt. And his bulky arms were so...

Oh, yum.

Why did he have to work *here* of all places?

Clearing my throat, I straightened my shoulders and tried to pretend it was perfectly normal for me to be here, wearing the most-revealing clothes I owned, and relishing some potent alcohol to ease my mangled nerves.

"Y-yes. I...I'll take a Bud Light Lime." There. That had sounded good...enough. Normal, average woman ordering a drink from a normal average bartender... who just so happened to star in all the dirty dreams I'd had this past week.

He gaped at me a second longer, then shook his head and dully repeated, "Bud Light Lime," as if he was a recorder. But as soon as the words seemed to soak into his brain, he wrinkled his brow and snorted. "A Bud Light Lime? *Really*?"

"What?" I frowned, curious about the venom in his voice.

He shrugged. "I don't know. I just thought you'd be more the type to order a blushing champagne in a fluted glass." He fluttered his eyelashes to complete his mockery.

His contempt shocked me. I would've thought he'd despise me a lot less by now. I'd finally given him an A. I'd assured him I would keep his secret. I'd even pretended not to notice when he'd almost kissed me. It hurt to realize he *still* thought of me as the bitch of the century.

"Well, I'm not," I mumbled, trying to hide the pain. "May I have a Bud Light Lime or do I need to go somewhere else for a drink?"

"No, no need to go. I can hook you up." A smirk twisted his lips, and his eyes went hard. "I.D. please."

When he held out his hand, I gaped at his extended palm. "You're kidding me?"

His expression glittered with evil relish as he slowly shook his head. "No, ma'am. I am not. Underage drinking is serious business, and we here at Forbidden don't allow that kind of activity."

Muttering under my breath, I snapped open the clasp on my purse and began to dig around. "You're getting a kick out of this, aren't you, Gamble?" I ripped my driver's license free and thrust it his way.

"You have no idea," he murmured as he slipped the plastic from my fingers before lowering his gaze. A second later, his eyebrows crinkled. "Aspen, huh?"

Folding my arms over my chest, I scowled. "That's right. What about it?"

Noel shook his head. "Nothing. I just didn't know your first name."

I ground my teeth and held out my hand. "May I have my ID back, now? *Noel*?"

He pulled it away from me and shook his head. "Hold on. I still need to check your age." When his gaze flickered to my birth date, his jaw dropped open. "Holy shit, you're only twenty-three?" His face zipped up. "How the hell do you have a PhD at *twenty-three*?"

I sighed and flicked some hair out of my eyes

impatiently. "Let's see. I graduated high school at fifteen, earned my bachelor's degree at eighteen, my masters at twenty, and I received my doctorate at the top of my class *last year*. Add that up, and that makes me...what do you know, twenty-three."

Shaking his head slowly back and forth, he gawked. "Well, shit. Graduated high school at *fifteen*? Fuck, I should've known you were one of those freaky girl geniuses." Then he hissed a derisive snort.

"I'm also thirsty." I leaned forward and yanked my driver's license from his hand. "How about that drink now?"

"Sure, *Professor*." His voice was contemptuous as he turned away and sauntered off. I glared after him, upset to realize everything I thought we'd shared yesterday must've been nothing but a figment of my imagination. And yet I wasn't quite upset enough not to ogle his tight ass in those blue jeans.

Seriously. Wow.

Forcing myself to look away, I opened my purse and pretended to dig around, though I'd already had my money ready to pay before I'd even seen who was behind the counter.

"Here." His voice was none too polite as he clunked an open bottle on the counter before me.

"Thank you." I gave a regal nod and took a tentative sip.

He stayed in front of me after I paid, watching me drink. His stance brooded as if he couldn't wait for me to leave, but his eyes...oh God, his eyes.

Growing warm under his direct stare, I motioned around us, hoping to say something that would at least get him to look away, because his captivated attention on me was making the insides of my thighs tingle. A slow burn spread from the pit of my stomach and out to the tips of my toes. "I didn't realize you worked here."

"Huh." His lips twisted with scorn even as his

eyes continued to devour me. "You mean, there was one thing I forgot to mention in my paper?"

I smiled despite his glare. "Apparently. Though actually, you did say you worked at a bar to support your siblings. You just didn't name which one."

"Right." He nodded slowly, and his gaze followed my every move as I took another sip. While he tracked the bottle in my hand to my mouth, my stomach tangled into knots. I gulped nervously, and I swear his stare tried to follow the liquid down my throat. What was even more discerning, his attention returned to my lips when I lowered the bottle. If his eyes had been a tongue, he would've just licked me from my mouth and down my chin, over my throat to just between my breasts...and back up again.

"I can't freaking believe you're only two years older than me."

The comment surprised me so much I spilled a little beer down my chin on my next sip. Moving quickly to wipe it away with the back of my hand, though he'd seen the entire thing, I cleared my throat. "Why? How old do I look?"

His lips tipped up in amusement. "Nineteen. But that's not the point."

"Then what *is* the point?" I glanced away, beyond antsy to be stuck under his direct perusal.

Leaning in close, he lowered his voice. "You act more like you're fifty in class."

I turned to study him. Periwinkle eyes gleaming with an emotion I couldn't name, he just stared back, the challenge in his gaze commanding me to return fire and come up with some kind of retort.

"Wow," I said, internally cringing because I could detect a catch in my voice when I'd tried so hard to make my tone sound as dry and unimpressed as his had. "You must charm all the ladies with that kind of flattery."

He just chuckled. "Bet I get laid more than you

do." And now even his words dared me to duel with him.

With a roll of my eyes, I snorted and pulled my shoulders back, putting more space between us. "I wouldn't say that's anything to brag about."

I couldn't believe I'd answered him that way. I should've gotten affronted and called him out for being out-of-line with such an unprofessional comment to his teacher. In fact, I should still call him on it now. Yes. Yes, I think I would.

But as soon as I opened my mouth, another customer called him away. He continued to hold my gaze as he held up a hand to the other person. Then he smiled slightly at me. After he skimmed a quick gaze down my body, he turned and left to help someone else, leaving me bereft and heated in all the wrong places.

CHAPTER TEN

"You know," Clary said, "most psychologists agree that hostility is really just sublimated sexual attraction." - Cassandra Clare, *City of Bones*

~NOEL~

I KNEW I WAS PLAYING with fire. But I just didn't care. Every time I had a free moment, I found myself wandering back to *Aspen's* end of the bar.

Aspen. I loved her first name. It wasn't at all what a staid, stuffy professor's first name should be. It was unusual and unique, just like the effect she had on me. Why she did things to me no one else had ever done, I had no idea, but I wasn't going to question it. I liked it.

Telling myself it was only to keep an eye on her because she ordered a new beer every time I returned, I almost convinced myself that sticking nearby was noble or some such shit. But being close to her just felt right, like that was where I belonged. Or maybe she'd put some kind of homing spell on me. I couldn't move too far away before I was reeled back in.

Worse yet, she kept talking to me every time I engaged her in conversation. I had to keep going back. Had to.

"I can't decide if you two are going to start strangling each other or making out right there on the bar," Pick murmured to me the third time I was dragged away from her because of an irritatingly interfering customer.

I glanced up from the glass I was holding under a flowing beer tap. "What do you mean?"

I knew exactly what he meant. I just hoped it wasn't quite as obvious to an outsider.

Pick lifted his eyebrows as if he couldn't believe I had to ask. "You keep glaring at each other and saying things that look like you're exchanging insults. But they're the hottest damn insults I've ever seen two people dish out. Like every little 'fuck you' is just code for 'fuck me' instead."

Shit, he *was* seeing exactly what I was feeling.

I glanced at her because I couldn't help myself. She had turned slightly so she could glance out into the crowd and people watch. But even seeing her do that caused a shock of arousal to ripple through me.

"Yeah," I murmured absently since Pick didn't attend college and couldn't know she was one of my teachers. "Maybe."

Admitting it aloud didn't simmer any of my lust, though. After verbalizing it, my brain seemed to accept what my body already knew, and I just wanted her more.

I slid the overflowing drink to the guy waiting with a lifted bill in my direction. "Keep the change," he called.

"Thanks." I didn't even pay attention to which bill he'd handed me. I just opened the cash register and shoved it inside. My mind and body could only focus on one thing right now.

Returning to her without her noticing, I leaned against the bar and called over the music and commotion. "So, what're you doing here on the college scene, since you're obviously too advanced to be one us mere mortal students going through classes at the regular pace?"

She jumped slightly and turned back to me, thrilling me with her amazing green gaze. The private smile she flashed teased me on every level possible as she refused to answer my question.

I nodded, knowingly. "Ah. A date, huh?"

She blushed, stirring me up into a hot and heavy arousal. Jesus, her blush was addictive. And damn it, why the hell was I *stirred* over my frumpy English professor? This was all wrong. She shouldn't be allowed to wear a dress like that, or put her hair up like that, or paint her face that way. Or lick her damn succulent lips, like ever, but especially not after every drink she took.

I wanted to drag her into the back and fuck her senseless on the rickety old couch in the break room. From behind. I could already imagine how it would feel to bury my face in that naked nook on the back of her neck as I tugged up her skirt and slipped down her panties.

And now I was wondering what kind of panties my frumpy English professor was wearing.

Was she wearing panties?

Dear God.

"I didn't say I was here on a date." Her shoulders straightened in that haughty way they were so used to doing in class. But without the too-big shoulder pads of her outdated blazer hiding them, they looked too pretty when they hitched up in outraged indignation. Too sensual. Too fucking hot. I wanted to put my hands on her. Bad.

But I smirked to hide my raging horniness. "Ah.

So it's girls' night out..." Glancing around her to make sure she was alone, I added, "*Without* the girls?"

She locked her jaw and then took a quick drink. Damn, the way her mouth puckered over the head of that bottleneck was driving me insane.

Enjoying how easy it was to make her uncomfortable because she was making certain parts of my anatomy so very uncomfortable in return, I leaned forward to rest my forearms on the bar. "Or were you just looking to pick up a little strange for the evening?"

"Oh, my God," she gasped and sent me a scowl to beat all scowls. "It's a date, okay? I'm here to meet *a date.*"

I smirked in victory and gave a careless shrug as if it made no difference to me why she was here, even though the thought of anyone else kissing that exposed skin on her shoulder made me want to commit a felony of murderous proportions. "When were you supposed to meet him?"

She darted an uneasy glance around as she twirled a dark piece of hair around her finger. "I showed up a little early. That's all."

I nodded. So, the idiot was running late. Stupid-ass douche. I bet if he knew what she looked like right now, he would've been here hours ago.

"Hey, can we get a drink over here?"

When a pair of college guys waved to get my attention, I nodded toward them and straightened, sliding my gaze back to Aspen. I hated the fact I had to leave her, even for a few seconds. "Sure thing. Hang on a sec."

***

"I hope she'll be a fool -- that's the best thing a girl can be in this world, a beautiful little fool." - F. Scott Fitzgerald, *The Great Gatsby*

***

~**A**SPEN~

He kept coming back to me. I knew I shouldn't, but I relished every little visit. I let myself dream that he wanted to be near me because he found me so irresistible and exciting. And with every beer I drank, that dream infiltrated itself into my system until I was downright giddy with it. He wanted me.

Even though he was serving a girl that looked as if she had to have a fake ID, and fake boobs too, his gaze roved to my end of the bar. He accepted his fee, barely glancing at her, even though she was making it obvious she was interested in him. Then he made his way back...to me. Watching him saunter closer was such a rush.

This was why I lingered here. I craved every time he was pulled away from me, just so I could watch him come back.

"Need another one yet?"

I shook my head. "No." But as soon as the words left my mouth, I blurted, "yes."

Noel grinned and another bottle of Bud Light Lime appeared in his hand. As he tugged the cap off and set it in front of me, I tilted my head just enough to make my hair spill over my shoulder.

"How did you guess I was here for a date?"

He rested his elbows on the bar to lean in toward me. "Maybe because I don't need a PhD to read minds like you do, Professor."

Something molten, hot, and way too yummy swirled through me as I recalled the conversation we'd had on campus over a week ago. I loved it when someone remembered something I'd said to them and referred to it weeks later. It meant he'd paid attention and soaked in just enough to carry a part of me away with him.

Resisting the urge to shiver and sway toward him, I grinned. "That or you have amazing deductive reasoning."

He chuckled. "Or that." Straightening away from the bar to toss his white hand towel over his shoulder, he picked up my empty bottle and pitched it toward the trash. The sound of breaking glass followed, making me shudder.

"You're wearing more makeup than you ever do in class," he finally said. "Your hair is all pretty and tempting. Your dress is flirty and seductive. You smell good enough to devour." Once again, he leaned forward onto the bar so he could see down on the other side and get a peek of me feet. After he glanced at them, he looked up again, and our eyes were only inches apart. "And you're wearing the most tantalizing pair of fuck-me shoes I think I've ever seen. Add that up, and it spells date."

I drew back aghast, but more aghast by the way my nipples tightened at his words. "*Fuck me* shoes?" I'd heard that term once or twice before. But no one had ever accused me of wearing a pair before. It made me feel alive. Warm. Dangerous.

Wanton.

Giving the source of those rampant feelings all my attention as he slid back to his side of the bar, I said, "And here, all I was going for was *kiss me silly and mess up my hair a little.*"

Noel shook his head. "Trust me. From a guy's point of view, they shout a very definite *fuck me.* Hard. Maybe even in the backseat because waiting until you went inside to find a bed would take just too...long."

The image he painted should've freaked me out. In the backseat with a date was where my darkest nightmares had originated. But hearing Noel describe it, with his hot voice and his engaging blue eyes pinned on me, I only grew more aroused.

Wow. But seriously, wow. That's definitely what my shoes meant now. For him.

What? No. That's not what they meant for Noel Gamble. Not at all. But, still. Wow, it kind of was.

God, he had me so confused right now.

How much had I drunk?

Managing to act a lot less scatterbrained than I was feeling, I lifted my chin and murmured, "Hmm. Thanks for the heads-up. I guess it's a good thing he didn't show then. I'm not sure I wanted to go quite that far on a first date." Then I couldn't help it, I added, "with him," and the way I looked at him made it clear I might not have been so discerning on a first date with a certain someone else.

"Damn." His lips parted and cheeks began to look a little flushed. His heavy-lidded gaze traced me and made me ache because he looked almost...tempted.

God, I was in so deep right now. Unfortunately, I loved the sensation of drowning in his presence. I never wanted this moment to end.

***

"Only those who try to resist temptation know how strong it is." - C. S. Lewis

***

~NOEL~

My control was slipping. I swear I tried to remain a gentleman, but inappropriate things kept slipping out of my mouth, and then she'd come back with something just as—

Damn. I was almost relieved when I was called

away from her because anything I would've said to Dr. Aspen Kavanagh next would've been an unmistakable, totally inappropriate proposition. Hell, I probably would've gotten down on my knees and begged for a piece of her.

Fortunately, The time away cooled me enough to keep my sanity. But I still returned to her as soon as I could.

It was winding down to one thirty and the closer it drew to closing, the more restless I grew. Once the bar shut down, she'd have to go, and our night would be over. I dreaded that.

"I thought you guys didn't win the national championships this year," she said an instant before her light fingers grazed my forearm.

A shudder racked me as I felt her caress explode out every pore of my being. She'd barely touched me; I should've barely felt it. But I did. I felt it more than the time I'd been sacked during playoffs and had ended up in the hospital with a concussion. Her fingers set off a live, electric current through every nerve ending inside me until I was so hard my dick throbbed in synch with my heartbeat.

We'd never had skin-to-skin contact before, I realized. And I had to say, the first impression of my bare flesh against hers was, shit...intense.

This woman, right here, was dangerous.

Her gaze lifted as she waited for my response, reminding me what had caught her focus in the first place: the stupid-ass tattoo on my forearm.

"That's the result of pre-celebration...drunk style," I told her, nodding toward the mark.

Her hand and all those pretty fingernails painted a sexy pink lingered on my skin, right over the tattoo. Shaking her head, she kept petting it. "I don't understand."

I sighed deeply...for two reasons. One: Well, fuck, she was petting me. It felt too good to concentrate on anything else. But two: I hated to confess my stupidity, and that damn tattoo was one of the stupidest things I'd ever done.

"The night before the championship game," I said, unable to take my gaze off her fingers that seemed attached to my arm. "A bunch of us got rip-roaring drunk, and we all got these to celebrate our win."

She stared at me a second before finishing, "And...the next day, you lost instead." When I rolled my eyes and nodded, she threw her head back and laughed.

If it wasn't for the fact that she was laughing at me, I would've been totally captivated by that honest, open sound of amusement. Oh, screw it. I watched, wanting my mouth on that exposed throat.

It took me a second before I could cluck my tongue and shake my head. "Go ahead." I waved her on as if disgusted even though I began to chuckle lightly with her. "Laugh it up. But next year, when we do win the title for real, I plan to change the last digit on the year and this baby will be a reminder of our accomplishments...not our failures."

She leaned in, her green eyes lit up like sparkling emeralds. "And if you lose again?"

I wanted to kiss her so bad. Her lips were perfect, practically begging me to dominate them. But I drew in a breath and reined myself in. I decided to answer cutesy instead of serious. So with a grin, I flexed my bicep she was still holding onto. "What? With this golden throwing arm? That's just not possible."

She didn't laugh as I'd planned for her to. No, the delicious, tempting woman sucked in a breath and her touch became bold as she slid her hand up the tight muscle. "Oh, God," she breathed out the word. "I bet women love to clutch these guns when you push inside them?"

Holy...

My mind blanked out.

Or more accurately, it didn't blank out at all. It merely lost all reasonable thought as images of every way she could clutch my biceps as I pushed inside her crammed every available space in my synapses. Hell, in some of the images, she didn't even have to touch my arms. She just had to scream as I made her come.

After mentally screwing her every which way known to mankind, I shook my head and cleared my throat. I had to glance away before I tried to act on my impulses. Not that it helped much. I still knew she was there. I still knew she wanted to clutch my arms while I—damn, I probably shouldn't go there. But I went there again and again.

So looking away didn't help my dick relax, but it did help me realize...I spun back to her. "Shit. You're completely wasted, aren't you?"

I knew she'd been downing bottle after bottle, but she hadn't been acting all giggly drunk like most of the co-eds I was used to. What she'd said, however, was like nothing I could ever picture Dr. Kavanagh saying to me...ever. Not even drunk. Since she *had* said it, though, she had to be totally out of her mind.

And now that I was looking for the signs, her eyes were bright and glassy And her posture was a little too loose for her.

"I've never been wasted before in my life." She tried to straighten her spine in her prissy, professor way, but she only ended up tipping to the side. Realizing what she was doing, she let go of my arm to brace her hand on the top of the bar, catching herself. As her eyebrows puckered with irritation, I reached out and helped her straighten up. I already missed the loss of her hands on me. The phantom warmth of them still heated my flesh.

"Did you put something stronger in my drink?" she accused, scowling at me. "Because I suddenly feel a little...tipsy."

I snorted. "Tipsy? Honey, you passed tipsy and headed straight to plowed the moment you asked me details about my sex life."

Her back tried to stiffen all self-righteously again. "I beg your pardon? I most certainly did not—oh shit." Her face flooded with color as her mouth dropped open. "I just asked you about your sex life."

Watching her lips form the word *shit* was my downfall.

I scuttled backward away from her, aching for her so hard my muscles vibrated from the tension they were using to restrain me.

"Don't worry about it." I waved my hand to excuse her behavior, to make it not as hot and sexy as it really was. "I know all about alcohol-induced slipups. Remember?" I flashed her my forearm and then immediately swung away, in petrified retreat.

I didn't want to leave, but I needed space before I did something unforgiveable.

I shoved Pick in her direction, grabbing a strawberry daiquiri out of his hand. "You gotta keep me away from her," I gasped, tempted to down the drink instead of deliver it to its owner. "If she goes into the back for any reason, do not let me follow her. Do you understand? If she tries to give me her number, do not let me keep it. And if she...Jesus!" I glanced at her just in time to see some guy tap on her shoulder, gaining her attention. "And keep that little asswipe sniffing around her away too. Got it?"

Pick blinked. "Uh..."

"Thanks." I turned away, leaving him to his new duties.

CHAPTER ELEVEN

"There is a charm about the forbidden that makes it unspeakably desirable." - Mark Twain

~NOEL~

PICK DID HIS JOB FOR the most part. With me constantly talking to her all night, I must've been keeping away the prowlers. Because as soon as I immersed myself in work, serving drinks, the men flooded in, trying to hit on her. Pick didn't exactly field the losers away, but he didn't really have to either since she brushed them off all on her own. God bless her.

I told myself that didn't mean anything. So what, she had welcomed my attention and practically asked me how I liked to take my women, but she'd turned others away. That didn't mean...except maybe it did. Even drunk, she preferred me over everyone else.

When she asked Pick where the restroom was and disappeared into the back, every fiber of my being wanted to follow her. But my damn, annoying co-worker grabbed my arm.

"You told me not to let you go, man."

I jerked my arm out of his grip and sent him a dirty look but stayed behind the bar like a good boy. But when she didn't return within five minutes, I was ready to chew my own arm off.

"What if someone caught her back there and is harassing her?" I growled to Pick, needing to check on her safety, which surprised the shit out of me. Outside of my brothers and sister, and okay, maybe my teammates on the field, oh, and possibly my coworkers, I'd never felt protective of anyone before. Not over a girl I wanted, anyway.

"*I'll* check on her," Pick said, lifting his eyebrows in that fatherly way, telling me to back off.

I glowered at him even as I practically shoved him toward the hallway. "Well, get to it, then."

He left and returned almost immediately. "She's fine," was his only answer.

I opened my mouth to demand details. She was fine how? Fine with some other guy? Fine, as in not puking her guts out? Fine, as in passed out peacefully and untouched in the back office? I needed to know more. Everything.

But last call came, and work stole my attention for the next half hour. I kept looking for her, but I never saw her again. She must've slipped out between people when I wasn't looking. Which aggravated me to no end. I couldn't even get one final glimpse of her in that unforgettable backless number.

Pick found a pair of sloshing drunk girls and offered to help them home, leaving me behind to clean up behind the bar. More people filtered out, and the waitresses got busy sweeping and straightening the main area.

I was wiping down the bar when I saw someone from the corner of my eye stumbling out of the hall that led to the bathrooms. Since we had closed ten minutes ago and the place was empty of customers, I glanced over to tell *whoever* that they needed to clear out.

But Aspen Kavanagh was too busy digging into her purse and pulling out a set of keys to notice me.

My mouth fell open. She hadn't left yet. I soaked in my last glimpse, so occupied with my perusal that it took me a second to realize exactly what she was doing.

Christ, she wasn't seriously going to drive in her condition, was she?

Sorting through the ring full of metal until she found the key she sought, she tripped on her fuck-me heels, bumped into the side of a table, and then straightened herself before weaving a crooked path toward the door.

Oh, hell, no. "Hey!" I called. "Dr. Kavanagh."

She didn't hear me, or just plain ignored me.

As she pushed her way outside, I cursed. "Vick." I turned toward a waitress who was pulling out bills and counting them at the cash register. "You guys okay here?"

She didn't even pause her count, but nodded and waved me on. "Yeah. You can go ahead and go."

"Thanks." I didn't wait around for her to change her mind. Setting a hand on the counter, I leaped over it and dashed toward the door.

A nip in the wind bit through my shirt as soon as I exited, reminding me I'd left my jacket inside. But I didn't care; I'd get it later.

Glancing around for my professor and spotting her instantly, I cupped my hand around my mouth. "*Aspen!*"

She faltered and whirled around, dropping her keys in the middle of the street. A car had just turned down the block, but she didn't seem to notice its approach as she bent over to retrieve her key chain, startling me with a view of just how nice her ass looked in that short little dress. Panic leapt into my veins as I worried the car was about to turn her into a pancake.

Popping off the curb, I raced forward, grasped her elbow and manually helped her back upright just as she got ahold of the keys. The oncoming car slowed when it caught us in its headlights, but I hurried her out of its path anyway.

She brushed my hand away as soon as we made it to the parking lot and the car sped up, driving past.

"What do you think you're doing?" she demanded.

I set my hands on my hips and loomed over her. "I'm trying to find out what the fuck you think *you're* doing."

She attempted to stand erect, tightening up her shoulders, but ended up stumbling a step to the left. "I..." She paused to hiccup. Damn, why did I have to think drunk chicks hiccupping was so adorable? "I'm going home. The bar closed. My...my date stood me up."

A wrinkle between her eyebrows formed when she confessed that. She looked confused and hurt.

I sighed. Shit. *Shit, shit, shit.* "You weren't seriously going to *drive* home, though, were you? By yourself?"

She turned to look at her car as if considering her answer. Then she weaved sloppily back around. "Well, it certainly won't *fly* me home."

"Dear God." I rubbed my forehead. "How can you have a PhD at twenty-three and be this naive?"

With a gasp, she pressed the flat of her palm against her chest. "How am I being naive?"

"How do you think? You can't just drive home drunk. What if you got into an accident? What if you were pulled over? You'd go to jail and lose your job. Then you'd never be able to give some poor, dumb schmuck like me another D in your life."

"You have a point," she admitted. Then she turned her green eyes my way and looked so lost I wanted to sweep her up and soothe all her troubles away. "But how'm I supposed to get home?" Her shoulders drooped. "I jus' wanna go home."

I sighed. Damn it. If only there hadn't been a catch in her miserable, despondent voice.

"I'll call you a cab," I offered, already digging into my pocket. After working at the bar for as many months as I had, I had my favorite cab service listed on speed dial.

"But I can't leave my car here." She sounded aghast.

I paused, my thumb hovering over the dial button. "It's okay. People do it all the time. This is a fairly safe parking lot. You can come back and pick it up in the morning, no problem."

Chewing on her bottom lip, she eyed her dark sedan with worry.

"Damn it," I muttered under my breath and pocketed the phone. "Okay, fine." Jesus, I couldn't believe I was actually going to offer this. "Give me your keys, and I'll drive you home."

She whirled to me with hope on her face, even as she said, "But what about your car? How will *you* get home?"

Shaking my head, I tried not to be charmed over the fact she was still cognizant enough to think about me. "I'll just stay the night with you."

"*What*?" She stumbled sideways as her mouth fell open.

I snickered. "Kidding. I'll call a cab from your place and have them bring me back here for my ride."

Okay, so I was too embarrassed to tell her I didn't have a set of wheels. Since I only lived eight blocks away, I'd planned on walking home. But I could always call a cab from her place if I had to.

She blinked, and the move made her look like an owl. Cutest damn owl I'd ever seen. Glancing away because she still held me under her homing spell with her prettied-up face and sexy clothes, I blew out a breath, half-hoping she'd decline and let me call her a cab, and half-hoping I could spend another few minutes in her company while she was like this.

"You would do that for me?" The way she slurred her words sounded foreign coming from her perfect mouth because her speech was always so succinct in class. It was as if she was a completely different person. A person I was allowed to desire.

"Why would you do that for me?" She stared at me, all lost and confused again. "You hate me."

"I don't—" When I shook my head, I had to shove my hair out of my eyes. "I don't hate you," I said, softer this time. *Far, far from it.*

Her lips parted and I wanted to bite them—especially the fuller, lower one—then suck it into my mouth and lick the sting away.

Silently, she held out her keys to me. A surge of awareness sparked through my system.

I shouldn't do this. It was dangerous. Tempting. She still had one side of her hair pulled up, though after the past few hours in the heat of the bar and in between the press of so many people, it had started to sag in places. Still...it looked tempting, as if someone had had his hands in it.

If only they could be *my* hands.

Giving in to her draw, I took the keys and sucked in a breath when her fingers brushed mine. God, this was going to be bad. I could already tell.

CHAPTER *T*WELVE

"These are the times that try men's souls." - Thomas Paine

~*N*OEL~

"Don't you love how the streetlights reflect through the windshield?" Aspen leaned forward in the passenger seat to stroke the glass above the dashboard of her car. But her safety belt caught before she could quite touch it, and she fell back into her seat with a sad sigh. "It's so pretty," she mumbled, eyeing the view longingly.

I shook my head in amusement as her navigation system told me to turn right at the corner. "Yeah, you've definitely had one too many to drink," I said to myself more than to her, since she wasn't even listening to me, too enrapt in the pretty lights to notice my presence.

"They look like carnival lights." She sent me a sidelong glance. "Have you ever been to a carnival?"

I blinked. "Umm...sure." Who'd never been to a carnival?

Whenever they'd come to my hometown, they'd always set up in the open lot not far from our trailer park. I used to sneak down and take Caroline, and Brandt too when he'd gotten old enough to go on the rides. I'd never gotten around to taking Colt, though, before I'd left for college. I hoped Caroline did that for me. Some of my happiest memories were of buying candy and tickets and watching my siblings when we'd gone on the rides. Colt needed a memory like that. Hell, everyone needed those kinds of memories.

"I've never been to a carnival," Aspen said softly. I glanced across the quiet interior of her car to watch her face fill with even more longing. "My parents said carnivals were foolish and a waste of time."

Damn. Her parents sounded like complete assholes.

"Do you think if my date had shown up, I would've gotten lucky tonight?" She paused and bit her lip. "I could be having sex right now. Wow, I can't even remember when the last time I had sex was."

Shit. Bad topic.

She'd been talking nonstop since I'd helped her into her car, changing subjects faster than I could change speeds. But we hadn't dipped back into this taboo territory since she'd squeezed my bicep in the bar.

"But I do remember the last time I dreamed about having sex," she kept on. "You were doing me on my desk at work and—"

What? She'd had that dream too? Unreal.

I shifted in the driver's seat because my erection felt pinched in my jeans.

"—and I was sprawled on my back with all these graded papers digging into my spine while you were standing on the floor between my legs so you could...you know. Then you hit this spot in me...Oh, my God. It felt so good. I somehow kicked over the monitor of my computer screen. But you just kept going, and I think I was about to come, but then I woke up all wet and aching, and I never did find out how that dream ended."

Oh, I knew how that dream ended.

But damn. This was not good. Hearing about how I'd made her wet and aching snapped the chains around my control as if they were scissor blades plucking apart a tendril of hair.

"You probably shouldn't be talking about this to me," I told her, my voice gruff.

She glanced over. "Why not? You've had sex, haven't you?" Then she snorted and threw her head back to laugh outright. "What am I saying? You're Noel Gamble. You've probably had sex more times this month alone than I have in my entire life."

I scowled. "Okay, now you're just being insulting."

"Six," she said.

I shook my head, not following. "What?"

"I've had sex six times in my life. Three different guys."

My mouth fell open. Jesus. I hadn't needed a head count. But hell, now that she'd given me one, I thought maybe I *had* had more sex in this month alone than she'd had in her entire life. Okay, not *this* month or even last month, exactly. But definitely during a football season month.

She tipped her head to the side and frowned thoughtfully. "Wait. If you're not willing, does that count?"

Zipping my attention to her, I almost ran a red light. Stomping on the brakes, I exploded, "Excuse me?"

"I said—"

"I heard you! Jesus Christ. If you're not willing, I don't think it's even considered sex. It's called *rape.*"

She had not just told me she'd been...No. No way.

Frowning thoughtfully, she murmured. "No. No, my parents told me very specifically I couldn't call it that. Told me I couldn't tell anyone, couldn't go to the police or talk about it ever again. No." She gave a vigorous shake of her head. "It wasn't rape. I deserved it. I agreed to go on that date with him, after all. I even climbed into the backseat with him on my own free will. They said I should've expected it."

Should've expected...?

Jesus. I thought I might vomit. But, what the fuck?

With my fingers choking the steering wheel and pretending it was her goddamn rapist's neck, I managed to ask, "How long ago was this?"

"Nine years. I was fourteen. It was my first time." she pressed a finger to her lips thoughtfully before adding, "I don't think a girl's first time should ever be like that."

"No," I agreed quietly. "No, it shouldn't." I thought about Caroline for some reason. Shit, she'd had that dance tonight, hadn't she?

What if that Scotini boy expected more from her than she was willing to give? What if she agreed to climb into a backseat with him for a couple kisses then got scared when he wanted more and tried to put on the breaks, but he didn't let her? I'd break every bone in his fucking body. I was tempted to pull out my phone and check on her, but I wanted to be here for Aspen, too. She was obviously going through some-thing right now, and I liked being the one to hear her drunk disclosures.

"Have..." I licked my dry lips as I turned down her block. "Have you ever told anyone about this before, besides your parents?"

I prayed that she'd tell me she'd gone to the police, despite Mommy and Daddy's wishes, and the asshole had been thrown behind bars, where he'd stayed until he died after being gang raped himself by twenty other inmates. When she didn't immediately answer, I glanced over at her as soon as I pulled into her drive and parked.

She'd curled up in her seat with her knees bent to her chest and her arms wrapped protectively around her legs. It gave me a view of silky black panties, but at the moment I was too worried about her to ogle them.

Looking a decade younger than twenty-three, she sent me a wide-eyed glance. "Of course," she said. "I told my therapist. It's very chic in my parents' world to have a therapist. But mine actually helped me get over it. I mean, the first guy I was with after it happened didn't reap any benefits. He didn't even stick around to finish our one encounter together because I freaked him out so bad. He pulled out as soon as I started crying. Then he ran off and never called me again. But the second stayed through more than one encounter before he stopped returning my phone calls. That's something though, right? It's progress."

I hissed a curse under my breath. Bastards. All three of them. I could tell every one of her past partners had hurt her, even if they hadn't been like the first prick. I wanted to pull her into my lap and just hold her. Or maybe even show her what the good side of passion was like.

But I restrained myself.

She'd been staring out the front window, probably at the lights again, when suddenly, she looked over. "I read your paper."

Her quiet words made my already unsettled stomach roar with anxiety. "Yeah. You already graded it and gave it back to me, remember? We had an entire discussion in your office over whether I deserved an A or not. And how you're going to keep my dirty little secret for me."

"Right," she murmured softly as if suddenly remembering. "Yeah, I guess I owed you a secret, then, didn't I?" She smiled but it wasn't very happy. Her green eyes lifted. "I was so turned on the entire time you were blowing up at me, telling me to take that A back if you didn't deserve it. If you'd have kissed me that day, I would've kissed you back. And more."

Holy fucking shit. I shoved open the driver's side door and hurled myself out of her car. The cool air was a welcome shock to my arousal. But then she opened her door and got out too.

"I, uh, I'm going to call my cab now." God, that sounded lame, but she was drunk. I couldn't do anything about all her confessions. Not now.

She nodded, then shivered and hugged herself before she started toward the sidewalk, which led to her front porch. When she stumbled and nearly went down, I cursed a little louder and shoved my phone back into my pocket.

"Wait," I called, darting after her and catching her arm just as she tripped again. "Let me help you."

She swayed my way until she was leaning against me fully. I had to slip my arm around her waist to keep her upright. Fuck, who would've guessed she'd have such a tiny waist?

Tipping her face up, she grinned engagingly. "It was the best essay I ever read, you know."

"Hmm." I swallowed, refusing to respond, and helped her up the steps onto her porch. When she couldn't seem to find her keys in her purse, I jiggled them to let her know I still had them after driving. She grinned and stepped aside, gladly letting me take over.

"Your grammar still sucked ass," she went on as I unlocked the door. "And you'd probably lose a spelling bee to a first grader, but...oh my God. It made me cry. I read it over, and over, and over. I even photocopied it like a creepy stalker, so I could continue to read it after I gave it back to you. And every time I look at it, I bawl my eyes out. For you."

Lifting her hand, she caught a piece of my hair and idly brushed it across my forehead to sift it out my eyes. The sensation of her fingers on me was like an electric shock. Powerful, startling. A complete rush to both my hormones and my heart.

My mother had slapped me before for saying something out of line, or she had shoved me aside for getting in her way. Girls I'd hooked up with had dug their nails into my ass when I made them feel good. My siblings had huddled close to me when they were frightened. Teammates had slapped my back in congratulations. But no one had ever touched me like this, with pure, honest affection as if they wanted to take care of me.

"You've been through so much," she murmured, sympathy ruling her tone. "Have so much to deal with. I want to hunt down your mother and hurt her for what she put you through."

I sniffled out a sad smile just as I pulled the key free of the lock. But I was no longer in such a hurry to get her inside...away from me. I forced my attention back to the front door, but I wanted to keep looking at her. Stare at her just like she was—soft, sweet, and a little vulnerable—for the rest of my life.

Her hand dropped from my hair only to land on my arm. Warm and soft, her fingers teased and seduced as they slowly trailed a scorching path down to my elbow.

"I'm so sorry," she whispered. "I thought you were like him. But you're not. You're nothing like him."

Say what? I glanced from her fingers on me and up into her eyes. "Like who?"

She didn't answer. Instead, she sniffed and wiped her palm over her cheek, the move making her look like a little kid instead of an accomplished college professor. "He made me hate football players. Especially quarterbacks. He made me...he made me cold and lonely. Hollow inside. But you would never do that. You would never hurt anyone the way he hurt..."

When her words trailed off, a burning hot pile of anger uncoiled in my stomach.

"What did he do?" I coaxed softly. She didn't answer. It only enraged and worried me more. "Aspen? Is he the one who...who raped you?" Shit. No wonder she'd always given me such a hard time. I reminded her of *that*.

I hated knowing I did that to her.

She turned to me and smiled softly. "You're not like him at all. You're...I don't know. You're something amazing."

I choked out a harsh laugh and pushed her door open with a savage shove. "Yeah, real amazing. I'm dirt broke, barely keeping my football scholarship afloat and about to let down the three people I care about most in the world if I can't keep my shit together. And let's not forget how I cheated my way to get here...or remind you of the boy who raped you. There is nothing amazing about that at all."

"Come here." Aspen gently took my hand and led me inside her dark house. I followed. I have no idea why I didn't even hesitate, but I went wherever she led.

Once inside, I reached out, fumbling until I found a light switch. When a pale glow brightened the corner of a tidy living room cast in shades of bright blue, I glanced at her just as she glanced back at me.

Framing my face with her hands, she looked into my eyes and said, "You are amazing, Noel Gamble." Then she let out a drunk grin. "Geesh, I would've thought the star football player of the university's undefeated team would be a little more cocky and sure of himself."

I shook my head. "You grow up the poor, dumb kid of the town whore and your peers beat arrogance right out of you at a young age. Literally."

She leaned in and rested her forehead on my shoulder. "But you have every right to be proud of who you are. You're a survivor."

The tight ball in my chest made it hard to breathe, and the way her soft fingers felt on my neck as they moved down from my cheeks and over my shoulders was doing a number on my dick. "Why?" I demanded, my voice a little too rough. "Because I know how to throw a ball?"

She looked up again. "No. Because you're not just a pretty face in an empty shell. You love. You fear. You feel things so...so strongly."

When one hand landed just over my heart, I sucked in a sharp breath.

It took everything I had to keep my hands off her in return. "Everyone feels, Aspen. Some are just better at covering it up."

"But you feel good things. Might be a little rough around the edges, but you have a good heart. A compassionate heart." Then she kissed my chest, right through my clothes and over my heart. It would've been so easy to bury my fingers in her hair, to tip my face down and inhale her scent. But I didn't, no matter how much it killed me to restrain myself.

"Aspen, we should—"

She lifted her face, startling me as she gave a pleased sigh. "I love how you say my name."

"Aspen," I murmured, saying it again because I just couldn't help myself.

God, what was I doing?

She closed her eyes and sighed again. "You make me tingle every time I see you."

Damn, if she wanted to talk about tingling... She licked her lips unconsciously, and my dick tingled from base to tip, turning as hard as stone.

"I think I've been perpetually wet since the first moment I saw you walk into my class."

Jesus.

A groan slipped from my throat. I gripped her shoulder, telling myself to push her back, but instead, I held her right where she was.

"The first time you walked into my class, I felt this zing, like a hot flash, cover me from head to toe. I remember stuttering when I introduced myself because I was so flabbergasted. You flabbergasted me. No one flabbergasts me. But then I learned you were Ellamore's precious quarterback and it all became clear. He was the football star too, and I had such a huge crush on him. I think that's my curse. But he only paid attention to me to make me think he was interested, so he could humiliate me...and then he hurt me. I thought you'd be exactly like that. I mean, I had the same first impression of you as I did him. Except with you, it was like...fifty times stronger. I just...I love looking at you. I love the sound of your voice. The way you walk. The way you smile and brush your hair out of your eyes. But I will never get over the way you love your family and how you'll do anything to save them. I just...I wish someday, someone would love me like that."

The look in her eyes was obvious. She wanted me to love her like that. Strangely, the idea didn't scare the shit out of me. I mean, I didn't fall head over heels that instant or anything. But after listening to her spill the crap she'd just spilled to me, I wanted her to be loved like that almost as badly as she did.

When I swayed forward without meaning to, she lifted her face. But I paused and closed my eyes, my jaw bulging as I swallowed down the temptation to take greedily. I had to stop thinking with my dick, because this had gotten way too personal, and way too emotional. And she was still way too...

"You're drunk," I reminded her.

She nodded, agreeing. "Really drunk."

"I can't kiss you. I'll be taking advantage." Fuck, why had I mentioned kissing? We hadn't been talking about kissing at all.

But she didn't seem to notice my subject change. "Okay," she slurred. "Then...how 'bout I jus' kiss *you* instead?"

It happened like that. I didn't tell her no in time so she lifted onto her toes and pressed her mouth to mine. I closed my eyes, trying to resist it. But the palm she'd been cupping my cheek with slid around until it caged the back of my neck. When her fingernails grazed the base of my skull as she combed through my hair, I shuddered. And her lips, Christ, her lips were soft and pliable. She tasted like Bud Light Lime and sunshine, and I couldn't help myself. I opened up to taste just a little more.

She mewed out a hungry sound, which had me cradling her face as I plunged my tongue in. God. Warm and wet, her kiss was everything. I could've done this all night. But...

"If we don't stop now, I'll be an asshole."

"Don't worry." She tugged me back to her. "I already considered you an asshole."

I laughed only for her to kiss me again. A groan smothered my chuckle, and I drowned in her lips until I could pull myself back...only to curse and go back for more. She was so tiny, I grew tired of arching down to kiss her, so I picked her up, and she immediately wound her legs around my waist.

Crushing her back against the wall, I kissed her some more, scoping out the cavity inside her mouth until my tongue felt as comfortable there as it did in my own. My lips didn't want to part from hers, but there was so much more I wanted to taste.

Living out my fantasy I'd had at the bar when I'd first seen her tonight, I buried my fingers into the part of her free-flowing hair she'd left down and kissed my way to the exposed side of her throat, and then onto her shoulder.

I had no idea she'd be quite this soft, or smell quite this good. It fogged my head so that when I slid my hand down her perfect bare spine, I just kept going until I cupped her ass and grinded us together.

Seriously, I didn't mean to forage inside her skirt, but her dress had just sort of naturally worked its way up when she'd lifted her legs. When I did get a handful of her amazing ass, I found myself palming her silky black panties instead of her skirt. Realizing I was right there, my hand had to keep exploring up between her legs until I found the material damp, soaked with her slick, wet arousal. She was ready for me. Aching for me.

From that point on, I was pretty much screwed. "Where's your room?" I gasped, moving my fingers until she was squirming against me, her body demanding more.

"Hall." She pointed sloppily over my shoulder. "First door. Right side."

Fusing our mouths back together, I peeled her off the wall and carried her through the dim front room, only tripping once when I ran into a chair.

She laughed and buried her face in my neck, which afforded me a few moments to focus on where we were going and delight in how warm and soft and perfect she felt wrapped around me.

When I entered her bedroom, she reached past me to flip on another light. Her sanctuary was brightly colored and a lot less neat than the front room. The sheets were barely thrown over the mattress and clothes were strewn across the floor as books lay piled in every nook and cranny they could fit.

This was her. The real her, not some stuffy, uptight teacher in front of a classroom. This room represented the woman in my arms, and I had a feeling not a lot of people saw the real Aspen Kavanagh.

I carried her to the bed. Once she'd been placed gently on her back, she smiled up at me and lazily kicked off her fuck-me heels. When she reached out with both arms, I was drawn back in. Without thinking of consequences or morals or rules, I climbed on top of her and crushed our mouths back together.

Unlike most of the guys I knew, kissing wasn't just some pre-show for me to get a girl ready for the big event. Kissing was its own affair. I'd been known to do nothing but kiss a girl all night, until she was the one begging for something else. I could do it until my lips were numb and it was impossible to tell whose tongue was whose.

Finding a girl who kissed just right was like a goldmine. And Aspen Kavanagh was the goldmine of all goldmines. She sighed into my mouth, her body warm and pliable. I buried my fingers into her hair, ruining the tempting way she'd fixed it.

I have no idea how long we kissed, our mouths mating and forging a bond that went far beyond mere physical companionship. But when she found the hem of my shirt and skimmed her fingers up my abdomen, I was more than willing to repay the favor.

"You're so hard," she murmured, the awe in her voice killing me.

"And you're not even touching the hardest part." I grinned as my lips found her jaw, then worked their way down to her throat while my fingers explored under her shirt.

"Feels so good," she murmured just as her hand went limp and flopped onto the mattress beside her.

My tongue paused on her pulse as my gaze darted to her fallen hand.

"Aspen?" I glanced up to find her eyes closed and lips parted, her face canted away.

The woman had passed out on me. My body

screamed in denial while a far distant part of my brain tried to tell me this was a good thing. But I agreed more with my poor, throbbing body. This sucked.

"Jesus." Beginning to tremble, I rolled off her and landed on my back. Wiping my hand over my face to cool my heated skin, I blew out a breath before counting to twenty in my head.

Then I craned my face around to check on her. Yep. Still out cold.

This had to be a new low for me. I'd taken advantage of a drunk girl until she'd passed out in my arms. And not just any drunk girl, but the most forbidden one I could ever want.

My dick throbbed in my jeans, pinching painfully as it crowded against the back of my zipper. After readjusting myself, I glanced toward Aspen to check on her again.

Well, at least *she* looked at peace. For the life of me, I could not get my body to calm down. My hormones continued to rage, and watching her dewy lips part as she breathed did not help.

Twisting my head the other way, I scanned her room for something to divert my attention so I could combat the lust once and for all and be on my way. One of the paperbacks on her nightstand caught my eye. On the cover, a bare-chested, long-haired dude leaned over to hover his face into the plunging neckline of some chick in a big, frilly dress. The title was something about denying a Highlander.

A smile cracked my lips. I bet she didn't teach about these kinds of novels in her classes. I reached out and flipped the cover around to study it a little more fully. The woman lying next to me was a romance junkie. Strange. I hadn't been able to detect that during any of the classes she taught. She seemed so clinical and profession when teaching, I never would've guessed she had a daydreamer inside her.

Turning back, I studied her passive face as my

chest filled with sympathetic pangs. Things started to add up. Her asshole parents had never taken her to a carnival. They hadn't given her a proper childhood, but they had probably pushed her in school until she was skipping grades and excelling in education. I couldn't picture her with a lot of friends if she'd always been the freak genius girl. And if the fucker who'd hurt her when she was fourteen was any clue as to what her life had been like, she hadn't felt very loved or protected. She'd probably been alone a lot.

And yet she read romance novels until the corners were frayed and worn. She still hoped for some kind of happily ever after.

She was so much like me it was frankly freaky. We were split between two worlds. She was the frumpy, genius professor hiding romantic hopes and dreams. I was the stud playboy football star working my ass off to save my poor, broke family. What a pair we made. And what an ass I felt like. She wasn't just some piece of fruit I wanted to sample because she was forbidden. She was a lot deeper than I had ever imagined.

Slowly, I reached out until I barely touched her cheek. She sighed in her sleep and rolled onto her side facing me. When she found my warmth, she snuggled in close. I wound my arms around, hugging her against me, and she ended up with her cheek on my chest and her arm wrapped around my waist.

It was sweet and comfortable and so damn agonizing to lay with her like that, I ended up kicking off my shoes and burrowing in, closing my eyes and burying my face in her hair.

We fell asleep wrapped in each other's arms, and I couldn't remember a night I slept so soundly.

CHAPTER THIRTEEN

"Worry never robs tomorrow of its sorrow, but only saps today of its strength." - A.J. Cronin

~ASPEN~

MY HEAD FELT LIKE IT was going to explode.

Rolling toward the heat source that had kept me cozy all night, I curled my legs up, expecting to find something solid and tangible radiating warmth and shelter. But all my fingers found were cold, empty sheets. Wrinkling my forehead, I winced when little axes in my head hacked at the interior of my temples. With a groan, I buried my face further into my pillow to block out the light flooding my room.

Inhaling a new smell, something spicy and masculine, I breathed in deeply, wondering where such a lovely scent had originated and what it was doing on my pillow. Until I remembered...

Noel Gamble. In my car. Driving me home. Then Noel Gamble. On my bed. Kissing me. With tongue. His hand between my legs.

Dear God, I'd kissed Noel Gamble and led him straight to my bedroom. I'd arched under him and begged him to— Oh, God. This was bad.

Already fearing the worst, I jerked upright, opening my eyes and checking out the other side of my bed, knowing I'd find him there. But when I found nothing but more sheets and a smashed pillow, I felt disappointed and disheartened.

My head pounded, and I swayed dizzily.

That's when I noticed the glass full of water on the nightstand next to a bottle of aspirin with a folded sheet of white paper propped against them.

Groaning as my headache roared back to life, I swiped up the note

"There ain't no sin and there ain't no virtue. There's just stuff people do." - John Steinbeck (From *The Grapes of Wrath*).

Hey. I just wanted you to know you did nothing wrong last night, and there is no reason to regret anything that happened...like I know you are. But don't sweat it. We could have done so much more. I know the right thing to do now is probably apologize for not stopping you immediately when you drunk kissed me. Except I'm not sorry at all. It was...amazing. Really, don't sweat it. Everything will be okay. Just take care of yourself. Drink the whole glass of water and don't take more than three pills. If you need anything, call. N. G.

I soaked in his phone number he'd scribbled in at the bottom of the page, memorizing it even as I commanded my eyes to look away.

But, oh wow, he'd left me a sweet, considerate letter. And his words actually worked. The panic I'd been experiencing a split second after waking up unwillingly drained from my system.

We hadn't done anything that bad after all. Or had we and he just wanted to sugarcoat it? Shit, I couldn't remember much of what had happened, but Noel seemed to think we were still in the clear, so I refused to get worried.

Except all day long, little puzzle pieces of my memory kept returning, reminding me of some of the things I'd said to him. I seriously couldn't believe I'd squeezed his arm at the bar and asked if women liked to clutch his muscles while he had sex with them. No, I must've dreamed that one up. I don't care how wasted I'd been, I would never say—

Oh, God. I had, hadn't I? This was so horrifying. How was I supposed to show my face in class again? How could I even step foot on campus?

As Sunday progressed, I kept biting my fingernails and glancing at the phone, just knowing some university administrator was going to call and fire me.

Then another memory would plague me, like the one where Noel Gamble had picked me up, and I'd wound my legs around his waist while he'd kissed me senseless against a wall. Or when he'd rubbed me through my panties. My stomach heated and thighs turned rubbery. Even as vague and blurry as the memories were, they had the power to stir me until I was a hot, wanton mess.

I knew I should be utterly embarrassed and scandalized. I'd just thrown my code of ethics and morals out the window, and I'd chosen one of the biggest playboys on campus to do it with. I *was* appalled at myself. Kind of. All the flattery kept choking out my honorable thoughts, though, because I was utterly thrilled that Noel Gamble, the guy who turned me on like no one else, the man who'd charmed me with his literature essay and entrusted me with his biggest secrets had actually *wanted* me. He could have any girl on campus—prettier, younger, and more fashionable with a personality much more lively than mine.

Wait. Noel Gamble *could* have any girl he wanted. So why had he chosen me? I wasn't all that and a bag of potato chips.

With a dreaded gulp, I pressed my hand to my chest and tried to combat the sinking feeling dropping heavily into my gut. This didn't have anything to do with that essay he'd written, did it? Because he now had insurance that I would never spill his secret to university administration. I'd be fired for sure if anyone found out I'd fooled around with a student. There wasn't any such regulation for students. Just for faculty. If I even thought about telling anyone about his false high school GPA, he could wave *this* in my face; it would get me kicked out of Ellamore just as surely as if I'd had sex with him.

And smart Gamble, he hadn't even had to lower himself to go all the way with me.

God, was that messed-up thinking or what? Was I honestly *insulted* because he hadn't taken complete advantage of me in my inebriation? What was wrong with me?

Probably that note. He hadn't sounded like some conniving bastard who only wanted to cover his bases. He had sounded like he cared. That note had been sweet and concerned, trying to help me through my guilt. He knew exactly how I felt, and I loved that.

But crap, wouldn't any guy who wanted to play into my good graces, say something sweet and seemingly concerned like that?

Okay, I had to stop thinking about this. It was driving me crazy. And all it was, was speculation. There were no good, hard facts to prove any part of last night had been genuine. Or false.

But thinking about them just being an act was depressing because the parts I remembered had been so amazing. I'd gone to that bar hoping to connect with someone, have a decent conversation, and if my stars aligned right, maybe have a decent make-out session. And I had. I'd gotten all of that.

It'd just been with the wrong guy.

Speaking of which, Philip didn't call all day Sunday. The jerk. But that didn't even faze me. In fact, it was a relief. I was a little too freaked out about my worrying whether I'd still have a job the next day to bum out over the fact I'd been stood up last night.

The universe must've thought I hadn't had enough to worry about, though, because I did receive *a* call before the day was over. My parents' house-keeper, Rita, rang me. She knew my mother was currently giving me the silent treatment; she'd had to field calls the few times I'd tried to contact either of my parents. So it made perfect sense when she said, "I'd probably get fired for calling you if anyone found out, but I thought you should know. Your father's developed a nasty case of pneumonia. His doctor admitted him to the hospital this morning."

I'd always had an iron stomach, but all the alcohol I drank the night before suddenly tried to make a reappearance. Nausea rising, I slapped my hand over my mouth before lowering it to demand, "How bad is it? What hospital? I think I can make it there by nightfall. Are they letting in visitors?"

"No, no. Please don't come. If you show up, they'll know I called you."

I closed my eyes and gritted my teeth. My instincts were screaming at me to hop into my car and see how my father was. But I didn't want Rita to lose her job. She'd always been the mother I'd wished I had. She'd been kind, or at least as kind as she could be without risking her own neck in the process. She had slipped me food when they'd locked me in my room for too long, but that was as far as she'd go. She'd been widowed with three children of her own to take care of. She couldn't put too much effort into caring for me. And I understood that.

"I'll let you know if anything changes." Rita's hushed voice filled my ear before the line clicked, going dead.

I nodded but didn't lower my phone as I stood there. What if my father died before I ever saw him again? What if he died before telling me he loved me?

What if he didn't love me?

Though I knew it was a fruitless effort, I called the hospital. They could tell me nothing, except that Richard Kavanagh was indeed checked in as a patient. I debated calling my mother, but she'd probably catch on that I knew, and Rita would get into trouble, so I slept badly, checking my call history every hour to make sure I hadn't missed any incoming messages in between stressing about how long it'd be before I was fired from my job.

I felt worse when the alarm woke me Monday morning than I'd felt from my hangover the morning before that. My father's heath, my employment uncertainty, and Noel Gamble were going to give me an ulcer; I just knew it.

But not a single wrinkle marred my work outfit. My suit jacket was loose enough to hide my girlish frame, and my skirt was long enough to be staid and professional. I looked the same as I had every morning I left before work. My mirror could detect nothing out of the ordinary. I'd even amazed myself by successfully covering the bags under my eyes with makeup. But I still had an uneasy sense as I walked from my car to the English building that I was making the walk of shame.

Everyone who looked at me would know exactly where I'd had my mouth only two nights ago. They'd glance into my eyes and see me slipping my hands over Noel's biceps and into his hair. I'd open my mouth and my voice would reflect all my guilt and shame. I had kissed a student and taken him to my room, into my *bed*. Just thinking that in my head felt so bizarre and unreal. I was not that person. I would never do that.

Yet I had.

I fully understood all the paranoia was just that, junk in my brain I couldn't shove out. But when Dr. Frenetti popped his head into my office first thing before I'd even taught my first class, I squeaked out my alarm and nearly peed my pants as I leapt to my feet.

"I just checked Gamble's current grade online. Looks like he's doing better already."

Hearing Noel's name right out of the gate like that didn't help my anxiety. Heartbeat whooshing loudly through my ears, I could barely hear myself answer after I cleared my throat. "Y-yes, he...he did very well on the make-up paper I let him turn in."

The dean lifted an eyebrow. "And he actually earned it?"

I blinked. What the hell kind of question was that? "Of course."

Smile a little gloating, Frenetti gave a knowing nod. "That's what I thought. He just needed a little time to warm up to the curriculum. I glanced over your syllabus, and it did look pretty strenuous."

I turned my attention to my computer to keep from rolling my eyes. "Yes, well...it took a pretty intensive one-on-one session to finally get through to him."

My face heated as soon as the words left my mouth. God, did that sound like a sexual innuendo or what? All I could think about was the intensive one-on-one session we'd had Saturday night. In my bedroom. But my supervisor didn't seem to notice any naughty meaning behind my words. He nodded, pleased. "Good to hear it." Then he disappeared before I had to bumble my way through any more mortifying dialogue.

Beyond grateful it wasn't a Tuesday, so I wouldn't be teaching *his* class, I skimmed over my lesson plans for the day until I was almost late to class. Yet still, I felt utterly exposed when I stepped in front of the room. Eyes turned to me, and I knew—just knew—they'd see everything. Know everything. Each time a pair of students leaned toward each other to whisper conspiringly, I knew they were talking about what I'd done. Every unexpected abrupt noise had me leaping out of my skin. And every dark-haired guy I saw had my insides jarring with an instant adrenaline rush.

I hated it. This was too much drama, and I was *not* a drama seeker. My muscles were so tense by the time I finished teaching for the day, I took a handful of painkillers as soon as I retreated to my haven. Leaving my office door open, I collapsed into the chair behind my desk and closed my eyes, relieved it was over. I'd survived one day, and no one seemed to know a thing.

"I would so not make it as a spy," I muttered to myself.

Covering truths and pretending everything was fine and dandy wore the snot out of me. Like a ragged, limp doll, I just sat there, trying to recover my scattered senses.

And then someone tapped on my doorframe, giving me heart failure.

I yelped out an embarrassing girl-scream and jumped to my feet.

"Sorry." Raising both hands in apology, Philip stepped into my office. His eyes begged forgiveness as he cringed. "It's just me."

I sank back into my chair, setting my hand over my heart. Wow, did I need to relax or what?

Seating himself across my desk from me, Philip drew in a deep breath before asking, "So, how much trouble am I in, and what can I do to get you to forgive me?"

Huh? Forgive him? "For what?" I asked dumbly before it hit me. Oh, Lord. I'd lost it. The date, of course.

"For Saturday?" he asked, looking uneasy. Then he gave a nervous laugh and shifted in his chair. "You don't have to pretend it wasn't a big deal. I know I was unforgivably rude for not even phoning you, but something came up and I was called out of town, and..." He looked to be all out of excuses. The helpless expression remained as he finished, "What can I do to make this up to you?"

I was already shaking my head and waving my hand before I began talking. "Really, it's okay." I mean, I had my own guilty burden at the moment. Who was I to be holding anything against anyone else? "I'm sure your...uh, situation was unavoidable."

Plus I kind of felt bad about already forgetting our date that never happened.

He blinked and straightened his back. "So...you forgive me? Just like that?" He arched an eyebrow and sent me an untrusting glance. "Really?"

His perplexity was adorable. I laughed. "If it makes you feel better, I could give you twenty lashes, but whips and chains aren't really my thing."

When his gaze turned heated with interest, I suddenly realized just how bad a double meaning *those words* had sounded. God, why did I keep blurting out tawdry things today? Head heavy from all the horrified blood rushing to my cheeks, I slapped my hand over my mouth before muffling out the exclamation, "Oh, my God. I just said that out loud, didn't I?"

Chuckling in delight, Philip inspected me from a pair of brown eyes glittering with approval. "I didn't hear anything if you didn't want me to."

Clearing my throat and grasping for the last shred of my dignity, I dropped my hand and discreetly murmured, "Thank you."

He nodded. "Does this mean we can try for another date again...soon?"

I opened my mouth, startled by the question. "Uh...I...Well, I'm not sure. You *did* stand me up and neglected to contact me again for *two* days."

My naughty whip slip-up must've given him some confidence, though, because he merely winked. "I'll give you some time to think about it, then. So...call me whenever you change your mind."

I didn't answer. He waved and turned away, sauntering from my office. I stared at the empty spot in my doorway where he'd vanished, chewing on my lip, unsure if I should give him a second chance or not. The man was pleasant enough with a good sense of humor and easy to talk to.

I'd never been good at the dating scene, so he would be an ideal choice of guy to go out with. But he *had* stood me up. He'd abandoned me in a place where I'd felt completely uncomfortable, and I'd ended up making the worst mistake of my life because of it. I should be totally pissed at him. I never would've drunk so much to ease my nerves if he'd asked to meet at a nice restaurant or a boring cocktail bar. And I wouldn't have let Noel Gamble drive me home if I'd been sober. And I certainly wouldn't have stuck my tongue down his throat and made out with him on my bed if he hadn't driven me home.

Holy shit, I could blame this whole thing on Philip, couldn't I? Perfect. Except no, no, I couldn't. I was too much one of those masochistic people who got off on taking all the blame for everything that happened in my life. I'd gotten myself in this mess. And I couldn't pin it on Philip Chaplain, no matter how nice that might temporarily feel. The lucky jerk.

But seriously, the idea of going on another date with him just didn't...thrill me. I'd only been mildly interested the first time around. And now, with all that worry about my father and worry about my job, and worry about Noel Gamble, no way would I be able to concentrate on Philip if we spent any more time together.

"Please don't tell me *that's* the douchebag who stood you up Saturday night? Dr. *Chaplain*? Really?"

I blinked, realizing I was staring right though a blurry figure standing in my doorway.

His voice hit me first. I knew exactly who'd come to my office before my gaze cleared enough to bring him into sharp, amazing focus.

Seeing him standing in the threshold of my office sent my nerves haywire. Lurching to my feet, I glanced wildly behind him, expecting to see Frenetti charging forward to fire me.

"What the hell are you doing here?" I hissed in way too guilty of a tone.

He stepped inside and shut the door, sending my heart crashing against my ribs in a panic, like a frightened bird desperate to escape its cage. I made a sound of denial in the back of my throat, but that was all I could manage.

"I came to talk about what happened..."

I gasped and crushed my hand to my heaving chest. He wouldn't dare. Not here. Not about *that*.

"Between us," he continued, "on Saturday night."

Okay, so he dared.

But the worst part was how he looked as he dared. I felt ragged and raw, unsettled to my very core. And he looked utterly amazing. His dark hair remained fashionably messy as if he'd finger-combed it before leaving the house. His blue eyes with that precious hint of lavender were bright and alert, full of vivacity. And his body. Sweet mercy, I was freshly reminded how it had felt against mine, caging me to my bed as his mouth absolutely leveled me.

Rattled by the physical aspect of my attraction and unhinged over the fact he wanted to discuss the worst thing I'd ever done out in the open, in my *office*,

I stared at him through eyes that refused to blink. But my vision went gray around the edges. God, I hoped I didn't pass out.

Wait, maybe passing out would help me avoid this conversation. Would it be too childish to hold my breath right now?

"What're your plans then, Mr. Gamble?" I demanded, horrified to realize I couldn't control how quickly my breathing had picked up. "Blackmail me? Threaten to tell the administration that I came onto you *in my drunken state* if I don't give you an A?"

His mouth fell open. "Wow." He let out a short hard laugh. "But..." Running his fingers through his hair, he barked out another cynical sound. "Wow. You honestly think I'm that big of an asshole, don't you? I just came here to make sure you were okay."

Immediately realizing I was wrong by the way his eyes glimmered with—what was that, *pain*?—I gulped down my shame. No way could he fake such emotion.

Lowering my gaze, I held my breath as the idea of hurting him ripped me open. "I don't... That's not... You aren't..."

"Breathe," he commanded softly.

Surprisingly, I did, sucking in air, my body unconsciously following his commands and easing the tightness in my muscles that had been there all day. When I looked up, I opened my mouth to apologize for my accusations, but nothing came out.

"So, I'm guessing you're not," he said, lifting his eyebrows, "okay, that is."

"Of course I'm not okay!" I exploded with a harsh whisper before glancing toward the closed door. "I got totally wasted and hit on one of my students." Flapping my hands to show him just how okay I wasn't, I hissed, "I'm completely wigging out right now."

Noel did the worst thing he could possibly do. He cracked a smile. "God, you're cute when you wig out."

"Noel!" I screeched, scandalized by how well he was taking this. His blasé attitude only unsettled me more.

"Right." Turning serious, he nodded and cleared his throat before he blew out a deflated breath. "So, what're we going to do?"

The way he said "we" stirred up an emotion that almost brought tears to my eyes. I don't think anyone had ever used that word on me before. Not a parent, or friend, or...anyone. I'd always done everything on my own. Being part of a team, a pair—God, it was what I'd always wanted. But being a part of anything with *him* was wrong.

Blinking rapidly, I tried to control the racing of my heart by breathing deeply. Purposefully. "Well," I said and took one more deep breath. "The right thing to do would be to confess. So, if you want to tell the dean of the English department what I did to you, so there are no secrets or lies, I...I'll understand. I can go with you right now, if you'd like."

"I don't—" He dodged in front of me to block my way to the door as if he feared I'd dart past him to go talk to Frenetti without his approval. "I mean, whoa. Hey." He gave a nervous laugh and lifted his hands. It reminded of me of an animal whisperer trying to calm a scared, cornered creature. "There's no reason to do that. No one saw us. No one knows. And you certainly don't need to get yourself fired because of this." He squinted his eyes. "And you would, wouldn't you?"

I nodded. "Yes." My voice cracked when I tried to add, "I'd be..."

"Fired," he repeated with a decisive nod.

When I managed a single stiff nod in return, his shoulders fell. "That's what I was afraid of." He sucked his bottom lip in between his teeth in a brooding gesture. It really was too bad he looked so yummy doing it. I just wanted to— Gah! I had to stop thinking that way.

"So, what do you think?" I found the courage to ask, since I really did like thinking in this collaborative "we" term.

He looked up, his eyes startled. "About what?"

I swallowed, flushing. "About what we should do."

"Oh." He exhaled softly. "Uh..." His gaze slid over me, heating as if he remembered how my skin had felt under his hands. The look he sent me said exactly what he wanted to do. The fervor that passed through me as his stare traveled down my form made my nipples bead up, tight and tingly.

"Are you insane?" I gasped, suddenly very breathless.

"Yeah." He blew out a hard breath as he took a step back. "I think maybe I am. Just a little." Then his gaze raked over me again. "Or maybe a lot. Jesus, I can see how hard your nipples are through that blouse."

Slapping my arms around my chest to cover the girls, I glared at him, hissing, "We are *not* starting some illicit affair, Mr. Gamble."

"We're not," he repeated, but he made it more like a question than a repetitive statement.

I flushed. "No! Oh, my God. It...it would be unethical, dangerous, sleazy, and...and...and besides. We're completely not compatible."

"What?" The last comment made him blink back to reality and scowl at me. "You think not? And here, I can't help but remember how *very* well we fit together."

"Will you stop that?" Heat suffused me from head to toe, knowing exactly what he meant.

He cocked his head to the side, looking confused. "Stop what?"

"Stop...stop the flirting and references to what happened. We're forgetting it. Remember?"

But he only grinned. "If I'm supposed to forget,

then how can I remember?"

"Oh my God, you're impossible."

"If you'd let me, I'd finish what we started right here. Right now. You're not drunk any longer, and that was the only thing holding me back." An ornery grin curved up the right side of his mouth. "Didn't you tell me how you dreamed about me taking you on this very desk?"

Color leached from my face. "I did not." But Christ, had I? What had I told him?

"Oh, but you did. In very colorful detail." He looked too happy to report my horrendous behavior, and I wanted to smack him and then kiss him and then probably tackle him onto my desk so he could take me in colorful detail.

"We shouldn't be talking about this." I spun away, facing a wall of bookshelves. Holy God, there was nowhere to go. I'd have to shimmy around him if I wanted to escape through the only doorway. There was the window, but we were on the third floor.

Maybe I should try it anyway.

"So then...I guess that means we're not going to do anything about it, huh?"

"You need to leave, Mr. Gamble. This conversation is...it's wrong."

"I don't see how it's any more wrong than you agreeing to go out with a guy who's already engaged to be married."

"*What*?" I twisted my torso to face him.

He cocked a challenging eyebrow. "Dr. Chaplain. Are you telling me you don't know he already has a fiancée?"

My mouth fell open. "Excuse me? No, he most certainly does not."

Oh, my God. Did he? No, he would've taken her to the scrimmage with him if he had. Wouldn't he? Or was she one of those women who didn't get into sports?

"He proposed to her in one of the classes I took from him last semester." Noel's voice shocked me back to the present.

Disappointment spiked through me. And Philip had seemed so promising. I didn't care that he hadn't interested me the way the irritating student in front of me did, but he'd been...nice, simple. Doable. Well, aside from the whole ditching me at a bar by myself thing. Oh, shit. He really was a bastard.

"But why...why would he ask me out if he was already engaged?"

Noel shrugged, something akin to regret flashing in his eyes, as if he felt like hell for enlightening me to the truth. "Maybe he thought you knew. And didn't care."

"Oh, God." I whirled away again. Could someone really take me for that kind of person?

"Seriously, why do you keep spinning to face the bookshelf?"

Crap. Now Noel knew what a lunatic I was. "Because I'm looking for a book," I ad-libbed at the last moment, surprised and proud of myself for thinking up that answer so fast. And you know, now that I thought of it, there *was* a book I'd needed to check. It was one of those second copies where I'd made notes in the margins. And if I remembered correctly, they'd been pretty damn good notes. Except, I was almost positive that particular book was tucked away in a box...on the top shelf.

Oh, well. I'd gone this far. Might as well keep on. I grabbed the chair sitting on the other side of my desk because it didn't have rollers and would hold me firmly.

"What the hell are you doing?" Noel asked as I stepped up.

"I thought I asked you to leave." Lifting my arms, I used the tips of my fingers to wiggle them under the box and draw it further out from the shelf.

"For God's sake. Here. Let me get that before you hurt yourself."

"I put it up here; I think I can take it down. And you're supposed to be gone...like I asked."

"You didn't ask. You demanded and—Jesus, Aspen." His voice filled with warning. "Don't. You're going to hurt yourself. I'm six three. I can reach it a hell of a lot easier than you."

"Well, I'm five four. What's your point? I can reach it just...fine." Crap. My fingertips barely touched the surface. I hiked myself up onto my tiptoes and tried again.

"No, you can't. Just let me... *Aspen*!"

"Stop calling me by my first name. It's not proper."

"Damn it, woman. Get down!" He grasped my hips and yanked me back just as I grasped the edges of the box. It came flying off the shelf at my sudden heave backward and tipped forward with all its contents raining down on both of us.

CHAPTER FOURTEEN

"I suspect the most we can hope for, and it's no small hope, is that we never give up, that we never stop giving ourselves permission to try to love and receive love." - Elizabeth Strout

~NOEL~

I TAPPED MY FINGERS against my knee as I pressed my phone to my ear, waiting for someone to answer.

Pick took his sweet time before giving a sleepy greeting as if I'd just roused him from bed at four thirty in the afternoon. "Yeah?"

"Hey, can you cover my shift tonight?"

"Fuck, you have the worst timing ever, Gamble. Why can't *you* work it?"

"Long story." I glanced over at Aspen laid out on the bed next to me, her arms resting placidly at her sides while her feet stretched out toward the end of the mattress. I suspected she was awake even though her eyes were closed. "I'm at the hospital...with a friend."

"Everything okay?" The concern in Pick's voice made me smile. He could act like a thug all he liked, but the guy's heart was as soft as a kitten's. He'd cut off his own leg to help a friend in need.

"Nothing a couple stitches can't fix." My gaze found the gauze patch at the top of her arm almost to the curve of her shoulder. Fifteen stitches to be exact.

"Okay, fine. But you owe me."

"Thanks, man." I hung up and lowered my phone just as Aspen's lashes flickered open. The pain medicine they'd given her must've kicked in because her green gaze looked glassy and incoherent.

"You don't have to stay. Really. I'm fine. If you need to go to work, go to work. They're probably going to release me pretty soon anyway."

"And you're going to need someone to drive you home once they do," I argued in a soft, reasonable tone.

I felt like shit for getting her hurt. But who knew corners of cardboard boxes could slice open such deep, nasty gashes? Jesus, I should've let her pull the damn thing down off the shelf by herself. She'd no doubt be *un*injured right now if I had. And I know it had hurt, a lot. She'd let me drive her to the hospital without a word of resistance.

"I can drive just fine. I have a small nick. It's not like they cut off my whole arm." But as soon as she spoke, color seeped from her face. Her eyes went sallow and lost as if her own words had elicited a painful memory. Slamming her lashes closed, she let out a regretful whimper. "I shouldn't have said that."

I tilted my head to the side, confused. "Why not?"

She blinked me back into focus. "Because..." She didn't answer, just stared at me with wide eyes. "My dad," she finally added, but that was all she said.

From her purse, a phone started to ring. Since it

sat on the cart next to me, and I didn't want her to move, I reached into it without asking for permission and snapped open the top clasp. Her phone rested near the top. As I pulled it out, I saw the call was from *Parents*.

"Here." I handed it over, but she just stared at me. You'd have thought I was handing her a poisoned apple or something. So I tried to be helpful as I said, "It's your folks."

"Oh, God." If she'd been pale before, she was sheet white now. "It's karma."

I grinned, glad to know I wasn't the only person who blamed all my bad shit on karma. "Why would karma use your parents' phone to call?"

I was trying to be cute enough to make her smile. It didn't work. If anything, she looked even sicker. "If you only knew."

For some reason, I did want to know. "So tell me."

Aspen stared at me, her expression startled. The phone continued to ring between us. She blinked and shook her head before taking it with shaking fingers.

"Hel...hello?" Her voice sounded so young and afraid. I didn't like that. I thought I hated it in class when her pitch turned professor-ish. But right now, I would've given anything to hear her powerhouse, self-confident tone again.

From where I sat, I heard a muffled woman's voice tell Aspen her father was in the hospital. Hmm. What a coincidence. Must run in the family to visit a hospital today. National Kavanagh Hospital Day. I waited for her to explain she was in one too. But she didn't.

"I...um, how long has he been there?" She nodded as a muted answer came through the receiver. "And his leg?" she asked next. "Is this going to affect that at all? He still has it, right? They haven't amputated anything yet?"

Oh, so that was why lost-limb jokes were taboo in her book. Good to know.

When she closed her eyes and crossed her fingers, I experienced this unavoidable urge to reach out and clasp that hand, or at least cross my fingers right along with her.

She looked so alone and small on that bed, her fingers crossed with hopeful, childlike anxiety. It made me uncomfortable to watch her this way, mostly because I couldn't do anything to help her, or more accurately because I shouldn't.

Thinking *screw it, she needs this*, I reached out and took her hand. Her fingers were cold and gave a startled jerk under my grip. But I didn't let go. Her eyes flashed open to peer up at me, but I just nodded, letting her know I was there. When her fingers finally squeezed back, I swear I felt the grip tighten around my heart instead of my palm.

"Well, that's good," she said into the phone only to wince as if she knew that was the wrong thing to say. But it must not have gotten the response she feared because she let out a relieved breath a second later. "Okay, then. Thank you for calling."

And that was that. I glanced around the room before turning back to her. "Is that all?" I asked. "Why didn't you tell them you were in the hospital, too?"

She flushed and handed the phone back to me. I regretfully let go of her fingers to take it. "I..." She shook her head and waved her bad arm. "This isn't a big deal. She only would've derided me for being clumsy."

"But you *weren't* clumsy. It was my fault you got hurt."

"No..." She sighed as if exhausted. "It wasn't your fault. And even so, she would've somehow found a way to blame me."

I frowned, which only caused her to glance away. Her fingers fidgeted with the blankets.

From listening to her drunken rumblings on Saturday, I already thought her parents were complete assholes. But now, I really didn't like them. I didn't like the way they affected her, making her stammer and turn placating. This was not the woman I'd seen lead a class for the last few months. And it certainly wasn't the woman I'd held in my arms all Saturday night.

"After everything they've done to you, I'm surprised you still talk to them at all," I blurted out before I could stop myself.

"What?" Her face once again leached of color. "How do you know—I mean, what're you talking about? You don't know anything about my relationship with my parents."

I winched. "Yeah, and you obviously don't remember everything you told me Saturday."

"Oh, God." Her eyes looked too large for her head as she gaped in horror. "What did I say?"

No way could I repeat what she'd told me. My mouth opened, but no words came.

"Noel?"

My first name on her lips slayed me. It made me want things, like hurting her parents or that other asshole football player who'd hurt her. It made me want to reach for her hand again or lean down and kiss away all the pain in her eyes by touching my lips to her brow.

Yeah, I definitely loved how she said my name. But before I could make a fool of myself and react to it, the door opened, and a nurse walked in.

"Okay, Miss Kavanagh. You're free to go."

"It's doctor," I said before Aspen could, not that she looked as if she was going to correct the nurse. Both women blinked at me. "She's a doctor, not a miss. She's..." Crap, now I felt like a pretentious ass for making a big deal about her fucking title. But Aspen deserved the respect of such an address. She'd worked her ass off through school to earn it. "A literature professor," I finished lamely.

The nurse flushed. "Oh, I...excuse me, Dr. Kavanagh." She turned to Aspen apologetically, but Aspen waved it away before sending me a strange look.

I shrugged, not caring if I'd sounded prissy. Right now, I wanted everyone she encountered to worship her and treat her as if she was the only thing that mattered.

It took a few minutes after that for us to leave the hospital. When I drew her car keys from my pocket, she zeroed in on them.

"I can drive, you know."

"Oh, really?" Flipping her off, I asked, "How many fingers?"

Instead of getting offended and telling me to behave, she squinted and leaned toward me, stepping off balance and nearly falling into me. I caught her around the waist, keeping her upright.

"Wrong answer. I'm driving. Besides, we came here together. How do you expect me to get home?"

Instead of pulling away to walk on her own as she would have if she were completely coherent, she leaned a little more heavily against me. "I could drive you back to campus to get your car."

There she went again, thinking I had my own set of wheels. I sighed. "You can't even see three feet in front of you. *I'm* driving." When she frowned at me, I merely sent her a saccharine smile. "Deal with it, sweetheart."

She sighed, giving in, and rested her head on my shoulder as I led her the rest of the way to her car. It felt nice, but I still had to glance around to make sure no one saw us. I doubted anyone would fire her just because she was hurt, and drugged, and had no idea what she was doing. But I knew I shouldn't risk it, except she felt too nice in my arms for me to let go.

***

"There you go." I handed Aspen a glass of water.

"Thank you." She accepted it and popped a pill into her mouth before swallowing the contents.

I sat on the edge of her bed beside her, my hip dangerously close to hers, even though she was covered by a few layers of blankets. I could still feel her warmth soaking through them.

While she set her cup on her nightstand, I fluffed her pillow before she could lie down. "Need anything else?"

She twisted her torso to watch me with a half-smile. "Noel Gamble, nursemaid," she teased.

I grinned back. "What? Didn't you know I doubled as one in my other secret life?"

"Just how many other secret lives do you have?" She lay down, but not on the pillow I'd just readied. She curled into me, wrapping her warm arms around my waist before placing her cheek on my thigh. Then she closed her eyes and sighed in contentment.

"Damn it, Aspen," I groaned, unable to stop my own arms as they folded around her in return. Lifting her lightly, I scooted down so I could lie next to her and provide my shoulder as her pillow.

Pressing my lips to her hair, I sighed. "Why do you always turn so sweet and cuddly when you're half out of your mind?" *When I couldn't in good conscience do anything about it?*

"I'm always cuddly," she answered, her voice thick and slow. "You only notice it when I'm half out of my mind."

I chuckled and pulled her blankets up to her chin. Eyes still closed, she sighed again and a smile spread across her face.

No way could I leave her like this. Besides, she was hurt. Someone had to watch over her. But I kept my shoes on, letting my feet hang off the edge of the mattress, thinking that somehow made this not so taboo.

Burying my nose back into her hair, I closed my eyes.

"Want to hear a secret?" I whispered, hoping she was fully out so I could confess everything to her subconscious instead of her.

"Hmm. Wha's that?"

I grinned fondly at the way she slurred. It reminded me too much of Saturday when we'd kissed and she'd been drunk. And it helped me to spill out my confession more freely. "I had a crazy-ass crush on you the first day of school."

She lifted her face and looked up at me, her lashes flickering open to reveal glazed, drug-fogged eyes. "No way."

I nodded. "Way. I was looking down, doodling in a notebook or something. Then I heard your voice, introducing yourself, and I had to look up. You sounded so...I don't know. Compelling. Even wearing one of those gawd-awful suit things you wear to class, I wanted you."

Her lips curled with pleasure. "Really?"

I nodded. "Absolutely. Some guys may be leg-men, or ass-men, or breast-men. But I am most certainly a confirmed mouth-man. And your mouth..." I reached out to barely press the pad of my index finger to her lips. "Christ, Aspen. I think I had about fifty split-second visions of everything I wanted to do to your mouth." Shaking my head, I grinned as she continued to watch me from lazy, tired, but transfixed eyes.

"I wanted to impress you with my first paper you assigned us. I wanted you to remember me and think of me as one of your favorite students. But you hated my paper. I don't think I'd put so much effort into a stupid literature assignment before, and I got a freaking C. It blew my mind. Then, when I was answering a question you asked in class one day and you found out I was on the football team, you looked at me as if I was complete slime. That kind of hurt, you know."

"I'm sorry," she mumbled, letting her cheek drop glumly onto the pillow. "It wasn't really you I didn't like." She lifted a hand to reach for me, but her fingers fell listlessly as if they weighed too much for her to handle. So I caught her wrist and lifted her hand for her, bringing her knuckles to my mouth so I could kiss them.

"I know that. *Now*. But with every C and D you gave me, I began to dislike you more and more until I hated you with this burning passion. It pissed me off so bad that I could be that attracted to you, and all you saw in me was a big, dumb jock."

"You're not dumb, Noel. The furthest thing from it."

I shook my head and smiled derisively, keeping to my own subject. "Didn't matter what I felt for you, though, it was always intense. Intense attraction, intense loathing, intense everything. I have been intensely aware of you since the first day you came into my life. Every time you assigned us anything, it was like a personal challenge for me to impress you, but my grade just kept dropping. I felt so stupid. I just..."

I gathered a piece of her hair and smoothed it out of her face. "I wanted you to look at me and see the success I wanted to be. Not the failure I knew I was."

"But I do see a success." Since I was still holding her hand up by my mouth, it was easy for her to open her fingers and cup my cheek. "You've accomplished so much."

"No. I only wish I have." I leaned forward to press my forehead to hers, adding a few more goals I knew I'd never reach onto my wish list, and all of them relating to her.

Her touch slid up my jaw until soft fingers curled around the back of my neck and urged me down, bending until I was face to face with her. When she tried to reel me in for a kiss, I resisted.

"Aspen," I whispered in warning, gritting my teeth. "You're not in your right frame of mind again. I can't take advantage of you like this two times in a row."

"I won't tell if you don't," she whispered back and pulled on me a little harder.

Resisting her mouth wasn't something I could do so I kissed her, lightly. But damn. Her mouth. My lips couldn't get enough. They turned hungry and moved a little more insistently until I had her opening up under my urging. My tongue was right there alongside hers, curling up with hers and snuggling inside.

I groaned, deep and low, trying to soften the kiss so I could safely pull away. But her hands swept over me, and I only kissed her harder.

My fingers ached to explore. My heart pounded, and my body yearned to covers hers. Before I knew it, I was rolling her onto her back and crawling over her.

"You're so beautiful." I traced the delicate curve of her jaw before sweeping down her throat. She lifted her chin, allowing me access, so I leaned in to kiss her pulse.

With a sweet moan of acceptance, she buried her fingers into my hair. My mouth found her collarbone and my tongue delved into the little indention between the two. I tugged gently at the sleeve of her blouse with my teeth to expose more skin on her chest. And as my lips foraged a path south, my hand smoothed up her arm to her shoulder, only to encounter the gauze patch, covering her stitches at the very top of her bicep.

It was the slap back to reality I needed. "Shit," I breathed against her throat and closed my eyes as I eased my mouth off her.

"What's wrong?" Her palm cupped my cheek.

I remained hovered over her a second longer before I cracked my lashes open and met her concerned, yet cloudy, gaze. "Nothing." I smiled. "Rest now, okay?"

When I went to crawl off her, she grabbed a handful of my shirt and clung on. "Stay."

Nodding, I tucked a piece of hair behind her ear. "Don't worry about a thing. I'll watch over you."

Her hand relaxed and her body settled. "Thank you," she murmured one last time before she was completely out of it.

The smartest thing would've been for me to leave. But there was nowhere else I wanted to be. And I'd promised to stay. So I settled down beside her, ignored the pissed-off straining erection in my jeans, and I slept next to Aspen Kavanagh for the second time. And it was just as amazing as the first night I'd held her until dawn.

CHAPTER FIFTEEN

"I generally avoid temptation unless I can't resist it."
- Mae West

~ASPEN~

"SCIENCE IS ABOUT HYPOTHESES, theories and laws made from facts that have been proven over time. Mathematics is made up of absolutes, where there is only one correct answer to each equation. But with music, art, *literature*, the possibilities are endless. There is no specific law or equation that makes a piece of literature so-called *good*. There are literally millions. And here's the real kicker. It's all completely subjective. One song may please the ear of one person, while it completely irritates the ear of another. So, does that make it good or bad or merely average? What do you think? What makes truly good literature *good*? What makes it stand the test of time until here we are, years, decades and centuries later, discussing it in a classroom?"

From the back, a male voice guessed, "It's got to be boring enough?"

Folding my hands together at my waist, I waited patiently for the laughter to die down. Then I nodded to the student, allowing him his answer. "It may be boring to you, Mr. Tenning. But obviously it wasn't boring to someone, or it wouldn't have been published, and republished, and then republished again so many times, so...try again."

He didn't have another witty answer ready, so he shrugged and slumped lower in his chair. I shrugged too, which pulled at the stiches in my arm. With a wince, I reached up to cup it briefly, my gaze straying not far from Mr. Tenning to where Noel sat.

It'd been a week since I'd fallen asleep in his arms, drugged just enough to say things I knew I shouldn't have but sober enough to remember everything I'd said. I knew he had stayed until morning too because I'd gotten a drink at three due to a dry throat and he'd still been there, next to me, keeping me warm, protecting me. But he'd been gone when my alarm clock had woken me at five thirty.

And now, here we both were, eight days later, on either side of the room, a line of propriety separating us from being together.

He sat sprawled in his chair with his long legs kicked out in front of him and crossed at the ankles while he tapped his pen again the notepad on his desk. His eyes were on me, though. And they narrowed as they darted to my hand cupping my injury.

I dropped my fingers and turned my attention to a girl in the front lifting her arm. "Yes?"

"It reaches our emotions," Sydney Chin answered.

With an approving nod, I gave her a brilliant smile. "Very good, Miss Chin." Turning back to the others, I began to walk toward the other side of the room. "People turn to the arts to find the height of an emotion. We go to a scary movie to be frightened, or a comedy to laugh. Books are the same, except without all the special effects on a screen. Instead, you have to use your imagination."

I tapped the side of my head. "And the best part of using our imagination is that each and every person in this room can read the same line on a page, and you will all picture something totally different in your heads. You'll all feel something different about it, because you've all come from different parts of the world, been raised by different standards, influenced by different people, taught from different back-grounds. No two people are the same, so no two opinions can always be the same, which is exactly why I grade on essay papers only. I fully believe there is no wrong answer to your opinion about a story...as long as you have sufficient reason to back that opinion up." I glanced up at the clock on the wall. "Which reminds me, I'm halfway through reading all the papers you handed in last week, so I should have them back to you by next Tuesday at the latest."

Spreading my arms wide, I gave the room a large grin. "And with that, I'll see you guys on Thursday."

A collective sigh spread over the class. By the way they scrambled to collect their things and leave, a girl might think they were thrilled to escape her room. Humph. I shook my head. Tough crowd. Oh, well. Sidney Chin had seemed interested in what I'd had to say. One fan was better than none. My shoulders slumped, making the ache in my wounded arm throb even more.

I massaged the tender spot as the group of jocks from the back made their way out of the seating area. I couldn't help but glance toward Noel. Mr. Tenning was talking animatedly to him, but he must've sensed my gaze because he looked over. Everything inside me sparked to life. It was as if this one man held the switch to my happy endorphins.

"Mr. Gamble," I said, nodding to him with a stony stare, "may I have a moment, please?"

He paused and kicked at his friend when Mr. Tenning murmured something in his ear. But he stayed behind, not moving until everyone in his group had made it to the door. Then, and only then, did concern fill his eyes as he approached me.

"Are you okay? You were rubbing your arm. Does it hurt?" When he went to reach for it, I pulled back and glanced behind him to where a few stragglers were still lingering.

Noel ground his teeth together as he took them in, and turned back to me, lowering his voice. "I can't believe it's still bothering you after a week. You need to go easier on yourself so you can heal. You're remembering to take your painkillers, right?"

I frowned. I hadn't called him after class to get my own lecture. I'd actually had something important to say. "I can't. They make everything...muzzy. And I need a clear head to teach."

He stepped closer, coming right up to the edge of my personal space. It was...nice, but this was so not the time or place. "You *need* not to feel any pain. I don't like knowing you're still hurting because of something I did."

"Oh, for God's sake." I cringed and drifted my gaze over the students who were now milling toward the doorway, not paying us any attention. More quietly, I hissed. "My arm is fine. The stitches are healing and everything will be okay. This is *not* why I needed to talk to you."

Eyebrows lifting with interest, Noel cocked his stance with smug arrogance. "It's not? Well, then... what's up, *Professor*?" Folding his arms over his chest, he waited for me to continue.

I sighed and held out his essay I'd read last night. "I can't accept this paper."

His gaze lowered before lifting again. "Why not?

Didn't I get the meaning of the assignment this time?"

"You *know* why not," I hissed. "You're treading on dangerous ground here. You risk too much."

His lips twitched as if this all amused him, as if there was nothing to worry about at all. "But you asked for an essay about how certain events change a person's goals. And you just said, two minutes ago, there were no wrong answers. Didn't I give you sufficient enough reason why I have the opinion and feelings I do?"

I did not like my own words used against me, but I did like how he'd been listening and soaking them in.

Grr. So not the point.

"You can't just write something like that. What if someone else had gotten their hands on this and read it?"

He shrugged. "So what? I didn't name you specifically." But he had written about how someone who was forbidden to him had just come into his life and changed some of the major things he wanted. I had altered his hopes and dreams. It was frankly flattering to know I made him question what he really wanted out of his life and how the only thing holding him back from pursuing his newest dream was my security.

But he'd come right out and announced he wanted to date one of his teachers, writing the line: *I stay away only because the consequences of fraternizing with a student are too great for her.*

"You actually wrote the word *fraternize*," I accused.

He gave a wide, proud grin. "I know. I even shocked myself on that one. Good word, huh?"

"Noel." I shook my head. He was impossible. *Impossible*! "I can't accept this essay."

"Okay, fine." With a roll of his eyes, he blew out a harassed breath and slipped a stapled stack of papers from his messenger bag to set it on my desk. "How about this one, then?"

I glanced down, blinking at what looked like another essay. "Wha...?" I looked up at him, completely confused.

He winked. "I had a feeling you'd be demanding a different version. So, there it is, without a single word of what you do to me on any line."

"You...you wrote *two* versions of your essay?" When he nodded, I shook my head, baffled. "Why?"

His blue eyes filled with an intense emotion that made my throat go dry. "Because I wanted you to know. I wanted you to understand."

My heart wrenched in my chest as he turned away and walked from my classroom.

***

Okay, fine. I admit it. Noel Gamble's freaking mock essay had gotten to me. So had that honest, seeking look in his eyes when he'd said *I wanted you to understand.*

He'd just placed the ball *firmly* in my court. And it was just too tempting not to leap toward it. So, there I was, doing something unspeakably crazy.

Forbidden was an apt name for this club, I decided. I knew I shouldn't be in it, but a thrill of naughty anticipation danced over my scalp as I opened the front door and stepped inside. I couldn't believe I was giving into this so easily, coming here in the hopes of maybe only catching a glimpse of him.

He probably didn't even work tonight. God, I hoped not. I didn't need anything else making me fall under his spell. I didn't care how much I really did want to see him, even if it was just stolen little longing glances from across a room without him knowing I was there. I needed to nip this fascination in the bud.

Easier said than done.

He was the first thing I saw. Being a Tuesday evening, the place was a lot less crowded than it had been the last time I'd been here. So I had a straight shot, wide-open view to the bar in the back. Blue fluorescent lights sprayed down on his dark hair, and the black cloth of his T-shirt looked especially nice stretching across his wide, thick shoulders.

A pinch in my chest had me sucking in a breath. He was busy, absorbed in his work, setting up a row of shots. His hands were fluid and graceful as he flipped over each glass with adept speed and then poured his way down the line. Everything about him was so freaking captivating. When he sprawled in his seat during class, doodling in his notebook with lazy strokes as if he wasn't paying attention to a thing I taught. When he directed his team on the field, calling plays and pointing out commands to his teammates. And definitely when he played Tom Cruise from *Cocktail.*

My parents would disown me if they knew how much I loved eighties movies. But I didn't care. I'd always had a thing for bartenders because of that one. I liked them almost as much as I'd been drawn to football players.

This was bad; he sucked me in way too easily. I should go. He hadn't seen me come in. I still had a chance to escape before he noticed I'd turned into a total creeper. But, nope, I didn't budge.

A waitress approached me and tried to take my order, but I waved her off with a smile and shake of my head. And returned to my stalking.

Noel Gamble really was a sight to behold. As he handled his own customers, he still had time to pause and help the other bartender mix his drinks correctly.

When the flow of traffic to the bar died off, I was drawn closer. I nibbled on the corner of my lip, telling myself to stay back, but yeah, that didn't work out so well. I kept drifting toward the light. Except another woman passing by the other side of the bar caught Noel's attention. He glanced briefly at her, only to do a double take.

Jealousy slapped me right across the face. It was so easy for him to notice other women. I obviously didn't mean as much to him as he'd made it sound in his essay.

But then his eyes narrowed on her. "Hey, Jess," he called, tipping up his chin as he tried to catch her attention.

She ignored him and kept walking, entering a hall in the corner and disappearing down it.

Ripping off the drying towel he had slung over his shoulder, he slapped it against the bar and growled, "I'll be right back. You got the bar okay?"

The dark-haired guy working with him lifted his face in surprise. "Umm…"

"Thanks," Noel called, not even glancing at his coworker as he dodged out the back side of the counter and streaked into the hall in hot pursuit of the woman.

Who was she? How well did he know her? How much of his naked body has she seen?

All questions I had no right or business asking, even as they repeated through my head with a stupid obsession I couldn't turn off.

Since I'd already given in to so much of my inner stalker tonight, I figured it couldn't hurt to give in to a little more. I wandered to the opening of the hall, trying to appear as casual and nonchalant as possible, and was rewarded to learn he hadn't gone very far down. Slapping open the first door on the left side, he barged inside what looked like an office from the brief glimpse and angle I saw of a filing cabinet.

He left the door wide open and stopped in the threshold, jamming his hands to his hips, his shoulders braced with anger. "Nice to see you, *Jessie*." Clipped with sarcasm, his voice floated back to me perfectly. "What's it been? Two weeks? Yeah, that sounds about right, since I've worked here every fucking night since then and haven't seen you at all."

"What's this?" The woman's voice came through a little more muffled, but I could still hear her clearly enough. "The employee's actually lecturing the boss?"

He gave a hard laugh. "Boss? That's funny. Because from what I can tell, we haven't had a damn boss since your dad's been here."

"Are you trying to piss me off, Gamble?"

"You know what, let me tell you what's been going on here since you last decided to grace us with your presence, and you tell me which one of us has the right to be pissed off? Last week, we ran out of our most popular lager, but don't worry." He lifted his hands as if to ease her panic. "I reordered more. You're welcome. But they shipped us the wrong batch, so I had to straighten out that clusterfuck. You're welcome. Then, the fire marshal stopped by. Our quarterly inspection was overdue, so all your dedicated employees worked our asses off to make sure everything was kosher for the inspection we had *yesterday*. Which you're welcome for...again. Next, Tansy was in a car accident and broke her leg. She's one of your best servers, by the way, since I'm sure you have no clue. But yeah, don't worry about that. I called every girl who works the floor and we rearranged things until all of Tansy's shifts are covered for the next six weeks, which, oh yeah, you're welcome for that too. And I made an order for all the other liquors we're running low on."

He paused before nodding and adding one last, slow, taunting, "You're welcome."

Instead of gushing out an apology or thanking him for everything he'd done, his boss only snorted. "If you came to tell me all the issues have been handled, then what the hell are you whining about?"

Noel jerked a hand off his hip and slapped the

door. "I'm not getting paid to take care of your job and mine both. You're lucky it's not football season, or you'd be shit out of luck right now. I can't keep doing this, Jess. And by the way, you're scheduling it all fucked up. Steffie's only signed up for two hours a week, while Gracie's working her ass off with fifty."

"So? I don't like Steffie."

"Well, you didn't hire Steffie. Your dad did. And if you don't want him to disown you after he gets back and find out how shitty of a job you've done, you'd better pull your head out of your ass and actually work once in a while."

"I'm here now, aren't I?"

"Just..." Stepping backward out of the office as if he couldn't bear to talk to her a moment longer, Noel muttered, "Fix the damn schedules, will you? I can't keep working this much. And hire another bartender while you're at it. I need a night off, or some goddamn sleep, sometime this year."

"I'd say so. You've turned into a fucking crab."

"Jess," he growled warningly.

"Jesus, if you're so all-fired to get a better schedule and new bartender, then you take care of it. Seems like you've gotten used to running this place, anyway."

The muscles in his back tensed, but he merely growled, "Fine. I will."

"Oh, and here are the fucking notes everyone gives me, whining for all the days they want off."

Noel stepped inside only to reemerge a moment later, his hand fisted around a ball of paper scraps. "Unbelievable," he muttered, storming right toward me. But he seemed so mad he didn't even notice me. I ducked out of the way just as he exited the hall and marched back behind the bar. Dumping the pile of notes onto the counter in the back, he began to organize them.

"Is a fuzzy navel made of peach or orange juice?"

his clueless coworker asked a minute later.

"Both," Noel answered without looking up. "Ice it, add one and a half ounces of peach schnapps and top that off with orange juice."

"Thanks. What're you doing, anyway?"

"Fixing the damn schedule."

"Really? Hey, can you get me more than sixteen hours a week?"

Noel stopped what he was doing and lifted his face. "What the hell? She only put you in for sixteen hours a week? Figures." He went back to work. "But yeah, you got it." Then he paused and lifted a slip of torn paper to his eyes, squinting.

"Yo, Lowe," he called as his coworker began to leave. "What's this say?"

Lowe came back and took the sheet. He blinked and turned it upside down before handing it back. "No clue."

Noel sighed and rubbed his face. "Great."

"Noel, table eight needs refills."

He glanced at the waitress who'd approached. "Sure. Oh! Hey, Mandy. Can you read this?"

He let her look it over while he pulled up a round of bottled beers.

With an apologetic smile, she shook her head and gave the paper back. "Sorry, sweetie. But it looks like Julia's handwriting if that helps."

"Julia," he murmured, scanning the tables. "She's not working tonight, is she?"

"Nope." Mandy grabbed the beers and was gone.

He looked so defeated as he set the note on the bar and shook his head, I couldn't help it. I couldn't handle seeing him like this. He worked so hard, at everything. The guy needed a break. Or better yet, he needed my help.

"Let me see," I said and came in close enough to slide the paper across the bar away from him. "I'm used to trying to decipher sloppy handwriting."

When he glanced up and only blinked at me, I sent him a nervous smile, rolling my eyes. "And usually it's other professors' penmanship, not students, that are the worst."

A breath rushed from his lungs. "What're you doing here?"

Ignoring the questions because I couldn't handle the answer, I studied the slip of paper before looking up. He looked so thunderstruck, I was actually afraid of the force of joy that pulsed through me. I should not get a thrill out of pleasing him, but oh God, I felt like a junkie. I had to do more to make him smile.

"It says 'need off every Friday for son's ballgames.'" Then I glanced away, unable to take the pressure I felt in my chest from simply looking into his periwinkle eyes.

CHAPTER SIXTEEN

"What you risk reveals what you value." - Jeanette Winterson, *Written on the Body*

~NOEL~

"YOU CAME BACK." THE words echoed though my head. She'd come back. Holy shit. Aspen had come back to Forbidden.

She handed the slip of paper back to me. "Yeah, I...I..."

"Thirsty for some more Bud Light Lime?" I guessed, making sure my fingers touched hers when I retrieved the note.

She flushed green and sent me a horrified glance. "God, no." But even as she shook her head, her fingers seemed to slide deliberately over the outside of my thumb when she retracted her hand. God damn. I shuddered from the obscene amount of pleasure it gave me. "I don't think I could drink that particular poison again for quite a while. I'll just stick with cola tonight." When she seated herself, telling me she planned to stay awhile, my heart almost cracked itself open it beat against my chest so hard.

I nodded and tossed the work memo aside before setting my hands on the counter between us. "You know, they make a mean cola just across the street at that *non*-alcoholic restaurant there. It's cheaper too."

She nodded and slipped off her stool, getting to her feet. "You're right. I don't...I don't know what I'm doing here. I should go."

Oh, hell no. I caught her hand just as she touched the bar to push away from it. Trapping it against the countertop, I waited until she lifted her large, startled gaze. "Don't go. I'm sorry. I shouldn't have teased. I just wanted to hear you admit you were here because of me."

Her eyes narrowed. "Why? Because you like to torture me?"

"No." I shook my head, feeling plenty tortured enough for the both of us. "Because it would've made my entire day."

She glanced away. When she dismissed me entirely and dug into her purse to pull out her phone, my disappointment almost ate me alive. She was probably telling her date to hurry his ass up because she didn't want to be stuck here alone with me a second longer than she had to be.

If she'd agreed to give Dr. Chaplain another chance, even though he was already fucking engaged, I didn't know how I would handle that. Probably very badly.

But about as soon as she put her phone away, my butt vibrated. Frowning, I tugged my phone from my back pocket and scowled at the unknown number. Curious to see who was texting me, I opened the message and my mouth fell open when I read what was written.

I AM here because of you.

"Oh." The air rushed from my lungs. *Fuck*. The pleasure, and longing, and anxiety that roared through me was way more intense than I wanted it to be. I looked up at her.

She bit her lip and stared back, and this overwhelming sensation roared to life inside me.

God, she just had to go and do this, didn't she? "You know, I was fully prepared to leave you alone. You convinced me this was a bad idea. I wasn't going to gamble your entire career away just for my own pleasure. But you coming here tonight..." I blew out a breath and shook my head. "That's a little too tempting to resist."

Her eyes filled with panic. Lifting her chin regally, she said, "There's nothing wrong with stopping at a bar for a drink."

I leaned in until I could get a whiff of lavender oozing off her. Then I tilted my head to the side and grinned. "No, there's nothing wrong with that at all."

She sat down slowly, her gaze leery, as if she suspected I had an ulterior motive. I sent her an innocent smile, but she only narrowed her gaze more. Paranoid woman. I loved how easy it was to make her suspicious.

"I'll be right back with your...cola."

Turning away, I hummed to myself as I pulled down a cup and opened the ice chest.

"Thought you said you *weren't* sleeping with your teacher."

I looked over to catch Lowe sending me a curious sidelong glance as we both scooped glasses into the ice. He lifted his eyebrows. "Not that it's any of my business or I'm judging or anything," he was quick to add. "You just sounded pretty adamant the other night that you weren't."

"What makes you think she's my teacher?" I evaded, curious to know how he'd come to such a conclusion. Risking a peek over my shoulder, I took her in. In blue jeans and a cashmere top with her hair pulled up in a perky ponytail, she looked like an undergraduate. Not a single professor vibe seeped from her.

Lowe just grinned. "My girlfriend and I take World Masterpieces from Dr. Kavanagh together. And Ten said her name the first night I worked here, so..." He let me figure out the rest of his deductive reasoning for myself.

Well, shit. If one guy could figure us out so effortlessly, then how easy would it be for anyone else to? Just how perilous to her job was it for me to even talk to her?

Feeling fiercely protective, I scowled at Lowe. "I think you're reading too much into something that's not there." The look in my eyes and tone in my voice told him to back the hell off.

"Hey, you don't have to worry about me." He lifted his hands, trying to tell me everything between us was cool. "I wouldn't say anything, and besides, I was just teasing you."

No. *Ten* teased me, thinking I wasn't even interested in her. I could tell Lowe *knew* I actually was.

I looked her way, every muscle in my body tense. I didn't want to cause her trouble. I didn't want some guy I barely knew and couldn't trust yet getting her into trouble either. But then she turned her attention our way as if she could feel my gaze on her, and we made eye contact. Christ, but I couldn't stay away from her either. The pull I felt toward this woman was crazy, and I knew I should fight it, but I kept forgetting why.

When the tops of her cheeks flushed and she darted her glance away, I jerked my elbow Lowe's way. "She doesn't seem to recognize you from one of her classes." And that's when it hit me. Aspen *didn't* recognize Lowe. In fact, she didn't even seem to be aware of him working alongside me.

Since the bastard had started, every woman had skipped over me to check him out first. Without fail. Everyone but Aspen. She didn't even realize he existed because she was busy sneaking another discreet glance my way.

Heat seized me. I wanted to go to her, and grab her, and just...brand her as mine. Such barbaric, caveman urges had never afflicted me before, but they roared to life now. She preferred me over Mason Lowe. Hot damn. Made me want to prefer her over every woman I'd ever known too.

Or maybe she just hadn't really looked at him yet. A scowl marred my brow as I studied her. I didn't like the self-doubt these thoughts caused. I hadn't experienced anything like it since I'd been here. In Ellamore, I was treated like royalty. Strangers loved me for my football skills. Ladies loved me for my looks. And guys loved me for my cool-ass attitude. I never had to wonder who thought I was a piece of trash, because they told me I was amazing. Until Aspen Kavanagh came along. And now the uncertainty was creeping its way under my skin and making me itch for answers.

Her fingers tapped idly against the countertop to the beat of the music playing as if she was waiting for something. For me.

But I didn't go to her.

"Hey, you take care of her for a little while," I told Mason, tugging the drink from his hand and handing him the one in mine so we could trade places.

He sent me a surprised glance. I didn't give him a chance to refuse, because I was already delivering his order to his customer. I barely paid the middle-aged guy any notice as I covertly watched every move Lowe made. He approached Aspen and set her soda on the counter. She turned to him with a ready smile, which only faltered when she discovered *he* was serving her.

Then she glanced my way and I rushed to look busy.

Lowe stuck around for a couple minutes, saying something I couldn't hear from my end. She responded with a nod and vague smile. His posture turned flirtier than I'd ever seen it before, and I had to scowl, ready to kick his ass. What the hell did he think he was doing?

Instead of batting her lashes at him, or blushing, or even—God, help me—giggling, Aspen merely slid her gaze to me. Jesus, she sat right in front of Catnip Lowe and her eyes still wandered my way. I wasn't quite sure how to deal with this. Awareness spiked through me and I wanted to claim my woman so badly I actually balled my hands into fists to fight the urge. Tugging her attention back to Lowe as if it took everything she had to focus on what he was saying, she nodded and replied to whatever he'd asked.

I rested my hands on the bar to catch my breath. It felt as if I'd just run a mile. And my skin was alive with this oversensitive prickly sensation. Jesus, I hoped I wasn't breaking out into hives. It wasn't exactly the most comfortable feeling. It was too new to be cozy, but I craved more of it. I wanted to look at her again just to hoard up more of the rush that just looking at her gave me.

"So, did she pass your test?" Lowe asked quietly as he appeared at my side.

I hadn't even realized I had been testing her until that moment, but hell, she'd passed. "With flying colors," I uttered. Jesus. I glanced sideways at him, needing help. Seriously. "What the fuck am I supposed to do now? I shouldn't—" What was I saying? I couldn't confide in Lowe about this. The less people who knew, the better. But I kept blustering, because I was so damn rattled. I needed some kind of guidance. "We can't—"

He patted my back dolefully. "It's always the one you shouldn't want that you end up wanting the most."

With a lift of my eyebrows, I waited for him to elaborate. He didn't. He just sent me a knowing grin and leaned in confidentially close. "But if she's worth it, nothing else matters. You'll find a way. And you'll sacrifice whatever needs to be sacrificed to get there."

Realizing he was talking about him and his girlfriend, I watched him thoughtfully as he turned away and stacked a couple dirty glasses into a tub to be taken to the back for washing. I swear he'd just given me his blessing to mess around with my freaking professor.

If she's worth it, his words rumbled through my head. I sent her a glance, and everything perked to attention. No one had ever affected me the way this woman did. She stole the breath from my lungs with a single glance, and made me feel more alive and more aware of every sense I possessed than anyone I'd ever met. She could even piss me off more than anyone else had ever pissed me off before. She had a power over me that should've scared the shit out of me, but it only drew me to her harder.

"You seriously like being with just one girl?" I grabbed Lowe's arm when he tried to pass by. "Monogamy, and relationships, and all that shit. Is it really worth it?"

He paused and lifted an eyebrow. After studying me thoughtfully for a moment, he grinned. "If it's *the* girl, then hell yes." Shrugging free of me, he took off down the hall toward the kitchen.

And I started toward Aspen without even thinking. I was halfway across the bar before I realized what I was doing. I was going to go after her, and I was going to make her mine.

But something on the television screen over the bar caught her attention. She tilted her head and squinted her eyes as if trying to hear what was being said. When her eyes widened and lips parted, I knew it was bad.

"What?" I demanded, stopping across from her at the bar and trying to crane my neck around to see the television.

The words on the bottom of the screen had my skin icing over with dread. *Ellamore Sex Scandal.*

I sliced a look to Aspen. When she met my gaze, her face was sheet white. So I scrambled for the remote under the counter. When I found it, I pushed the closed caption button.

ESU assistant volleyball coach, Vander Wilson, was fired this afternoon for having illicit relations with freshman volleyball player, Allison Belfries. According to allegations, Wilson and Belfries's affair started early in the season and lasted until this week when Wilson's wife caught the two together. But when Wilson tried to end the relationship, Belfries went to the head coach to confess everything. University officials dismissed him immediately and have declined to make a comment at this time. More on that later...

"I need to go," Aspen gasped, jerking her purse off the bar as she hopped off her stool. "I can't... This is... I'm sorry. Can I pay my tab now?"

I turned to her, already knowing what I'd see and dreading it. She wouldn't even look at me. Her cheeks were stained with guilt and her throat worked as she swallowed convulsively.

"Aspen," I started, ready to fight for her. But what the hell? I'd just decided she was worth it; why would the universe pull the rug out from under us like that?

"Don't," she pleaded, her voice strained and eyelashes damp.

I crumbled. Here, I'd been all prepared to argue our case. We weren't like them. Neither of us was

184

married; we weren't being unfaithful. And if I remembered correctly, Coach Wilson was in his late thirties. He was probably twenty years older than Allison Belfries.

But the bleak, troubled, guilty gleam in Aspen's green eyes reminded me our situation would probably be worse, actually. Volleyball wasn't nearly as big of a deal at Ellamore as football was. And Aspen was actually one of my professors, responsible for giving me my literature grade. The media would make a hell of a lot bigger deal out of us than they would from some coach/player relationship. And it'd all fall back on her. She'd get the heat, the dirty names, the ruined future. She'd get everything, while I'd get off scot-free.

No matter how much I wanted her, no matter how amazing she made me feel, I couldn't do that to her. The sacrificing part was all hers, not mine.

I hated that.

Taking a physical step back, I nodded my understanding and relinquished my fight to try to keep her. But God, it sliced me in two to let that hope go.

"Here's your tab, Dr. Kavanagh." Lowe appeared beside me, already back from his kitchen trip.

I knew he was probably trying to be helpful because he'd seen everything that had just happened. But his actions irritated me. I didn't want anyone to know what was going on between us. And even more, I didn't want him to realize how much this fucking hurt. Showing my vulnerabilities pissed me off. I wanted to ball my hand into a fist and punch Lowe in the face. Actually, any kind of violence to get this clawing sensation out of my chest would do. And since he was handy...

Aspen sputtered, her face coloring as she blinked at him. "You know...you know who I am?"

"My girlfriend and I take World Masterpieces," he explained. Then he shrugged and gave her a bashful smile. "You're actually her favorite teacher."

She paled, but nodded and tried to smile back as she handed him a twenty to pay.

Lowe turned toward the cash register and sent me a glance as he did. But his gaze was unreadable, and I felt abandoned as he turned away.

Though Aspen stood just on the other side of the bar, she was suddenly unreachable.

We didn't speak as we waited for Lowe to return with her change. And we didn't look at each other. I watched her from the corner of my eye as she hugged her purse to her breasts. I folded my arms over my chest, frustrated because I could do nothing to fix this.

Lowe returned too soon. Now Aspen would leave. My mind whirled to come up with the perfection solution to fix this, but I had nothing.

After stuffing a ten in the tip jar, she spun away and hurried off. Without even saying goodbye.

I clenched my teeth and glared at Lowe.

He blew out a long breath. "Well... That sure sucked for you."

With a harsh laugh, I shook my head. "Yeah." Damn it. I still wanted to hit something. "I need a drink." Yanking up the first bottle of bourbon I found, I flipped over a glass and splashed in a liberal amount. After downing it in one swallow, I hissed out a breath through my teeth, only to discover Jessie had actually come out of her office. She narrowed her eyes. I narrowed mine right back and watched her with a challenging arch of my brows as I poured myself another.

She pointed her index finger threateningly. "You're paying for those, Gamble."

After she turned and started for the exit to leave for the night, I glared after her. "No, I'm not." Then I drank the next shot.

CHAPTER SEVENTEEN

"Dreams come true. Without that possibility, nature would not incite us to have them. " - John Updike

~ASPEN~

MY COZY, TWO-BEDROOM, bungalow-style home sat in the middle of a street with trees in the front yards and kids' toys in the back. Middle class's version of the American dream. This was the first place I'd lived on my own, the first place I'd lived away from my parents.

I'd gained my freedom here. Within the first few weeks of moving in, I'd gone a little wild. Well, my version of wild, anyway. I'd painted my walls crazy colors like tangerine and robin's egg blue. I bought towels and silverware that totally mismatched *because* they mismatched. I even went out and bought a bottle of wine to celebrate.

If only my parents had seen me then...

But that's exactly why I'd done it, because I knew they'd disapprove. Well, that and because I'd loved those colors and I loved my mismatching menagerie of things, plus I really had wanted to do something commemorative to celebrate.

It was a small rebellion, but big enough in my book. Finally living for myself now, I cherished every little independent thing I got to do.

So, reading in the bathtub? Oh, you know I did that every chance I got. In the four months I'd resided in Ellamore, it had become my Saturday morning ritual. Besides, I really needed something this morning to get my spirits up. I'd felt depressed since Tuesday when I'd left Forbidden—and Noel—for good.

All my lavender-scented aromatherapy votive candles were set up around the rim of the tub and lit, casting a lazy splash of warmth across the walls of my bath, while mist from the heated water steamed up my mirrors and caused my pores to bead with perspiration. My feet rested by the drain while I propped my back against the other end, and the towel turban I'd used to wrap my wet hair also seconded as a nice cushion for the back of my head.

I'd kicked most of the bubbles to my feet because they'd been messing with my paperback—*bad* bubbles—but now that I was nearing a fairly intense and wildly physical part of the story, I was suddenly very aware of my breast floating just below the surface of the water. I slid my thighs past each other and shifted, wet warmth lapping my body as the hero's tongue lapped over the heroine's skin. Growing even more restless, I turned a page, anxious to find out what he was going to do to her next, because I had to say, the man was inventive with some of the things he liked to lick.

It reminded me of Noel Gamble's tongue and how he'd glided it across my collarbone before he'd nipped at a freckle with his teeth. Swallowing when my nipples began to tingle, I shifted my legs again, rubbing them together to alleviate some of tension growing between them. But that only aggravated the situation more. In the novel, the hero's hand wandered down a taut stomach and then between soft thighs, and I had to tighten my own together in response.

"You're mine now, Isabelle," he growled in her ear, his voice rough but his fingers tender.

Damn, why couldn't some guy say cheesy crap like that to me?

But then an echo of Noel's voice stirred my memory. *"Want to hear a secret? I had a crazy-ass crush on you on the first day of class."*

A whimper left my lips and I slapped my book closed. The big m-word filled my head.

To help me recover from the trauma of my first sexual encounter, my therapist had suggested self-pleasure so I could learn that sex could also feel good, not just painful, scary, and debilitating. I'd been fifteen and utterly mortified by the entire conversation. Took me three months to look her in the eye again after that and then another three years to even consider the idea.

The few times I'd tried to get off by myself had been awkward and embarrassing. It hadn't warmed me to the idea of sex in the least. The only thing that had worked had been time and romance novels. But right now, I wouldn't be going at it cold turkey as I had before. My body was already receptive to the idea. Setting my paperback aside, I decided one more attempt couldn't hurt anything. So I closed my lashes, and a face with blue eyes and dark windswept hair filled my head.

I'd only seen him once in class since I'd left the bar on Tuesday. And our gazes had clashed twice during that hour. Each time, we'd both glanced away as if even a single stare was too much temptation. It broke my heart not to even be able to look at him because Noel Gamble was art, like God's apology for all the regular men in the world.

As my fingers found a sweet spot, I moaned and arched my back, upsetting the water along with every nerve ending in my body. While in my mind, I saw him, cheek pressed against my pillow as he lay beside me, whispering about the way I'd affected him the first time he'd seen me.

I came on a gasp, accidentally splashing water out of the side of the tub and snubbing out all the candles as well as drenching my poor book. But it was worth it. Oh my, was it worth it. Okay, nothing was worth damaging a hallowed book, even though at the moment, I was like, "I'll jus' buy another one."

But, seriously. My first orgasm. It felt nice. Amazing. I'd never relaxed enough to allow the two guys who hadn't forced themselves on me to ring my bell, and I'd always stopped prematurely when trying on myself. But with a little Noel Gamble stimulation and the drenched paperback beside me, life was good.

I should celebrate. With ice cream. Maybe some chocolate. And wine. Ooh, yes. Wine sounded good right now.

Energized instead of relaxed as my lavender candles should've made me, I pulled out the drain's plug with my toes and stood up. Water streamed off me, making me feel raw and sensual. Sexy.

Mmm, I wondered if a good orgasm always made a girl feel beautiful.

Humming to myself, I shook my head to loosen the towel wrapped around my hair, and I used it to dry myself. And for once, I didn't think of how much I needed to tighten my abdomen, or do something about the jiggle in my thighs. All self-critical thoughts I usually had when I was naked were blissfully silent.

Damn, why the hell had I waited so long to do this?

I laughed aloud. "Thank you, Noel Gamble."

In answer, the muted sound of my doorbell peeled through the closed partition of my private bath.

"Crap!" I dropped my towel and dove for my clothes, wondering who the heck was at my door. I *had* ordered some new shoes online, but I swear the tracking information had said they wouldn't arrive until Monday. But it was the right time for my mail to be delivered. And it wasn't like I had any casual friends who'd drop by unannounced. Could be a door-to-door salesman or Jehovah's Witness, but I figured it was probably the postal guy.

Not expecting to receive anyone who would be staying long, I bypassed my bra and tugged on my cotton panties before jerking on the cutoff blue jean shorts and a striped peach and cream long-sleeve I had sitting at the top of my laundry hamper. With my feet bare and hair still wet and uncombed, I flung open the bathroom door and hurried through the house.

I didn't even think to check the window before receiving my visitor. I just unlocked all the bolts and pulled the entrance open, expecting a deliveryman's greeting smile. When I saw Noel instead, I yelped out a startled gasp and jumped back, covering my braless chest with both hands.

The afterglow of my orgasm which I'm sure was still staining my cheeks fled to be replaced by horrified embarrassment. But, oh my God, had touching myself while thinking of him somehow drawn him to my house? What the hell kind of voodoo shit had been in those candles? I needed to buy more.

"I..." he started, opening his mouth wide as if ready to deliver some big long explanation of why he was here. But then his gaze shifted down and he left his mouth hanging open. No words came. The appreciation in his gaze as they traveled down my bare legs and back up stirred every organ in my body.

Now that my body knew how liberating and amazing release was, it was ready to experience another. And this time, forget the memory, I'd take the real deal: one Noel Gamble hand-delivered to my front door.

Which was totally, insanely wrong.

"What the hell are you doing here?" I exploded, pulling my arms tighter around myself because my nipples didn't seem to care that the man in front of me could doom my entire career. Tight and pouted into hard points, all they wanted was to dive into Big O, Number Two. The selfish bitches.

"I..." he tried again, not getting much further this time because his gaze froze on my arms, where the skin had started to prickle into goose bumps. "Oh, fuck me sideways. You're not wearing a bra, are you?" He glanced over my face before paling. "And you just got out of the shower, too."

Keeping my girls securely covered with one arm, I released the other so I could push wet hair out of my face. "Bubble bath," I corrected.

He whimpered, literally whimpered. Lifting one hand as if to command me to speak no more, he turned to the side so he wasn't directly facing me and then covered his mouth with a fisted hand. "Jesus, you're evil. Now I'm picturing you naked, covered in bubbles and surrounded by all these candles and shit while you're reading a book."

Damn, he was good.

"Don't forget how incredibly wet I was," I said because, hell, I always said stuff I knew I shouldn't to this man. Why stop now?

He sliced me an incredulous glance. "You're trying to kill me, aren't you?"

Backing away, he sank into the wicker chair on my front porch, exactly where I sat on Sunday mornings and drank my cappuccino while I read. It usually swallowed me whole. But holding Noel's large frame, it seemed small and ridiculously girly. Making him look even more masculine than usual.

"What the fuck am I doing here?" he muttered to himself as he buried his face in his hands.

I swallowed, feeling slutty and evil for what I'd just said and torturing him more than I should have. But he was the one who'd come to me; *he'd* started this.

As much as I wanted to rail at him for stirring up the hornet's nest of our chemistry, I couldn't stop thinking about how he'd been driving over to see me while I'd been getting off to a picture of him in my head. The person I'd been craving had actually been wanting me back. He still wanted me now. It was thrilling and heartbreaking and so beautiful to know; I slid down in the opened doorway to sit and pulled my legs up to my chest, hugging my knees as I watched him struggle through whatever battle was going on inside him.

He lifted his face to look at me, and seemed to crumble. "God, you are so..." He shook his head.

A warm glow flushed my skin. No one had acted so enthralled by me before. It sucked that the first person to show a spark had to be forbidden, but I loved the sensation it had on my ego, regardless.

He watched me for a second before shaking his head and saying, "Spend the day with me."

I wanted to grin and sigh even as my shoulders fell. "Noel, we discussed this on Tuesday."

"No, actually, we didn't discuss anything. You just left and—" When I opened my mouth to argue, he held up his hand, "I totally understand why. But something's happened since then."

"Okay." I nodded, hoping it was a miracle that had happened and Ellamore had changed their school policy to allow student-teacher relationships. "What happened?"

He didn't answer immediately. Frowning after a

long gap of silence, I opened my mouth to ask if he was okay, when he said, "I just got out of weight training...like, I came here straight from there."

"O...kay," I said slowly. He didn't look as if he'd come straight from training. The other day, he'd been wearing his sweatpants and had wet hair. Today, he was rocking dark brown pants and a black and gray-striped shirt with long sleeves, which molded to the contours of his chest and made him look too yummy to be sitting on my front porch.

He blew out a loud breath.

"Coach corralled all of us together and had a little talk." By the ominous tone of his voice, I knew I wasn't going to like what his coach had had to say. "After the big scandal on the volleyball team and how much media attention it caught, he decided to make a new rule that if any guy on the team was caught with any staff or faculty member on campus in any inappropriate way, we'd immediately be kicked out of the football program. And since I have a football scholarship..."

"You'd lose your funding and have to leave Ellamore entirely," I finished for him.

"Right," he said with the faintest tremor in his voice.

I closed my eyes. "Well, I assure you that I'm not going to go to your coach and tell him—"

"I know that," he muttered, clearly irritated. "That's not why I'm here."

Flickering my lashes open, I frowned at him, confused. "Then why did you come here?"

"Because...because I wanted to see you," he rushed the words as if saying them fast would give him the courage to mean them.

I blurted out a startled, nervous, confused laugh. "I'm sorry but...you just told me the risk for us has just *doubled*. This would affect both of our lives now, Noel, not to mention what it'd do to your brothers and sister, who are *counting* on you."

"I know." He groaned and gnashed his teeth. "You just had to mention them, didn't you?"

"Well, someone has to. And since I'm the one in the position of authority, I should be the one to take responsibility and say no. We've already gone too far. It stops here."

"No. Just listen to me. Please." The desperation in his voice tore me up. I hated knowing I was causing him misery. "I let you go on Tuesday because you were the only one who'd pay the consequences if anything happened. I didn't like that. But now...now, we'd both be putting in the same risk. I have just as much to lose as you do. So...we have equal footing."

With a high-strung laugh, I shook my head. "You're not making any sense. How could you even suggest...I mean, after you just completely spelled out the consequences for both of us?"

"Because I *do* know the consequences. I know exactly what would happen if we started something and were caught. But now...now I want to know the consequences if we *didn't* do anything."

"Noel," I whispered. He must've heard the rejection in my voice because he was quick to cut me off.

"I've been going crazy, Aspen. My sister calls daily with problem after problem. My mom hasn't been home in weeks, and it's making me feel like the guiltiest piece of shit because I'm not there for them. Meanwhile, I've been working my ass off every night to make enough money to help them, while trying to keep my grades up and...and everyone around here has completely different expectations of me, thinking I'm some carefree football hero who has nothing to worry about except the next game or keeping myself in shape, or which girl I'm going to take home tonight. You're the *only* person who understands everything, both sides. And I...I feel things for you, like there's this connection with you. I...fuck, I don't know how to say this. You know how much I suck at putting words together."

I hugged my knees tighter to my chest because it felt like my heart wanted to explode out of my ribs. Telling myself to keep quiet, I said, "You're doing a fair job so far."

He glanced at me, and his eyes swirled with emotion as his lips tipped with pleasure. "It's not just physical," he said. "I mean, sure, the chemistry is like, *pow*. But I just...I like being around you. I like that you know...me. And I like learning about you. I just...I want to know what we'd be like, what we'd be missing if we did nothing. I want to know if maybe there's... more. What if...fuck, I don't know. What if it's *worth* risking everything to be together?"

It didn't seem possible that anyone wanted to even consider such a risk for me. Rita, whom I loved like a mother, certainly hadn't felt that strongly for me. She'd never risked her career or her family for my benefit. So hearing Noel say what he'd just said completely melted my defenses. Torn, I bit my lip and glanced at him. And, damn, his eyes were pleading.

"I've had a really shitty couple weeks," he said. "I'm tired and stressed, and this is the first day I've had off in a long time. But all I want to do is spend it with you." Lifting both hands in a sign of surrender, he shook his head. "No funny business, I swear. I won't even mention sex. I just I want to be around you. We'll keep it completely platonic."

I told myself I had to be the stupidest girl on the planet just before I asked, "What did you have in mind?"

His body sagged as if the relief had been overbearing. But then he grinned. "There's this park on the edge of a river one of my teammates took me to during my freshman year. It's about an hour away from here. No one would recognize us, and we'd be out in the open where I wouldn't be tempted into trying anything...untoward." He lifted his eyebrows and sent me an ornery grin. "So, what do you say? Give me just one day?"

CHAPTER EIGHTEEN

"There's nothing more intimate in life than simply being understood. And understanding someone else." - Brad Meltzer, *The Inner Circle*

~NOEL~

"THIS PLACE IS AMAZING."

The awe in Aspen's voice made me grin across the cab of Ten's truck as I parked at the edge of the grounds in the visitors' parking area. "I had a feeling you'd like it."

A long sloped lawn extended before us before dropping down steeply into the banks of the river. The grass was short and green; patches were beginning to grow, promising new vegetation.

A couple families were already enjoying the day, spreading out picnic blankets or walking their pets, or letting their children chase each other across the wide-open expanse. And beyond that sprawled a strip of small kiosks and vendors, peddling their wares on either side of a cobbled walkway.

"How'd you ever learn about all this?" Aspen asked, opening her door as I opened mine.

"My roommate, Ten, brought me here once. He lives in this area and wanted one of their corn dogs they sell. I think I made fun of him the whole way he dragged me here until we actually made it." I grinned at her. "But the damn corn dog wasn't half bad, so I had to shut up."

She laughed. "So you brought me out here because you were craving a badly processed meat sausage on a stick deep-fat fried in cornmeal batter?"

"Hell no." Snagging the ball I'd thrown into the backseat before heading to her house this morning, I held it up and twirled it on my finger before catching it. "You, my dear professor, are going to learn how to play football."

Aspen arched an eyebrow, seemingly interested instead of horrified. "Really? What makes you think I don't already know how to play?"

Okay, that one caught me off guard. I arched a suspicious eyebrow. "Do you?"

Her lips curved, and they looked so hot with that knowing little twitch tightening them. I had to remind myself again I wasn't going to touch her today. Nothing sexual. Just friendly bonding. Getting to know each other.

Realizing what that smile meant though, I groaned. "Hell, you *do* know."

Her entire face lit up. "I kicked ass in fantasy football last year," she confessed, sounding rather proud of herself.

I threw back my head and laughed. "Holy shit. I had no idea you actually *liked* the game. I mean, the way you acted in class, I thought you hated everything to do with football, but..." Then it dawned on me. Her behavior hadn't had anything to do with her opinion of the sport itself, but with her history with a certain *player* of the sport. I blew out a breath. "Right. Well, wow. If I'd known you were a fan, I would've bugged you into coming to our scrimmage we had a couple weeks back."

"Don't worry, I went."

"So you saw...?" My eyebrows lifted as I pointed at my own chest. She nodded and I had to know. "Well, what'd you think?"

Eyes lighting with flirtation, she strolled around Ten's truck to meet me on the other side. "I thought you could be the next Rodgers."

"Shit," I said, shaking my head. "No way."

She slipped the ball out of my hand, and I watched her, frankly turned on by her interest in it.

"Hmm." She practiced holding it different ways before glancing at me. "You know, I just now realized I've never actually *touched* a football before."

I couldn't believe it, and yet I could. Shaking my head, I took it back from her. "Well, this calls for a lesson, then." Reaching for her hand, I started us off toward the grass. "I'm going to teach you everything you need to know about how to throw a ball."

For the first five minutes, I just talked and demonstrated how she needed to position her shoulders and waist, where to keep her elbow, and how to hold it in her hand. When it was time to show her an actual throw, I spotted a boy about twenty yards away.

"Hey, kid," I called. "Catch this." When he immediately nodded and scrambled into position, I wound back my arm and sent him a nice, slow, lob. He caught it without any effort and threw it back. Aspen cheered and clapped for him, telling him what a nice job he'd done.

When I handed the pigskin over to her, she began to look nervous.

"I feel ridiculous," she admitted when I stood behind her and basically got her into position.

I wiggled my eyebrows. "Trust me. You look hot." I was very glad I'd only let her put on a pair of shoes and a bra along with what she was already wearing before I'd dragged her out of the house this morning because her outfit was casual and comfortable and perfect for both our practice and *my* view. The ensemble broadcasted the best features of who she really was.

With a laugh, she jabbed her elbow back into my gut. "I'm probably going to throw like a girl."

"You are a girl, so who cares?" Satisfied with how she was set up, I took a step back and let her throw to the kid. He had to run and jump for it, but he caught it with a happy shout. "Not bad," I said, nodding my approval.

She turned to send me a skeptical glance, but I just grinned at her. She totally threw like a girl. "Want to play now?" I asked.

Our catcher and a couple of his friends were up for a game of touch ball. And they didn't seem to mind letting the "girl" in on the fun. Actually, I think they all grew crushes on her within the first five minutes. She was just so fun about the whole thing. She laughed at her own mistakes, and playfully bantered with her opponents whenever we lined up before a snap, telling them she was going to take them down. And fuck, she was adorable to watch whenever she got the ball. She'd laugh as she dodged away from someone. I'd never in my life seen someone laugh while playing football before.

It was a little impossible to believe she was the same strict, no-nonsense, straitlaced woman who taught my literature class. But when Aspen Kavanagh loosened up, she loosened up.

By late afternoon, the kids had to leave and I was starving. So was she. Covering her stomach when it let out a hearty growl, she said, "Where's this corn dog stand you were raving about again?"

Our exertions had left a rosy glow on her cheeks. And her eyes...damn, her green eyes were alive and glittering. I think I could've stared at her all day, just like that.

"What?" she asked, sending me an odd glance as she took down the ponytail she'd put her hair up in earlier when we'd started the game. As she finger combed the mass and let it spill down her back, I shook my head. Who was this woman, and how had I gotten lucky enough to get her for an entire day?

No one would believe me it I tried to tell them Dr. Kavanagh ate corn dogs, and finger combed her hair, and flirted with a bunch of preteen boys before sticking her tongue out at them after making a touchdown. But I was glad they'd never suspected. I was glad I had her all to myself.

"Nothing," I murmured, reaching out to take her hand. "Let's find that stand."

After buying six corn dogs between the two of us, we found an empty picnic bench and sat across from each other as we ate. I liked seeing her appetite. She didn't seem shy about eating in front of me, or ordering two sticks. And the way her lips puckered when she took a dog between her teeth was, well, I just couldn't watch much of that. My head was already in a place it didn't need to go. But even after I glanced away, I was still keyed up and aching to touch her.

"You know," she said, thoughtfully, as she polished off her first corn dog and started on the next. "I don't think I know what your major is."

I glanced over. "Business management. Why?"

Her eyebrows lifted. With her mouth full, she muffled out the word, "Really?"

I shrugged and tossed one of my empty sticks toward a nearby trashcan, sinking it. "Well, you know, I'm not good at English. And math and science aren't my thing either. History's never interested me, but I'm decent in social situations, and I really like leading the team on the field. They listen to me, and I don't know, kind of look up to me. That was one thing I know I can do, so I stuck to that in case, you know, the NFL doesn't want me."

"But you really do like football, don't you." She said it more as a statement than a question, as if she was just then realizing the answer.

"Of course. Why would I play if I hated it?"

"I don't know." One side of her shoulders lifted. "You just...after that day in my office when you said it was about desperation, I didn't think it was what you loved more than anything in the world."

"It's..." Fuck, how did I explain this? "I don't know. Getting into football in high school is what finally earned me the respect of some of my classmates. My natural talent gave me this rush that was...addictive. I love the game and crave that split second you have to think and react, strategize what the best play for that moment is before five hundred pounds of the defensive line tackles you. I like learning more of the tricks of the trade since I came to Ellamore, but...there's a lot more pressure now. A lot more on the line. It's not just fun anymore. Now, it's everything, which takes out a little of the pleasure. But, yeah, to answer your question, I still like it. I love it."

Aspen nodded, letting me know she understood. "If you could do or be anything in the world, without any consequences or worries, what would you do?"

The first thing that popped into my mind was her. I'd be with her. But I knew she meant occupation-wise. I shrugged. "Don't know. I can't really think of anything I like more than football."

"Would you teach it to others if you couldn't play anymore? You did really well with those boys today. I think you'd make a great coach."

"Huh." I hadn't thought about that before. "That's actually not a bad idea."

Her back straightened as she preened. "I know. But seriously, you're smart enough to do anything you want. I just wanted to make sure football was what you loved most."

I blinked and shook my head. "Did you just call me...smart?" *Someone color me shocked.*

She furrowed her brow. "Of course you're smart. I always knew that. It takes a mad set of brains to always say the exact thing in class you know will tick me off the most."

Laughing, I shook my head and finished off my fourth corn dog, but inside I was still flattered she'd called me smart. When I spotted another food stand not far away, I dusted the crumbs off my fingers and turned my attention back to her. "Okay. Enough about me. I want to hear more about you."

Her smile was a little uncertain. "Me? What do you want to know about me?"

Leaning a little across the table, I sent her a look as if to tell her to brace herself because this was a serious question. With my voice lowered, I asked, "What's your favorite flavor of ice cream?"

She blinked and then threw her head back and laughed. "I don't know. Vanilla?"

Wrinkling my nose, I exploded, "Vanilla? Who the hell prefers vanilla over all the other flavors out there?"

"Hey!" she scolded, half-laughing and half-insulted. "Don't bash my tastes. What's *your* favorite?"

"Easy. Rocky Road."

"Interesting." Making a sound in the back of her throat, she tapped her chin with her finger and studied me. "Is that some kind of symbolism for the way your life has gone?"

I snorted and rolled my eyes. "Okay, Miss Literature Professor. Enough of that shit. Not everything is an analogy on life. Sometimes, we just like the way something tastes." Licking my lips, I swayed toward her as my attention dropped to her mouth. "Kind of how I like the way *you* taste."

"Don't," she warned instantly, all smiles gone as she pulled back and arched me her nervous glance.

Fuck, I'd forgotten I was keeping this strictly platonic.

"I forgot." Lifting my hands, I instantly backed off. "My bad, seriously. I'm sorry. But now you have me craving ice cream. If I can't have the other thing I crave right now, you owe me a big, double-scooped cone full of Rocky Road."

Standing up, I reached across the table for her hand and pulled her up behind me. I'd never been a hand-holder before today, but I liked twining my fingers through hers and pressing our palms together. There was something wholesome and innocent and yet utterly erotic about swinging our arms in sync as we walked side by side.

***

"Mmm, now *this* is why I dragged you here," I said after we both had cones full of ice cream. "I couldn't very well buy ice cream by myself."

Aspen tempted me out of my mind with the flash of her tongue as she lapped up her vanilla coated in chocolate and crushed M&Ms. "Why's that?"

I snorted. "How lame is it for a guy to visit an ice cream stand by himself? Hell, it's even wrong for a guy to take another guy. It's only right when some chick is unwillingly dragging him along."

Wrinkling her nose, she bumped her shoulder against mine. "So, I'm your ice cream beard, then?"

"Exactly." See, she totally understood me. I didn't even care that the entire idea made her laugh at my silliness. I loved her laugh.

We wound our way through the strip together,

holding hands and eating our ice cream cones, checking out all the strange shit people had for sale. Homemade jewelry and odd little knickknacks mostly made us laugh. But then Aspen found a used books rack.

I watched her scan through the frayed paperbacks, charmed by the fascination on her face. She was in her element and looked good there. When she found a story I knew had caught her interest, I paid the vendor for the paperback before she'd realized what I'd done.

"You didn't have to do that." Her words said one thing, but her eyes said another as she gratefully hugged the book to her chest.

I rolled my eyes. "You're welcome," I said, bumping my shoulder into hers. "Now let's find a grassy spot and stretch out for a minute so you can read."

Her eyes grew big. "You...did you just offer to let me...read?"

I shrugged. "Sure. Why not? It's our lazy day to relax and do whatever we want. And I've seen your bedroom, remember? I know how much you like to read."

"But...you're just..." She shook her head, at a loss for words. "That's probably the sweetest thing anyone's ever offered me."

I couldn't believe she was so touched by the suggestion. I didn't see it as a big deal. Trying to play it down, I said, "Actually, I have a selfish motive. I was thinking a nap in the sunshine sounded like heaven right about now. So...if you were reading—"

"Wait, wait, wait. You brought me on a date to take a nap?"

When she arched her eyebrows, I laughed and raised my hands. "Hey, whoa. Who's calling this a date? I thought I made it very clear I wasn't going to try any of that hanky-panky that happens on dates. I just wanted to hang out with someone I enjoyed being with and do things we both wanted to do together. And since I can see in your eyes you're dying to open that book, and I'd kill for an hour of rest, the two would go good together."

And apparently that was all the explanation she needed.

"Okay, then," she agreed before I could try to cajole her any more.

So that's what happened. We stretched out together, side by side with our faces basking in the sunshine and our backs propped up by a huge ornamental rock, and I closed my eyes while she opened her book.

I don't know how much time passed, but dusk was approaching when I came to. I felt more rested than I'd felt in a long time. It might've had something to do with the fact that my face was pillowed on her thigh or that she was running her fingers through my hair, but damn, it felt good. I lay there a second, just soaking it in, wondering how the hell my face had gotten down there and how I could get it there again, sans clothes.

I heard a page flip above me and decided to sit up, yawning. Aspen's hand fell from my hair, which was a shame, but she smiled at me in a lovely manner as she lowered the book and asked, "Better?"

"Much." I stretched, realizing she'd made it halfway through her story. Damn. "What time is it?"

I'd taken my phone out of my pocket before I'd gone to sleep to be more comfortable. When I spotted it nearby in the grass, I went to reach for it, but Aspen answered, "It's almost seven."

"Fuck." Ten was probably having a shit fit.

As if he'd just heard my thoughts, my cell phone went off.

"And oh, yeah," Aspen added. "Someone named Zero keeps calling and asking where his truck is."

I groaned and answered my roommate, telling him to hold his damn horses. Aspen read the reply over my shoulder. "I take it *Zero* is a friend?"

"Yep." I pocketed the phone. "My roommate. He goes by Ten, so I of course label him as Zero. He takes Modern Lit with me, actually. Oren Tenning."

Her eyebrows lifted. "Oh." The way she said it told me she knew exactly who Ten was. "He writes very...interesting papers."

Laughing, I leaned into her to smell her hair. It smelled exactly as I imagined it would, like lavender and warm sunshine. "I'll bet. Chock full of f-bombs and crude comments, huh?"

She tensed.

Alarmed by her reaction, I pulled back. "What's wrong?" Then it struck me. "Shit. I'm sorry. I know better than to ask you about anyone's papers or grades. I told myself not to even mention school today."

"No, it's okay. That's not why I was freaking out. I mean, not that I was..." She cleared her throat and glanced away, the tops of her cheeks turning pink.

I took her hand, worried about what was ruining our perfect day. She didn't think I'd told Ten about what I was doing with her in his truck, did she? I opened my mouth to assure her my roommate was clueless when she finally lifted her gaze.

"Did you just...did you just lean in and *smell* me?"

Shit. I had, hadn't I? Another thing I'd promised myself I wouldn't do today. But I hadn't even thought about it. After waking up relaxed and rested with my head on her thigh and her fingers in my hair, it had felt like the most natural thing in the world.

"Maybe," I hedged, only to turn the tables on her. "Did I just wake up on your lap to you scratching my head?"

Blushing madly, she bit her lip. "Maybe."

I swayed toward her. I wanted to steal a kiss. So bad. But my phone buzzed again, letting me know I had another text. With a groan, I lifted it, and we both read Ten's message, wanting to know when I'd bring his truck back.

Aspen puckered her brow. "Why do you have his truck, anyway? What's wrong with yours?"

"I don't have a truck," I answered her as I wrote Ten back, telling him I'd be home by midnight.

Aspen's eyes widened. "Midnight? What do you plan on doing with me until then?"

I shuddered, thinking up all the things I'd love to do with her until then, and had to remind myself I'd promised to behave. "Dangerous question," I warned.

"And why don't you have a truck?" Then she rolled her eyes. "Oh, I get it. You're a motorcycle guy, aren't you? I should've guessed."

Shaking my head, I just grinned. "I wish."

Her teasing grin fell. "You mean, you don't—?" With a gulp, she flushed guiltily. "Oh, my God. I'm sorry. I just assumed..."

"Hey, you didn't say anything wrong. I just don't have a set of wheels, that's all. It would've felt, I don't know...selfish, I guess, if I'd bought a car while my family was..." Well we didn't need to go there. "I usually send all the extra money I have home to my sister to take care of stuff there, anyway, so it's not like I can really afford one."

"Well, that's just...you know, you surprise me all the time, Noel Gamble. As soon as I discover something good and altruistic about you, you go and top it with something even better."

Instead of flattering me, her words only fed my guilt. Because bringing her here today had been incredibly selfish and wrong, threatening both her future and that of Caroline, Colton and Brandt. What was worse, it didn't bother me enough to take her home *quite* yet.

We were already here; what was another couple hours? Besides, I wanted her to experience the one thing I'd brought her here to do.

"Come on." I took her hand and helped both of us to our feet. "I think it's about time for the main event."

"Main event?" Her smile was curious with a hint of eager excitement. "What's the main event?"

I pointed to the lights behind us on the other side of the vendor's market strip. In the distance, the brightened outline of a Ferris wheel rotated slowly.

Grinning, I lowered my mouth to her ear. "You're about to experience your first carnival, Dr. Kavanagh."

Her beautiful lips parted with awe. The colorful lights from the amusement park reflected in her dazzled eyes. Spinning to me, she sputtered. "But how did you know I've never...?"

Damn, she must not remember anything from the drunken conversation we'd had together, which was too damn bad, because I couldn't forget a single detail of it.

Lifting her fingers laced with mine to my mouth, I kissed her knuckles lightly and winked. "It's an old ESP trick I learned from my literature professor."

CHAPTER NINETEEN

"Love is like the wind, you can't see it but you can feel it." - Nicholas Sparks, *A Walk to Remember*

~NOEL~

SHE LOVED IT. ASPEN didn't say anything aloud, but all I had to do was watch the expressions flit across her face to know the whole experience thrilled her.

"Oh, my God. Look. They do actually sell cotton candy at carnivals. I thought that might just be one of those movie clichés."

I felt like a dog walker who was being drug around by my overeager pet when she took off, hurrying toward the food stand, her hand tugging me along behind her. I laughed and hurried to keep pace. She was so freaking adorable, letting her inner child free. As she ordered a ball of big pink sugary fluff, I got a Coke because I knew she'd need a drink soon.

"Oh, funky." She smacked her lips together after

the first taste and scrunched up her nose. "I didn't realize it would melt like that as soon as it hit my tongue. But, wow, it really is pure sugar, whipped into a fluffy ball, isn't it?"

"Here." I handed over the drink and she gave me a grateful thank you before snatching it away and sucking down half the contents.

She nursed the cotton candy a lot slower after that, and together, we browsed the carnival stands, watching a short sock puppet show before another vendor called out to us, coaxing us to try his ball throw.

Aspen nudged me in the ribs. "Come on, Mr. Quarterback," she teased. "Why don't you show us what you got?"

"Hey, you're the champion ball thrower now; you've had an entire day of practice. Why don't you try it?"

"Ooh." The vendor eyed us with relish. "I smell a challenge. You two want to go head to head?"

So, we did the ball throw. I kicked her ass, of course, and she called me a sore winner. I just shrugged and told her I'd go easy on her here whenever she decided to go easy on grading my essays.

She murmured, *"Touché,"* and then rolled her eyes, laughing.

When the vendor congratulated me and thrust a blue stuffed bunny with floppy pink ears into my chest, I stared at him as if he'd lost his mind.

Aspen held her belly and laughed harder. "Aww. You two look so cute together. And look, his fur's almost the same color as your eyes. I think it's a match made in heaven."

"Okay, smartass. You better take this thing because I'm sure as hell not carrying it around."

When I pushed it at her, she looked at it as if it had rabies. "But...I've never had a stuffed animal before."

Her arms fumbled to keep it from falling to the ground when I let go of it.

"Never too old to start," I said, feeling smug that I'd managed to give her the bunny without being sappy about it.

She still looked completely flustered. "But what do I do with it?"

"Hell if I know. Toss it on your bed like all those throw pillows you have."

"Well..." she still acted undecided, but I could see the yearning in her eyes. The girl wanted her stuffed animal. Finally, she relented with a quiet, heartfelt, "Thank you." She blinked and I swore to God, if she dropped a single tear, I was going to drag her to the first quiet, shadowy nook and kiss her senseless.

But, really, what kind of heartless parents didn't give their kid a stuffed animal? Even my freak show of a mother had tossed a dirty, dog-mauled teddy bear with an ear torn off at me one year for Christmas.

Needing to steer us away from anything emotional, I tugged on her hand. "That's it. Time to take you on the rides and see how sturdy your stomach is."

"Oh, I don't... No, that's okay." Eyes widening, expression instantly leery, she shook her head and resisted my lead.

"What? You're not scared, are you? Don't worry. We'll start out easy. How about the Ferris wheel?"

"*The Ferris wheel?*" Her eyes bulged even wider. "But that's the biggest, tallest thing in the entire park."

"Oh, come on. You have to try it out at least once."

It was surprisingly easy to talk her into it; I think she secretly wanted to go but was nervous.

After buying tickets, we got into line behind a bunch of kids. We were by far the oldest two people waiting to board.

Leaning toward me, Aspen murmured, "This is silly. Let's just go."

"Nope. You're not chickening out on me." I tightened my grip on her hand, keeping her close as I stared up at the Ferris wheel as it slowed to let a pair of giggling girls off.

Her back immediately stiffened, and I saw some of her professor-self sprout on her features. It was kind of hot. "I am not chickening out. I'm—"

"Chickening out." I grinned smugly, daring her to contradict me.

"Fine," she snapped, turning to face the ride. "Let's go on the Ferris wheel ride, then."

"Good," I spit back. "Because it's our turn to load."

"What?" Her fingers squeezed around mine as she whimpered. "Oh, God. Noel, wait."

Pulling her along, I helped her into the seat the guy was holding open for us before I hopped up beside her. She looked so nervous, her fingers wrapped around the safety bar until the bones in her knuckles tried to poke through her skin.

Needing to distract her, I bumped my elbow into hers. "You know, the first kiss I ever had happened on the top of a Ferris wheel."

Aspen turned wide eyes to me. "What was it like?"

I bunched up the features on my face as if to say *meh*. "Wet and sloppy. We were both pretty clumsy, but then, we were only eight." I winced. "And her parents saw the whole thing. They dragged her off as soon as we landed, chastising her for going anywhere near the nasty Gamble boy." With a sigh, I shrugged. "She never talked to me at school again."

When I noticed Aspen was giving me an odd stare, I asked, "What?"

The corners of her lips fluttered up with a smile. "I actually meant, what was the ride like."

"Oh. Well..." Just as our cart jerked into motion and we were lifted into the air, I reached out to cover her hand. "Time to find out."

She sucked in a breath and leaned toward me. As the wheel paused to let more people on, Aspen gulped audibly and leaned forward to gaze out at everything we could see from this height. "Wow."

"I know." I couldn't take my eyes off her. "Pretty amazing, isn't it?"

"I think...I think...it's the most beautiful sunset I've ever seen." Tears glistened in her eyes and there was no way I could do nothing.

Leaning in, I pressed a brief, polite kiss to her cheek. As I pulled back, Aspen touched her damp skin with two fingers and glanced at me.

Feeling more self-conscious after this small peck than all the open-mouthed, heated kisses we'd shared before, I cleared my throat and tried to shrug it off. "What? It's a tradition for me. And your parents aren't here to take you away afterward, so...why not?"

Her lips lifted into a smile, and I blew out a relieved breath, glad she wasn't pissed.

We spent the rest of the ride in quiet contentment, taking in the reflection of the sunset off the water of the river below.

"Okay, that was fun," she admitted once our feet were back on solid ground.

"Aren't you glad I made you try it?"

Lifting her chin, she tightened her lips as if to hold in a grin, but I saw it anyway. "Yes. Yes, I am."

"So what now? Bumper cars? The scrambler?"

"I have a better idea." Grasping on my hand, she started off. I followed, charmed by this carefree, eager side of her.

When we passed a tent, she dodged right, taking me into the quiet, shadowed spot next to it, squeezing us between canvas and the hut holding the puppet show.

"Wha...?"

She stopped abruptly and faced me. That's when I realized... Oh, shit.

My skin rippled with buzzing energy. I refused to react. I'd promised her I wouldn't try anything untoward. But I'd never said she couldn't. And obviously, she wanted to.

She lifted her hand, and I held my breath. But then her fingertips barely grazed my cheek, and air hissed from my lungs, unable to stay in. It sawed through my teeth until my nostrils flared.

She didn't say a word; I didn't either. Turning her hand over, she brushed her knuckles up my jaw and over my short sideburns. When they combed through my hair, I closed my eyes and bowed my head so she could reach me easier.

"Aspen." Her name cracked on my lips. My body was so wired I just knew I'd see electric sparks igniting over my flesh if I opened my lashes.

"Aren't you going to touch me back?" Her voice was husky; she was just as turned on as I was.

"You asking me to? Because I promised I wouldn't."

Her breath heated my lips. Fuck, she was right there. "Noel," she whispered. I opened my eyes just as she added, "Touch me."

Her mouth met mine, and I felt it zap through the entire length of my dick.

As I hardened in my jeans, her lips parted and a warm, moist tongue darted cautiously forward.

Gasping, I clutched her face and tipped her jaw until she was following my lead, clutching my arms and straining onto her toes to press against me. She tasted of cotton candy and cola. Thrusting my hips against her softness, I tried to alleviate some of the insistent throbbing. But she was so warm and pliable right now, nothing except release was going to bring me down from my high.

"God, you know how to kiss." She was driving my mouth crazy with her shy, curious exploration.

She pulled away to pant against my throat. "I do?" Since she didn't sound as if she believed me, I thought I'd just show her.

"What do you think?" I returned my mouth to hers and took things a little deeper. She seemed eager to go where I took her, her hands smoothed up over my chest, along my arms, into my hair...

"Jesus." I broke off to catch my breath. My shallow gasps stirred her hair. She shivered and cuddled into me, so I wrapped my arms around her. We held each other as the music from the Ferris wheel poured over us and a cool breeze from the setting sun brushed past. The scent of popcorn and hot dogs made it almost surreal, but we were really here, really doing this, a college football player and his literature professor fraternizing.

I rested my mouth against her temple and soaked her in.

"I'm in this if you are, Aspen. I know we have a lot to lose. But I fully believe we have more to gain if we start something. So, it's up to you completely. You have to make the final decision."

CHAPTER TWENTY

"Angry people are not always wise." - Jane Austen, *Pride and Prejudice*

But...

"Even a fool learns something once it hits him." - Homer, *Iliad*

~ASPEN~

I HADN'T SEEN, TALKED TO, or heard from Noel in three days, not since he'd driven me home from the carnival, walked me to my door, and kissed me senseless on my front porch. I guess he'd been serious when he'd told me the next step was completely and totally up to me, which freaked the crap out of me.

The smartest thing to do was stay away. I knew that and my head was on board. But my body just didn't understand, and I don't think my heart had caught the memo either. I was restless all day Sunday and Monday. I kept checking my phone to see if I'd missed a call. I kept glancing out my living room window to see if anyone was walking up my front walk. At work, I perked to attention in my office every time I heard footsteps in the hall. But no Noel, or any student or professor for that matter, stopped at my door.

Today, though...today I'd see him. In class. I was so on edge relaxing was impossible.

All my classes took place in Morella Hall except one, a beginning literature course I taught remotely through telenet to a local community college. I had to cross the street and walk half a block to the campus library, which had the closest video broadcasting system to the English department on campus.

As soon as I was finished with that, I had ten minutes to return to Morella to lecture for Noel's Modern American Lit class.

Keyed up to see him, I hurried from the library, nearly galloping in my heels. I knew I couldn't tell him I wanted to start a relationship, but that didn't mean I wasn't having some serious withdrawals. I needed a Noel fix...soon.

So when I spotted him as I was nearing Morella where he leaned a shoulder against the building with his back to me and his cell phone pressed to his ear, everything inside me soared.

I started his way so he would see me pass...until I heard what he was saying.

"Shh, sweetheart. Just calm down and tell me what's wrong?"

The concern in his voice and the feminine pet name he used made me pause. A thick layer of jealousy tasted like acid on my tongue. Who was *Sweetheart*, and why did he sound so invested in her?

That's when he hissed, *"Pregnant?* You're *pregnant?* How can you be... Jesus Christ. But you said—"

Pregnant.

My ears rang with a hollow pain I couldn't even brace myself against. But he'd gotten some girl *pregnant*? I couldn't...this was just...

No.

"Just save it, okay," he growled savagely into the phone. "You can apologize until the cows come home, but that's not going to change the fact there's going to be a...Jesus, how are we going to afford a kid? Holy fuck."

He jerked his hand over the back of his head, his fingers shaking. "Stop. Stop crying right now. You got yourself into this one. And now we're both going to pay. Fuck. I can't...I just can't..." He let out a world-weary sigh and messaged his temples as he bowed his head. "I can't talk about this right now. I have to get to class. No...no... Damn it, *no*! I'll call you later."

He hung up and shoved his phone into his pocket. Glancing to his right as if to make sure no one had overheard him, he didn't bother looking left, or he'd have seen me not moving, staring right at him with my heart shattering to pieces in my eyes.

The pain of knowing he'd impregnated someone else splintered until a fresh anger rose. He'd been nothing but rude to that poor girl. She'd been crying and apologizing, and probably scared out of her mind, and he'd yelled at her, scolded her, made her feel like shit.

What a total douchebag.

My disappointment rose up my throat. I couldn't believe I'd been falling for this man, thinking he was noble and good.

Curling my hands into fists, I wanted to hit him, and make him hurt the same way I hurt. Hell, the same way his *sweetheart* hurt.

But for now, I had to get to class too.

After marching the rest of the way to my room, I set my briefcase on my desk hard enough to make a student in the front row who was lying her head on her desk to jump and sit up. Crap, I needed to cool myself down before I did something stupid.

Easier said than done because Noel walked into the room a second later, igniting every pissed off nerve in my system. I glanced at him, and he met my gaze. He looked very solemn and grave, and I wondered if he was going to confess everything to me. But then his lips twitched as if he was trying to force them to smile for my benefit but couldn't quite get the job done. All the while, his eyes remained hooded and troubled.

As he passed, he flipped a folded slip of paper my way. It landed perfectly in my closed briefcase. He didn't even slow his pace as he kept going, finding a spot in the back of the room.

Thinking he was going to ask me to meet him somewhere so he could tell me what had just happened, I reached for the note with unsteady hands and unfolded it. But it was just another quote for my board. And a cheerful, happy quote at that.

"A smile is a curve that sets everything straight."
- Phyllis Diller

I frowned, the straight line of my lips showing that everything was indeed not straight.

How dare he? After what he'd just done to that other girl, after what he'd just found out...how fucking dare he try *anything* with me? Awful, no good, rotten, cheating bastard.

Opening my case, I slid out my pile of notes. Blood seethed through my veins as I shuffled through them without a clue as to what I was actually looking at. Then, calmly, I stood in front of the room, my hands curling around the notes as I watched seat after seat fill until it looked as if everyone was present.

Noel sat low in his chair, his eyes closed, and his

face in his hands as he rested his elbows on the desk. It was more than obvious news of his fatherhood was bothering him. Well, I decided that clearly wasn't enough for him to worry about.

Cramming my notes back into my case, I clicked it shut and rested my hands on top.

"In Nathaniel Hawthorne's work, *The Scarlet Letter*," I started, with my chin high, "the protagonist, Hester Prynne, has to wear a red letter A on her clothes to show everyone she committed adultery and had a child out of wedlock. She became an outcast for the rest of her life. While her *lover*, who committed the very same act, got off scot-free because she refused to name him. But even though he lived out a life of good reputation, he ended up driving himself insane and dying from the guilt. *Mr. Gamble*." I lifted my voice and shot him a hard stare. "Which do you think is worse?"

His jerked his head up from where he obviously hadn't been paying attention to anything I'd just said. Eyes ravaged with torment, he croaked, "What?" Then he glanced around and turned back to me. "I'm sorry, what?"

"*The Scarlet Letter*," I reminded him. "Nathaniel Hawthorne. The woman sleeps with her minister and gets pregnant. She's publicly scorned for *three* hours, then thrown in jail, and then forced to wear the letter A to show her shame to everyone for the rest of her life. Or her lover. The local minister she refused to indict. He comes away with a clean reputation but can't handle all the guilt. So...which character do you think had it worse? Would you rather everyone know what you did and hate you for it, but end up with a fairly clean conscious? Or would you prefer to hide it and let it fester, where you always worried about it coming to light, and were always ashamed to know someone else paid for the very crime *you* committed?"

His face lost all color as his mouth fell open. But

he had nothing to say. He stared at me hard for a good twenty seconds, and torment filled his eyes, before he blinked rapidly and shook his head. "I...I thought we were starting on Tennessee Williams today."

Around us, the class tittered, and my face filled with red, hot shame.

Dear God. What the hell was I doing? This had to be the most unprofessional, immature thing I'd ever attempted. If I was upset with Noel for something, trying to take it out on him in the classroom was the worst thing I could possibly do. Feeling sick to my stomach with my own shame, I glanced away and brought the back of my hand to my mouth as I tried to pull my dignity back in around me.

It didn't work. Drawing in a deep breath, I lifted my face, trying not to bawl. "Very good, Mr. Gamble," I said, my voice raspy with emotion. I nodded once. "I guess you were paying attention after all."

Though everyone else let out an amused chuckle, Noel just kept staring at me as if I'd betrayed him.

Still too rattled to continue class, I fluttered out my hand. "I still expect you all to have *The Glass Menagerie* finished by the end of next week. So today, I'm giving you the rest of the hour to find a nice quiet corner to read. We'll continue our classroom discussions on Thursday."

For a beat, no one moved as if they thought I was teasing them. I wasn't one of those teachers who let class out early, but today, there was no way I could stand up here the entire hour.

Not bothering to wait on them, I yanked up my briefcase and streaked toward the exit. Behind me, I heard them finally begin to gather their things, but I didn't wait around as I usually did. Like Hawthorne's minister, I had my own guilt to nurture.

CHAPTER TWENTY-ONE

"They slipped briskly into an intimacy from which they never recovered." - F. Scott Fitzgerald, *This Side of Paradise*

~NOEL~

WHAT THE HELL HAD just happened?

I was already in a fuck-tacular mood. The call I'd just received had flipped my world upside down.

I'd woken up this morning, planning on being the perfect student in Aspen's class and being playful and cute and shit so she'd stop resisting me. I'd even found the perfect quote to make her smile. But then all hell had broken loose, and it had taken everything I'd had to even look at her in all her stunning glory while my guts felt like they were being jerked up toward my tonsils.

She'd called my name while I was in the middle of deliberating whether I should go home and try to help clean up some of the mess my sister had made.

But Jesus, how were we going to raise another kid in that place? Caroline would be eighteen soon. Maybe I could bring her out to Ellamore with me. Except the idea of leaving Colton and Brandt alone made me cringe.

Then Aspen happened. I have no clue what had changed between Saturday night and this morning, but this was not the woman I'd kissed goodbye on her front porch. That woman was warm and receptive and could send me to my knees with her smile alone. But *this* woman...fuck, I don't know. But I was going to find out what her fucking deal was.

As she raced from the room as soon as she dismissed us, I grabbed my things and followed in hot pursuit.

"Hey!" I called. But there were still too many people around. I wasn't sure if she ignored me for propriety's sake or because she was just that pissed. Clenching my jaw, I followed. She hit a stairwell that led up to the top floor where the offices were kept. We left the students behind and as soon as we reached the landing, I grabbed her arm.

She whirled around, glaring at me. So I glared back and yanked open the first door I saw. It ended up being a supply closet. Perfect. I shoved her inside.

"What do you think you're doing? Stop man-handling me."

After making sure we were good and locked inside, I came around slowly. "We are *going* to talk about this."

"I said get your hands off me!" Panting, she twisted her elbow out my grip.

I clenched my teeth. "Christ, what is going on with you? Why are you suddenly so pissed off? Saturday night—"

"No! How *dare* you mention Saturday to me? *Damn you.*" She shoved against my chest. "Even the idea of you coming into my class with your flirty little note just *minutes* after hearing you're going to be a father disgusts me."

"A father?" I took a step back and ran into the door. "Say *what*?"

"Yes! A father." Her green eyes shot hateful daggers just before they filled with pain. "I *heard* you talking to that poor girl on the phone, *yelling* at her. Jesus, Noel. How could you treat her that way? You're just as responsible for this as she is, yet you didn't seem to have an iota of remorse or—"

"Okay, stop right there." I lifted my hands, glaring at her. "Maybe you should know all your facts before attacking me." I snorted out a bitter laugh. "Jesus. Your faith in me is incredible. I can't fucking believe you automatically thought that was *my* kid."

"Well, you sounded pretty fucking sure you'd have to take care of it, going on about how much harder this was going to make your life. Why *wouldn't* I think it was yours?"

"Well, I'm sorry to disappoint you, but I'm not into incest. That was my seventeen-year-old sister, *Caroline*, and yes, I was furious to learn she was knocked up. I'm also fairly certain the baby's daddy isn't going to be there for her, so I *will* have to help her take care of it and this *will* make our lives that much harder to handle."

"Oh." She blew out a harsh breath. Apology hung heavy in her gaze, but she didn't beg for any kind of forgiveness. "I..."

When she couldn't even say sorry, I snorted.

"This is just great." Spiking my hands through my hair, I whirled away but couldn't even step a foot from her; the closet was too small for me to escape. I felt sick to my stomach. "I can't believe I'm falling so hard for you that I'm willing to risk school, my family, my entire future—*everything*—and you still think I'm capable of juggling you and a new kid. Fuck, I was even willing to try a monogamous, committed relationship with no qualms whatsoever, which I've never even considered before."

Rage consuming me, I spun back to her and pointed a finger into her chest. "I may have had drunk sex with complete strangers more times than I can count, but I have *never*, not even once, forgotten protection. I'm a safe fuck, got it? And if I did manage to impregnate some girl, I sure as hell wouldn't turn around ten minutes later to send secret love notes to my goddamn English teacher! Is that perfectly clear?"

Her green eyes were so wide I could see every remorseful thought inside her. "Yes," she whispered. Then her face crumpled. "I'm sorry. I'm so sorry. Why do I keep misjudging you?"

"The hell if I know." I clenched my teeth and glared. "I fully realize this thing between us is doomed, okay. I know we can never..." I closed my eyes and bowed my head. "We might not stand a chance, but I can't stop thinking about you. I can't stop craving that connection we share. It's so fucking strong, I've been willing to... God, I would do anything for little stolen pieces of you, Aspen. But if you can so easily assume I'm... Christ, if you don't feel the same way about me—"

"I do. I feel the same."

"Then prove it, damn you. Show me I'm risking everything for a reason. Because, right now—"

Warm lips crashed into mine, cutting me off. Aspen clutched my face and rose up onto her toes, pressing herself against me and fitting us together like two halves of an inseparable whole.

"I do. I swear it," she rasped against my mouth between kisses. "I feel the same. Exactly the same. Please. Please. I'm sorry. I feel it, too. I'm just scared and—"

"So am I." I literally shook from fear, and some residual anger, as well as growing lust. The lust won out. Hauling her up into my arms, I slotted our mouths firmly together.

Every molecule in my body ignited. As heat consumed me, my brain shorted out and my body took over. Or maybe it didn't quite short out, but it definitely went into caveman mode.

Mine.

Must possess.

My words hadn't gotten through to her, so I was compelled to just *show* Aspen how much she affected me. How different she was from every other woman. I had to somehow cement what we'd started so she'd know this wasn't merely fluff.

My mouth attacked hers, forcing her to open and let me in, to accept every piece of me. My fingers imprisoned her face, trapping her in my kiss. I turned into some kind of madman, unable to get enough. The fact that she was just as frantic for me only fed the beast.

Blood pumped through my veins like rushing lava. Hot and explosive. Unable to control my staccato breaths, I backed her into the small space of wall next to the closed door. But that wasn't enough for either of us. Not nearly enough. She climbed me, clinging to me with her legs as she wound them around my waist.

I bumped my hips up between her thighs and ground against her hard. The way she gasped and arched into me, throwing her head back and pulling taut in my arms as she bit her bottom lip, was so fucking hot I almost came in my jeans.

Sinking my teeth into the base of her neck, I thrust against that warmth I wanted to burrow into. Her fingers in my hair tried to yank me bald. The resulting pain was so damn hot I growled and caught her knee, spreading her just a little wider.

Before I knew quite what I was doing, my palm skated up bare skin until my hand was under her skirt. Damn, I loved this skirt. And with no pantyhose in my way, I found my way inside the barrier of her panties as soon as I encountered moist cotton.

She was wet. So wet. For me.

"Noel," she moaned, writhing against me, grabbing fistfuls of my shirt and yanking me closer.

I thrust a finger into her and we both let out a sound of shocked abandonment. "Oh, fuck. Oh, fuck," I breathed. She was so... "Fuck." I nudged another finger in and, damn, it was so sweet. So fucking sweet.

Aspen knocked the crown of her head back against the wall and closed her eyes tight. Her lips parted as these quick, shallow pants exploded from her, each breath heaving out her pleasure. She was so beautiful as I kissed her neck. Fingers pumping hard and fast, I nearly came every time I went deep.

When my lips caressed the shell of her ear, I asked, "Do you feel that? Do you feel what we do together? This isn't normal, Aspen. We are a force of fucking nature. How can we keep fighting this? How...God. I want to be inside you so bad right now."

"Uhn..." That seemed to be her tipping point. She shuddered and the muscles hugging my fingers contracted. Crying out, she came so hard and fast it shocked the shit out of me. I kissed her to muffle the sound, my digits penetrating until they were soaked and cramping. She kissed me back, and kept kissing me until I was breathless and dizzy.

As soon as her body began to quiet, I slipped my hand free and grappled for the top button of my jeans. Mindless with lust, I didn't think the next step through. I just knew I had to be inside her as soon as possible or I was coming in my damn jeans.

When she scurried to help me, fumbling for my zipper and completely on board with my idea, I let her take care of that part so I could cradle her ass in both hands and secure her a little higher against the wall. Her legs spread open, allowing me all the access I needed, and with her skirt rucked up to her waist I could see how the crotch of her panties was still pushed aside from my fingers.

The dark curls between her legs were wet and glistening. My mouth watered as I caught a glimpse, and my dick pulsed in her hand when she tugged me out of my pants.

I needed this so bad. I needed her.

Holding me at the base, she guided me to her entrance. Our cheeks brushed as we both stared down, watching our bodies join.

"Do it," she whispered, sounding as eager as I felt.

I shoved forward, impaling her.

She was so wet. And warm. And oh, my fucking God. The tightest thing to ever take my penis. When she keened out a high sound as if she was in pain, I jerked my head up to watch her bite her lip and close her eyes. I wondered if maybe it hurt, because, Christ, she was so snug I probably felt like I could split her apart.

Somewhere in my head, I knew I should stop for some reason, pull out, go slower...something. There were multiple reasons to end this and think things through. But I couldn't concentrate on a single one because fuck, she was *so*... I pushed in a little deeper, groaning at the way she gripped and squeezed even tauter around me.

"It's okay," I told her, instead of asking if she was really okay. Why didn't I ask? I had no clue. Then I kissed her hair and stroked the side of her neck as I held her by the ass with one arm and pulled out just enough to ease back in. "You can take it, baby."

Actually, I wasn't so sure she could. This was...this was...intense. But I made myself believe it, because, damn, stopping was not an option.

When I pumped her again, she made another sound, which I couldn't quite tell whether it was pain or pleasure. I was trying to go as slow as possible, even though I had to keep moving because I couldn't just *not* move.

"Noel," she whimpered, clutching my head and turning her face in toward my neck. Her breath on my throat made me swell inside her.

"What's wrong, baby? Hurt?"

"No. God, no." She moaned and shivered. "It feels so good. I just...I need...I need..." The way she tightened around me and wiggled, her body demanding more, had me groaning and moving a little faster. "Yes," she breathed, her sigh a gasp of thanksgiving. "Faster. Harder." And then she bit me. She freaking bit me, right on the jugular.

From that point on, I was a goner.

I fucked her against the wall, raw and primal, without tenderness or mercy. Every thrust I delivered was fraught with a savage thirst for more. We attacked each other, touching and kissing, biting and licking. I cupped her breast in my hand, and sank my teeth in the swell of her breast, right through her blouse because I couldn't take the time to remove her clothes. I needed it all, right then.

Just as urgent as I was, Aspen caged my hips between her thighs and wrapped her legs around me until the pointy ends of her high heels stabbed me in the ass every time I pulled out.

When she came a second time, I was right there with her, flooding her with everything I had. It felt so good and right as I buried myself as deep as I could go. I almost passed out as soon as I was done. Sagging into her, I buried my nose in her hair and let the wall support us both while it took me a moment to recoup even an iota of my strength.

I hadn't expected it to be quite that powerful.

"Jesus," I breathed, taking another few seconds just to get my wind back. Zapped of energy, I snuggled against her, not sure if I was trying to give comfort or take it. I just knew I loved sharing this moment with her, loved nestling into her warmth and inhaling her scent.

She was quiet and compliant, and so soft in my arms, I think I could've held her just like that for the rest of my life. I whispered her name because I needed to hear it aloud. Then I cradled her face with a hand that wasn't quite steady.

I wanted to tell her...so much. But there weren't words to express what she'd just done to me, what we'd just done together. It couldn't even compare to what I'd always imagined.

Tilting her head in toward me, Aspen kissed my palm, so I pressed my mouth to her throat. When she threaded her fingers through the hair at the back of my neck, I lifted my face.

"You okay?"

Now I ask.

If my mind wasn't scrambled to hell and back, I might've smacked myself in the head and apologized for my stupidity, but Aspen only laughed. The sound shot through me, making my exhausted dick pulse with one last aftershock inside her.

Her glazed eyes widened, but then she rubbed her nose against mine and made a satisfied hum deep in her throat. "I am so absolutely okay, I think I could live with being this okay for the rest of my life." Her voice was husky and sexed up. It ignited yet another aftershock from me.

We both grinned those goofy happy grins and kissed slowly, lazily, as if we had all the time in the world. Something loosened in my chest. All the pressures, and worries, and desperations in my life just sort of floated away. For the first time in too long to remember, I didn't care about anything but this moment. Aspen had taken it all away.

Wanting to thank her for the bliss, I slipped my tongue between her lips and stroked the roof of her mouth. She was everything. Everything I needed. And the way she clung to me and caressed me made me feel cherished and needed in return. We were perfect for each other.

She sighed my name, and I knew. I'd do whatever was humanly possible for this woman.

It didn't immediately compute when something wet and warm dripped down the inside of my leg. I was too busy floating in our shared high, amazed she seemed to be as punch drunk on our aftermath as I was. But whatever that shit was just kept running. I blinked a few times before I realized...

I'd just ridden her bareback.

And...here came fucking reality, walloping me with a full bitch smack of what-the-fuck-did-you-just-do right in the face.

"Shit." I yanked my hips back, pulling out of her.

She gasped from the sudden separation. Her eyes were still dewy with passion, glazed over and soft, her expression full of elation and utter relaxation. Then she looked at me. Brows knitting with confusion, she cupped my cheek with one soft hand. "What's wrong?"

Jesus. Where to start?

***

~ℐSPEN~

Noel flinched when I touched him. It killed a part of me. After what we'd just done, what we'd shared. I'd never felt anything like that with anyone before, as if we were no longer two separate people, but one binding whole.

Torn in half by his small rejection, I began to withdraw my hand. But he caught my fingers and squeezed them hard. His eyes went frantic, darting around my face as if he was scared...for me. "Are you okay?" he asked, and his breathing was no longer steady but coming in short bursts.

I nodded, confused. He'd just asked me that. "Of...of course. Why? What's wrong?"

I'd been floating, absolutely high off life. Nothing could top the sensations alive and abounding inside me. Noel had been right; we *were* a force of nature together. Because that had been...that had be better than every amazing word in the entire dictionary. I couldn't even describe—

But he still looked scared out of his mind. It made no sense. How could he be scared? There was nothing to fear. Life was wonderful.

The fear eased from his eyes as he blinked and then he blew out a breath as if forcibly reining his emotions under control. When he leaned in and tenderly cuddled me, my muscles relaxed. "I swear to you, Aspen, I wasn't lying when I said I never forget. I don't. I mean, I never have before. But this was...wow. Shit. It wasn't like anything I've ever done before. And you have to admit it was totally unplanned. And we weren't exactly thinking rationally, and... If I'd been in the right frame of mind to remember, then...Jesus, we probably wouldn't have done anything in the first place."

I pulled away and looked up at him with a crinkle in my eyebrows. But what the heck was he talking about? He cringed in apology. "I'm clean. You don't have to worry about that. They make sure of that frequently while you're on the football team."

I nodded. "Okay," I said, still not catching on until he added, "Are you, by chance, on the pill?"

The pill?

The meaning finally took root, and every muscle in my body tightened. For a moment, I felt like a complete idiot. I didn't have a lot of experience in this, but still...I'd read enough and watched movies, and...I totally should've realized what he was talking about from the beginning. I had a PhD, for crying out loud.

What was it with smart girls turning stupid

whenever a hot guy smiled at them?

Stunned that I'd just put myself in this situation, and it was really happening...to me...I started to pull away, needing space to deal with...everything. But Noel tightened his arms around me.

No longer steady and comforting, his voice shook slightly as he whispered, "Aspen?"

He stroked my hair with those sigh-worthy hands of his just as something thumped against the door of the supply closet we were in.

I yelped, and the people on the other side laughed amongst themselves, their muffled voices filling our tiny space and jerking me back to the present with a malicious vengeance, before they moved off again, obviously not realizing we were inside.

"Oh, my God," I whispered, absolutely horrified. My mouth fell open. I tried to deny what had just happened, but I couldn't. My skirt was still hiked up to my navel and something wet was slipping down the inside of my thighs.

"Don't freak out," Noel commanded in a soft, warning voice. He reached for my arm.

I squeaked out a sound and shoved him away, then gaped at him in utter horror. But...don't freak out? Was he *insane*?

"We just..."

He blew out a long breath and nodded. "Yeah. I know."

"At *school*," I hissed, completely losing my cool. "*Omigod, omigod, omigod.*" Flapping my hands, I walked in a circle because there was nowhere else to go in this cramped closet, and I certainly couldn't leave and risk anyone seeing me in my just-had-the-best-sex-of-my-life look. Realizing how rearranged my clothes still were, I beat them back into order, shoving my skirt down over my legs and jerking it around until the zipper was back where it belonged. My blouse was a disaster, there was no way to get the wrinkles out, but I desperately tried to iron it into submission with my hands.

"I can't believe I just had sex with a student. I'm going to be fired before I even make it back to my office. Oh, shit. Damn. My parents are going to find out, and probably everyone else." Eyes widening, I looked up at him. "Oh, hell. You're Noel Gamble. This is definitely going to make the news. It'll be even bigger than the coach with the volleyball player. Oh...my God. I'm going to be a scandal. How can I be a scandal? I've never even gotten a parking ticket. I drive the freaking speed limit and use my blinker to change lanes. And this one time, the telephone company refunded me too much money on my cell phone bill, but I caught the error and gave it back. I. Gave. It. Back. I always do the right thing. I never... Oh, my God. This is the worst thing I've ever done. I can't even—"

"Breathe," Noel ordered, catching my shoulders and pressing my back against the wall. "Just calm down, okay."

I drew in a heaving breath, realizing I hadn't breathed since I'd started my panic attack. I looked up into Noel's eyes, seeking reassurance. He appeared calm enough for both of us, so I took comfort in that...for like a microsecond. But then it all hit me again.

"Your coach," I gasped. "Oh, my God, Noel. Your coach said he'd kick any player off the team who was caught—"

"Then we just won't get caught," Noel spoke over me, determination lighting his gaze as he gritted his teeth.

"But—"

He kissed me silent. Rough and quick, but it effectively shut me up. Gripping my face in his hands, he forced me to look at him. "What we did was amazing," he said as if willing me to believe that as

236

fiercely as he did with his stare alone. "It was just between you and me, and it was no one else's fucking business. I know you won't show me any favoritism in class, and I sure as hell won't ask for any. I'll work my ass off to earn whatever grade I get. We can keep the two separate; that's all that matters. And we're two consenting adults who—"

"Who just did it in closet like a pair of irresponsible teenagers without any protection. Oh, my God. I'm supposed to be some kind of role model for all the young girls on campus. What kind of message would this send? Damn it, Noel, you know this is wrong. This can never happen again, not that it matters. We're going to get caught as soon we open this door, and it's all going to be over, anyway."

He shook his head insistently. In that moment, I wasn't sure if I'd ever met a more stubborn person in my life. "Look, okay, the condom thing was, yeah, a mistake. I'll admit that one. Neither of us were thinking. Things happened. But it did happen, and we can't undo it. So we'll just...we'll deal with those consequences if there are any. And we're not going to get caught in here either. We'll wait until everything settles down between classes. We can slip out after—"

"But I have another class to teach." Oh, God. Just saying that aloud made this that much more real. And awful.

I'd just had hard and dirty sex, on campus, with one of my students, and I had another class to teach in...shit, twenty minutes.

My hands began to shake. I was one of *those* women now. It didn't seem real.

Noel choked out a sound of pain and his expression crumbled as he reached for my face. "Jesus, don't cry." When he wiped wetness off my cheek, I realized I already was.

A sob worked up my throat, and I shuddered with fear.

"No." He hauled me against him, my forehead bumping hard against his clavicle. "I'm sorry." His fingers sank into my hair and rubbed my scalp. "I lost my mind and before I knew it, I was inside you. I'm so sorry, Aspen. I'll make this right. I swear it."

I let his words calm me. I even rested my cheek on his chest until he seemed satisfied I was okay. Then I let him crack open the door and check the hall. He took my hand and led me from the stuffy supply closet that now smelled like us. But as soon as we were out, I shook my fingers away from his.

He glanced back at me as if he wanted to argue about it. I knew he wanted me to follow him so we could go somewhere else together. But this had to stop here. And he must've seen something in my face, known I wasn't going anywhere with him, because he clenched his jaw but silently nodded his acceptance.

So, he took off one way down the hall, and I went the other, telling myself this could never happen again. No matter how amazing it had been, no matter how much I loved being with him, no matter how great I felt just looking at him, this could never... happen...again.

CHAPTER TWENTY-TWO

"I want to know everything about you, so I tell you everything about myself." - Amy Hempel

~NOEL~

I GAVE HER TWENTY-FOUR hours. I knew Aspen. She needed time and space to wrap her head around what had happened. It killed me to give it to her, but I allowed it. But only for one day. I knew there was no way I'd be able to enter her class on Thursday and watch her teach without imploding, so on Wednesday afternoon, beyond grateful I didn't have to work that night because I'd reorganized the schedules at work, I hiked to her place as soon as I thought she'd be home for the day.

She answered her door, cracking the entrance open and peering out at me with her large, adorable owl eyes. As her mouth fell open, I stepped forward. She had to scurry backward and pull the door open wider to let me in, but she did, without any kind of fight. The shock might've prevented her from trying to bar my way.

I was okay with that, because I was inside.

Shutting the door behind me, I held her shocked gaze. "You about done freaking out yet?"

She swung her head back and forth. "No."

"Well, I'm done waiting." Cupping her face in my hands, I added, "What we're doing is wrong. Making it a one-time deal is wrong. Trying to convince ourselves it was dirty and tawdry and something to be ashamed of is *wrong*. It was the best damn sex of my life, Aspen. I felt connected to you, like hell, I don't know. I wasn't just getting off in some random girl; I was sharing something deep and meaningful...with *you*. I don't care how many school policies tell us no. *I'm* saying yes."

She drew in a loud breath and shook her head. "Why do you make it so hard for me to resist you?"

Hot damn, I was winning. My lips kicked up at the side. "Because you want to say yes just as badly as I want you to."

A groan, telling me her will was crumbling, exited her lungs. "This is going to end badly." She leaned forward and thumped her forehead against my chest.

"Maybe." My arms swooped around her as I kissed her hair. "Maybe not." Then I kissed her cheek. "I hope not."

Looking up at me, she showed me all the faith she had in me. "So do I."

Finally, I kissed her mouth. Her lips trembled under mine, so I eased up on the pressure until she was the one straining forward for more.

Her fingers settled in my hair. I walked her backward to her couch and settled her down. There was so much I wanted to do, and touch, and see. The closet had been nothing but a giant tease. I hadn't been able to undress her completely, or taste her nipples or kiss the inside of the thigh. I planned to rectify all that right now.

But about as soon as we were both horizontal and I was slowly peeling her shirt up over her head, a buzzer went off somewhere in the back of her house.

Lifting my head in absolute confusion, I glanced around. "What the hell?"

Under me, Aspen laughed and swiped at my hair with fingers as if smoothing it back into place. "Oven timer." She wiggled under me to let me know she wanted up.

I sat back, blinking at the concept of an oven timer going off. Nothing had ever been cooked in the oven at my apartment, and it sure as hell hadn't back home. I'd had home-cooked meals a few times when the neighbor lady three trailer houses down had taken pity on us kids and invited us over. But to think of Aspen making a home-cooked meal was...unreal.

"Food," I said dumbly as my stomach rumbled happily over the idea. Well, hell. She cooked too? This was too good to be true. "What're we eating?"

"We?" Aspen arched her strict, professor eyebrow at me as she stood and smoothed her shirt back into place. "I don't remember inviting you to supper?"

"Oh, come on." I popped up after her and trailed her into the kitchen like a begging puppy. "I'm a poor, deprived college kid. Are you really going to deny this face?" I pointed out my puckered lip and batting eyelashes.

When she glanced over and caught sight of them, she laughed. "Oh, my God. You're pathetic. Okay, fine. You can stay for supper. I have plenty."

After she turned off the timer, she grabbed a set of hot pads, but I snatched them from her. "You're injured. I'll do it."

She frowned. "Injured? What're you talking about?"

"Your arm," I reminded her as I opened the oven. "Falling box of books. Gashed shoulder. Fifteen stiches. Ring a bell?"

Her hand fluttered to her shoulder. "I don't even notice them anymore. They've stopped pulling when I move."

"Well, that's good. But just wait until they start itching. After one of my mom's *friends* put me in the hospital one time, I—oh, shit. Lasagna. You made *lasagna*?"

She blinked. "I..." Shaking her head, she glanced at the lasagna before turning back to me. "Yeah, I made lasagna. What were you saying about being put in a *hospital*? How old were you?"

I kind of liked the fierce expression on her face, as if she wanted to go defend the past me. I waved a hand. "Oh, ten or so. The point is, I ended up with stiches, and they irritated the hell out of me when they were ready to come out because they itched so much. But, seriously, how did you know lasagna was my favorite meal?"

"I just craved lasagna tonight."

"Well, you made enough for an army." I slid it free and set it on the hot plate she'd already set up on the countertop. "So, I'm saying your subconscious knew I was coming and your telepathy told you to make me this."

Crossing her arms over her chest, she rested her hip against the counter as she faced me. "And I'm saying you're completely ridiculous." She shook her head, her eyes twinkling. "You know, when I first saw you, I had no idea you'd be quite this...playful."

I caught her waist and pulled her up against me. Anchoring her bottom against the counter so I could press into her, I ducked my face and brushed my nose against her neck. "I had no idea about a lot of things about you, so I'd say we're even on that score. You are nothing like I thought you'd be. You're better. So...so much better."

When I grasped the hem of her shirt and yanked it up over her head, she yelped out her surprise.

"Noel!"

I grinned. "What? I think we should eat topless." Her hands went to cover her plain white bra, but I caught her wrists. "Don't." My voice was soft. Pleading. "I want to see you."

I heard her swallow. Her body trembled against mine. Then she lifted her bright green eyes and confessed, "Then I want to see you too."

I breathed easier. "Done." My own shirt was off half a second later.

Eyes widening, Aspen ran her gaze over me with a look of complete awe. "Wow."

"Feel free to touch," I told her. "Because I plan to."

I smoothed my fingers over the ugly black stitches on her shoulder. She shuddered and closed her eyes, so I kept on, shifting my hand up until I caught hold of the strap of her bra. I slid it off and kissed the patch of skin it'd been hiding. Kissing my way down to the breast it no longer supported, I brushed the cup aside and took her nipple into my mouth. There, I suckled, making her groan until finally she touched me back. She curled her hand around the back of my neck, and clung to me while I tugged gently on her breast.

As my tongue worked over the hard peak, she trailed her hands down my back. When she reached the waistband of my jeans, she came around to the front, made a tentative sweep over my six-pack and then popped open the top button of my jeans. That's when I couldn't take it any longer.

"You know, we should wait for that lasagna to cool down before we eat it."

"We really should," she agreed and kissed my pec, right over my heart as she made a humming sound in her throat and slid my zipper down.

Gripping her hips, I picked her up. "I have the perfect idea of how we could bide our time."

Teeth nipped my earlobe before she whispered, "Take me to bed."

***

~*A*SPEN~

Noel laid me almost reverently on my mattress. Then he stepped back and ripped open his jeans. I sat up, utterly captivated. He was perfectly formed, his body a sculpted piece of art. As he pushed stiff denim over his hips and down his legs, I swear my mouth watered. I swallowed and let my gaze drop down every blessed inch of him, then back up to his bulging boxers.

"I like how you watch me." He put on even more of a show by hooking his thumbs into the waistband of his shorts.

"I like watching you." Holding my breath, I waited and then...wow. He pushed the boxes down until he was gloriously naked.

"You like?" Holding his hands open at his sides, he turned slowly to give me a three-hundred-and-sixty-degree view. His tight, narrow butt was just as impressive as what bobbed out the front.

I could barely tear my gaze away. But I managed to meet his eyes. "You'll do."

He laughed and crawled onto the bed, pausing when he bumped his knee against the paperback I'd been reading last night before going to bed. Scowling at it, he picked it up and tossed it over his shoulder.

I gasped in outrage. "Hey! My book."

"I'll apologize to it later, I swear." Then he hulked over me and stared down into my eyes.

I narrowed him a half-hearted scowl. "That's two paperbacks now that have been harmed because of you. I hope you realize that's not a good way to start a relationship with a book junkie."

He merely arched an eyebrow. "*Two* books?"

"Yeah. That one, and the one I drenched in the bathtub when I—" Remembering he knew absolutely nothing about the bathroom incident, I snapped my mouth shut and flushed a deep scarlet.

"Bathtub?" He caught on to my distress a little too easily and gave a wicked grin. "Were you perhaps...*naked* in this bathtub?"

I gulped unable to take my eyes off his. "I usually am when I'm in the bath."

"Hmm." He pulled his bottom lip in between his teeth. "I'm having a hard time picturing you that way. Can you give me a better visual?"

Without asking, he opened the top clasp of my shirt. Then he slid it down my legs. "Damn," he murmured once I was completely unclothed. "You are so...beautiful."

I blushed under his stare, and my nipples pulled tight. He focused on them hungrily. "So, about this bath where you ruined a perfectly good book." Voice husky, he ran his gaze over me yet again His fingertips lightly flicked over one nipple. "Were you perhaps doing...this...when it happened?" He cupped me between the legs and rubbed his fingers against my clit.

I arched and groaned, grabbing a handful of sheets under me as my body pushed up against his touch. "Maybe," I panted.

"And you were thinking about me while you did this?"

When he leaned down to replace his fingers with his mouth, his tongue sliding mercilessly over my aching flesh, I cried out and grabbed his hair. But, oh, my God. "Definitely," I confessed on a high voice.

"Jesus, Aspen." His voice was unstable and frantic. "You completely undo me."

His hands spread my thighs wider as his tongue

lapped deeper. I dug my heels into the mattress under me, feeling his touch from the tips of my toes to the roots of my hair. Then he pushed a finger inside me, and I cried out my shock. The wave of pleasure was overwhelming. I tried to fight it and embrace it at the same time, unable to stop writhing as Noel took me to a new level of delirious.

Sagging onto the mattress when the muscles in my body went into a post-coital coma, I stared at Noel in dazed wonder while he scrambled off the bed, jerked up his pants and dug through the pockets until he pulled out a folded line of condoms.

"Look, I remembered this time." He was so boyishly adorable as he sent me a proud grin that I had to grin back. In fact, I had a feeling I was glowing from head to toe I felt so sublime.

He tore one off from the others and glanced at me, smiling as he shook his head. "You look like you've just been fucked silly."

At the moment, I couldn't feel insulted if I wanted to. I simply kept beaming. "Haven't I?"

"Not yet." A new determined gleam lit his eyes as he crawled back onto the bed. Hovering above me, he leaned in to kiss my lips. His tongue mated with mine as he suited up. And then his warm palm clasped my knee, nudging me open just a little more.

When he pushed inside, I threw my head back and breathed through my teeth. He was always just so...there. Huge and filling, like he wanted to take over every available space I had to give and then demand more.

Gripping my thighs, he wrapped my legs around his waist and curled his arms around me. Knotted together until I didn't know where I ended and he began, we made love.

***

The room was quiet. Feeling too lethargic to move, I lounged sideways across Noel's chest, completely nude as he ran his hand over my warm, sensitive spine.

"That feels..." I managed a moan. "So good."

"Oh, yeah?" He sat up enough to lean over me and kiss my jutting hipbone. "Feels good to me too. You're soft all over."

I closed my eyes and smiled, unable to control the giddiness roaring through me. But I'd never had an after-sex experience like this before. With the two guys who hadn't forced me, they'd left with excuses as soon as they'd finished. Actually, since the first hadn't even bothered to finish, I guess only the one guy had pulled out as soon as he'd finished his business, and then he'd gone on his merry way.

But this...this was nice. I liked after-sex cuddling.

Noel rolled me from my side onto my back so he could kiss my belly button next, but a lump under my spine had me wiggling until I reached back and pulled up the blue bunny he'd won at the carnival.

Arching an eyebrow, he picked it up and sent me a smug grin. "I knew you'd keep this thing." Then he used the soft cloth of the bunny's ear to caress me from my navel and up between my breasts.

I sighed and stretched languidly under him.

He hummed in contentment. "I'm suddenly very, very glad you wear those frumpy clothes you do to school. I think I'd flip my shit if any other guy on campus had a clue what you looked like under them."

I glanced at him, lifting my eyebrows. "What, you don't like my power suits?"

He gave a quick laugh. "Power suits? Is that what you call them?"

I shrugged. What else should I call them? I wore them to gain the position I wanted on that campus.

"I know that's not what you usually wear," Noel went on. "At the bar in that sexy, black backless thing and to the carnival in those adorable jean shorts. I have a feeling you only wear your *power suits* to the university."

I smiled with pride and kissed his cheek. "And you would be right."

"Hell, I know I'm right. But why? Why do you do it? You know how...unflattering they look, right?"

With a roll of my eyes, I laughed. "Yes. That's the point. I would rather be overlooked and misjudged with low expectations than to come in my first semester with a bunch of flash to intimidate people and make them think I want to roll right over them. Besides, I want them to know I care about my job, not fashion."

"You have funny reasoning, Professor, but I'm still glad you don't let everyone else see these curves." He flung the bunny over his shoulder so he could use his fingers to stroke a knot on my hip. Pausing at it, he furrowed his brow. "What's this?"

Ice formed in my veins. As he leaned down to examine the old knife scar and then kiss it, I jerked away. "Don't." The panic in my voice had him looking up and studying me, reading every uncomfortable, memory-laden expression on my face.

"Aspen," he said softly, his sharp eyes seeing more than I wanted him to. "Was that a trigger?"

"Tr...?" I blinked. Why would he use that word? My therapist had always used that word. Shaking my head, I tried to laugh off the concern in his gaze. "I don't know what you mean?"

"I mean..." He drew in a deep breath and then exhaled. Setting his fingers against the scar, he asked, "Did you get this from your rape?"

I blacked out. Seriously, for a split second, I saw nothing but absolute black. But I remained completely, horrifyingly conscious.

"Aspen?" Warm fingers cupped my shoulders. Blinking the black away, I watched a fuzzy image of

Noel's concerned face slowly fill my view. "Do you remember telling me about that?" he asked.

"No," I whispered in horror. "I didn't..." Oh, God, I hadn't, had I? Why would I tell him about *that*? Opening my mouth to speak, I shook my head, completely aghast. "W...why would I tell you about that?"

"You were drunk. We talked about a lot that night."

"But..." I pressed my hand to my chest. That wasn't something I ever wanted him to know...wanted *anyone* to know. "What exactly did I tell you?"

"Not much. You were fourteen. He was a football player. Your parents refused to do anything about it."

I brushed my hair out of my face, surprised how cold my fingers were. "But..."

"I'm glad I know." He took my hand and kissed my knuckles. "I'm glad I understand why you were so judgmental of me at first. And I'm relieved to see just how strong you are. You survived this and overcame it. I don't...shit. I don't know how much you think about it when we're together, but the fact that you can still find pleasure with me is..." He shook his head. Eyes gleaming with emotion, he smiled. "You just impress the hell out of me, that's all."

I curled into him and ducked my face into the hollow between his neck and shoulder. "I don't think about it, *him*, not when we're together, except maybe to marvel over how good it can actually be compared to..." I shivered, remembering just how bad it could get.

"I'm glad." Noel kissed my cheek. "But if I ever do hit a trigger, or do *anything* that reminds you...you'll tell me, right?"

I nodded, and strangely enough I wasn't lying. How we'd moved so effortlessly from teacher and student who completely despised each other to personal confidants, I have no idea. But I'd be forever grateful for it. Not only had I just gained a lover, but it also felt as if I'd made a friend. So, I confided in my friend.

"It was my senior year." Resting my cheek on his heartbeat, I ran my fingers idly up his chest, marveling over how hard and smooth he was. "I was a couple months shy of fifteen. Zach was a senior too."

"Zach." Noel snarled the word as if he wanted to commit the name of his next victim to memory.

I smiled softly and nodded, loving the protective sound in his voice. "He was eighteen, like most normal high school seniors, and was the 'it' boy. Back then, I wasn't very good at concealing my emotions. Everyone knew I had a raging crush on him. The first time he smiled at me and said *hi*, I think I literally sighed aloud. When he asked me on a date, I was just...over the moon."

Noel's arms tightened around me, but he didn't interrupt as he combed his fingers gently through my hair.

"I had no idea there was a bet going around over who could take the freak girl's virginity."

Cursing fluidly, Noel tucked his face next to mine and pressed our cheeks together. He hissed out a breath as if he needed to release some of the anger building pressure inside him.

"He was a complete gentleman most of the night. We watched a movie; he paid and bought me popcorn and a drink. I was pretty much in love by the time the ending credits rolled. I think he had paid more attention to me during that one action flick than my parents had paid me in my entire life. He let me pick the film and put the popcorn in my lap so I'd always have access to it. He even got me a soda refill half way through the movie. After that, I would've run away from home and joined a band of traveling gypsies just to be with him. Whatever he wanted. So when he asked if I'd like to go to the local make-out spot before he took me home, I was all on board. But I'd never even had my first kiss up until that point. I kind of thought he'd be okay with working our way through the bases, one step at a time, you know."

Noel nodded and kissed my temple. "Of course," he agreed with me, his voice soft and tender. "That's how it's usually done."

"The kissing was okay," I went on, wondering why I didn't feel awkward talking about kissing another guy while I was lying in my current lover's arms. But spilling everything to Noel just seemed... natural. "I'm not sure I would've dove straight into French kissing right off the bat if I'd had the choice, but I wanted to make him happy, so I tried to catch up. It was when he went up my shirt that I started to get uncomfortable. I just..."

"You weren't ready yet," Noel finished for me.

"Right. I wasn't ready. Except when I tried to slow him down..." I shook my head and squeezed my eyes closed.

Burying his nose into my hair, Noel murmured, "You don't have to talk about the rest."

But I wanted him to know. "He completely changed," I plowed forward. "If he'd continued to be nice, if he'd just tried to sweet talk me a little more, I probably would've given in willingly. But at the first sign of my hesitance, he turned brutal. He grabbed my face hard with one hand, called me a frigid little freak, and pulled a knife out of his pocket."

"Shit." The arms banded around me constricted even tighter.

"I think threatening me with a blade turned him on more because I went stiff and compliant after that, but he just kept sliding it over my skin as he cut off my clothes. He had it against me when he first, you know, forced himself in. That's when I jumped, and he nicked me—"

"Okay, no more. *Jesus.*" Noel breathed heavily

against my hair as he held me hard against him before he rasped, "I'm sorry, I just can't...I guess I didn't realize hearing about you go through something like that would this..." He shook his head.

I'm probably sick and twisted, but I loved knowing how difficult it was for him to hear this. But it meant he cared. Noel Gamble cared about what had happened to me. Not even my parents had cared that much.

"It's okay." I twisted in his arms so we were lying belly to belly. Needing to comfort him, I touched his cheek. When he met my gaze, his blue eyes swirled with torment.

"How the fuck did you survive through that?"

"It's been a long time," I said. "Directly afterward, I drew so hard into my shell, I didn't even care when Zach bragged to the entire school about winning the bet. I didn't care about much of anything. But time and therapy helps more than you'd realize."

Noel nodded. "I still don't understand why the hell your parents wouldn't do anything about it?"

I shrugged. "Zach's father was one of my parents' colleagues at the university where they taught."

"Fuckers." Snorting, Noel just shook his head. "Please tell me Zach ended up dying a slow and painful death."

"No. He became a corporate lawyer, and is doing very well, so I hear."

"The prick. He probably brags to this very day about how he popped the freak girl's cherry too."

I had to smile over the acid in his tone. I loved how upset he was on my behalf. "Probably." Leaning in, I brushed my nose alongside his. "I wish I had grown up in your hometown. And you'd been the star football player I had a crush on."

His lips caught the corner of my mouth. "I do too. I mean, other than the fact, I would've been a sixth grader when you were a senior and I wasn't a star anything at that point. I was still short and scrawny and getting my ass kicked every other day."

"I still would've preferred you over him, any day." Leaning in, I kissed him briefly on the nose.

"Then I guess it's a good thing you have me. I'm all yours, Aspen Kavanagh. And if Corporate Lawyer Zach ever comes near you again, I'll kill him. I will literally snap his neck."

Grinning, I kissed his lips this time. It was on the tip of my tongue to say, "I love you," in a soft dreamy sigh. But then I realized what I was about to blurt out. Swallowing down the words, I hooked my arms around his neck and rolled us until he was on top of me, pinning me to the bed. "Make love to me," I demanded instead.

His grin was cocky and pleased. "Yes, ma'am," he answered as his mouth descended toward mine.

CHAPTER TWENTY-THREE

"Three may keep a secret, if two of them are
dead."- Benjamin Franklin

~NOEL~

AND SO I STARTED an illicit affair with my
literature professor. Except it didn't feel illicit. In my
book, it wasn't dirty, or wrong, or in any way
shameful. It was the purest relationship I'd ever had
with anyone.

I hated that we had to keep it secret, but I had to
admit, I loved hoarding her all to myself. She showed
me the parts of her no one else got to see. She opened
up and talked, and in return, I talked too.

Our nights together were always short and never
lasted long enough. I usually had to wait until late,
after work, until I could go see her. Then I woke at the
butt crack of dawn for training. I hated leaving her
bed while she was still warm and sleeping, all curled
up and beautiful under the covers. I just wanted to
crawl back in with her and stay there the entire day.

But what I despised most was spotting her on campus. It was more difficult than I could've ever imagined to walk by the woman I'd just spent the night with and couldn't wait to spend the night with again without even acknowledging her. I also loathed hearing people bash her because she graded so strictly. I couldn't defend her. I couldn't kick their ass. Everyone still assumed I didn't like her.

And I really despised not being able to tell other girls who hit on me that I was no longer available. It was strange. I'd never even considered being a one-woman kind of guy. But now that I was, I didn't miss the other way. I was so obsessed with Aspen I didn't even want anyone else.

So when Tianna started flirting with me one day in the quad just as Aspen walked past in her frumpy power suit and black briefcase, my body instantly ignited. I couldn't help but glance over T's shoulder to watch my woman pass. But when she briefly glanced back, I could see she was pissed to see the groupie hanging around me.

I was able to ward Tianna off without too much drama; I tried to convince her she needed to give my boy Quinn some attention, maybe pop the poor kid's cherry. But just to make sure Aspen still knew I was thinking about her, and no one else, I made a risky move and dropped another quote on her briefcase when I passed her desk later that morning as I entered class. Something I knew would make her mood lighter.

"Why do people say 'grow some balls'? Balls are weak and sensitive. If you wanna be tough, grow a vagina. Those things can take a pounding." - Sheng Wang

My plan worked; she couldn't stop smiling as she started class. But I still hated how we had to hide so much. When she called me that evening, I was sure she was going to mention Tianna, but she merely said my name and sniffed, letting me know she was crying.

Heart instantly leaping into my throat, I pushed up from the couch where I'd been writing my latest literature essay for my hard-ass, totally hot English professor. "Aspen? What's wrong?"

"My...are you...I just really need to see you right now. Can I come up?"

"Come up?" *Wait, what?* "You're here? Outside? Right now?"

"Yes, I...it's a bad time, isn't it? I'll leave."

"No! Don't go. My roommate just left. Come up. Your timing's perfect." I rushed to the door without bothering to end the call. She'd never come to my place before, so whatever was bugging her must be big. As soon as I popped my head into the hall, I saw her exit the stairwell. Her face was white, eyes swollen and red, and her hair was a scattered mess.

"Baby? What's wrong?" I yanked her into my arms, kissing her unkempt locks. "Are you okay? Are you hurt?"

When she burrowed into me and buried her face into my chest, my heart twisted painfully. I hated seeing her this way.

"It's my dad," she finally croaked.

I squeezed my eyes closed. She'd told me all about his diabetes and pneumonia. Sounded like the guy was going to bite the big one any day. "Is he—"

"They're going to amputate his leg. But his circulation's so bad they're not certain if that will even help."

"Jesus. I'm sorry." Kicking the door shut, I carried her into the apartment and sat on the couch where she coiled into my lap.

"And the worst part is my mother didn't even call to tell me. It was their housekeeper, Rita. She...she thought I should know. And now I can't go see him

256

because then they'll know Rita's feeding me information, and I don't want to get her into trouble because she's always been so nice to me, but why...*why* wouldn't my own mother tell me about this? How could she possibly think I didn't deserve to know?"

Probably because she was a cold, selfish bitch who never considered her daughter's feelings, I wanted to say, but held my tongue. "I don't know." I rubbed her back and kept holding her, trying to show her the best support I could.

"I don't think they'll ever tell me they love me," she whispered. It broke my heart. My mom had never said the words either, but I'd always had Caroline, and Colton, and Brandt. And strangely, I was glad I'd ended up with the parent I'd had. At least I'd had freedom to do whatever I'd wanted. I'd never been controlled and brainwashed the way Aspen had. I'd never felt alone or repressed while I was being neglected. Not the way she had.

Loathing her parents with a burning passion, I laced our fingers together, palm to palm, and pressed my forehead to hers. "Not saying it to you is *their* loss."

She studied me, her lashes still wet from the tears she'd cried and her nose red. But she still looked beautiful enough to take my breath. Anyone had to be stupid not to tell her how they felt about her.

I opened my mouth to tell her...shit, I don't know. She'd completely altered my world in the past few weeks, and I wanted her to know how amazing she was. I wanted her to know what she did to me. It reminded me of the next quote I wanted to slip to her.

"When we find someone who is brave, fun, intelligent, and loving, we have to thank the universe." -Maya Angelou

But Aspen set her fingers over my lips to keep me quiet. Then she smiled softly and leaned in, dropping her hand from my mouth so she could kiss me. I groaned against her lips and slid my palms into her hair. Her bottom shifted until her warmth covered my erection. Then she ground down on me, and hell, I had to bump back up into her. My fingers found their way under her shirt and to the back of her bra where I opened the clasp.

Just as I began to swoop my way around to the front, the door to my apartment rattled before swinging open.

Aspen yelped out a scream and dove against me, hiding her face in my chest, and I scrambled to sit up, pulling my hands out of her shirt.

Ten stepped inside. "Man, I forgot my fucking wall—" He jerked to a stop. "Shit. Sorry. My bad."

He stuck his hands in the air and began to back out of the apartment, but Aspen lifted her face and glanced at him. Slamming to a halt, he stared at her hard.

"Get out!" I yelled, and grabbed a couch cushion to throw at him. But it bounced off his head unnoticed.

Tipping his face to the side, he studied her from a different angle. "Why do you look like...?" Then it hit him who she was. His eyes bugged. "Holy shit."

"Out," I ordered, scooting her off my lap so I could jump to my feet and block his view of her as well as charge toward him.

The fucker still didn't move. "Jesus Christ, man. She's—"

I pushed him into the hallway and shut the door.

And that's when he lost it. "You're banging the teacher. Oh, my fucking God, you're banging the fucking teacher. Holy shit, Gam, this is so...*boss*. You are the man. The *man*!"

Slapping my hand over his mouth, I gritted my

teeth and cast him a warning glare before glancing worriedly toward the closed door. "Shut. Up," I hissed, threatening him with my eyes.

He pushed my hand away. "*Shut up?*" he hissed right back. "Are you kidding me? My roommate's officially badass. You're doing her for the grade, aren't you? So you can keep your scholarship? Damn, you're brilliant. I mean, I knew you could charm the ladies, but to get hard-ass *Kavanagh* to drop her panties is...epic. Wait till the guys hear—"

"No!" I grabbed a fistful of his shirt and pulled him close. "No one can know, Ten. Jesus, if you tell anyone...fuck. There's nothing to tell, okay? You didn't see anything. Nothing is going on. This is a...non-issue. Got it?"

"The hell with that. You're banging the fucking teacher. You're going down in history as—"

"Did you not hear Coach after the volleyball scandal? If we're caught with any faculty member on campus, we're off the team. I'll lose my scholarship. She'll lose her job. Everything will go to hell. Tenning, please. You. Didn't. See. Anything."

I begged him with my expression, and he finally growled out a sound. "Damn it. You know how to suck the fun out of everything."

He stormed past me and ripped open the door to the apartment before I could stop him. "I'd say hi," he told Aspen as he entered. "But apparently I don't see anything."

She was pacing the floor in front of the couch, her face pale and arms crossed tightly over her chest with her hands tucked into the sleeves of her shirt as if she was cold. Without speaking to him, she watched him march to the hall and disappear into his room. He returned seconds later, waving his wallet and looking at neither Aspen nor I, before he moodily slammed out of the apartment again.

I blew out a breath and sagged against the wall,

rubbing my hands over my face. "You're freaking out, aren't you?"

"I should go." She hurried toward the exit, her face down. But I grasped her shoulder and pulled her close so I could press my mouth to her cheek. She remained stiff in my arms.

"I can trust him," I whispered.

She lifted her chin, her eyes wet and scared. "I'm glad *you* can."

"He won't say anything. I promise you." I'd kill him if he did, and I was sure he knew that.

She just shook her head. "I shouldn't have come here tonight. I was...what was I *thinking*?"

"I'm glad you did." I kissed her cheek this time. "I'm your boyfriend, Aspen. I want to be there for you when you go through rough shit."

"My *boyfriend*?" she choked out and incredulous sound. "How can you be my boyfriend when I can't tell a single soul about you?"

Growling through clenched teeth, I scowled at her. "I'm your boyfriend because I'm your boyfriend. We don't need any more explanation than that. It just is. I'm the one who's there when you're happy, and when you're sad, and when you come apart in my arms. This..." I slammed her body against mine so she could feel what she did to me, "makes me your boyfriend."

A tear trailed down her cheek. Lifting her fingers, she gently touched my lips. "I wish I had your confidence."

I kissed her fingertips and brushed the tear away. "You don't need it. I have enough for the both of us." And with that, I had her talked off the ledge. She stopped resisting me and leaned in to me when I kissed her. When I led her back to my bedroom, she smiled and tugged my shirt off.

It wasn't until after she was asleep later that night and curled around me in my bed that my own doubts rose. With Ten knowing, our risk had just doubled. It was selfish of me to keep her, to keep doing this, because it could so easily end up hurting her *and* my family. But then I realized I still didn't care enough about the *what ifs* because my determination to remain hers had also doubled. Aspen had gotten so deep in my blood I was more than willing to take any chance I had to just to be with her another day longer.

CHAPTER TWENTY-FOUR

"It is easier to forgive an enemy than to forgive a friend." - William Blake

~NOEL~

"LET'S GO OUT TONIGHT."

It was a Friday and neither Ten nor I had to work. This had to be the second time in over a month we'd had the same night off, and it being a weekend made it even rarer. But I'd been planning on going to Aspen's. Nights I got to spend the entire evening with her were few and far between. I madly craved some quality time with my woman.

"Can't," I said, rushing to finish the assignment I had for History. "Got plans already."

"What? You going to *Dr. Kavanagh's* to earn your next A?"

Slamming my pen down, I stood up glowering at him. "That is enough of that shit. Don't talk about her that way again. Fuck, don't even think about her. You and I are not going there."

"Dude." With a nervous laugh, Ten shifted a step back and lifted his hands. "You know I'm just messing with you."

My hands fisted at my hips. "Well, it's not funny."

"Hey." Growing serious, Ten set his hand over his heart. "When—and I say when, not if—this thing between you two goes south, I'm going to be right there for you, man. I'll hand you every woe-is-me beer you need and find you that next rebound chick to get her out of your system. But until then, it is my God-given right as your best friend to lovingly harass you about it as often as possible."

I let out a long, weary sigh. "So, basically, there's no shutting you up?"

He grinned, wide and ornery. "Oh, Hell no." Then he plopped down into the seat next to me. "So what's she like, anyway? She make you do it with the lights out? Cut away a little hole in the sheet to fit your whacker through?"

"Seriously." I waved him away as if swatting off an annoying fly. "You're not getting anything out of me. You might as well zip it."

"But I'm dying of curiosity here. This is big. Like huge. And if I can't talk about it with anyone else, I'm talking the shit out of it with you."

I groaned. "Dear God, save me." Picking up my pen again, I tried to get back to my homework. But my roommate just wouldn't stop.

"So really, have you actually seen her naked? Like total birthday suit nude? She have a decent little body under all those clothes or what? I could get that, you know, her hiding her light under a bushel. I bet she turns into a fucking animal once you strip her down. Bam!" He slapped his palm on the top of the table. "She has nipple rings, doesn't she?"

I rolled my eyes. "She doesn't have..." Realizing I was about to confess that I had indeed seen her nipples, I quickly revised with, "...a belly button ring."

"But her nipples?" Tenning pressed, leaning in and really getting excited as he slapped the tabletop. "Oh, fuck. They *are* pierced, aren't they? I knew it! God damn, you are the luckiest son of a—"

I cut him a glare. "I didn't say they were pierced."

"But you didn't say they weren't."

"I didn't say she didn't have a tattoo and you haven't automatically assumed she has one of those, now, have you?"

"Oh, hell. She's got a tat too? I think I'm in love. Where is it? Is it a tramp stamp? Bet it's a butterfly."

With a groan, I tried to concentrate on my history lesson, but Ten slapped the tabletop again. "Seriously, cut that studying shit out already. Watching you turn scholarly gives me hives. Now get your ass into your room, change into some club-thumpers, and come with me to drunk it up." When I just glared at him, he grinned. "I'm not going to stop harassing you about her until you agree to hang with me tonight."

***

So Ten talked me into going out with him. When I called Aspen to bemoan my change of plans, she sided with my roommate, saying I needed to socialize as I always had or people might become suspicious. I still didn't want to go, but I did.

I was bombarded as soon as I stepped into the frat house. I guess it'd been a while since I'd been out partying. Fellow football players slapped me on the back and stopped me for a chat. Girls slid me sidelong glances. And people kept refilling my cup as soon as it was close to being empty.

It was all so very typical, and yet now it felt off. Nothing here had changed, but I felt as if I had. I yearned for a quiet, peaceful evening at Aspen's, watching a movie on her couch or experimenting on different takeout foods in the kitchen.

We'd cooked together. We'd showered together. We'd eaten and slept together. Worked on homework together—her grading, me writing. It was all so very domestic and maybe even boring, but I'd never been bored with her. And I'd always wanted to go back for more. And right now, in this crowded, music-thumping, party-blasting house, I just wanted to head to her place.

"Hey, Noel, baby." Warm feminine fingers crept up my arm, making me jerk away and spin toward the redhead grinning at me.

Tianna's friend. Marci, if I remembered correctly. "Hey," I called over the noise, tipping my head to greet her in a vague kind of way.

She reached up on tiptoes and leaned in to talk into my ear. "Ready to cash in on the rain check?"

The threesome. Shit, I'd totally forgotten about that. As I glanced around, I spotted Tianna closing in on us. She waved, and my stomach swirled with unease.

Feeling cornered but wanting to let the girl down gently, I smiled at I shook my head. "Bad night."

Biting her lip, she wrapped her arms around my bicep. "Tomorrow then? Please."

Great. She wasn't going to give up, was she? I winced. "Look, I appreciate the offer but..."

Her eyes narrowed slightly. "Who is she?" she asked, no longer smiling, and actually looking as if she was ready to cut a bitch.

Alarm raced up my spine, but I kept playing it cool. Clueless. I wrinkled my eyebrows. "Who's *who*?"

"The new girl you're fucking? I haven't seen you with anyone around campus."

"Marci," I gritted out, growing annoyed with this conversation. "I didn't want to be an asshole and say this, but I'm just not interested in you."

She snorted. "Not interested?" Backing up, she

splayed out her hands to encompass her body. "In this?"

Meh. I actually preferred Aspen's look more. But I couldn't say that. I could, however, put a dent in Marci's inflated ego.

"Look, Tianna told me how obsessed you are about me. And I'm not looking for anything like that. I don't do relationships, or clinging women, or sobbing midnight phone calls, begging me to give you another chance. And you have exactly that kind of drama written all over you."

When her mouth fell open, I realized I'd probably gone a little overboard. I sent her another apologetic wince and friendly pat on the shoulder. Then I turned and got out of there as quickly as possible without looking as if I was bolting. She didn't follow, but I had a feeling I hadn't heard the last from her. I'd never been into cutting down a woman like that before, so whatever she did to me in response, I'd probably deserve.

I faced a whole new set of problems when I entered the next room, though. Less crowded, it had a couple couches sitting around a coffee table and facing a television. And my roommate was in the center of the action, drinking from a funnel and looking completely lit.

"*Ow!*" he shouted when he saw me. Jumping onto the coffee table, he pretended to strum a guitar like a rocker. "*I got it bad. Got it bad. Got it bad. I'm hot for teacher.*" Then he fisted his hands and pumped his hips, dry humping the air as he continued to sing the golden oldie Van Halen song.

I shook my head and sighed. "I'm gonna kill him. I am seriously going to kill him."

"Hey, Gamble." He cupped his hands around his mouth and yelled. "Sing it with me. *Got it bad, got it bad, got it bad—*"

"You're fucking drunk," I shouted back.

266

"No, *really*? How'd you guess? Hey, does she like to play naughty schoolgirl? That way, you could be *her* professor every once in a while."

Quinn appeared next to me, holding a red plastic cup as he peered up at Ten. "What's he talking about?"

"I have no idea." I couldn't stop glaring at my roommate, thinking up the quickest way to silence him.

Death.

Yes, it'd have to be death.

"What kind of stuff does she make you do for extra credit? Write *fuck me silly* fifty times in a row? Do you call her *Dr*. Kavanagh when you're inside her? Hey, do you even know her first name?"

"Enough!"

"Think she'd lift my grade too if I offered to lick her—"

With a roar, I launched myself at Ten's legs. When we both toppled over backward off the table, someone screamed and about a dozen players surged forward to break us apart. But I still got in a couple decent punches before I was pulled off him.

Quinn was the only one with enough muscle to drag me away. Breathing hard, I pushed him off me as soon as he got me alone in a brightly lit bathroom. But Jesus, I couldn't believe my best friend on earth had just ousted me like that.

"I'm gonna kill him," I muttered even as I grew sick to my stomach. Aspen would never forgive me for this. Oh, God. Had I just ruined her entire life? "I can't believe he...he..."

"Jeez, Noel." Hamilton tugged at my arm to get me to face him. "He's drunk. He always talks stupid when he's drunk."

My chest heaved from how strongly I was breathing. "But he said—"

Quinn laughed and shook his head, looking completely unconcerned about how shit was about to hit the fan. "You're not honestly worried we *believed* a word he said, are you? We all know how much you hate Kavanagh."

When I shot him an irritated scowl, everything inside me was still too open and raw. The truth must've reflected on my face because his eyes widened.

"Oh," he breathed, his mouth falling open as he gaped in absolute shock.

I hissed, "Shit," and squeezed my eyes closed.

Damn it. Hamilton did not need to know about this. Too many people already knew. Hell, after Ten's little show, I'd be surprised if everyone *didn't* know. When I risked a glance his way, Quinn was still staring, badly.

"Look, it's not what you think."

He immediately lifted his hands and shook his head. "No. No, of course not," he agreed. "I mean, after Coach Jacobi's decree and the scandal on the volleyball team, you'd never risk her job and your own future like that, just to..." His eyes were wide and seeking. "Would you? You love her, right?"

It struck me just how truly innocent Quinn Hamilton was. I'd never heard the kid cuss, or say one disparaging thing about anyone else. He had that pure, boy-next-door edge about him and thought the best of everyone. We all teased him about being a virgin, and looking at him right then, I had to wonder if he really still was.

He stared at me with his hero-worship gaze on. I was the leader of our team, and he'd always looked at me as if I could do no wrong. If I said the wrong thing right now, I could wipe out his entire belief system.

"Fuck, yes, I love her," I hissed. And then it struck me what I'd just admitted, but what shocked me most of all was that I hadn't lied. All feeling drained from my limbs, and my face probably went sheet white as I stumbled back to sit on the closed seat of the toilet. "Oh, shit. I love her."

I loved Aspen.

"Don't worry." Ham leapt forward and patted my shoulder to support me when I buried my face in my hands. "I won't tell anyone. I swear. I mean, you're really one of the only friends I have here, so..." He shrugged and offered me a pathetic smile. "I don't have anyone to tell anyway."

God, he just seemed so...young. I couldn't remember ever being that young. I'd been wizened to the world since birth, always feeling responsible for someone, or avoiding a fight, or working to keep my nose clean. I'd never been able to gain such blind devotion for anyone the way Quinn seemed to have for me.

"Are you seriously only nineteen?" I wondered aloud, finding it hard to believe someone could stay that pure for that long.

Quinn flushed and cleared his throat before he scratched his ear. "Actually, I'm twenty-one."

"Huh? But you're a—"

"Yeah." He shrugged and glanced away. "I was held back in school a few years."

For some reason, that reminded me of Aspen, who'd been pushed forward in school. It must really fuck with a person socially to mess with their schooling timetable.

I stared at him with a new set of eyes, and opened my mouth to say shit-knew-what when the door to the bathroom opened.

Ten stumbled inside. A cut on his lip looked like it'd just finished bleeding. His eyes were bloodshot, but he seemed to have sobered quite a bit, because he immediately started apologizing.

"Gamble, man, I am so sor—"

Rage boiled in my bloodstream as I surged to my feet. Winding back my arm, I punched him right in the eye. "You son of a bitch."

He moaned and clutched his face. "Shit," he muttered, bending over and dancing in place as if that would alleviate the pain. "Fuck, man. That hurt." He straightened, clutching his eye.

I pointed my finger at his nose and growled. "If she gets *any grief* because of what you just did, I will never forgive you." Shoving past him, I opened the door to leave, but caught a wide-eyed Hamilton watching us.

"And you." I pointed to him. He gulped and shifted a step back. I still couldn't believe he was twenty-one. Old enough to drink alcohol, or more importantly, serve it. "Do you need a job?"

CHAPTER TWENTY-FIVE

"Only those who will risk going too far can possibly find out how far one can go." - T.S. Eliot

~ASPEN~

THURSDAY NIGHT. Ladies' night. The Forbidden Nightclub was crowded as usual.

After I splashed on a little makeup and slid on my favorite pair of tight pants with tall leather boots and dressy top, I strolled into the club, unable to stay away from my man.

Hugging the edges of the crowd, I kept close to the dark walls, wondering whether he'd be working tables or the bar this evening. I scanned the tables first, until I spotted a server. Noel's roommate stood at one small table pulling some bills from his black waist apron to give a table full of girls their change. I had a bad feeling I knew exactly where he'd gotten the black eye he'd been sporting all week, so I'd never asked Noel about it.

As Ten handed the change back, he leaned in to speak into the ear of one girl. But whatever he said must've been pretty offensive because her mouth dropped open right before she slapped him. He merely grinned, blew her a kiss, and sauntered off.

Shaking my head, I wondered how Noel had ever befriended such a character.

The next waiter I spotted happened to be another student of mine. Another football player too. He must've sensed my gaze because he glanced over as he passed, and nearly tripped over his feet. He gaped a second before stepping toward me.

"D...Dr. Kavanagh," he greeted. Shit. My cover was blown. "Do you need a drink?"

"No, I—" I started before cutting myself off. Great, if I didn't need a half-priced drink on ladies' night then what possible reason did I have for being here? So I opened my mouth to order something—anything—when he nodded his head toward the back of the club. "Noel's working the bar tonight."

My jaw sagged. "I...*excuse me*?" I wrinkled my brow as if I was überly confused. Inside, my nervous system went haywire with panic.

But why in the hell would he automatically tell me where Noel was? He should not know I was here to see Noel.

As if realizing he'd just misspoken, his eyes grew big. "I mean..." He coughed into his hand. I watched the wheels in his brain churn, trying to come up with a cover. "I just meant...my friend, *Noel*, was at the bar...you know, in case you changed your mind and wanted to order anything. You could go up there, no problem, and order something from him...if you wanted...later on."

He had to be the worst liar on the face of the planet. An instant sheen of sweat had already coated his face and his eyes darted as if begging me to believe him. But at least he seemed to know he was caught because he whirled away before I could answer and darted off into the crowd of people.

I stared after him, my heart pounding. He knew. He knew about Noel and me. My flight instincts kicked into gear. I wanted to race toward the door and keep running, because if this guy knew, then who else knew? Noel's roommate knew. More were bound to find out.

I suddenly felt as if I was standing on a ticking time bomb. This was going to end badly. There seemed to be no way around it.

"Hey there, pretty lady?" a voice said to my right, startling me back to the present. "Can I get you a drink?"

I turned slowly, mechanically, to see another waiter approaching. This one had a tattoo on the side of his neck, more running up and down both arms and too many piercings for me to count. I looked at him but really didn't see him. The certainty of my impending doom weighed down on me, and I couldn't breathe so well.

But the waiter merely grinned and snapped his finger as if he recognized me. "You were here a few weeks back, flirting with Gamble, weren't you? He's working the bar tonight." Winding his arm around my waist, he applied the lightest pressure to the base of my spine and urged me forward as he accompanied me to the bar.

He wasn't being pushy, but actually really considerate, so I knew I could back away and escape if I wanted to. The bad part was, I did want to escape. I wasn't sure if I could face Noel just then. My mind was spinning and the object in my purse seemed to heat right through the leather and burn into the side of my leg.

But I let Noel's coworker sweep me along anyway. He bent slightly to talk in my ear. "He's a little crabby tonight, so maybe you can cheer him up for us, huh?"

I wanted to ask why Noel was crabby, but all too soon, there we were, at the bar.

"Yo, Gamble," the man at my side called as he pulled out a barstool and offered me a hand to help me climb up and sit down. Noel's back was to us. He was busy mixing a drink, so he didn't turn immediately. I'd just settled my purse in my lap and straightened my spine on the stool when he finally glanced over.

His coworker leaned one arm on the bar and another loosely around my waist as he shouted over the noise. "Got some orders over here."

Never taking his eyes off me, Noel carried his drink to the bar and set it on the countertop in front of the person who'd ordered it. And then he came directly to us.

"I need two beers from the tap, Corona in a bottle, and a fuzzy navel," the tattooed waiter started.

Noel didn't even give him the time of day. His lips twitched and his eyes brightened into a smile. Finally, he asked, "What're you doing here?"

He looked too pleased to see me for me to start slinging questions about how many people knew about us. Hell, I even forgot about what lay in my purse. I was too thrilled to be in his company again. Our secret stolen time together had been rare this week. A few longing glances across the classroom was all we'd been able to manage.

My body flooded with awareness. I wanted to grab his tight black shirt and drag him to the nearest supply closet to reenact our first time together. From the way his eyes glittered, I had a feeling he was having similar thoughts.

"I came for a drink," I managed to say.

His half smile turned into a full grin. With a wink, he leaned across the bar and in a husky voice said, "Then you came to the right place."

"Hey." His coworker tapped on the top of the bar

between us. "Did you hear me, princess? I said I needed—"

"Heard ya," Noel snapped, but he kept looking at me. Voice dropping again to address me, he said, "Be right back. Don't go anywhere."

He returned with a whole batch of alcohol. "Two house beers, Corona, and a fuzzy navel," he said, setting them in front of his friend. "And a Bud Light Lime for the lovely lady." As he set my drink in front of me, he added with a wink, "On the house."

I took a drink, relishing the way the cool liquid wet my dry throat. Noel stuck around to watch, his gaze dipping to my lips. Knowing how much he liked mouths, I drew my bottom lip in between my teeth and sucked a drop of beer off it.

He lifted his gaze. "Stay till closing," he said, wording it as a half-question, half-demand. "I'm going home with you tonight."

The futility of our situation flooded me again, but I nodded anyway. I just couldn't keep away from him. And I didn't want to.

So I remained until last call, and then I stuck around a little longer. By the time only a handful of customers remained, all four of Noel's coworkers had curiously glanced my way, but none of them ever asked to me leave. I'm fairly certain they all knew exactly why I was here.

Though I'd been excited to spend time with him after he clocked off, I grew worried as I sat there. Did everyone he worked with know about us? We were being too obvious, weren't we? God, how pathetic was this? We knew each other inside and out, had shared more intimacies than I'd ever share with another living soul, and we had to sneak around and hide everything like a pair of pathetic teenagers.

This had to stop.

As if sensing my mood, Noel glanced over. His gaze seemed to see everything inside me, and he started forward just as someone else approached the bar. I could tell by the way his jaw bunched that he gritted his teeth in frustration as he glanced at the middle-aged woman who interrupted us.

"Sorry, ma'am," he told her. "But we're closed."

"That's okay," she answered, slowly and methodically setting her hand on the bar. "I didn't come for a drink."

Warning bells screamed inside my head as I turned more fully toward her and took all of her in. Something about her, from the neat, precise way she dressed to each and every calculated move she made, reminded me of my mother. This woman was a cobra, and she was coiled tight, ready to strike her next victim. When she turned to look directly at Noel's coworker behind the bar, I had to turn and look too. Mr. Lowe, who took World Masterpieces from me with his ever-cheerful, energetic girlfriend stood at the cash register, counting the drawer, with his back to us.

As if he sensed eyes on him—or maybe he'd heard the woman's voice and recognized it—his hands froze in the pile of twenties.

A breath passed before he turned slowly and stared straight at the cobra. Then he locked up tight as if she'd somehow immobilized him and trapped him in her sights. The color drained from his face, and a handful of twenty-dollar bills fluttered from his limp hand, scattering the air as they drifted to the floor.

The look on his face was so familiar to me. I'd seen it too many times in the mirror after I'd been attacked by Zach. Every time I'd wondered to myself, *why did this happen to me, why does the world hate me so much, what have I done to deserve this,* I'd had that very same expression on my face.

Tossing him a conniving smile, the woman murmured, "Hello, Mason."

Directly across the counter from me, I could actually feel Noel stiffen. A glance at his face told me he could sense the unease between Mason and the woman just as thickly as I could. His gaze darted between the two and he looked as if he wanted to jump in and defend his friend, but wasn't sure how...or why.

After taking a large swallow, Mason finally opened his mouth. "Leave," he said softly, except the steel behind that one word sent shivers through me. If I were the woman, I'd have been gone, see you later, bye-bye now.

But she merely smiled as if his hard command amused her. Then she gave away her tell when she blinked, fluttering her eyelashes rapidly. He'd managed to make her nervous.

"I need to talk to you, darling."

Mason's face went from white to green so fast I thought he might vomit all over the floor. "Not interested," he said and bent down to gather the fallen bills, his hands shaking enough to make him fumble.

Growing impatient with him, the woman leaned over the counter. "Don't you want to know what I have to say? I came all this way just to see you."

"I don't care what you have to say," he growled, still scrambling to collect all the cash he'd dropped. "I just want you gone. Forever."

She narrowed her eyes and ground her teeth. She didn't like being ignored...just like my mother.

Noel bent down and helped Mason pick up the money. I couldn't hear what he said, but he murmured something, and Mason nodded his head in return. About as soon as he did, Noel bobbed back upright, straightening and spinning to send the woman a pleasant smile.

"So, like I said," he started again, "the bar's closed. If you could leave now—"

"I'm not leaving until I talk to Mason."

Noel's smile fell and his jaw bulged again. "Well, he doesn't want to talk to you, so...get lost."

She glared, a sound of repugnance hissing from her nostrils before she turned back to watch Mason stand and ease the twenties back into the cash drawer.

"He doesn't know what you are, does he?" she called past Noel's shoulder. "I doubt anyone in this room knows what you've done." She turned to glance at all the other guys who'd worked ladies' night. They were the only people left now. She and I were the last two remaining customers. All the boys who'd played waiter and were wandering around the floor, picking up trash and sweeping, paused what they were doing, their attention on her.

Having gained her audience, the evil woman laughed and turned back to Mason. "I bet they'd be very interested to know how you *used* to make your money."

Mason slapped the cash register closed, making me jump. He whirled around to glare daggers at his visitor. "What the fuck do you want?"

Pleasure bloomed across her face. In a mellow voice, she murmured, "I told you; I need to talk to you."

"Then say whatever you're dying to tell me and go away," he growled. "And never come back again."

She glanced at Noel and then me before tactfully licking her lips. "I think you'd rather hear this in private."

He laughed, hard and short. "So not happening."

"Fine." She tossed her hair and gave a brittle smile. "Since you're forcing me to speak out among your friends, then I will. I'm pregnant. And you're the father." She took a step back from the bar and untied the sash on her coat to let it fall open, revealing the bulging waistline under her blouse.

CHAPTER TWENTY-SIX

"Man may have discovered fire, but women discovered how to play with it." -Candace Bushnell

~NOEL~

WELL, FUCK. IT WAS NEVER a dull night at Forbidden, but usually the action happened *during* hours, not after.

After Lowe's cougar friend dropped her little bomb, Mason stared at her as if frozen for a good five seconds before he turned away and disappeared down the hall without saying a word.

The woman moved to follow him, but I growled, "Don't even think about it."

"Dude." Ten appeared at Aspen's side. "Doesn't he have a girlfriend he moved all the way from Florida to be with?"

I sent my roommate a shut-it scowl and turned back to Mason's...problem, who wouldn't stop glaring at me. "Well, you heard the man," I told her. "He said to say your piece and get out, so...time to go, lady."

I had tried being polite with her, but that hadn't worked. So I didn't mind being direct. Hell, I was eager to get downright rude to this...person. She left a nasty aftertaste in my mouth for some reason. Maybe it was because she looked at me as everyone from my hometown had always looked at me. Like I was trash.

"Did you not hear what I just told him? We need to discuss this...together."

I chuckled. "Honey, if he'd wanted to discuss anything with you, he would have. But he didn't. So go."

When she didn't budge, I stared her hard in the eye and called out to Ham, "Yo, Quinn. Escort this *fine* lady to the door, would you?" The virgin needed a nasty task for his first night on the job.

Lowe's problem was too busy killing me with her glare to notice the way Ham jumped and widened his eyes as if he wanted to piss his pants rather than go anywhere near her. But he calmed himself just in time to scare the shit out of the bitch. She spun around when he approached and yelped out a sound as the six-foot-six, two-hundred-forty-five-pound receiver made eye contact with her. She didn't need to know he was as harmless as a kitten. His size was as intimidating as his gravelly voice when he said, "This way."

She hopped into gear without complaint and was out of the club in moments.

After the door closed and silence descended in the bar, I glanced toward Aspen. She lifted her face, and we shared a look as if to say—

"Well, shit," Ten exploded. "Guess Lowe isn't as devoted to that girlfriend of his as he pretended to be."

I sighed and shook my head. "I wouldn't go making assumptions about something we know nothing about."

"Was it just me, or did that woman creep anyone else out?" Quinn asked, appearing on the other side of Aspen at the bar. Shivering, he rubbed his arms and glanced back toward the front door as if to make sure all the evil was gone.

"I thought she was kind of hot," Ten said and wiggled his brows. "Don't blame Lowe for bumping uglies with a cougar like that. I'd certainly bang her."

At the word cougar, I explicitly remembered Lowe saying he didn't like cougars. At all. Eyebrows furrowing, I frowned, utterly confused about what had just happened.

"Well, he's puking his guts out," Pick announced, strolling out of the back hall. I guess he'd gone back to check on Lowe. "Impending fatherhood must not suit him."

Aspen let out a breath and opened her mouth as if she was going to say something, but then she closed her lips and remained silent. I sliced her a glance. "What?"

With a small shake of her head, she sent me a tight smile. "Nothing."

I knew it wasn't nothing and studied her a second longer, but a ringing by the cash register interrupted the quiet room.

"Is that Lowe's phone?" Ten asked.

The five of us in the bar shared a glance. I think we all knew the ringing of his cell phone couldn't be good news. Since no one else was budging, I stepped forward and glanced at the lit screen as it continued to chime. The picture of a girl with long, silky brown hair and a nose ring peered up at me with a cute, carefree smile. The name under her picture read Reese.

"It's Reese," I said, wondering if—

"That's his girlfriend's name," Pick answered, confirming my suspicions.

Shit.

"Should we answer it for him?" Quinn was the

first to ask.

I spread my arms. "And say what? Sorry, but your man can't come to the phone right now; he just found out he's going to be a daddy...to another woman."

Ham winced and shut his mouth. I glanced at Aspen. She lifted her brows as if telling me she'd support any decision I made. But I didn't answer the phone, and it finally fell silent. The room exhaled a collective breath of relief.

Until the phone started ringing again.

"I have a feeling she's going to keep calling," Pick said. "She must know something's up."

Damn it. I glanced toward Aspen again. Her steady green gaze gave me the boost I needed to pick up the phone. I pushed *Accept*, still wondering what to say to Lowe's woman, when Ten shouted, "Shit! Are you really going to tell her some *old* chick just came in, claiming Lowe knocked her up?"

"Say *what?*" a girl's voice screeched from the other end of the line.

Double shit. Panicking, I punched the *End Call* button and glared at my roommate.

"You moron," Pick exploded, slapping Ten on the back of the head. "He'd already answered the phone; she probably heard everything you said."

"Oh...fuck." Ten hunkered his shoulders and sent me an apologetic cringe. "My bad."

"You mean, *Lowe's* bad," I muttered. "Damn it." I shouldn't have tried to answer the phone.

When it rang again, I jumped, set it back where I'd found it, then lifted my hands and backed away slowly. Lowe was going to kill me for this.

Mason didn't return to the bar until after the phone had stopped again. No one had seemingly moved, so when he exited the back hall, rubbing his face, we all turned to stare. He was busy wiping the back of his hand across his mouth and didn't immediately notice all the attention until he glanced up.

When he caught us gawking, however, he jerked to a stop and dropped his arm.

His face was still pale and his skin looked damp as if he'd sweated out a bucket of anxiety. "What?" he croaked, his eyes darting fearfully to each of us. "Jesus, she's not gone, is she?"

"Um," I started and tossed him an apologetic grimace. "No, *she's* gone, but...uh, we might've just...accidentally told your girlfriend what happened." When he merely blinked, I cleared my throat. "Your phone rang...and then it rang again. I was only going to let her know you were away for a minute, but...yeah...sorry, man."

Lowe dashed around the counter to swipe up his phone. After fumbling in his haste to dial, he pressed it to his ear. "Reese?"

"Let me guess," a muffled female voice spoke from the entrance of the club. "Mrs. Garrison just showed up to announce you'd put a baby in her."

I lifted my face to see the picture of the girl off Lowe's phone step inside Forbidden, followed by a blonde, who was also very pregnant.

Damn, how many women had Lowe put a baby in?

Dropping his phone to his side, Lowe let out a lengthy sigh. "Yeah. Pretty much."

After a quick glance between the two, I decided Lowe wasn't going to get beaten to a bloody pulp for his transgressions. He looked like shit with his apologetic puppy dog eyes and his expression a mask of shame and regret. But other than the tensing of her jaw, his girl didn't look like she wanted to kill him.

I glanced at Aspen, wondering what she'd do if we found ourselves in the same predicament. Though we kind of already had, hadn't we, when she'd assumed Caroline had been one of my party girls. And no...no, she hadn't been very forgiving. Lowe's Reese looked pissed, but she remained rational.

"I had a feeling we hadn't gotten rid of her so easily." Reese stormed forward, her pregnant friend trailing behind her. Stopping next to Quinn, she set her hands on the countertop and let out a world-weary sigh. "I say, if a stake through the heart doesn't work, we try cutting her head off."

While everyone else gaped at her as if she'd lost it, Lowe actually laughed. He approached and took her hands in his so he could lift them to his mouth and kiss them reverently. Falling serious, he said, "I am so...so sorry."

Tears glistened in her eyes, but she tried to shrug it off. "Hey, if there isn't some insurmountable obstacle in our path, we wouldn't be us, would we?"

Lowe shook his head and kept her hands by his mouth. "You shouldn't have to deal with this," he said and drew in a deep shaky breath. "You shouldn't—"

"I think she was lying," the pregnant blonde spoke up, breaking him off. After tossing her hair over her shoulder, she slid onto the stool next to Reese and reached for bowl of beer nuts, but Pick snagged them away before she could reach them.

When she sliced him a dirty look, he merely winked. "Let me get you a fresh batch, Tinker Bell. Who knows what kind of filthy fingers have been in these all night."

Her mouth fell open as she watched him jump over the bar and toss the old bowl, only to pull up the box and sprinkle out a new pile, just for her. Then he slid it toward her with an indulgent smile.

"I'm inclined to agree with her," Aspen spoke up, startling me.

I turned, curious about her input. "What do you mean?"

"I mean, I think she was lying, too."

"Exactly," the pregnant blonde cried, lifting her hand in a thank-you gesture to Aspen. Her mouth was muffled by nuts as she added, "I mean, hello, she'd have to be nearly as far along as I am, right? Everyone I needed to tell about my baby was told *months* ago. Why would she wait this long to drop the bomb *now*?"

Reese zipped her gaze to Lowe, her eyes sparkling with hope. "Eva has a good point. And what about her fiancé? How does she know it's not *his*?"

Lowe pulled his bottom lip in between his teeth, looking thoughtful. "Maybe it took her a while to find me."

"Yeah, right." Reese snorted. "You know, good and well, that bitch has known every step you've made since leaving Waterford. She found out everything there was to know about me within a month. There's no way she lost track of *you*."

"So wait, wait, wait." Ten waved his hands. "Lowe, you seriously fucked another woman, maybe even knocked her up, and you..." He set his gaze on Reese, "aren't pissed as hell right now?"

"Oh, I'm pissed," Reese was adamant to claim. "But not at Mason. Besides, this particular...event happened before we hooked up." Then she cleared her throat and lowered her face before mumbling, "Technically."

Lowe winced and reached out to run his hand over her hair before leaning over the bar to kiss her temple. "I can't believe this is happening. You are the only person I've ever wanted to have babies with. Jesus, Reese..." He squeezed his eyes closed and pressed his brow to hers. "Can't we just rewind everything so I can go back do it right the first time?"

I glanced at Aspen because, hell, seeing Reese and Mason's connection simply drew me to her, wanting a taste of the same bond they shared.

She glanced at me as if she felt the same pull. Her eyes glittered with tears. Then she turned back to the grieving couple. "I've had a lot of experience with people like this...Mrs. Garrison, is it?"

Reese turned toward Aspen, wiping her wet

cheeks. "That's right."

"Right," Aspen murmured on a soft note. "And I've come to learn they give away certain *tells* when they're lying. Each person's may be different, but they always do something to denote the lie. And from her behavior, I don't even believe she was pregnant, much less honest about the child's paternity."

Lowe blew out a relieved breath. "Really?"

She shook her head.

"But her fucking belly was out to here." Ten held out his hand and pretended to waddle. Next to him, Ham nodded, thinking the cougar had looked pregnant too.

"It wasn't shaped quite right, though," Aspen insisted. She pointed at the blonde. "Her stomach looks almost perfectly round, while the other woman's was more...oblong."

Propping his elbows on the bar, Pick leaned over the counter to check out the blonde's belly. "You do have the most adorable baby bump I've ever seen."

"And the other woman's breasts didn't look nearly as swollen as hers," Aspen went on.

Pick snorted. "I'd say."

The blonde shot him a glare. "Who the hell are you, anyway?"

He grinned at her. "Pick."

She blinked. "Pick what? I'm not picking out your name."

"No, that's my name, Tinker Bell. Pick, short for Patrick Jason Ryan. You like?"

"Anyway." Aspen lifted her voice to speak over Pick's strange flirting with the preggo. "She didn't have any of the water retention this girl has in her face."

The preggo gasped, grasping her cheeks as she whirled to Reese. "I have water retention?"

"What? *No!* No, sweetie. Barely any at all."

"So I *do* then?"

Gritting her teeth, Reese sent Aspen a scowl. I thought I was going to have to jump over the bar to defend her, but the front door opened again.

Mrs. Garrison had returned.

"Hamilton," I growled. "Go lock the fucking door before someone else wanders in here, will you?"

If Jessie learned we had this many non-employees in the building after hours, she'd flip. But then, I guess she wouldn't have to worry about it so much if she bothered to come in once in a while. She could deal with this scene instead of leaving it to us to handle.

"Anyone have a hatchet handy?" Reese growled, stepping away from the bar to face off with Mrs. Garrison. "Because I'm feeling the compelling need to hack a bitch."

"Dude." Ten bumped his elbow into Hamilton's, looking jazzed as he bounced on the toes of his feet. "Chick fight. Awesome."

Lowe hurtled the bar and was at his woman's side in a microsecond. Wrapping an arm around her waist, he tugged her back against his chest as he glared at the newest arrival. "I told you not to come back. And I made it crystal clear before I even left Florida that I never wanted anything to do with you again. Why are you doing this?"

She ignored him, smiling almost pleasantly at Reese...almost being the key word because there was nothing pleasant about the glitter in her eyes. "Reese," she murmured, nodding her head in acknowledgement. "It's been too long since I last saw you."

"I know, hasn't it?" Reese answered with the same fake pleasantry before she sneered. "My hand's stopped ringing from the last time I bitch-slapped the shit out of you."

"Ohh!" Ten cried, smacking his knee and hooting. *"Burn."*

Mrs. Garrison narrowed her eyes. "You need to

release him, dear. He doesn't belong here."

Reese cracked off a laugh. "Me? Release *him*? Are you kidding me? You're the one who—"

Lowe covered her mouth with his hand, muffling her words. "We're not getting into this," he told the old crow. "The only person who needs to leave Illinois is you."

Mrs. Garrison's voice broke as she asked, "But what about our baby?" just as her lashes did their fluttering thing.

Visibly shuddering, he shook his head. "You're not even pregnant. I don't know why you're making up this lie or what you think it'll accomplish, but nothing you can do will get me to leave my life here or split me away from Reese."

"Oh, I can guess why she's doing it." Reese pulled Lowe's hand off her mouth. "I bet her fiancé left her, and she had no one left to torture."

By the way the older woman glared, I figured Reese must've hit the nail on the head.

"If I'm not pregnant, then how do you explain this?" Again, she made a dramatic performance of ripping open her coat and showing off her stomach.

"Oh, please." The blonde Reese had called Eva laughed. "That's the fakest pregnant belly I've ever seen."

When Mrs. Garrison pierced her with a frown, she pooched out her own stomach. "This is the real deal, honey. So why don't you stop picking on Mason and my cousin Reese, crawl back home to Florida, and find someone new to harass. In fact, look up Madeline and Shaw Mercer why don't you? They actually *deserve* your brand of attention."

The woman merely sniffed at her. "I should've guessed you were Reese's snooty little Mercer cousin. Eva, isn't it? The one who tried to trap Alec Worthington into marriage by getting herself knocked up—"

"Okay, that's enough," Reese snapped. "Why are you still here? No one wants you."

"And no one believes you either," Lowe added.

"So, you're really going to bank on the chance that this bump might be fake?" Mrs. Garrison lovingly rubbed her belly. "Are you sure you can live with the uncertainty of knowing whether you have a child out there or not?"

Lowe's eyes grew tormented. He tugged his girl in closer to his chest. Reese impressed the fuck out of me when she rubbed his arm soothingly. It made me wonder what would happen if I were ever put into this situation. After nearly raising Caroline, Brandt, and Colton, I knew I could never turn my back on the likelihood of being a father. But now that Aspen was in my life, it'd kill me think of having anyone else's child.

Realizing what I'd just thought, I sliced her a startled glance. But had I really just—? Did this mean I wanted no one's babies but hers? Whoa. I think I had just thought that.

That was whacked out.

"Hey, I'll volunteer to find out if the bump's real." When Ten rubbed his hands together with a leering grin and took a step toward Mrs. Garrison, she yelped and hopped away from him, raising her finger threateningly.

"Come near me, and I'll call battery so fast your head will spin. No one touches me."

"Then I'm not convinced you're pregnant." Lowe nestled his face against Reese's, seemingly emboldened by her presence. His skin tone was no longer ashen, and now he looked more pissed than scared.

"It's a boy," the persistent woman went on. "I bet he'll have your eyes and your beautiful hair. I'm thinking of the name Christopher Mason."

When Lowe once again went sheet white, I decided I'd had enough. Someone needed to take control of this situation and nip it in the bud.

"Stop already," I said, glaring down Mrs. Garrison.

"You've already gone too far," Aspen added, slipping off her stool and opening her purse. "Because this is one lie you can't support. We can stand around here, bantering all night and accomplishing nothing. Or we can prove whether you're telling the truth within minutes." Pulling a small brown paper bag out of her purse, she opened the end and extracted a box. When I squinted to focus on it, I realized it was a home pregnancy test.

What the—?

Stunned speechless, I gaped at it, my mouth dropping toward the floor. Lifting my gaze, I met Aspen's apologetic cringe just as Ten exploded, "Shit, Gamble. You knocked up *Dr. Kavanagh*?"

CHAPTER TWENTY-SEVEN

"With enough courage, you can do without a reputation." - Margaret Mitchell, *Gone with the Wind*

~ASPEN~

NOEL WOULDN'T STOP staring. Unable to answer the blaring question in his eyes, I turned toward Mason and Reese. "Here. Get your answers."

They looked about as shocked as Noel did, though. Finally, Reese shook her head as if to clear it and slipped the box from my hand. "Thanks." Her jaw setting with determination, she faced the woman who was too freakily like my mother. "Well, alright then. Where's the bathroom in this place?"

"I'm not taking that thing." Mrs. Garrison took a horrified step back.

"Yes, you are," Mason said, his voice determined and hard. When she looked as if she was going to object, he smirked. "I'll tell you what. You take that test, and if it comes out positive, I'll go with you right now."

"Excuse me?" Reese spun to gape up at him. He clasped her shoulder as if begging her to trust him.

"But if you refuse, I want you to leave and never enter this state again."

A moment of indecision crossed the older woman's face, but she finally nodded.

"Okay, then," Reese said. "I'm watching every step you make until this is over."

"You're not going with her," Lowe insisted at the same moment Mrs. Garrison bristled and said, "You're not coming with me."

"I'll go." Eva, the true pregnant woman, raised her hand.

But Pick grasped her elbow. "I don't think so, Tinker Bell. If Lowe doesn't trust his woman alone with that broad, then you sure as hell aren't going near her. Not in your condition."

I had a feeling Mrs. Garrison would try to trick Eva into peeing on the stick for her. So, I drew in a deep breath and took matters into my own hands. "Give me the box." When Reese readily handed it over, I glanced at Mrs. Garrison. "This way."

"And who do you think you are?" she sneered, not moving.

"She's *Dr.* Kavanagh," Reese answered for me, emphasizing the doctor part as if she wanted Mrs. Garrison to think I was a medical doctor, not an academic one.

Mrs. Garrison merely narrowed her eyes. "Well, isn't that nice?"

"Pleasantly so." Well acquainted with how to treat her kind, I gave a stoic nod, demonstrating my stiff indifference. "Now, shall we?" I turned away, not waiting for her and not surprised when I heard her fall into step behind me. "Mr. Gamble," I called, notching my chin high. "Would you please escort us?"

He was out from behind the bar before I could blink, taking my elbow gently. Without saying a word, he directed us into the hallway. No one else followed. We were halfway down the dark corridor before he leaned in close and whispered into my ear. "We are so going to talk about this."

I nodded. "It's the reason I came to see you tonight."

He blew out a long breath. "Shit. Do you really think you're—"

"I hope you don't expect me to pee on a stick in front of you, *Doctor*?" The grating voice behind us caused Noel to dig his fingers a little deeper into my arm. I could tell he was about to say something degrading, so I quickly spoke up.

"Oh, you won't be going near the stick. But I do think you can handle the rest on your own." I paused in front of the bathroom door and held out a cup I'd swiped off the bar. "All we need is a sample."

Mrs. Garrison glared at the cup a moment before snatching it from my hand. Then she threw it against the wall, seething. As the cup shattered, she demanded, "Where's the fucking back door in this place?"

Noel just chuckled. "Sorry, we don't have one."

She glared at him for a moment before spinning away and stalking off.

Sharing a glance with Noel, I lifted my eyebrows. "Well, I guess she *was* bluffing."

He looped an arm around my waist and kissed my hair. "She might not be pregnant, but what're the odds that *you're* not?"

When his hand settled low on my stomach, a wash of heat spread through me. "I...I'm not sure. I'm only a few days late, but..."

"The closet," he said. "No protection. I remember."

"Yeah." I closed my eyes and breathed through

my teeth. "I've never been regular. So it might not mean anything. I just...needed to know."

Noel cradled me close, burying his face in my neck. "It's strange. But I'm not nearly as freaked out as I thought I'd be."

I lifted my face as his fingers lightly traced my jaw. "What're you saying?"

"I'm saying if you are, it'll be okay. Maybe better than okay. A little premature, but I'd be...okay with this."

My breath caught in my chest. But had he just told me he actually *wanted* to have babies with me? I didn't know how to answer. An immediate joy bubbled in my chest just knowing he felt that way, but I knew the idea of a baby right now would be bad. Worse than bad.

And yet...a part of me wanted it to be true, wanted Noel and me to stay together and make a family. Someone to love and love me in return.

"So," Noel prodded, catching my chin and lifting my face until I was forced to look at him. "Would *you* be okay with it?"

I opened my mouth, but I still wasn't sure how to respond. My initial gut instinct was to scream yes and jump into his arm so we could hug and live happily ever after. But every time I tried to picture our future, it just looked doomed.

"Dr. Kavanagh!" Reese Randall's ecstatic voice hurtled down the hall before she raced to us and hugged me tight. "You did it. You were right. She was totally lying. Oh, my God. Thank you."

I was too startled by the contact to hug her back before she was pulling away and pushing her hair out of her face. "I don't think we could've handled that so diplomatically without you. You're such a lifesaver. Oh, and thanks for, you know, going along with me when I made it sound like you were a medical doctor."

"Not a problem," I told her, trying to sound

gracious and teacherly, even though I totally ruined it by grinning and adding, "It was kind of fun." There was just something eternally perky about Miss Randall; she always filled my World Masterpieces class with a cheerful vivacity and drew out the carefree goofball in me.

But then she completely killed my glow by leaning in to whisper, "And good luck on your own test, however you want it to go." When she glanced conspicuously toward Noel, I realized she knew... *everyone* here knew he and I were together.

And Noel didn't help the situation in the least when he walked me out of the hall a minute later, calling across the bar to his roommate that he didn't need a ride home while he proprietarily set his hand at the small of my back to lead me toward the exit.

Mr. Hamilton waving us goodbye and politely calling, "Good night, Noel. Night, Dr. Kavanagh," only made the situation worse.

If I ended up being pregnant, everyone would know my student was the father.

***

"You don't love someone because of their looks or their clothes or their car. You love them because they sing a song only your heart can understand." - L.J. Smith

***

"So why do you think she did it?"

Biting my bottom lip, I pulled out of the parking lot of Forbidden. In the passenger seat, Noel nervously drummed his fingers on his knee. He did that a lot when he wasn't quite comfortable. Well, I wasn't exactly ready to put on my fuzzy, bunny slippers and curl up with a good book myself.

After the anticlimactic departure of Mrs. Garrison from Forbidden, I was ready to move past that scene though, while Noel obviously was not.

"I mean, what the hell?" He glanced across the interior of my car toward me. "I don't get it. The woman came all the way from Florida to tell Lowe a lie he would've caught on to eventually. Why even bother?"

I focused on his question because I didn't like thinking about how perilously public our relationship was becoming, and that was the only thing zooming through my mind right now.

"Women like her use whatever they can to manipulate people," I told him. "She knows she's a quick thinker. Maybe she was hoping Mason would blindly follow her back to Florida so she could bank on the chance she could come up with something else to use against him to keep him there."

Noel snorted. "Yeah, but...why go through all that trouble for someone who wants nothing to do with you?"

I shrugged, picturing my mother. "It's all about control. She thrives on managing the people in her life. And every little thing they do."

"I like control," he argued. "I'm the freaking quarterback of my team, and I consider myself the head of my family. Hell, I've practically taken over at Forbidden. But I've never—"

Reaching out, I set my hand on his to stop his drumming fingers. "That's because you know the difference between leadership and dictatorship. And you have a rational functioning brain. She does not. I doubt either of us could understand the way she thinks. She's gotten so used to manipulating, blackmailing, and doing whatever she wants to get her way, she has this whole ego trip going on and thinks she can't fail at anything. In her own mind, she's invincible."

Turning his hand over so our palms were facing, he laced our fingers together and gave a warm squeeze. "You sound like you have some experience with people like her."

I nodded and paused at a four-way. "I do. Mrs. Garrison is the spitting image of my mother. I know her type well."

He brought my knuckles up to his mouth to kiss them. "I knew there was a reason I already didn't like your mother." Then he changed gears, holding up the bag containing my pregnancy test and shaking it. "You're still taking this when we get home, right?"

A rush of air exited my lungs. "Of course."

His fingers returned to tapping. Silence filled the car. I was actually tempted to reach out and turn on the radio to kill the tension.

"So, tonight kind of turned into baby-palooza, huh?" Noel glanced over and sent me an unreadable look. "I mean, what with that lady coming in to harass Lowe, then the chick with his girlfriend who really was pregnant. My sister's knocked up. And now you..."

When his eyes revealed just how nervous he was, I realized that was why he'd been rambling about Lowe's problems. He'd been afraid to bring up the real issue.

Us.

"I'm probably not," I tried to reassure him. "Like I said, I've never been regular. But it's been long enough to get some accurate results, so—"

"No, it's fine," he told me. "I get it. And I'm with you one hundred percent. I don't want to wait to find out. I want to know tonight."

I nodded and pulled into my drive. After I killed the car, we both continued to sit there, facing forward without moving, until Noel burst out, "Okay, is it totally weird that I'm completely turned on right now?"

I twisted to gape at him. "What?"

He turned to me, too. "I can't stop thinking about it." He reached out and touched my shoulder tentatively before his fingers slid down my arm. "What if a part of me is growing in there? In you? I feel like I branded you, like we're just so explosively amazing together, a whole new life form developed to contain the overflow." His touch scaled my abdomen before pressing lightly. "It's so fucking hot. We could've just created art together, Aspen. A masterpiece."

Leaning across the center console, he nipped at my mouth and then slid his tongue inside. The kiss started warm and slow, but it didn't take long to gain heat and fervor. Before I knew it, we were both panting and straining across the front seat to reach for more of each other.

"I can't wait." He peeled my shirt up over my head and flung it into the backseat before grasping my waist and hauling me into his lap. "Get over here, woman."

"But what about—" We were still in my car, the front steps were only a few feet away. It was dark, yeah, but still...anyone could walk by and see.

"I don't care," he rasped, pushing down the cups of my bra. "I need you. Now."

When he sucked one of my aching nipples into his mouth, it rendered me brain dead from thereon out, and suddenly, I didn't care either. I cupped his head and gathered fistfuls of his hair into my hands as I rode his erection through our clothes. The suction he had on me seemed to tug on a nerve linked directly to the bundled core between my legs because it lit me up until I was writhing against him, begging him as I fumbled between him to tear open the fly of his jeans.

Pulling him into my hand, I pumped him, loving the feel of velvet over steel. His mouth popped free of my nipple so he could groan and slam his skull back against the seat's headrest.

"Damn, that feels good." He jerked his hips up, letting me know he wanted more. I squeezed harder and went faster. "Yes," he hissed, bowing his head forward and straining. But just as quickly, he grabbed my hand and pulled me away. "Wait. I want to come inside you."

Getting my pants off was quite a trick. We both fumbled clumsily, he cursed in frustration, and I had to throw my head back to laugh over the silliness of it. But as soon as they were out of the way and smacked against the driver's side window, Noel grasped my hips and led my body where he needed me.

Since my legs draped over his, he spread his own knees as far as he could in the confines of the seat so he could in effect spread *me* apart. Then he yanked me down and impaled me. The shock of it caused me to gasp. The muscles inside me clenched around him, needing something to hold on to, to ground me to this moment so I couldn't just float away.

"God damn." His fingers bit into my hips and he yanked me up, only to jerk me back down. It was just as filling as his first thrust. I bit my lip and gripped his shoulders, hanging on for dear life. "I love this," he panted. "I fucking love being inside you." His breathing was rough and eyes hooded as he met my gaze. "You're so gorgeous. Jesus, Aspen." He pressed his forehead to mine. "Nothing should be this good. I don't want it to end."

The literature professor in me immediately had a Robert Frost moment. *Nothing gold can stay.* Well, Noel Gamble was the golden pot of happily ever after at the end of my rainbow. Did that make him my fleeting glimpse of joy? My gold that could not stay?

His fingers found my bare, flat stomach as if seeking our child. What if there *was* a baby in there? What if he'd planted a piece of forever inside me? A piece of our legacy could survive from generation to generation. Maybe our gold *could* stay.

My body turned to liquid fire as he took me straight to the peak without mercy, driving me straight over the edge and into ecstasy. We came together, kissing and touching, united in more ways than I could probably count. As I curled into him and he buried his face in my hair, holding me close, the only thing I could think was, *Please don't let this end yet. Just a little longer.*

***

So, I peed on the stick.

After what had just happened in the car, my knees were already too wobbly to walk straight. Noel had always been an intense lover, but this time he'd left me rattled. But it must've affected him too because he didn't want to stop touching me.

Once we'd found all our clothes and gotten decent enough to dash inside without being caught *in flagrante delicto* by the neighbors, he'd taken my hand and hadn't let go. He wouldn't even let me into the bathroom by myself, which was a bit too personal for me. I shooed him out. But as soon as I finished, he opened the door, popping his head inside, embarrassing the heck out of me because just knowing he'd listened to me was awkward.

"Anything yet?" he asked, stepping close and smoothing his hand down my arm as he glanced at the test strip.

I shook my head. We fell quiet, staring at the stick. Another thirty seconds passed and finally a line began to appear.

Noel squeezed my bicep. "Here we go."

I held my breath, waiting, hoping. No second line appeared. My shoulders fell limp.

Noel lifted his gaze, his blue eyes probing. "This means it's negative, right?"

I nodded, unable to speak a single word. My throat closed over, going instantly dry. I tried to clear it delicately, but it didn't help.

"Well." He blew out a long breath, stared at the wall over my shoulder, then raked his hand through his hair before setting it on his hip. "Shit."

I lifted my face, surprised to hear him say that. Had he actually *wanted* it to be positive? Oh, my God. Had *I*? I'd been so hopeful. I thought negative was the result I'd been hoping for. But I felt so disappointed now that it was the result I'd gotten.

"I guess...I guess we just dodged a bullet there," he said, only to wince and glance away.

Unable to handle knowing he'd wanted it as badly as I had, I pushed past him, escaping the bathroom. "Aspen? What...?"

I rushed down the hall, needing space. Everything inside me felt like it was going to come out. But once I reached the front room, I realized this wasn't where I wanted to be. I wanted to be back in that car, on Noel's lap, holding on tight to my chunk of gold.

Tears burned the backs of my eyes but I refused to cry. I sat blindly on the armrest of my couch and grabbed the back cushions for support. My throat squeezed shut; I probably should've gotten myself a drink, but I just sat there.

I felt as if I'd just lost a child, when in actuality I'd avoided a complete disaster.

"Aspen?" Noel appeared cautiously in the opening of the hallway, where he stopped as if afraid to come closer.

I looked up at him and shook my head, "What were we thinking? If I'd been pregnant, that would've been it. The secret would've come out. You would've been kicked out of school. I would've lost my job. Your siblings...your siblings...Why were we in any way *hopeful* for this?"

Noel stepped forward, paused, then stepped forward again. Kneeling in front of me, he took my hands and lifted them to his mouth to softly kiss my knuckles. "Because we wanted to create proof of how amazing we are together. We wanted a living legacy of our bond."

His words were the absolute truth. I had wanted something tangible and real that was half me and half him. I'd ached for it, needing to make us as permanent as possible.

"But it's the most irresponsible thing we could've done. This has gotten completely out of hand. We forgot protection again, just now, in the car. And we're letting way too many people know about us. Damn it, everyone in the bar tonight *knew* we were together. And now they know we're risky enough to possibly get pregnant. Hell, four of them were even *students* of mine."

Noel winced. "If it's any consolation, I'm fairly certain we can trust all of them."

Fairly certain? I closed my eyes and bowed my head. Jesus, wasn't that just great. "It's too dangerous. Too reckless. We need to be rational."

He groaned and pressed his forehead to our clasped hands. "I hate it when you're rational; you always try to leave me when you're rational."

With a harsh laugh, I yanked my hands out of his grasp. "Because it's the smart thing to do, Noel. My God, do you not realize how much we lose control when we're around each other, how much we put at risk? This is the second time we've gone without any kind of protection, and you said you've never—"

"I know what I said," he snapped irritably as he ran his hand through his hair and pushed to his feet. "And it's not like I mean to forget. It's just...everything with you is different. That's the entire point of all this. If you weren't, if you were just any other girl, we wouldn't have any of these problems. I wouldn't lose my head when you're close, and I wouldn't forget my fucking condoms. But then, we probably wouldn't have to worry about remembering either, because you're my teacher and I would have no problem staying away. But you are *different*. You're more. And that's exactly why it's worth the risk."

"No." I shook my head, even though his words were getting to me. He always knew how to break my restraint. Because he was different too. He was more to me too. "It's not worth it." Since he *was* more, I didn't want him to get hurt.

"Baby." Cupping my face, he came in for a kiss. I knew the moment his mouth touched mine, I'd be a goner. We'd be right back where we started, sucked into the moment and forgetting reality...again. So I dodged away, making him seethe.

Letting me retreat, he blew out a hard breath and dragged his hand through his hair. "Okay," he muttered. "I know tonight freaked you out—"

"It didn't freak me out. It opened my eyes."

He didn't like that answer. His eyes narrowed and his teeth clenched. "Look, I know the chances of us actually making it through this unscathed seem impossible, but—"

"But what? You want to keep plowing forward as we are until we're exposed and everything explodes in our faces?"

Throwing his hands into the air, he shouted, "I don't care about exposure. I care about staying with *you*."

I slammed my fists to my hips. "Well, staying with me isn't good for you."

Noel barked out a laugh. "What the hell ever. You're the *best* thing that's ever happened to me. I had to raise myself with no guidance of how to be a good person, how to build good study habits, how to feel like someone actually cared about what happens to me without me needing to fix all their problems in return, how to depend on someone else. You taught me all that. I *need* you, Aspen. Jesus, you really have no idea what you've done for me in the time we've been together, do you?"

Hugging my waist, I paced across the floor, craving some space before I wavered. "I'm not saying what we had together wasn't...wonderful. But there are other very important things to consider here. Other *people* to consider."

Noel sat on the couch arm I'd just vacated and stared across the floor at me as a dawning horror list his gaze. "What we *had* together?" he repeated slowly.

Everything inside me clenched with dread over what I was about to do. "I think—"

"No." He shot to his feet and stalked toward me. "Don't you dare say it."

I scrambled backward, my eyes widening. But he caught me and clutched my shoulders tight. His eyes commanded me not to say a word. But I did anyway. "We need a break."

"No," he growled. "We started this together, fifty-fifty. We are not ending it unless both of us want out. And I say no."

"Noel." My voice cracked, and his face fell.

"Damn it, Aspen." He dipped his head and came in to kiss me. I set my hand against his chest.

We stared at each other, eye to eye, both of us breathing hard as my little cat clock on the wall with the swishing tail and shifting eyes ticked back and forth, filling the silence.

"Fine." His fingers eased off my arms as he took a step back. But his eyes remained intent, still full of fight. "You take your break. Take however long you want to think about it, or whatever shit you think you need to do. But I'm not. I'm still in this one hundred percent, and I'm not going anywhere until you realize we belong together despite everything there is against us."

Without waiting for me to respond, he marched for the front door and jerked it open. His footsteps pounded on the front porch, growing fainter as he left. Holding my fingers to my lips, I tried not to cry.

Noel cared so much he was going to fight for us no matter what. It made me love him more than ever, which broke my heart even harder.

CHAPTER TWENTY-EIGHT

"Never underestimate a pretty little liar." - Sara Shepard, *Pretty Little Liars*

~ASPEN~

FOUR GRUELING, AWFUL, incredibly long days passed. And I didn't see Noel once. I think he was torturing me on purpose. He knew my willpower was nil. He knew I'd have to see him soon. And honestly, tomorrow—when he walked into my classroom for Early American Literature—couldn't come soon enough. I needed my Noel fix. Now.

I tapped my fingers against my chin, unable to concentrate on my work as I stared longingly at the cell phone I'd set on the corner of my desk. When I started to reach for it, thinking I could send him one little text, just to say hello, I mentally slapped myself and snapped my fingers back to my keyboard.

No. Bad Aspen.

I turned my attention to the screen of my

computer where I was entering scores into the campus's grading system, and couldn't focus on a single thing. I hated entering scores. I might have to go completely paperless just to bypass the monotony of score entering.

The only class so far where I'd decided to go paperless was Noel's. And it was going surprisingly well. After we'd started our relationship, I'd had the students in his class turn in their next essay electronically. That way, I didn't see a name when I read their papers. I just read them as fairly as possible, assigned the score when I was done, and that was that, they were instantly in the system. That part, I loved.

The scary part came when I realized I'd had no idea what letter I'd given my own boyfriend, because I hadn't been able to discern which paper had been his. After I'd finished with everyone in the class, Noel and I had checked his score together. I think I nearly squeezed his fingers off I was so nervous by the time we saw he'd gotten a B.

I almost bawled because I hadn't given him an A like I'd hoped I would. He was the one who'd laughed and pulled me into a hug, telling me it was okay. He was making an overall high C in the class. All he had to do was pull another B in the last essay, and he'd be fine. He'd sounded so sure of himself I had relaxed. But, God, I'd had no idea dating one of my students would put this much stress on my job. When we'd begun this thing, I'd been confident I could separate school and personal life. Except I couldn't. I wanted to give Noel the biggest A possible.

A throat cleared, jerking me from my daydreaming. "Dr. Kavanagh?"

I lifted my face from my computer screen to find a pretty redhead standing in the doorway of my office. She looked familiar, but I wasn't sure where I'd seen her before. Swiveling my chair to face her, I pasted on a smile, always thrilled when a student sought me out. "Yes?"

She bit her lip, looking a little nervous. "I'm Marci Bennett. I'd really like to talk to you about my grade."

"Okay. Come on in." Since I was already in the system, I quickly typed in her name to pull up her file. "You're in World Masterpieces, right?"

"That's right." She stepped inside and shut the door behind her. It caught me off guard because students typically didn't do that when I met with them. Usually, we kept the door open, or I was the one to close it. Only Noel had ever done that to me, which only made me more uneasy about Marci doing it. But I shrugged off my apprehensions and continued to smile.

As soon as she seated herself, her demeanor changed. Her coyness melted away to be replaced by a smug little smirk. Confused by the transformation, I skimmed my gaze over her, taking in the entire picture. Her hair was her one shining feature, but it was so brilliant a red I wondered if she dyed it. Her boobs looked big, but again, they were nothing help from a good bra couldn't make. Most everything about her seemed fake and enhanced.

"So, how can I help you?"

She folded her hands precisely in her lap, reminding me of one of my mother's moves. "Well, for starters, I'd really like an A."

To keep from rolling my eyes, I gave a serious nod. "I see. Well, it looks like you have a C now." I flickered my gaze briefly to my computer, and yep, she was so rocking a C, a C minus at that. "All you have to do is attend all your classes, turn in all your papers, work really hard and raise it two grades, and you'll be set."

Okay, that might've been a bit smarmy of me, but she was giving me a pretty smarmy look herself. The spoiled brat.

"Actually," she said, twirling a piece of a hair around her finger. "That's doesn't work for me, 'cause I'm not planning to attend another one of your classes for the rest of the semester. And I'm sure as hell not writing another one of your damn essays."

Hmm, I'd been wrong. Spoiled brat was actually too mild of a term for this one. I was beginning to think raging bitch might work better. Continuing to smile, I lifted an eyebrow. "And you expect an A for that?"

She flashed me a grin. "Exactly." Then her gaze went serious as she leaned forward. "Oh, and one more thing. I'm going to need you to stop fucking Noel Gamble while you're at it."

I bolted upright in my chair as the blood rushed from my head. "*Excuse me?*"

With a little sniff, she rolled her eyes. "You don't have to play stupid with me, honey. I know everything. You see, Noel turned me down the other week." An aggravated sound gurgled from the back of her throat as she tossed her red locks over her shoulder. "And no one turns me down. I knew something was up then. So...I followed him until I got my proof. And *tada!*"

She drew up her cell phone, turning it to show me the screen. Noel and I were in my car, cozied up in the passenger seat. We hadn't reached the part yet where he'd ripped off my bra, thank God, but it was more than obvious what kind of relationship we had.

Wondering how the heck she'd gotten such a good shot, as dark as it had been and as close up as it was, I zipped my gaze up.

Marci smiled and nodded. "It's time to give me a chance with him now."

Dear God, she *liked* him. She liked *my* man.

Banking on the fact that she didn't want to hurt him, I said, "If you show that picture to anyone, Noel will get into trouble, too. After the scandal on the volleyball team, his coach told all the football players they'd be kicked off the squad if they were caught in a similar situation. And since he's here on his athletic scholarship, he'd have to leave Ellamore completely. Do you really want that to happen to him?"

Marci paused. I prayed I had her bluffed out; I even took a relieved breath. But then she came back with, "Then I guess I'll just have to show them *this* picture."

She used her fingers to scroll to a new image, and I almost threw up.

Noel's face didn't make this shot. It was all me. My bra was gone, and I'd thrown my head back until my hair was spilling down my back with my bare breasts arched out. The only part of my partner was a strong masculine arm wrapping around my back. I was probably in the middle of my orgasm, and...okay, I had to swallow a little bit of vomit there.

But, oh, my God. This was bad. How many pictures did this bitch have?

"No one can tell who he is here because his face is cropped." She sent me a little smirk, which I returned with a silent glare. "But you see...right there." She pointed to his tattoo. "About a dozen other players have that same exact tattoo. So, it's more than obvious you're fucking a current player on the football team, but no one has to know exactly which one."

I kept my expression bland. It was the only thing I could do at a time like this. I mean, sure, I could leap across the table to strangle her to death, and that's what I wanted to do. But that wouldn't help Noel, unless I finally did come up with a way to sneak a dead body out of my office.

Damn it.

After clearing my throat discreetly, I asked, "Did you want that to be a low A or a high A?"

***

"The only way to find true happiness is to risk being completely cut open." - Chuck Palahniuk, *Invisible Monsters*

***

~NOEL~

I decided to give Aspen some time. I know, that made no sense. Whenever she had time to reason things out, she decided against us. But I was banking on the fact she'd miss me.

Because I sure as hell missed her.

"Come on, man. You're killing me here." Ten reached past me where I sat at the table in our dinky kitchen with homework spread across the surface and slammed closed the textbook I was reading. "You've been working or doing homework all fucking weekend. It's driving me batty."

I sent him a glare and reopened my book, muttering under my breath because the bastard had lost my place. "I told you, I need to catch up with this shit. Back the fuck off."

Ten slowly tipped the book shut again, lifting his eyebrows in outright challenge. "You're not doing homework, pussy. You're pouting because she dumped your ass."

Clenching my teeth to keep my temper in check, I ground out, "She did *not* dump me." She'd specifically said the word break. Break meant we'd get back together...eventually. Break meant there was still a chance.

When I opened the book a third time, my roommate snagged it off the table and out of my reach, holding it above his head like some kind of eleven-year-old bully stealing his little sister's doll. "You just keep telling yourself that, bud. But we're still going out tonight."

I slapped the top of the table. "I don't want—"

"Well, I'm starving, and there's no food in the fridge. It was *your* turn to grocery shop. So you're taking me out to eat. I'm craving Guido's."

I shook my head, startled by how specific he was. He never craved one certain place. Hell, the guy never craved one certain type of food. He was one of those vacuums that ate whatever you put in front of him.

"What is this?" I asked. "You asking me on a date?"

He winked and blew me a kiss. "Buy me enough drinks, and you might even get lucky."

With a snort, I gave in and let Ten drag me out of my apartment. I wouldn't admit it to him, but it was nice to get some fresh air. I'd holed myself up in the apartment for too many days, and getting out to breathe for a minute actually helped clear my head.

We found a spot a block down and across the street from Guido's. Still flipping me hell about mooning after Aspen, my roommate bumped his arm into mine, trying to rile me up. But I ignored him for the most part.

Not until he breathed, "Oh, shit," did I look up and catch how wide his eyes had gone.

"What?" I began to turn to see what he was staring at, but he caught my arm. "Nothing. I changed my mind. Guido's sucks. Let's get some Mexican or something instead."

I rolled my eyes. How much more obvious could a guy get. I turned again. When he physically tried to bar me from looking, I shoved him back and faced the little Italian joint.

And there she was.

Across the street, in front of a wide, open glass window at a table for two, sat Aspen. In Guido's. With

Dr. Chaplain. On what looked like a fucking date.

"Motherfucker." When I stepped off the curb to cross to her side, Tenning grabbed my arm.

"Whoa, man. What do you think you're doing?"

My jaw set. I couldn't look away from *my* woman as she took a drink from a wineglass and smiled at something the douche across the table from her had just said. What did she think *she* was doing? That was the question.

"I'm going over there," I told Ten. But he jerked me back, pissing me off something major.

"Are you nuts? If you go over there and create a scene like some kind of *jealous ex-boyfriend*, people are going to realize you're actually a jealous ex-boyfriend. Do you *want* to get kicked off the team? Do you want her to lose her job?"

I snapped a hard glare at him. He lifted his brows, and I cursed under my breath. "Damn it." Digging my phone out of my pocket, I did the next best thing. I called her.

I could tell the moment her end of the line started ringing. She went stiff and her *date* made a gesture, probably telling her it was okay if she answered. But she shook her head. I ground my teeth. When it went to voice mail, I growled. "I see you. I see who you're with. And I don't like it. How is being with an *engaged* man so much better than dating a student?"

After leaving that message, I instantly dialed her number again. This time, she apologized and leaned down to check the ID. When she saw it was from me, she set her phone back in her purse. I could read her lips as she told him it was no one important.

Acid ate through my stomach. "No one important, huh?" I snorted and had to glance away because it suddenly hurt too much to look at her. "You told him I was no one important? Thanks. Thanks a lot." I hung up because I knew I would say something really awful next, and I didn't want to say anything awful to Aspen. I just wanted her to get her head out of her ass and get away from that dick.

But, damn it, I couldn't hold it in. I lit her phone the fuck up with text after text, damn near harassing her—or maybe it was flat-out harassment. Hell, I didn't know. I asked if she was going to fuck him, if cheating on his fiancée with him made her feel better about herself than having a faithful, monogamous relationship with me, if she always got over men as easily as she'd gotten over me. I don't know what all I said, I just couldn't shut up until I saw her grab her purse and stumble to her feet, probably heading toward the bathroom.

Taking that as my cue to follow, I stepped off the curb again. But Ten, damn him, wasn't about to let me get near that restaurant.

Growling at him until he gave me some breathing room, I paced the corner of the street, waiting until she made it to the bathroom, or wherever the hell she'd gone, and could reply to me.

But she didn't reply.

Fed up, I dropped the big bomb. I wasn't playing around anymore. Fingers shaking so hard I had to delete and retype the message three times before I pushed *Send*, I wrote, "*Don't do this. I love you, Aspen. Ditch him and come outside to me.*"

Anxiety shuddered from my lungs. There. Now she knew. I'd just bared my soul to her and made myself as vulnerable as I'd ever been. Only a cold-hearted person would ignore this, and I knew Aspen. She was the furthest thing from cold-hearted as a person could get. She loved me back. She just had to stop listening to reason and propriety, and she'd realize that.

Another five minutes passed. When she appeared at the table where her date was still waiting, the breath rushed from my lungs. I fully expected her to give him her apologies and come running out to me.

But she tucked the back of her skirt up to her legs like a proper lady and seated herself. And their date continued.

I couldn't look away. I couldn't blink. Everything inside me shattered. Swiping my hand over my mouth, I turned to my best friend.

His eyes were wide with, what...I didn't know. Shock, fear, concern, worry. "Gam?"

"Fuck it," I said. "Let's get drunk."

***

"It does not do to dwell on dreams and forget to live." - J.K. Rowling, *Harry Potter and the Sorcerer's Stone*

***

~ASPEN~

My head was pounding. As I let myself into my dark house, I kept the lights out and rested my back against the front door to catch my breath.

The night had gone exactly as I'd planned, which I hated. Philip had been eager to take me out when I'd called him. He hadn't even had a problem with agreeing to meet there.

I'd asked him about his fiancée straight off, and he'd told me they'd split in February. Then he'd bought me some drinks, and we'd talked university politics until the phone calls and texts had started. I knew it was Noel immediately.

When Philip had told me it was okay to answer them, I'd waved him off, trying to appear as if it'd be rude to answer a call on a date. But then it became rude to ignore my phone because it kept going off and interrupting us. I don't know what I was thinking; my brain obviously wasn't screwed on right because I should've just turned the entire thing off. Except I'd never been able to do that because subconsciously I'd always been waiting for "the call" from my parents.

I'll never know why I excused myself to go to the bathroom, either. But I did. And I read his texts. All of them.

It killed me to walk back to Philip.

As inconspicuously as possible, I found where Noel was outside, watching us, and thirty seconds after he dragged his friend off, I stood up, cancelling my date with Philip.

Drawing my phone out of my purse, I let the Prada drop to the ground as I opened the last message he'd sent me.

Don't do this. I love you, Aspen. Ditch him and come outside to me.

Over and over again, I re-read it, and it hurt more each time my gaze flowed over the words. Moaning, I brought my fist to my mouth and bit my knuckles. But that didn't help. The tears came anyway.

I slid to the floor and buried my face into my knees as pinpoints of agony stabbed me in the gut. I have no idea how long I sat there, trying to console myself and failing, but my joints were stiff and my head was muzzy. It hurt when someone pounded on my door, making the vibration of it rattle through my spine.

I yelped and slapped my hand over my mouth, hoping the caller hadn't heard me. Breathing hard, I remained perfectly still, hoping he'd leave without trying again. But thirty seconds later, more pounding followed.

"Dr. Kavanagh," someone shouted. "I know you're in there. Dammit! Get your ass out here. Now!"

Wait. That wasn't Noel's voice. What the hell?

I scrambled to my feet and slid aside the curtain

to peer out the window. Oren Tenning glared back, his hands on his hips. Worried something had happened to Noel, I scrambled to unlock the deadbolt and opened the door.

But he didn't spill any kind of word about his roommate. Fisting his hands and waving them erratically, he screamed, "*What the fuck?*"

I cleared my throat, licked my dry lips, and straightened my back. "What do you need, Mr. Tenning?"

"I need you to tell me what the hell happened tonight. When you texted me and asked me to make sure Gam was in a certain place at a certain time... Fuck, I thought you were going to try to get back together with him. Not rip his fucking heart from his fucking chest."

Tears slipped down my cheeks. I was grateful it was dark and he couldn't see my face, because my plan to appear unaffected was bombing.

"You *used* me."

Setting my hand against my diaphragm, I took a deep breath. "I needed him to hate me."

"Well, congratulations." He snorted and flung his hands at me. "He does."

I winced but nodded my head. "Good."

With a harsh laugh, Ten ran his fingers through his hair and spun around only to come right back to me. "I can't believe you. He was crazy about you. He...Jesus. Just...don't *ever* ask me to help hurt my best friend like that again. Because I refuse."

"I wasn't asking you to hurt him. I was asking you to help me *protect* him."

"Protect him? Protect him from *what*?"

I couldn't answer that one without breaking down. My fingers were already shaking too hard, telling me I was on the verge of a panic attack. With a stiff smile, I met Ten's gaze. "I guess you'll find out soon enough."

"Find out?" he echoed, his eyes going wide with alarm. "Find out what? What the fuck is about to happen?"

"Nothing that will affect you. Nothing that will touch Noel. I think." With a hefty swallow and metaphoric crossing of my fingers, I drew in a deep breath. "I think he's safe."

"You *think*? Jesus Christ. Now I'm freaked out. What's going on? What did you get him into?"

"Nothing. I'm ninety percent certain this won't affect him at all."

"Well, unless you're a hundred and ten percent certain, then I'm not convinced. *What* is going on?"

Standing steady, I lifted my chin and got my regal on. "What's going on is that I refuse to be one of those teachers who gives a student a grade she doesn't deserve." If I couldn't get my happily ever after, then neither would Marci Fucking Bennett. "I won't bow under pressure, or demands, or *blackmail*. And that's all you need to know. I appreciate your concern for your friend, and I'm glad Noel has someone who's loyal and concerned about him. But you really need to go now."

"Fuck," he breathed. "Someone knows, don't they? Shit. Who is it? It can't be any of the guys from Forbidden. They'd never do that to Gam. Just tell me who it is. Maybe I can talk to him. Wait, you said *she*, didn't you? Who is she?"

"You don't need to get any more involved than you already are." I touched his arm. "Just keep Noel...away from it. And...and if he does try to do anything *radical*, please remind him of his brothers and sister. He can't get himself kicked out of Ellamore if he wants to help his family. His siblings need him."

CHAPTER TWENTY-NINE

"The only thing worse than a boy who hates you: a boy that loves you." - Markus Zusak, *The Book Thief*

~*A*SPEN~

THE LONGEST NIGHT of my life passed in seconds. Thirty thousand of them. And I felt every single one. I didn't sleep. Didn't eat. Just sat on my couch, in the dark, wondering if I was doing the right thing. If I told Noel about Marci Bennett's demands, he'd try to do something sweet and noble, and he'd probably get himself kicked out of Ellamore because of it.

But it had hurt so much to do what I'd done. If he hurt half as much as I did, then this was cruel and unusual punishment. How could I do this to him? How could I make him think I didn't love him after he told me he loved me first?

Because I did *love him*, I had to repeat to myself every time I began to melt. I loved him so much I wanted him to reach his goals. I wanted him to graduate from college, get drafted into the NFL, and live out his happily ever after. He was going to accomplish every goal he ever set out to reach. I was going to make sure of it.

But my head throbbed as I drove to work. And it pounded as I started my first class. I was halfway through teaching Introduction to Literature when the door to the lecture hall burst open, slamming against the wall.

A couple girls in the room let out shrieks of terror and I nearly peed my panties as I whirled around to face the threat. I expected to see some terrorist toting a lethal-looking weapon or something equally dramatic. But what stumbled into the room was worse.

So. Much. Worse.

Clothes rumpled as if he'd slept in them, an unshaven Noel Gamble sent me a huge, sloppy grin as he tripped toward an open seat in the front row.

"Sorry I'm late, Professor." He slurred his words badly, and the scent of a brewery punctuated the air as he passed me to collapse into his chair. "I slept in." He held up his thumb and forefinger, holding them an inch apart, "jus' a lil' bit."

I couldn't believe my eyes. "You're drunk," I spat, appalled, stupefied, and frankly scared out of my mind.

Dear God, this was going to end badly. Panic gripped me, but I managed to keep it cool as I glared daggers at the man tearing my chest open in the front row.

"Shh." He smashed his index finger against his own mouth. "I won't tell if you don't. It could be our lil' secret."

As people in the class around him tittered, having no clue what he really meant, I blanched. I could kill him for this.

Noel glanced at the girl to his right who was still giggling, and his grin widened, encouraged. "Hey, you're kind of cute. Have we had sex before?"

Damn it. I *was* going to kill him. Right here and now.

When the girl blushed, giggled some more, and told him no, he set his hand over his heart, tsking. "Now, tha's a damn shame. We should toe'ly hook up." Then he glanced at me, his gaze mocking. "Tha' okay with you...Dr. Kavanagh?"

That's it. This was more than I could take. "*Mr. Gamble*," I shouted, unable to control my rage. My hand shook as I pointed toward the exit. "Get out of my classroom. Right. Now."

His drunken grin died and glassy eyes narrowed. "But I'm here to learn, *Professor*. So jus' go ahead and teach us somethin' useful. Like...like maybe about that Hemingway guy." Eyebrows furrowed in thought, he shook his head. "No. Tha's not right. Hemingway? Hathaway? *Hawthorne!*" He snapped his fingers, or at least tried to. "Yeah. Hawthorne. Why don't you talk about his red-letter book some more, or whatever it's called. I think I could relate to some of *those* fucked up characters."

Jaw clenched, I bit out, "You don't even take this class. Now leave."

His smile was bitter and his laugh even harsher. "Wow, you really get off on coming up with new ways to get rid of me, don't you?"

When I met his gaze, a vulnerable pain glinted from his eyes, nearly killing me. I needed him gone before I broke completely, shattering into a million pieces.

"Mr. Hamilton," I called frantically, my lashes beating like hummingbird wings to hold back the tears. Scanning the room, I searched the sea of faces for his friend I knew who took this course. "Could you please escort your *teammate* from my room?"

"Quinn?" Noel whipped around until he saw the other guy stand up and start toward him. "Hey, Ham!" he cheered, pushing to his feet to greet his pal with a pat on the back. "I didn't know you took this class too, bud. Why don't you go sit back down?" He waved Quinn away. "I'm good here. I got this."

"Come on, Noel," Quinn said somberly.

"But I'm here to learn some literature." When Noel resisted and tried to pull his arm out of Quinn's grip, a couple more bulky, football-player-looking guys leapt from their seats to assist.

This time, when three guys lifted him into the air, he just smiled and pointed at the girl he'd hit on. "Hey guys, have you met my new friend here?" he asked his fellow football players. "We haven't had sex yet but I'm sure we will." Glancing at her over Quinn's shoulder, he mimed a phone and pressed it to his ear. "Call me."

I fisted my hands down at my sides, holding my breath. At the last second before his teammates propelled him from the room, he reached out and grabbed the doorjamb, like a cat refusing to go into its carrier.

"Wait!" He struggled against the players until his gaze met mine. "I came to say something to you." Emotions boiled from the depths of his intense gaze.

My stomach knotted.

"Fuck you," he said, gritting his teeth as if he meant every letter of those two words with everything he had. "Fuck you for being a coward and giving up. Fuck you to hell, *Dr.* Kavanagh." He took a piece of paper from his pocket, wadded it into a ball and threw it toward me. I watched it land on the ground and knew I didn't what to know what it said.

When the door shut, silence fell over the lecture hall. Pressing my hand to my abdomen, I turned to face my students. I'd never seen so many people so adamant to hear what I had to say next.

I opened my mouth, but no words came. Clearing my throat, I ducked my face and tried again. "Sorry for the interruption. You may be excused now."

For a breath, no one moved. Then I lifted my eyebrows, and they suddenly couldn't leave fast enough.

One girl was even nice enough to bend down and fetch my note for me. I took it with a stone-faced nod and curled it into my fist. After the place cleared out, I packed my briefcase and walked to my office before shutting myself inside alone. I collapsed into my chair and sat there another five minutes before I opened my hand to read the note crumpled inside.

It was another quote for my board: "You know what the crummiest feeling you can have is? To hate the person you love the best in the world."- S.E. Hinton (from *That Was Then, This is Now*)

***

"Would 'sorry' have made any difference? Does it ever? It's just a word. One word against a thousand actions." - Sarah Ockler, *Bittersweet*

***

~ Noel ~

Sober and feeling like shit, I fisted my hand and pounded on Aspen's door. She didn't open it until about thirty seconds after I started shouting her name at the top of my lungs.

As soon as the dead bolt sounded and it cracked open, I set my palm on the surface and started to push...until the chain caught. Glaring at it, I lifted an eyebrow. "Really?"

"Stop pounding on my door or I'll call the police."

I pressed my forehead against cool wood so I could see her through the small slit and wedged my fingers into the gap. Risky move, but I knew she wouldn't smash my digits. My dick might be another matter, but my fingers seemed relatively safe. I hoped.

"Please. I just came to apologize. I'm sober now, I swear."

"You could apologize out there just as well as you could in here."

But I wanted to be in there. "Aspen," I choked out, dying a little from her rejection. My eyelids squeezed together. "I'm sorry. I'm so fucking sorry. Let me in. Just let me in."

She gave a surrendering sigh. To me, it sounded like the creaking of the pearly gates as they opened to allow me entrance into Heaven. "Get your fingers out of the way, so I can unlock the dead bolt."

I opened my eyes to consider her. She could be lying, but I decided to chance it.

"I trust you," I whispered before I slowly slid my hand free.

The door immediately popped shut. I swallowed, fearing that was it. I was forever forbidden entrance into her home. A second passed, and I just stood there, terrified, and not sure what to do with myself now, because everything I wanted was on the other side of that door.

Then the chain rattled and my heart lurched with shock and elation.

Grabbing the handle, I turned and bulldozed my way inside.

"Hey—"

She could scowl at me in disapproval all she wanted, but I was inside. With her.

"I'm sorry. I'm so sorry." I caught her by the back of the neck to yank her against me. She didn't get out much more than a surprised squeak before my mouth covered hers and my tongue dove deep.

One thing she'd never been able to deny me was a kiss. As I plundered, she crawled up me, clinging and digging her fingers into my hair as her nails gripped my scalp. It felt so fucking good, I slung my arm around her waist and picked her up. And as naturally as breathing, she wrapped her legs around my hips.

Anchoring her higher than me so that we had to change positions and she was the one tipping her face down, I lifted my chin to keep my mouth fused to hers. For now, that was my main goal. As soon as our lips lost contact with each other, she'd start in. She'd try to push me away. But I wouldn't let that happen.

I spun us until I propped her spine against the wall and there I dry humped her through our clothes. The warmth between her legs spread through all the layers of cloth and hugged my dick with a dirty tease. When she whimpered and ground back against me, I groaned.

Her head slammed back, making me lose contact with her lips.

"Stop," she breathed, even as her body rubbed against mine.

"Never." I kissed her throat and peeled down the collar of her shirt.

She shoved at my shoulder, but I kept licking and nibbling, determined to change her mind.

"Noel. I said stop." When she sucked in a breath, I glanced up. She'd closed her eyes and was biting her bottom lip. I knew her release was coming, so I pushed my hips harder against her, knowing I was hitting her sweet spot, dead on target. In mere seconds, she'd be breaking apart in my arms.

"No," she moaned, even as she started to come.

"Yes," I hissed right back, watching her face as she fell apart in my arms. She fought it, thrashing her head back and forth. But I could tell just how hard it hit her when she cried out and strained against me, seeking what she knew I could give her. She took it all, and was left panting and limp when she came back down from her peak. Finally cracking her lashes open, she gazed at me from glassy, dazed eyes.

"You. Are. Mine," I told her. "I don't care how many times you break up with me or how many other men you try to take on a date. I don't care how wrong we are for each other. I don't care that I'll never be good enough for you or that we're risking everything to be together. Your mother would never approve. Whatever. Fuck it all. You are fucking *mine*. And I'm yours. And we belong together."

"No," she whispered.

"Damn it." Fisting my hand, I pounded the wall next to us. "Yes!"

She jumped, and a tear slid down her cheek. "Noel, stop. Please. *Stop*. I don't want this. *I don't want this*."

She wasn't shoving at my shoulders anymore, but the glazed loss and defeat in her watery eyes undid me.

"Fuck," I whispered. I stopped pinning her hips to the wall and pressed my forehead to hers.

She unwound her legs from me and touched her toes to the floor before sliding down, probably to escape me. But I went with her, keeping our brows pressed together. Once she was sitting and I was kneeling in front of her, she let out a small sob.

Jesus.

"I'm sorry," I croaked. "Jesus, God, I'm so sorry. I know I crossed the line. So many lines. I know I went way past guy-fighting-for-his-girl and straight into harassment territory last night when I text bombed you, even though I'm still pissed at you for going anywhere with him. How I responded was uncalled for and just...fucked up. And today in class. Today was even worse. I know that. And then just now..." Cold hard dread settled in me as I realized what I'd actually

326

done just now. "I forced you to—"

I couldn't even admit it aloud. But oh, God. I was no better than Zach was. The very idea made me sick.

Scared as fuck of what I was capable of, I stumbled away from her. She must've sensed how close I was to completely losing my shit, because she looked at me, and even with her lashes clogged with tears that I'd made fall, she still had the compassion to reassure me. "You didn't force me, Noel. Not at all."

I still felt like shit, though. So, I bowed my head, trying to combat the nausea. It didn't help matters when she added, "But I do need you to go."

I winced. "I am more sorry than you can ever imagine. Aspen...please."

She didn't answer.

I wasn't forgiven.

"Fuck," I said a little louder this time.

When she sniffed and covered her mouth with her hands, I sat on my haunches to watch teardrop after teardrop stream down her face. I'd hurt her, and I hated that. She had every right to hurt me back, to never forgive me.

Realizing this was it; she wasn't going to let me in again, I surged to my feet and grabbed my hair with both hands.

Deep in my chest, my soul disintegrated as I heaved in a choked gasp for breath. It might've sounded like a goddamn sob, but fuck. Whatever.

She watched me for a second before she hugged her folded legs, squeezed her eyes closed, and dug her face into her knees.

"Aspen." When another pussy-sounding sob tore from me, I pressed my hand to my chest, trying to push everything back in. But nothing worked. All the pain, and fear, and desperation of losing her spilled out. "I don't know how to do this," I confessed, shaking my head back and forth. "I don't know how to give you up. I love you."

The features on her face fell. Hugging her ribs, she bowed her head and cried quietly. More lost than I'd ever felt in my life, I approached her slowly and gently set my hand on the top of her hair. When she trembled under the warmth of my palm, I knew there was only one thing left I could do.

I had to let go.

"Okay," I said, my voice breaking and my chin wobbling. "Okay." My fingers slid limply from her. My guts twisted as I wondered if that was the last time I'd ever touch her.

I wanted to fall to my knees and keep begging, but I'd already scared her enough. It took everything I had to turn away and walk to the front door.

When I opened it, I paused, giving her one last chance to call me back. When she said nothing, I murmured, "Take care of yourself," and left.

CHAPTER THIRTY

"The world breaks every one and afterward many are strong at the broken places." - Ernest Hemingway, *A Farewell to Arms*

~ASPEN~

THREE DAYS AFTER I GAVE Marci Bennett an F for not turning in her assignment, Dr. Frenetti rang my phone.

"Aspen, I need you to come to my office. Right now."

The pinched tone in his voice told me everything I needed to know. I spent a couple seconds closing all the programs on my computer and straightening my desk before I stood and brushed the wrinkles out of my skirt and blazer. Though my knees felt like cooked noodles, I kept my spine ramrod straight and walked the short distance to the dean's office in a sedate, orderly pace.

As I tapped on Frenetti's opened door and

glanced inside, I found another man wearing maroon wind pants and a T-shirt supporting Vikings athletics sitting back in a chair across from him. Both men turned to look at me. Frenetti scowled in his typical manner. His visitor leered and let his gaze travel down my body as if he'd seen me naked, which—oh, God— he probably had. I crossed my arms over my chest as if that could stop him from ogling.

"Aspen," Frenetti rumbled out as he motioned to the gawking pervert. "This is Rick Jacobi, head coach for the football team."

I nodded, and a piece of hot lead dropped into the pit of my stomach

This was it. My career was over.

***

"Lettin' the cat outta the bag is a whole lot easier 'n puttin' it back in." - Will Rogers

***

~*N*OEL~

My will to keep marching forward had seriously declined in the week since I'd fucked things up with Aspen. I didn't want to go to work each night, or attend classes each day, or keep sweating through these fucking workouts each morning. I didn't want to answer the phone when Caroline called. I didn't want anything. Except my woman.

But that wasn't going to happen, so I just kept doing all the shit I really didn't care about anymore.

With my bag full of exercise clothes to change into slung heavily over my shoulder, I trudged into the university's sports complex for my crack-of-mother-fucking-dawn weight training. Yawning, I rubbed my hand over my jaw. I hadn't shaved in days and winced at the pull of sore muscles.

I'd just turned down the hall toward the locker room when someone from behind me called my name frantically. Glancing around, I found both Ten and Hamilton skidding around the corner and racing toward me.

Frowning, I asked, "What the hell are you doing here for morning training?" Ten only trained in the evening or not at all. He refused to even pretend to be a morning person.

"Ham called me." Breathless as he reached me, he grabbed my arm and yanked me in the opposite direction of the locker room. "Man, you need to come with us. Right now."

Not used to my best friend acting so agitated, I glanced toward Hamilton. But he looked as if he might shit his pants any second. Unease stirred within me.

I resisted Ten's pull. "What's going on?"

"Just..." Ten yanked me along, none too gently. "Come on."

They led me to a bathroom. As Ten ducked down to check that all the stalls were empty, Quinn folded his arms and braced his back against the door so no one else could enter. Their behavior made it seem like they were preparing to kick my ass or something. And if I didn't know any better and trust these guys with some of the biggest secrets of my life, I might have been worried.

But then it struck me; they *were* the only two guys on the team who did know my one big secret. Acid filled my stomach, sharp and painful.

I nearly bent over double as I blew out a shuddery breath. My gym bag slid off my shoulder and slapped to the floor. "Aspen?" I said, knowing this couldn't be about anything else.

Ten straightened from the last stall and stared at

me for a moment before he said, "Yeah."

"Fuck." I clenched my eyes shut and rested my hands on my knees as I concentrated on not getting sick all over the place. But, "Shit. How bad is it?"

After a small groan, Ten admitted, "It's pretty bad."

I looked up and stared at him. When he didn't say anything, I glanced toward Hamilton. He'd gone white, but nodded, agreeing with Ten.

It was bad.

"Well?" I demanded, my voice raspy with fear. "What happened?"

"Shit, man." Ten set his hands on his hips and looked away. "Someone took a picture of you two together."

"A picture," I repeated. "What *kind* of picture?"

"What the hell kind do you think? You guys were fucking."

I nearly blacked out. Reaching for the wall to steady myself, I held on for dear life as Ten kept talking.

"But at least now I know she doesn't have pierced nipples."

"*What*?" Heat suffused my face.

Seeing I had on my you-must-die face, he lurched backward and held up his hands. "Hey, I'm just...calm down. *Gamble!*"

My breathing went erratic as I fisted my hands at my sides. "Where is this picture? What exactly does it show?"

"That's about it. I mean, just her top half. It was night, pretty dark and she was in the front seat of some car. Her head was thrown back and her tits were stuck out like she was in the middle of coming. You were cut out completely, except for your arm." He glanced at my arm. "And your tattoo."

"Oh, God." Someone had seen us that night? Taken *pictures*? Who would dare... Why would anyone... "Christ." I stared at Ten from what felt like bloodshot eyes. "How the hell do you know about such a picture? Did you *see* it? Who took it? Where—"

"Coach hung it on the board in the middle of the locker room. *Everyone* has seen it."

"*What!*" It was just hanging out in public for everyone to see Aspen in her moment of glory? No fucking way. I spun toward the doorway and charged. I knew Hamilton was still bracing the door shut, but that didn't matter to me. I wasn't on the team because I was afraid of being tackled.

His eyes widened, but he seemed to prepare himself for my attack. Damn fucking football player. I didn't let him down, bowing my head and charging with my shoulder.

Ten shouted my name and crashed into me from behind as I rammed Hamilton hard, causing him to grunt out a whoosh of air.

"What the hell do you think you're doing?" Ten tried to ask between curses as he and Quinn wrestled me to the ground and pinned me down.

I bucked under them, flailing and roaring out my rage. "I'm getting that picture."

My roommate sat on my back and Quinn contained my legs. "Are you insane? Coach put it up to get a reaction out of someone. Out of *you*. You can't go tearing in there and—"

"I need it down," I ground out. "Motherfucker, how *dare* he? How dare he do that to her? I need that picture ripped *down*."

"Okay! Okay, buddy." Ten patted my shoulder. "We'll get it down. Just...breathe."

I stopped fighting, but the guys kept sitting on me for another couple minutes before Ten nodded at Quinn.

Slowly, cautiously they let up pressure. When I didn't try to break loose as soon as I had an ounce of wiggle room, they leapt off me and jumped back. I stayed sprawled on the floor, panting and trying to calm myself before I sat up and glanced at Ten.

"I want it down."

"We'll get it down," he promised me, his eyes steady on mine with a look of pure assurance that I'd never seen him give anyone. "I swear to you, we'll get that picture down. But you can't go anywhere near it. If Coach finds out it's you, you'll be off the team and kicked out of school, bro."

"I don't care." I pushed to my feet and brushed off my clothes. "She shouldn't be put on display like that, like some kind of dirty whore. She's not—"

"I *know*," Ten said forcefully. He lifted his hands, back to placating me. "We both know that. But you going in there like this won't help anyone. It won't help you, it won't help your brothers or sister. And it won't help her. She's already gone, man."

"Gone?" I repeated stupidly. "What do you mean *gone*?"

"Do you seriously think they'd let her stay on campus after something like this? Besides," he glanced away and mumbled the last part, "there's a sign above the picture."

"A sign?" My heart sank. They'd labeled my woman, just like what had happened in that Hawthorne book. All her hard work to get a position at Ellamore had come down to a big scarlet A... because of me. This was definitely not the kind of A I'd always wanted from her. I tasted bile and wanted to get it out of me. "What's it say?"

Ten blanched and shook his head. Hamilton looked away.

"*What's it say*?" I roared.

"Jesus. It says, 'Who wants to join Dr. Kavanagh in leaving Ellamore forever?'"

"Oh, God."

I started for the door. This time, they trapped me against the damn sinks.

"Let me go, damn you."

"What're you going to do? Blow in there and confess, so you can go down with her? Man, you only have one year left of school. You're *this close* to getting everything you've worked so hard for. And don't forget your family. Jesus, Noel. Your *family*."

"So, what do you expect me to do? Take the coward's way out and let her take the fall for both of us? Fuck that."

"Think about this, Gamble. Think with your brain for a second. Nothing you can do will save her."

A growl escaped my throat. I gritted my teeth and closed my eyes, trying to combat the agony, but it just followed me.

"But you can still save Caroline. And Colt, and Brandt. *They* didn't do anything wrong and they'll be the ones who suffer right along with you if you throw away your entire future and admit anything to Coach."

His words penetrated my rage until it struck me what he'd just said. I squinted. "How the fuck do you know anything about them?"

Ten's mouth opened. And then shut. Appearing suddenly uncomfortable, he glanced away. "You've mentioned your brothers' and sister's names before."

"But I've never told you..." This didn't add up. "Jesus, what do you know?"

He ground his teeth and shot me a glare. "I don't know anything, man. You've never told me anything about your life back home, except those names."

I shook my head. "Then why do you keep bringing them up?"

"Fuck." He hissed. "She told me to, okay?"

Not comprehending at all, I just blinked at him. "What?"

"Dr. Kavanagh," he mumbled, scowling at me.

"Aspen? When the hell did you talk to *Aspen*?"

"Jesus Christ." Ten squeezed his eyes shut. "The night we caught her with that history professor douche. She texted me and asked me to make sure you were there, so you'd see them together."

My mouth fell open. I swung my head back and forth. This didn't make any sense.

"When I disappeared from you for a little while after that, I went to see her, to call her out on it, and demand to know why the hell she'd done that to you. I swear to God, man, I thought she wanted you there so she could hook up with you again. I didn't know—"

I waved my hand, shutting him up. "Then why...why did she want me to see that?"

"She said..." He growled out a sound of irritation. "She said you needed to hate her for this to work."

No. No way. That did not sound good. My heart sank to my knees as I asked the dreaded question. "For *what* to work?"

"Man, she knew then. I think she knew about the picture. I think someone wanted to fucking blackmail her for a good grade. And she refused."

She'd sacrificed herself. And made sure I would remain safe.

Black spots dotted my vision and my knees gave out. Both Quinn and Ten caught me and helped me back upright. I worked my jaw but that didn't relieve any of the distress flowing out my limbs.

"Did she say who?" I asked, my voice low but rational and steady. I think I totally had Ten fooled because his grip loosened as he shook his head. "She refused to say."

No, she wouldn't have, would she? Stubborn woman had done all this to protect me; she wouldn't give any information to Ten that might change her plans.

Fuck.

My head racing with all the things I needed to do, I stared Ten right in the eyes. He gulped but didn't say anything. Finally, I shoved roughly against both him and Hamilton. "Get off me."

Both guys released me in the same breath. I stumbled a little from the sudden loss of their restraining hands. Then I took a second to breathe in a fresh gulp and clear my head as I straightened my clothes. When I felt like I was in my own body again, I glanced at the two guys staring at me with blatant concern.

"Thanks for the heads-up. But..." I shook my head slowly. "I can't let her go down by herself. We started this together. We end it together."

Ten winced. "How did I know you were going to say that?"

He didn't try to stop me as I stalked out the door. Both guys dogged my heels, but I ignored them all the way to the locker room. When I shoved my way inside, I jerked to a halt, watching the crowd of guys, hooting and hollering as they clumped together in front of the message board.

I saw red. About fifty dicks were about to die.

But Ten pushed me aside and plowed forward. "*Coach!*" he yelled. "You piece of chicken shit bastard. Get that picture of me and my girl off the goddamn board."

With his roar echoing around the room, Ten rushed into the crowd of guys, shoving them aside to reach the picture. Then he ripped it down and tore it into shreds.

Coach Jacobi appeared in the doorway of his office, a clipboard in hand. "You saying that's you in that picture, Tenning?"

"Yes, sir, I am. Couldn't you tell by the look on her face? Only *I* can bring a woman that much pleasure."

I clenched my teeth and shook my head. "He's lying."

"No, they're both lying." Hamilton spoke up from beside me. "That's my arm, Coach."

"Jesus Christ," Jacobi exploded. "All *three* of you

fucked her?"

"No," I bit out, pissed off completely. How dare they tarnish her like that?

"But we'll all swear to it," Ten quickly jumped in, not letting me defend her. "We're a team, and we protect our teammates."

"Yeah." Shadow, one of my offensive linebackers, stepped forward. "We don't want to lose one of our own just because he got lucky with the hottest teacher on campus. So that's *me* in that picture." It obviously wasn't him. His arm was way too thick to belong to the arm of the person in the picture.

"No, it's me," my head running back shouted from his locker. Since his skin was too dark to match mine, he was just as blatantly lying.

A few others jumped in to protect me, and I just stared around me helplessly. They weren't going to let me go down with the ship.

With a disgusted grumble, the coach ripped off his hat and threw it on the ground. "Fine," he muttered to the room at large. "I'll let this go this time since it didn't make any media attention. But if I hear about one of my boys sleeping with a teacher, or coach, or a goddamn janitor on this campus, he's getting kicked off my team. I don't care if I have to get rid of every single one of you. This shit stops now." Then he stormed from the room. As he left, the guys around me clapped and hollered as if they'd actually accomplished something.

But I had gained nothing. Aspen had still been kicked out of Ellamore. And she'd known it was going to happen, had even taken measures to keep me from getting caught with her.

I whirled around to growl at Hamilton. "You don't even have one of these fucking tattoos."

He grinned and shrugged. "The coach didn't notice, though."

I shook my head and stalked toward the door.

"Hey, where're you going?" Ten raced after me.

I spun to point an ominous finger at him. "Just stop right now. You might've kept me from confessing, but you're not stopping me from this. I have to find her."

"But what about training?"

"Fuck training."

***

I tried her office first. Save for a desk, computer, and empty bookshelves, the room was completely bare. Cold, hard dread settled in the pit of my gut as I glanced around for even the slightest sign of her existence. But even her quote board was gone.

God, how long ago had she been dismissed? She couldn't have cleared out her office in a few minutes.

Sick to my stomach, I combed the halls until I found the name on a door I was looking for. Shoving it open, I barged inside, making Dr. Frenetti glance up in surprise.

"Noel! What brings you by?"

Narrowing my eyes, I glowered. How dare he act nice to me after what he'd done to her? "You need to bring Dr. Kavanagh back. Today. She is the best damn teacher your department has ever had." I let out a harsh laugh. "I mean, the woman actually taught me to appreciate literature. And I *hate* literature."

Expression frosting with ire, he slid his gaze over me. Then his eyes widened as they paused on my tattoo. I flexed the muscles under it, fisting my hands at my sides.

So the dick finally realized who I was. Good for him.

Mouth puckering with distaste, he looked up at my face. "I'm sorry, Mr. Gamble, but Dr. Kavanagh resigned. She wasn't let go. I'm afraid we have no control over bringing her back."

Resigned?

I blinked, thrown off by that piece of information. But something in Frenetti's smirk let me know it hadn't exactly been a voluntary resignation.

"No," I said through gritted teeth. "I think she left because you *made* her go. And if you think I'll be okay with you chasing her off because of my involvement with her, then you seriously underestimate me, pal. Right now, I could kick your ass without a second's regret."

Frenetti jerked back in his chair. "Excuse me?"

"Bring. Her. Back."

"Threats will not work with me, Mr.—"

"I'll leave," I said softly, stepping close. "I'll leave this whole fucking university, let you all scramble to find a new quarterback next year. Are you prepared to give up a very real shot at the championships...just like that?"

Glaring back at me, Frenetti pushed to his feet and kept his voice just as ominously low. "You leave this school, and we'll take it public, make sure every radio and television station in the country knows exactly why you and your little whore were kicked out of Ellamore. She'll never find another job in education anywhere, and you'll never get accepted into another university. Both of your lives will be over. So, just try it, Gamble. We have no problem destroying you."

CHAPTER THIRTY-ONE

"When you come to the end of your rope, tie a knot and hang on." - Franklin D. Roosevelt, *Choosing Simplicity*

~NOEL~

AND THAT'S HOW I LOST the woman I loved.

After outplaying me and figuratively handing me my ass, Frenetti ordered me from his office. I hiked to Aspen's house next. It was about two miles from campus. I'd made the trip a number of times before, but today, I couldn't move fast enough, couldn't reach her soon enough.

Her place was quiet and abandoned when I got there, her car gone and all the shades drawn. I pounded on the front door anyway without any success. I'd also texted and called her phone, but the line went straight to voice mail.

If it weren't for the gaping hole in my chest, I might've been able to convince myself she'd never existed at all.

***

I skipped the rest of my classes that week. The semester was rapidly coming to a close; I knew I really shouldn't have ruined all my forward progress. But I couldn't function properly. I wanted Aspen back.

The guys at Forbidden rearranged our schedules so I didn't have to work either. Hell, even my sister had stopped calling so much. I had hurt her a lot by the way I'd yelled at her after finding out about her baby. And no matter how many times I'd apologized for blowing up at her, I sensed we'd lost something vital in our relationship.

I probably should've called to check in with her, since she wasn't updating me any longer. But I just couldn't find the will. So, I did nothing but lie around, staring at my phone, waiting for Aspen to finally respond to one of my messages.

In the past two days, I'd toned my texts down to just quotes for her collection. I'd already said everything I could think to say about everything else. Now I just had to remind her I was still here. Waiting. Loving her.

When a knock fell on my apartment door Saturday evening, I leapt to my feet, breathless. I probably looked like shit. I hadn't showered in at least three days, maybe four. And I'd worn the same sweatpants and shirt since...who knows when. Probably lost my razor for good. But if Aspen was here...

In my haste to reach her, I tripped over the messy coffee table, overflowing with energy drinks and snack food wrappers. After banging my knee against the corner, I limped forward and finally caught the front doorknob to yank it open.

But it wasn't Aspen.

I squinted out at Pick, disappointment making my chest hurt. "What the hell are *you* doing here?"

He rolled his eyes. "Apparently I'm your babysitter. Zero and the virgin are worried shitless about you. They don't think it's safe for you to stay alone right now, and since they're both working tonight, I got elected to watch your unstable ass."

"Safe to stay alone?" I repeated incredulously. "Just what the hell do Ten and Hamilton think I'm going to do? Hurt myself?"

"Hey, I told 'em you were a big boy, but..." He shrugged. "Tenning insisted. I think the kid's got a big ol' man-crush on you."

With a heavy sigh, I stepped back and opened the door wider for him. "Well, you might as well come in if you're not going to leave."

"Uh..." Instead of stepping forward, Pick took one backward. "Actually, could you come with me instead? I had plans before my Save-Gotham Batman light went off to come running to your side."

Snorting out a laugh, I shook my head. "No way, pal. I'm not following you around on some raunchy date. I don't play third wheel."

He chuckled. "Contrary to popular belief, I do not get laid every night of the week. And lucky you, you happened to catch me on an off night. Mason needed help fixing up an old turd car he bought. I was headed over there tonight to check it out."

"Lowe?" I lifted my brows with interest. "I didn't know you two had gotten so cozy."

"Yeah, we're a regular pair of BFFs now." Rolling his eyes to match the dry sarcasm in his voice, Pick explained, "When he learned I also worked at an auto body shop, he asked for my take on his new ride, and I offered to look at it. That's where I was headed when your boys called. So...are you coming along or what?"

I paused. I didn't want to be gone in case Aspen came back, but hell, I knew she wasn't coming back.

When that realization hit me, I clenched my teeth and looked away. Suddenly, I didn't want to hang around here all night, feeling sorry for myself.

"Sure," I muttered. "Let me clean up first."

***

"So what's up with you and Professor Girlfriend? I'm guessing you guys split since we've all had to rearrange our schedules for you and now I'm stuck on suicide watch."

I glared over at Pick from the passenger seat of his car, some souped-up classic he had no-doubt fine-tuned to perfection. "You're not on—look, I'm not going to do anything to myself. I'm fine. But yes, we're..." The word caught in my throat and I had to rasp, "...over. It's been a week, but I'm past it."

Okay, I wasn't past it at all. But I no longer felt the urge to get drunk and crash her class anymore. That was, if she still *had* a class to crash.

Shit. The guilt slammed into on me all over again. She was gone, and it was my fault. I wiped a hand over my face, surprised to find my fingers shaking.

"Then why are Larry and Curly still worried about you?"

"Because they're pussies?" I guessed with a disgusted sigh. "How the hell should I know?"

"Well, what happened?"

Drumming my fingers against my knee, I turned to gaze out the side window.

"Might as well tell me," Pick cajoled. "I'm going to bug the piss out of you until you do."

I sighed and glanced at him. "Some anonymous *person* sent a picture of us together to my coach, and she got axed."

"Well, fuck," Pick breathed out quietly. "Why didn't you get into trouble, too? Or did you?"

My jaw hardened. "The picture only revealed her

face. Mine was cropped off."

"Wait. Then how did they even know it was a student she was banging? If they couldn't see you, she could've been fucking anyone."

Grinding my teeth, I pushed up my sleeve to show him my tattoo. "Back in October, about a dozen of us got these the night before our big national championship game. It was the only clear thing you could see of me in the shot."

Pick glanced at the tat, read it carefully, and snorted out a laugh. "National champs? Didn't you guys lose that game?"

"And didn't I say we got them the night *before*?" I muttered, pushing my sleeve back down to cover the humiliating mistake, a mistake that had ended up costing Aspen her job.

"So, the girl got stuck with all the heat, and you just...let her take the fall...by herself?" Pick shook his head, disappointed oozing off him in waves.

"No," I growled. Fisting my hand, I slammed it down on his dashboard. "I did not just *let* her take the fall. By the time I'd found out what had happened, she was already gone. Ten and Hamilton managed to talk me out of confessing to Coach. But that's what I should've done. Damn it. Instead, I went to Aspen's boss and tried to talk *him* into bringing her back. Big fucking mistake. Let me tell you. Coach would've just kicked my ass off the team and pulled my scholarship."

"But not this prick," Pick guessed.

I shook my head. "Nope, not this prick. When he learned *I* was the guy in the picture, not only did he refuse to reinstate her, but he refused to reprimand *me*. He's a big football fan, you see. So I threatened to leave school and drop out of the team if he didn't bring her back, to which he in turn threatened to go public if I even acted like I was going to leave. So, now she's gone, and I'm stuck here in order to save her reputation and make sure she doesn't lose all chance of getting a job anywhere else in the country. But in the meantime, yeah, I look like a complete bastard for letting her take all the heat for *our* relationship."

"Man." Pick shook his head and blew out a low whistle. "That's harsh. Sucks to be you right now."

"Yep," I muttered, turning my face away to look out the passenger side window again.

"And you haven't heard from her at all since that went down?"

Emotion overwhelmed me. I wanted to hit something again. Or break down like a pussy and cry. "No. I'm pretty sure she left town. She won't answer her door, and her mail has been piling up."

"You don't think *she* would hurt herself, do you?"

White hot panic roared through me. I glanced slowly at Pick, giving him the death glare. "Well, I hadn't...until now. Jesus, she wouldn't—wait. No. Her car's gone too. If she was in the house, her car would still be there. She's *okay*." She had to be okay.

"Unless—"

"Jesus, Pick," I snapped. "Stop freaking me out. She's okay. She just needs some time."

"Well, if you ever need to get into her place, just to check and make sure, I know how to jimmy a lock."

I shook my head. "God, man. Where'd you learn a handy trick like that? The state pen?"

"I never went to the pen, ass wipe. It was *county* lockup for, like, two weeks. And, no, I didn't learn how to break and enter in jail. You meet all kinds of interesting kids when you grow up in the foster care system."

I knew he'd done some time because he'd mentioned having to meet with his parole officer before. But... "I didn't know you grew up in foster care."

"Yep. From birth until I graduated out of it at eighteen."

With a shiver, I wondered what would've happened to me if my mother had been any more of a crappy parent then she'd been. I could've grown up in the same kind of life as Pick had. Hell, my little brothers, and maybe even Caroline, still might fall into that fate if I didn't watch myself.

Fuck, I should definitely call and check in on them.

"Here we are." Pick pulled to the curb of a split-level apartment complex behind a vintage jeep.

Rubbing my face, I followed him from the car and toward the opened bay door of a garage. As we approached, voices filtered out from inside.

"Oh my God. *Alec*? What're you doing here? How did you even find me?"

Pick caught my arm before I could step inside. After pulling me back a foot, he peeked around the corner to spy on whoever was talking. Curiosity getting the best of me, I crowded up beside him to look as well. The pregnant, blond cousin of Lowe's girlfriend stood there, her arms wrapped around her baby bump as some rich-looking douche hovered over her. He looked pissed, while she appeared to be shocked senseless.

"Mason told me you were here," her visitor answered her.

"You think he's her baby daddy?" Pick whispered to me. I began to shrug when she spat, "Well, he shouldn't have bothered. Because I haven't changed my mind. I'm not getting rid of this baby."

"I talked to your parents, Eva—"

"Oh, well, you know what? I talked to my parents too. And I know exactly what their position is. I wouldn't be here in BFE Illinois, sponging off my cousin if they hadn't kicked me out because I refused to get an abortion. And since I'm still here, *Alec*, I guess that means I haven't changed my mind. So, sorry for your wasted trip, but you came for nothing.

You can turn around and go right back to Florida."

Alec gave a low chuckle and stepped ominously close to her. When Pick tensed beside me as if he wanted to intervene, I glanced sharply at him and grabbed his arm.

"Don't. This is their fight, man. They obviously have issues to work out. If you get involved and break your parole, you'll land right back in jail."

Pick wouldn't take his steely glare off Eva's baby daddy, but he didn't move away from me either. He just popped his neck, probably to relieve some tension and kept watching the scene unfold with narrowed eyes.

"You're really going to play this all out, aren't you?" Alec hissed and caught Eva's arm, making me tighten my grip on Pick to restrain him. "Fine, I'm willing to play. What do you want, E?"

"This isn't a power play for me to get a pretty toy, Alec. The only thing I want is my child."

"Bullshit! What happened to the girl I met who said kids gave her the willies?"

"You knocked her up. So I guess I'm just going to have to learn to adjust."

"Good for you, Tink," Pick whispered, nodding his head in approval and smiling at the pregnant chick. "Good for you."

"Jesus Christ," Alec shouted inside the garage. "Why can't you just take care of this?"

"I am! I'm going to stay here and *take care* of my baby, like a mother should."

"A mother? Oh, my God." The douche let out a belly laugh. "Are you even listening to yourself? This is not you. You're not mother material, Eva. You're a fucking spoiled, rich cunt."

When Pick bristled, I tugged him closer to me, keeping him reined in. "Don't do it."

"Just because I didn't plan on this ever happening, doesn't mean I'm going to brush it aside like a minor inconvenience. I'm keeping my child."

"Well, I can't allow you to do that."

Fuck. That didn't sound good. From the muscles in Pick's arm tensing under my grip, he didn't think so either.

"Why not?" Eva shot back, glaring up at him, and clearly not alarmed by his threat. "I'm not asking you to do anything. In fact, I don't even *want* you involved."

Alec jerked her closer to him, and this time, I had to use both hands to keep Pick from charging. "How stupid do you think I am? Of course, you'll ask. You'll get the law on your side, too, and you'll fucking bleed everything from me. You could hold this over me for the rest of my life, suck me dry with some bullshit child support, make me pay for all kinds of shit I want nothing to do with. And I refuse to let you get away with it."

She gave a long, tired sigh. "Alec, believe me, I will not do that to you. I don't want anything from you. Actually, if I never saw you again, I would be overwhelmed with joy. I'll even sign a piece of paper, saying so."

"See, now." Alec shook his head and laughed softly. "I'm having trouble believing that. I know you, remember? I know what a conniving, manipulative bitch you are. And I refuse to let you continue this."

"Well, I've changed." Eva huffed out a sound of aggravation and tugged at the grip he had on her arm. "People can change, you know. Now...let me go."

"Not until you agree to get rid of it."

"Never!"

"Then you leave me no other choice."

Everything happened at once. Alec shoved her against a wall with enough force that I lurched forward right along with Pick to help her out. Eva's pained gasp haunted my ears as her douchebag baby daddy braced one forearm across her throat to choke her into place while he reared back his other fist and punched her in the stomach. Repeatedly.

She screamed, and screamed, and screamed. It echoed through my ears, telling me I'd remember that scream in my dreams for years to come.

Christ, the crazy bastard was serious when he said he wasn't going to let her keep her baby.

Pick roared out an animalistic sound of denial and lunged past me, beating me to the bastard. Surprising Eva's attacker with his shout, he ripped Alec away from her and spun him around.

"What the—" Alec stumbled, off balance.

Pick didn't bother to introduce himself. He snatched up a wrench that had been sitting on a nearby table and wound his arm back before swinging and catching Alec square in the face with the business end of his steel.

Now it was the douchebag's turn to scream. He grabbed his nose, and blood flew. Pick kicked him in the knee, making him stumble back into the wall of the garage not too far down from where Eva had crumpled to the floor, cradling her stomach. Then he pressed the flat side of the wrench hard against Alec's throat with both hands. Face immediately turning twenty shades of purple, Alec clawed at Pick's fingers, seeking oxygen.

"You just messed with the wrong girl, pal." Pick kneed him in the stomach, right where Alec had hit Eva in hers.

I grabbed his shoulder to pull him off. But he wasn't coming off.

"Doesn't feel so good when it's done to you, does it, fuck face?" Pick kneed him again, this time in the balls.

"*Enough!*" I had to use everything I had to yank him back, and I still barely managed to pull him away, wrapping both of my arms around his torso and giving a good, hard heave. But, Jesus, Pick was a hell of a lot stronger than I took him for. He might not have my mass, but there was a fuck-load of pissed-off muscle packed into his lean frame. I could only drag him a yard or two away before he absolutely resisted and tried to go back for more.

Alec choked out a sound and his eyes rolled into the back of his head. He doubled over and folded to the ground.

"Touch her again, and I'll kill you," Pick roared, struggling against me. "Got it? I will fuck you up beyond all recognition."

"Jesus," I muttered, yanking on him harder to shake some sense into him. "Stop."

That's when Lowe finally decided to show his lazy ass up, opening the garage door from his house and shouting, "What the hell?"

"A little help," I shouted back, still struggling to hold on to Pick.

When Pick spit at Alec, a wad of phlegm landed on the guy's arms he was using to shield his face.

"Damn," a struggling Lowe panted from beside me when he took one of Pick's free arms to help propel him backward. "What the hell just happened?"

Pick pointed at the bleeding pile of wasted space cowering on the garage flood. "He hit her. In the stomach. He fucking hit her baby."

Stunned silent for a good two seconds, Lowe finally said, "Eva?"

Remembering her, we all three turned to where I'd last seen Eva clutching her belly with her legs folded like broken table legs.

Crouching in front of her, Lowe's woman grasped Eva's shoulders. "E?" Reese's voice trembled. "What happened? Are you okay? Oh, my God. Mason. She's hurt bad."

"I...I think I'm bleeding." Breathing erratically, Eva removed her hand from her stomach to look down.

I looked down too and almost passed out when I saw the red drops splatted onto the concrete under her.

"Shit." If the bastard had succeeded in killing her kid, Pick really would destroy him.

"*No!* No, no, no." Shoving away from us, Pick nudged Reese aside and squatted in front of Eva. "Tinker Bell?" he said as gently as I'd ever heard him speak to anyone.

Eva lifted her face and stared at him from large, water-stained blue eyes. She looked so frightened and full of pain, I gulped down my own rising panic.

"Pick?" she whimpered his name in confusion as he slid his arms under her.

With a forced smile, he nodded. "Hey, beautiful. You want to take a ride with me? I got a real fast car, and we can get you taken care of in no time."

She sobbed and moaned, then buried her face in his shirt as her fingers clutched fistfuls of his sleeve. "It hurts."

"I know, baby. I know." Crooning, he pulled her a little closer and scooped her into his arms before standing up and turning toward me. "Well?" he demanded when no one moved. "Let's get her to the hospital."

"But..." I shook my head and glanced at the possibly unconscious guy slumped on Lowe's garage floor. "What about him?"

"Fuck him." Pick glared at Alec. "He can rot there and die for all I care. Did you not see him punch her *in the stomach*?"

"Yeah, but...shit." I ran my hands through my hair, not used to dealing with this kind of mess. "Shouldn't we call the police or something?"

"Someone can call them on the way to the hospital. Now let's go. She's *bleeding*."

That seemed to startle Lowe into action. "Come on." He grabbed Reese's arm, and they dashed toward

Pick's car. "Jesus, I can't believe this is happening."

That made two of us. I hurried along behind them, abandoning the half-dead baby daddy.

Reese rushed ahead to open the door for Pick and Eva. Gnawing on her lip, she glanced back toward the garage. "What if he's gone by the time the police show up?"

Pick glanced at her before he ducked his head and slid into the backseat with Eva. "Then I guess I won't have to go to jail for beating the shit out of him, will I?"

Reese swerved her attention back to me, her blue eyes wide with fear. "Will he really go to jail? For *defending* her?"

"Umm..." I winced and scratched the side of my neck. "He *is* on parole."

"Shit," Lowe muttered. "Fine. I'll stay here and clean this up." Grasping Reese's shoulders, he spun her to face him. "I assume you're going with Eva?"

She nodded and rose up on her toes to give him a quick kiss on the cheek. "I love you. Be careful."

Seeing them like that immediately made me think of Aspen. The crack in my chest broke open a little wider. Slapping the roof of the car as I opened the driver's side door, I called, "Let's go. Time's wasting."

Reese hurried into the front passenger seat, and I turned the key. When the engine roared to life under me, I met Pick's gaze in the rearview mirror.

He nodded in silent permission. "She'll go as fast as you tell her to."

So I put the pedal to the floor, and we screamed down the street in the direction of the nearest hospital.

Across the bucket seat from me, Lowe's woman was silent, chewing on her fingernails as Pick murmured something every once in a while from the back to the girl curled in the fetal ball on his lap.

"What is he on parole for?" Reese finally asked me a quiet voice.

I shrugged. "Beats the hell out of me."

She nodded and went back to biting her nails.

We made it to Ellamore General in record time. I pulled up to the emergency room entrance, and a couple orderlies came out with a wheelchair when they saw Pick drag a bloody Eva from the backseat. They swept her off, and the three of us left to wait loitered helplessly in the entrance.

Reese paced the floor, sending text after text on her phone, while Pick—his shirt and jeans a bloodstained mess—slumped in a chair and closed his eyes, his face pale and mouth drawn taut. I camped out against a nearby wall and crossed my arms over my chest.

And we waited.

CHAPTER THIRTY-TWO

"Whatever it is you're seeking won't come in the form you're expecting." - Haruki Murakami

~NOEL~

I OPENED THE DOOR OF my apartment, weary and defeated. The place was quiet and made me feel extra lonely.

Reese's cousin, Eva, had gone through an emergency C-section at the hospital, giving birth six weeks early to a four-pound, six-ounce baby girl. Mason had shown up only minutes before to report he and the baby daddy had made a deal: we wouldn't turn Alec in for what he'd done to Eva if he didn't turn Pick in for what Pick had done to him.

Apparently, that had worked for Alec, because Lowe said he was on his way back to Florida.

When a nurse had come out to tell Reese she could go back and see the new momma or the new baby through the window in the incubator where they'd put her, I decided it was time for me to head home. Since Pick didn't seem willing to budge from the hospital, I made the trip on foot.

Walking helped clear my head. Hell, the entire night had cleared my head. When a catastrophe like this happened, it made a person realize what was truly important. Opening my phone, I sent another quote off to Aspen. It was one I'd had for a while, but had been saving for the right moment. Well, that moment might never come if I didn't make it happen.

After I pushed *Send*, I blew out a breath and collapsed on the couch. I wanted to call and leave a voice message, just to tell her all the crazy shit that had happened tonight. I needed someone to share my day with. But I decided to wait until I could see her again. So I started to dial home and check in on Caroline, Colton, and Brandt. But I stopped myself. It was late, even in their time zone; I didn't want to wake them for no reason.

Lying there, I stared up at the water-stained ceiling of my broken-down apartment, wondering what the hell I was doing. My family was hundreds of miles away. The woman I loved was God knew where. I felt scattered. And trapped. My goals for a college diploma and an NFL draft no longer seemed relevant. But I couldn't leave. Not unless I wanted to destroy Aspen's reputation.

Scrubbing my hand over my face, I felt decades older than I was.

When the door open, a spark lurched through my chest, hoping it might be her. But it was only Ten.

He paused when he saw me. His gaze uncertain and leery. "'Sup?" he hedged. "Pick already leave?"

"Yep." I glanced at the ugly walls again. Someone seriously needed to paint this place. "How was work?"

"Fine." He remained wedged in the doorway, watching me cautiously. "Hey...I brought you something."

I lulled my face his way, wondering why he was acting so weird. But then he stepped into the room, leading someone else inside with him by the hand.

My gaze followed a feminine hand up a feminine arm, and hope sparked in my chest. But a mass of red hair killed it just as quickly as it had started.

Not Aspen.

"Hey, Noel," Marci said, sending me a shy smile as she continued to hold Ten's hand.

I rolled my eyes to my roommate, unimpressed, unmoved, and completely uninterested. "No thanks."

He growled. "Damn it. This has to stop. You're beginning to freak me out."

I narrowed my eyes. "Why don't you let me take care of myself? And hold the babysitters from here on out, too. A night out with Pick isn't exactly my speed."

"Well, maybe *I'd* be more your speed." Marci finally left Ten's side and strolled toward the couch, swinging her hips with a bit too much enthusiasm. She was wearing high heels, a short skirt, and low top.

I should've felt something. I was a guy. But I just sighed and rubbed my forehead. "No," I groaned. "No, no, no. I'm sorry I made you think I wanted something from you back in March. But I've changed my mind. I'm not interested anymore."

Jarring to a startled stop, Marci set her hands on her hips and scowled. "This isn't still about that ugly bitch teacher, is it?"

My mouth fell open. "Excuse me?"

"Oh...shit," Ten muttered from behind her. "You're the blackmailer, aren't you? I knew it was a chick, but...damn."

I was slow on the uptake because my brain didn't want to admit it. But if Marci had been the one to blackmail and then get Aspen fired, then it was because of me. It was my fault this had happened. I'd been the one to push Marci away and make her retaliate.

Deliberately, I sat up and pushed to my feet. "*You* got her fired?" Creeping around the coffee table, I started toward her.

Reading my face, Marci's eyes bugged. She skipped a step back and bumped into Ten. He grabbed her arm and shoved her toward the door. "Go," he commanded.

But she didn't move fast enough. I leapt, and the only thing that kept me from reaching a handful of pretty red hair and pulling it out by the roots was my roommate who jumped between us. She just gaped at me, her mouth fallen slack.

"You fucking spoiled brat." I pointed an accusing finger over Ten's shoulder. "If you weren't a girl, I'd mess you up right now. Got that? Don't you ever talk to me, or look at me, or think about me again. I want nothing to do with you."

"But..." Tears filled her eyes as she pressed a hand against her chest. "I protected you, Noel. I didn't give them a picture with your face in it. I didn't tell anyone it was *you*. I freed you from her."

"Like it fucking matters," I roared. "They goddamn know it's me, Marci. I *told* them it was me."

"You wha...*what*?" She frowned, still not getting it. "Why would you do that?"

"You hurt the woman I love," I told her, making it as clear as possible. "I will never forgive you for this."

I began to shake as she called me a bastard and ran from the apartment, bawling. I pushed away from Ten and ran my hands through my hair, tempted to chase Marci down so I could wrap my fingers around her neck and squeeze.

Behind me, Ten let out a breath. "Man, I swear to God. I didn't know—"

"Just shut up," I snapped. Then I cursed as my cell phone rang. Aspen *would* pick this moment to finally call me back, wouldn't she? Just when I'd learned exactly how much involvement I'd had in getting her thrown out of Ellamore. Just when I was feeling so shitty and guilty I wanted to curl into a ball and die.

But when I glanced at the screen and saw it was home, not her, I closed my eyes, not ready to take any more bad news from Caroline. But hell, whatever. It couldn't be worse than what I was already dealing with, so bring it.

"Hey," I answered, expecting my sister's voice.

Instead my middle brother, Brandt, sobbed in my ear, his voice shaking like crazy. "Noel. Something's wrong with Caroline. We need you."

***

The sun was beginning to rise over the horizon when we entered Bluebird Heights trailer park. I'd been driving for the past four hours while Ten had slumped passed out in the passenger's seat.

I owed him for this, big time. He didn't have to let me borrow his truck when I'd asked, and he certainly hadn't needed to volunteer to come along, but here he was. The annoying pain-in-my-ass roommate I'd had last week was gone, and this Oren Tenning seemed to be a completely improved edition.

Tapping his knee, I said, "Hey. We're here." Home, sweet trailer park, home.

He grumbled in his sleep before finally sitting up and rubbing his eyes. After stretching, he glanced out the window at the place where I'd grown up. "Shit, man. I had no idea."

I didn't answer, just parked and cut the engine. A torn dingy curtain had been sucked through a piece of cardboard covering one window. It fluttered in the breeze as if waving hello to us, while the scent of the nearby sewage plant had already seeped into the interior of the truck. I sat there a second, soaking in the feelings that always came with this place. The shame and anger and frustration of being Daisy Gamble's son.

With a soft curse under my breath, I opened my door and stepped out. Ten followed without a word. I almost wished he'd pop out with some dumbass sarcastic comment, but he said nothing.

There were no steps leading up to the front door, so I just turned the handle and vaulted inside. My brothers were camped out in the dim front room, Colt sleeping on the couch and Brandt on the floor. Though it seemed too early in the year for them, a swarm of fruit flies danced around the dirty dishes piled in the kitchen.

I nudged Brandt's leg with my shoe until he jerked awake and sat up.

He stared at me a moment before blinking and saying, "Noel?" When his voice cracked with emotion, I hauled him off the floor and into me for a bone-cracking hug. It took him a second, but he finally hugged me back, and when he did, he buried his face in my neck to let out one short sob. Jesus, but he'd gotten tall.

"How's Caroline?" I asked, pulling away to see he still had a bruise on his face, a fresh reddish purple one.

He shook his head. "She's bad. Real bad."

I reached out to touch his discolored jaw, but stopped myself at the last second. "Shouldn't that have healed by now?"

With a half shrug, he glanced away. "It's a new one."

New one. No one had told me he'd gotten beat up again. Hell, no one had told me much of anything in the last few weeks.

On the couch, Colton stirred. When he sat up, yawning and scratching his head, the holey blanket that had been covering him slipped down to reveal pale, boney arms. Shit, how much food did the kid eat? Looked like he only got fed once a week.

"Hey, kiddo," I greeted, my throat closing over, as I reached out to ruffle his grease-matted hair.

He'd been five when I'd moved away. So when he stared up at me with leery, untrusting sunken-in eyes, I realized I was akin to a stranger, his absent big brother who'd deserted him.

"Where is she?" I asked, turning to Brandt and unable to look at Colt without begging for his forgiveness.

Brandt pointed toward a narrow hall. "The bathroom, I bet. She's been in there all night."

I nodded and made my way to my little sister. The bathroom was dark, but the morning sunrise coming in through the window showed a human-sized lump on the floor, draped over the toilet seat. Reaching inside, I tried to flip on the light switch, but nothing happened.

"Light's broken," my sister's frail voice came from inside.

"Shit." I crouched down and scooped her into my arms. "Caroline?"

She slumped against me, so frail and limp I stopped short from pulling her in tight, afraid I might hurt her.

"I'm so glad you're here." Curling in close, she shivered and cuddled her face against my collar.

I kissed her hair and tried to keep it together, but fuck, my little sister. When I spotted dark splotches splashed around the rim of the toilet, I choked. "Is that...Jesus, is that blood?"

Made me think of Eva Mercer and the way she'd bled after getting punched in the stomach.

Caroline didn't even lift her face. "Probably."

"Oh, hell. Did you have a miscarriage?"

She wiped her nose with the back of her hand and sniffed. Wetness soaked through my shirt, telling me she was crying. "No. I...I...Sander's parents offered me money to get rid of it...so...I did." The last three words were whispered and clogged with tears.

The breath whooshed from my lungs. "You...I..." I shook my head, not sure what to say. My fingers trembled as I brushed the hair out of her face and kissed her temple. "Is this what you wanted?"

"I don't know," she croaked.

Squeezing my eyes closed, I ground my teeth together. "Fuck, Caroline. If you'd wanted to keep the baby, I would've helped you. You realize that, right? I know I lost it when I found out, but I was mad, and disappointed, and scared shitless."

"Well, what do you think *I* was?" She pushed back to glare up at me. "I was scared too, Noel. And you weren't here. What was I supposed to do?" Burying her face into her hands, she wept openly, her shoulders trembling from the force of her sobs.

Fisting my hand against my mouth, I watched her fall apart. This was my fault. I'd failed my family. I'd failed Aspen.

I'd failed, period.

"I'm sorry," Crawling the few feet she'd scooted away from me, I pulled her back into my arms. But she remained stiff, and it broke me. I buried my face in her hair. "I'm so sorry."

It took her a while to finally ease back against me, but when she did, I could finally suck in a relieved breath. I stroked her back as if that could somehow repay her for all the times I hadn't been here for her. With a gulp, I glanced over her shoulder, trying to pull myself back together, when I spotted more blood. Fuck, that was a lot of blood.

"Do we need to get you to a hospital?"

She shook her head. "No, I think...I think it's over now. They said I'd bleed. I just didn't expect so much." When her voice broke, I kissed her temple again.

"Does it still hurt?"

Her nod was all I needed to see. "Okay." I shifted

with her until she was sitting on my knees. Then I rose to my feet. "Let's get you somewhere comfortable, and we'll see about finding something for the pain."

I didn't even bother taking her to one of the two bedrooms. If the boys had been sleeping in the living rooms, I already knew I didn't want to go back there.

Ten met us at the end of the hall. "Hey, I'm—"

His words broke off abruptly when he saw Caroline.

She looked up at the new voice, and her eyes bugged. "Oh, my God!" Yelping, she clutched me hard and buried her face back into my chest. "Who is *he*?"

Snuggling my cheek against her hair in reassurance, I said, "That's just my roommate. Oren Tenning."

"Hey," Ten greeted, his voice hoarse. "How you doing?" When I saw the direction of his gaze, fixated on my little sister's bare legs, I scowled at him. Her oversized T-shirt didn't fall much past her thighs, giving him an eyeful.

Clearing my throat, I finally got him to tear his attention away from her. When he caught my death-glare, he spun away, putting his back to us. "Uh...the uh...I'm starving, so I was going to take the boys to the closest McDonalds for breakfast. Did you two want anything?"

"Yeah." I sighed. "Get us some biscuits and gravy, and breakfast burritos, and sandwiches, and shit like that. Let me put her on the couch, and I'll dig some money out of my wallet to pay."

"Don't worry about it." Ten turned to watch us as I passed him.

"I'm not hungry," Caroline protested.

"Well, you need to eat something and build your strength back up." I settled her down and sat next to her as I fussed with the blanket Colton had been sleeping under to cover her legs. "At least try, okay?"

After a reluctant nod, she glanced past me toward

my roommate. Standing awkwardly by the door with his hands shoved deep into his pockets, Ten peered back. But as soon as their gazes collided, they jerked their glances away. Blushing madly, Caroline rested her head on the pillow and rolled to bury her face in it.

I stood up, took a deep breath, and turned to my roommate. When I gave him a single nod, he rounded up my brothers, who were more than willing to go get something to eat, and left the trailer house.

***

As Brand and Colton sat on the couch, on either side of a pale Caroline, chowing down on all the food Ten had bought them, I stepped outside for a minute to catch some fresh air. My roommate followed me not long after.

He blew out a breath and rested his back against the metal walls of the trailer house as he set his hands on his hips. "What's that saying? *Karma*-sutra: fate fucking you in in all kinds of creative ways?"

I barked out a harsh laugh. "Yeah. Sounds about right."

Ten joined in with a short chuckle, but it didn't last long. Cursing under his breath, his ran his hand through his hair. "So, what happened in there was...shit, man. Is she going to be okay?"

"I don't know." Gazing at the rest of the homes in the trailer park, I sighed. They were all better maintained than ours.

"Where's your mom?"

I turned to Ten. "Good question."

He hissed out another curse and pushed away from the wall. "Well, this...this frankly sucks. No wonder you never told me about your home life. Or that your sister was fucking hot."

"Excuse me?" When I slid him a sharp glance, he lifted his hands as if surrendering.

"What? Whenever you mentioned her, I always pictured some five-year-old in pigtails carrying around a blankie and teddy bear. And...she's not five."

"She's not eighteen either," I growled. "So back off."

"Hey, I wasn't disrespecting. The walls in that place are thin as shit; I heard her tell you what she just went through. I'm just saying, I'm not blind."

"Well, you'd better turn blind around her."

"Fine, whatever." Ten lifted his hands once last time, telling me he was backing off. He let out a long, loud sigh and looked up at the sky. So did I. After a minute of neither of us speaking, he asked, "What're you going to do about this whole fucked-up mess?"

Kicking at a large rock embedded in the grass, I tried to quell all the rising emotions. But the more I thought about what I should do, the more I wanted to tear the trailer house apart with my bare hands. "You know, I always wondered how bad I'd let things here get before I had to give up on Ellamore and come back home. But shit, this is worse than I imagined. How could I let things get this bad?"

"But if you leave school now—"

"I know," I snapped, not needing the reminder. Pressing my hands to either side of my head to try to ease some of the pressure building inside, I closed my eyes. Except when I did, all I could picture were news reports with Aspen's face splashed all over the covers of newspapers and screens of televisions with the headline *Ellamore Sex Scandal Spreads from the Volleyball Team to Football.*

"I can't do that to Aspen," I moaned, shaking my head. "I just can't."

"Then what're you going to do?" Ten pressed. "Because you sure as fuck can't leave those three in there like that."

"*I know that.*" I glared at him and growled, flashing my teeth. "But what *can* I do?"

"Well, what do you *want* to do?"

"I *want* to go into that pathetic excuse of a house, scoop up my brothers and sister, and take them back to Ellamore with me. I want to protect *everyone* I love."

Ten flashed a sudden grin and dusted his hands off on his thighs. "Well, all right, then. Let's do it."

"What?" I blinked and gaped at him. "We can't do that. They don't...Their life is here. School. My mother...shit, I don't have any kind of custody. It'd be considered kidnapping if I—"

"If you got caught." He wiggled his eyebrows. "But I don't see your mom anywhere. Do you really think she'd contest it?"

A seed of hope sprouted inside me. It'd be rough...but so worth it.

Shaking my head, I frowned at my roommate for even suggesting the idea. "I can't bring three underage kids home with me." Caroline would turn eighteen in two weeks, but still. "Where the hell would we put them in our dinky, two-bedroom apartment?"

Glancing at the dinky, two-bedroom trailer house they were staying in now, he lifted his eyebrows and shot me a look. Okay, so he had a point. Even our shit-hole apartment was in a hell of a lot better condition than this dump.

"Look, my bed's bigger than yours. The boys can camp in my room, your sister can take yours, I'll get the couch, and you can bunk of the floor until we find someplace bigger to rent."

I just stared at him, unable to believe what I was hearing. "Are you serious?"

He made a face. "Fuck, yeah. I'm certainly not taking the floor."

With a short laugh, I shook my head. Only Ten could make me smile at a time like this. "I mean, about the whole thing? This is a big deal, Ten. This would fucking save my life, but it'd be a huge change.

For you too. Are you sure about them coming back with us?"

He shrugged as if it was nothing. "I mean, they're going to be squished in my half backseat on the ride there, but hell, why not?"

Squeezing my eyes shut, I covered my face with my hands as the relief nearly buckled my knees. "Thank you. Oh, fuck. Thank you so much, man. I'll never be able to repay you for this."

CHAPTER THIRTHY-THREE

"I wanted a perfect ending. Now I've learned, the hard way, that some poems don't rhyme, and some stories don't have a clear beginning, middle, and end." - Gilda Radner

~ASPEN~

I WAS HOLLOW. AN EMPTY SHELL.

Staring down at the graves of both of my parents, I wondered why I wasn't crying, why I hadn't shed one tear over their deaths.

Next to me, Rita sniffed into a tissue and dabbed her eyes. I reached out and patted her arm, trying to offer a measure of comfort, but how did I offer anything when I had nothing? Felt nothing?

The past few days had been a complete blur. After "resigning" from my position at Ellamore, I'd gone home and packed a bag, ready to leave town for a few days to, I don't know, find myself. Recalibrate my life. Make plans for the future.

Hide from Noel.

But my housekeeper had called when I was stuffing a handful of jeans into my luggage. And now my biggest fear had come true. My parents had died before telling me they loved me or even showing they cared. I knew I should've felt destroyed, lost, alone, hopeless. But no. Nothing. There was just a big, blank void, a vacancy where they'd never filled my heart.

I'd been braced to hear about my father. In the hospital with pneumonia, losing his leg to diabetes, I knew this fate was most likely coming for him. But that wasn't how he'd died at all.

Mother had actually been driving him home from the hospital when they'd had a head-on collision on the freeway. Both dead. Instantly.

Shocked much? Oh, yeah. I was definitely in a state of utter shock. Maybe that's why I was so numb. Or maybe I was just a heartless shrew. Maybe Mallory and Richard Kavanagh had rubbed off and I could never feel anything again.

But then I thought of Noel, and I knew that wasn't true. Because just from drawing forth his face in my mind, I was no longer numb. I was aching and broken.

My parents might not have ever shown me love, but I did know love now. I knew how it felt to find someone worth living for, to risk everything for that love, and to sacrifice everything for it. It was beautiful and amazing. So I no longer craved it from the two bodies lying in this cold, hard ground. They could take their brand of love with them, wherever they went.

I tossed a rose into each open grave and turned away, ready to be finished with this. Only a dozen other people were present at the cemetery. I recognized colleagues of Richard's and Mallory's—Zach's father stood near the back—but that was it. No friends, no other family. Just work ties.

A rustling came behind me, and I knew Rita was

hurrying to catch up with me. I slowed enough for her to reach my side, then I hooked my arm through hers, and we made our way to the black ride awaiting us.

"Am I an awful person, Rita?" I wondered aloud.

Warm fingers surrounded mine and squeezed hard. "Why would you think such a thing, child?"

"They raised me," I said. "They kept me healthy and clothed me, put a house over my head. They paid for my education and helped me get a good start on life. I wouldn't have anything if it weren't for them. So shouldn't I owe them more than this? Shouldn't I...mourn?"

"Oh, honey. You're just in shock. Denial is a very real stage in grieving."

I shook my head. "No. No. I know they're gone. I know..." I would never see them again. Stopping twenty feet from the car while it was still just the two of us, I turned to her. "I'm relieved," I finally confessed. "I spent my entire life, worried about disappointing them, striving to gain their love. And now...now I'm free. I lost my job this week, and my biggest fear was how I was going to tell them. But I don't have to worry about that now. I never have to worry about winning their approval again."

Rita clucked her tongue and pulled me in for a hug. "This is my fault. I should've nurtured you more. I never should've let them intimidate me into keeping my distance. You were always such a good obedient girl, and all you ever needed was a hug, just a little compassion."

"No. You did fine. I understood why you couldn't do much. And I'll always remember the times you did do something."

Grasping my shoulders, Rita stared up at me from pale, watery eyes. "They never treated you right. I don't know how you turned out as well as you did."

Finally, I had to blink back some emotion. This was my true mother, right here. And she'd just given me all the parental approval I'd ever needed. "Thank you, Rita."

After we returned to the house, my parents' lawyer came to read the will. Rita was left a thousand dollars for every year of service she'd worked for them, and then they'd left the rest of their financial worth to the university where they'd both worked.

As those words were read aloud, the cold inside me only grew deeper. Rita gasped and covered her mouth. "No," she breathed, turning to me with guilt in her eyes. "But...but what about Aspen?"

The lawyer winced. "I asked them about her when they had these drawn up. But they said they'd already given her all the tools she needed to survive. Their money was of no consequence to her."

I wasn't even that surprised. Still hollow, I merely lifted my chin and answered, "They were right. I don't need their money." It didn't even matter that I'd been planning to ask them for a loan until I found a new job. They really had given me all the tools I needed to survive. I could do this. Somehow.

***

It only took me a few days to see to my parents' affairs. As neat and tidy as they'd always been, they still needed someone to put all their wishes into action, so everything fell to me. I spent another day with their lawyer, making sure Rita was set, and all Richard and Mallory's things could be sold to auction. Then I made sure a fund was arranged with the university where their money could go.

I stopped by their graves one last time before leaving town to say a final goodbye and attain my closure. A weight lifted from my chest as I climbed back into my car. It was so strange. I'd hit my rock bottom. I'd lost the love of my life, my job, *and* my parents. I had basically no prospects for the future, and the money in my savings account would probably only last me a month or two.

But I didn't feel as if this was it, as if everything was over. Maybe I really was in denial. Except a seed of hope had sprouted in the voided place in my heart. It grew and budded, and I couldn't stop this feeling that a new start was awakening inside me.

My cell phone rang as I reached the city limits, making my bud of hope blossom into a flower. It'd been a few days since Noel had stopped calling and started leaving messages. He still texted every morning, providing me with quotes for my collection. Yesterday's had been my favorite yet:

"When someone loves you, the way they say your name is different. You know that your name is safe in their mouth." - Jess C. Scott, *The Intern*

But aside from those texts, he'd stopped begging me to call him back, or forgive him, or come home. He'd stopped apologizing for the loss of my job. He'd stopped fighting fiercely for me. Then again, I hadn't responded to any of his attempts, so he really didn't have a reason to think there was something left to fight for, except I still loved him. I'd always love him.

My heart jerked in my chest as I scrambled for my phone in my purse in the passenger seat. Maybe Noel hadn't quite given up after all.

The ID on the screen showed my old advisor and mentor, though. Shoulders slumping, I answered politely.

Dr. Thorn extended her condolences over my parents' death. After I excused her apologies for not making it to the funeral, she finally found her way to the meat of her call.

"I know you're probably getting along just fine over at Ellamore," she said, making me cringe because I didn't want to confess I was no longer employed there. "But we had a faculty member in the English department here decide to retire at the end of the semester, and you were the first person I thought to replace him with. You were always so enthusiastic about the curriculum, and you have the youth and vivacity I want here. So do you think it's possible you would consider returning to us...as a professor?"

***

It was late when I made it back to Ellamore. I'd driven straight through and should've been exhausted. But while my body just wanted to rest, everything else inside me perked to attention, exulted over the fact that Noel was close. I could have waited until morning, but I didn't. I had to see him now. I parked in front of his apartment building and hurried through the dark to the front entrance where a broken overhead light dangled limply above the front door.

I balled my hand and raised it to his door, but decided I didn't want to wake his roommate, so I took my phone from my purse to call, when I changed my mind again. I'd much rather wake him a different way.

I tried the lock and found it open. Tiptoeing through to the dark hallway, I reached his bedroom and turned the knob, pushing my way inside. The lamp by his bed glowed softly and the sheets rustled as I entered. I wondered if he was already awake, waiting for me, sensing I was coming. But when I lifted my eyes to the bed, I found a girl gasping and sitting up on his mattress instead.

Holding her blankets up to her chin, she gaped at me from a pair of wide, water-stained eyes.

I froze as the air was pummeled from my chest. She was beautiful with long, streaming blonde hair and stunning features. It hurt to look at her.

Acid filled my stomach, and I thought I might be sick all over the floor. Tears filled the ducts in my eyes.

But he'd moved on. I was too late. He—

"Are you looking for Noel?" she asked before sniffing and wiping at her cheek. "I think...I think he's in the living room, either sleeping on the floor or the couch. I'm not sure which."

She seemed friendly. I couldn't believe this girl— whom I didn't know but hated more than everyone else on earth—would dare be friendly to me, as if she wasn't crushing my soul into a thousand pieces. It took me a good five seconds to actually process what she'd just said.

Noel was sleeping in the living room. Not in here. Not with her.

The confusion must've painted my expression pretty obvious because she said, "You're Aspen, right? I've heard about you. I'm Noel's sister."

"Caroline?" I breathed. *Oh, Jesus. Oh, thank you, God.* "I...oh! Well, I've heard about you, too."

The relief left me dizzy and I had to reach for the doorframe and hold on to catch myself. And once again, my own overwhelming emotions kept me clueless from a few oblivious details for far too many seconds, otherwise it might not have taken me so long to realize Noel's sister was crying...and here. Why was she *here*, and where were the two brothers?

"Are you okay?" I asked, stepping forward, concern for her overriding everything else.

"Yeah." She nodded and hugged herself, dropping the sheet to reveal she was wearing one of Noel's Ellamore Viking shirts. "I...I...no. No, I'm not okay. I don't think I'll ever be okay again."

When she buried her face into her hands and dropped all pretenses of not bawling her eyes out, my heart broke for her. I crawled onto the mattress and pulled her into my embrace. As natural as breathing, she rested her head on my shoulder and accepted my solace. The smell of Noel on the sheets comforted me as I comforted his sister.

"Is it the baby?" I finally asked, smoothing her hair out of her face.

Her body shuddered as she cuddled closer to me. "There is no baby." The hollow echo in her voice told me that was exactly what the problem was. Instead of asking what had happened, I said, "How'd you get here?"

"Noel came and got me."

I nodded and continued to comb my fingers through her hair. I have no idea where this nurturing side of me came from, but this girl was a part of Noel, and she was hurting. I had to fix her. "Where are your younger brothers?"

"They're sleeping in Oren's room." Finally, she lifted her face and blinked at me. "Does anything hurt worse than getting your heart broken?"

"I..." The diplomatic answer caught in my throat and wouldn't come. So I went with honesty. "No, not in my experience."

She opened her mouth to say something else, but footsteps in the hall jerked both our attentions to the doorway.

"Caroline?" Noel's hushed voice woke every fiber of life inside me, making my muscles tense with anticipation. "Are you okay? I heard voices—" He entered the room and took a full step before seeing me. Jerking to a stop, he stared. And stared some more before rasping, "Aspen?"

I didn't know what to say. I suddenly felt lame and insecure. When the word, "Hi," fell from my lips in a tiny, uncertain voice, I internally winced.

"Hi," he breathed, glancing back and forth between Caroline and me. His voice was flat when he added, "You're back."

I nodded, worried it had been a mistake to come here like this. "I...I came to talk to you, but..." I motioned to Caroline. "I met your sister instead."

He turned his attention to his sister, and she scurried off the bed. "I'll just..." She hooked her thumb toward the door. "I'll let you two talk."

"No." Noel held up a hand. "You stay. We can go. You need your rest." Tipping his face to the side, he finally seemed to notice her wet eyes. "You okay?"

She nodded and tried to wipe the evidence off her face. "Yeah. Better. With a little help from Aspen."

When she glanced at me, I sent her a supportive smile. She started back toward the bed, so I took that as my cue to climb off it. But as we traded places, she gave me one last impulsive hug.

"Thank you," she whispered into my ear.

I nodded, gave her a farewell smile, and turned toward Noel. He stared at me, his eyes swirling with emotion but his expression hard. Then he spun away and stalked from the room. I followed him, down the hall and to the front door. He didn't slow down or hold out his hand for me, and that hurt. But I really couldn't expect less, could I?

Once we were outside the apartment, the dim lights from the exterior halls showed how stiff and uncompromising his shoulders were.

He kept walking, so I kept following down the stairwell. Hurrying to keep up, I finally called, "You didn't tell me Caroline had lost her baby in any of your messages."

Jerking to a stop, he whirled around. We'd just reached the landing between floors, where the stairs turned. He grasped my arm and urged me toward the wall until cool brick met my spine.

Stepping in close enough for me to feel his heat and smell mint on his breath, he growled, "Well, you didn't tell me you were leaving town. You didn't tell me Marci Bennett had blackmailed you. And you sure as hell didn't tell me you'd lost your fucking job...because of me. Christ, Aspen." He cupped my face and pressed his forehead to mine. "You didn't tell me shit."

He was so mad he shook with it. I felt every tremor move through him so acutely I might as well have been shaking too.

"Damn it," he muttered when I didn't respond. "Why didn't you *tell* me?"

I closed my eyes. "Because I didn't want you to do anything stupid."

He snorted. "Too late."

"Oh, God. *Noel.*" Shoving against him, I gasped. "I *lied* for you. I refused to tell them who you were, to *protect* you. Why would you...wait. What exactly did you do?"

Looming above me, he fisted his hand on his hips and scowled right back. "I told them it was me in that picture. What do you think I did?"

"No." Denying it, I shook my head adamantly. Fear raced along my skin, prickling my scalp. But if Noel had gotten hurt from this, after everything I'd sacrificed to keep him safe, I...I didn't know what I'd do. I'd probably lose all faith in the world. "Did they...did they kick you out?"

Shame entered his eyes. Bowing his head slightly, he glanced away and ran his hand over his hair. "No," he admitted in a low voice.

Air hissed from my teeth. "Oh, thank God."

"They wouldn't let me leave," he added on a frustrated sneer.

"Wouldn't *let* you? What did you—please don't tell me you *tried*. God, Noel. You *need* this scholarship."

He stepped toward me. "You know what? I'm tired of everyone telling me what I need lately." Setting his fists against the wall at either side of my head, he leaned in until our faces were inches apart. "What I need is *you*. No one gets me like you do. No one loves me like you do. You are everything. And when you went down because of me, a part of me died.

I feel fucking broken because I couldn't leave that damn place with you. I tried. I tried so hard to get them to bring you back. And when I threatened to leave, they threatened too. And now, if I go, they'll make this whole thing public and drag your name through the mud. You'd never get to teach again, *anywhere*. So, here I am, stuck, unable to do a single fucking thing, while you take all the heat for—"

"Shh." I touched his face and stroked his cheek, offering him a wet smile. "It's okay."

"No." He gritted his teeth, snarling at me, and he mashed his forehead more firmly to mine. "It's not fucking okay. What they did to you was *not* okay. They made what we had lurid, and dirty, and wrong. And it wasn't. It just...wasn't. I swear to God, you're the only thing that's ever been right in my life."

I leaned up onto my toes and smashed my mouth to his. He kissed me back savagely, grabbing my hair hard, and bruising my lips with his. I think he was trying to punish me, but it felt too good to be any kind of punishment. I ground back just as fiercely, needing to feel him and taste him and—

He ripped his mouth from mine and wrenched himself away, squeezing his lips together as if they'd betrayed him. Glaring, he said, "Don't ever do that again. If we were caught, we were supposed to go down together."

I shook my head. "I don't recall ever making that deal."

"Damn it." He came in close again, sinking his hands into my hair and cupping my head in his palms. "I could do *nothing*, Aspen. Do you even *understand* what that did to me? My hands are still tied, and I can't do anything for you, while you can just blithely sacrifice your entire life for *me*? That's not right. It's not fair. Why didn't you tell me what was going to happen? Some kind of warning—"

"I wanted to do this for you, Noel." Laying my

palm on his cheek, I let out a content sigh. It didn't matter what kind of turmoil was going on around us, right here in his arms, I felt home.

"But why didn't you tell me? And then after, why'd you leave without a word? Why didn't you answer even one fucking text?"

"Contact with you after this might've alerted the university that it was your arm in the picture. I didn't want that. Plus I thought we could use a little time apart, to clear our heads and look at everything from a fresh perspective." When his eyes narrowed and he opened his mouth, I rushed to add, "And I was a coward. If I'd gotten in touch with you, I knew I would've been tempted to come back."

"But you did come back."

My smile was tremulous. "I guess your power of temptation was stronger than I thought. I just can't stay away."

A sob ripped from his throat. He wrapped his arms around me and pulled us flush together. This kiss was softer but just as greedy. "Is this it, then?" he asked, nipping at my jaw. "There's nothing keeping us apart, so we can finally be together? Openly and permanently?"

I bit my lip, and he felt my hesitation. Lifting his head, he gazed at me. "Shit," he whispered. "I really don't like that look in your eyes."

"I was offered a job," I told him, "to teach at my university back home. Eight hundred miles away."

The breath rushed from his lungs as he stared. Then he dropped his hands from my face and slowly backed away. "So, you're leaving. And I can't follow. Jesus Christ." Gripping his head, he spun away from me. "How many times do you plan on breaking my heart?"

"No more, I hope." Hugging my waist, I took a deep breath and took the biggest leap of my life. "Because I turned the job down."

He whirled back, his gaze zipping to me. "You what?"

"I'm not going anywhere."

"*What?* Are you crazy?" He came back, gripping my arms. "You can't turn this down, Aspen. What if you can't find a teaching job nearby?"

I shrugged. "Then I won't teach. I'll do something else."

"But you love to teach."

This time, I nodded. "Yes, I do."

With a growl, he pressed even closer. "Do I have to throttle you, woman? You are *not* sacrificing anything else for me."

I just smiled. "Well, I'm not leaving you either. I may love to teach, but I love *you* more. Noel Gamble, my home is wherever you are, so I'm staying here."

He whimpered, and his hands on me began to tremble. "You should go." His voice was strained, but he kept urging, "I know you want the job, I can tell. You should take it."

"I do want it," I admitted. "But I don't care. Like I said, I want you more."

Shaking his head, he just kept staring at me. "You say that now. But...in a few years, when you're trapped here because of me, you'll resent me and everything I kept you from. I need you to follow your dreams, Aspen."

"I am following my dream, Noel. Trust me. All I've ever wanted is to be loved."

"God help me." He shuddered and I watched some of his resistance crack. "I do love you. I've never loved anyone the way I love you, but—"

"But that's all I need," I reassured him. Touching his face lightly, I repeated, "Believe me, I can get a job anywhere. It doesn't have to be at the university or even community college level. I just like trying to fill people with the same appreciation of literature that I have. I will find work wherever I am. But I won't find another you. I don't want to leave you."

He folded. His shoulders fell and his body slumped into mine as his lips caught my temple. "I don't want you to leave either."

"Then it's settled. We're all staying."

Noel kissed me again. "I love you. I love you so much. I don't know how I could ever prove to you how much I love you."

He'd already proven it. No one had ever loved me the way he did. With every word and gesture, he showed me his feelings, and I relished each and every moment with him. He'd taught me what it was to love and be loved. He'd unleashed my inner child and helped me live in the moment. But he'd also given me a future to look forward to. It might be uncertain, but I couldn't wait to start it. With him.

I knew he'd tell me about what had happened with his siblings while I was away, just as I'd tell him about my parents. We had a lot to discuss, but I had a feeling we'd have plenty of time to talk about all that.

Later.

For now, I was too excited to know we'd actually have a later. So, I kissed him back and relished the present.

*E*PILOGUE

"Don't cry because it's over, smile because it happened." - Dr. Seuss

~*A*SPEN~

"WE START ON *To Kill a Mockingbird* on Monday, which happens to be one of my favorite books, so if anyone wants to impress me, just do well on the essays for this story. Got it?"

When half the class groaned, I shook my head and grinned. There would always be the naysayers, but I usually found one or two people who loved literature as much as I did. And that's why I kept teaching, and why I kept coming back each day, excited to share my appreciation with them. I relished reaching students like the girl in the back corner who sat in a wheelchair as she eagerly listened to all my thoughts about the last story we'd just read.

I opened my mouth to tell my sophomore class how I sensed they weren't as enthusiastic to start the story as I was, but the bell rang, interrupting me. I still jumped every time that happened. It was one of the few things I missed about teaching at the college level. But other than that, I was extremely content here.

"Have a good weekend," I called above the blare of my students gathering their things and making plans with their friends.

For once, I was glad they were eager to leave, because so was I. This was my last class for the day, and I was anxious to check in with Noel to see how his day had gone.

I started sweeping up everything I wanted to take home with me when I saw someone approaching my desk from the corner of my eye.

Setting his hands on his hips and scowling from a familiar pair of periwinkle blue eyes, he hissed, "I can't believe you just gave me a C on that paper. What the hell, Aspen?"

I sighed. "Brandt—"

"I mean, I know you said you weren't going to show favoritism if I took your class, but really? A *C*? I actually *tried* to do a good job."

I knew I shouldn't because he was genuinely upset, but I smiled fondly at the memory this conversation brought. "And yet you completely missed the point of the assignment," I had to tell him.

He opened his mouth to zing something back at me. He was too much like his brother not to fight back. But a pair of passing girls caught both of our attention as they giggled.

"Oh, my God, did you see the new Econ teacher? He is *so* hot."

Brandt groaned as the other girl crowded in close to her friend and grasped her arm. "I know. I wonder what his name is, 'cause I want to enroll in *that* class."

"Hell, yeah. I heard he's the new football coach, too."

"He is," Brandt finally spoke up, startling them into breaking up their gossip session. When they lifted their faces and found Brandt Gamble speaking to them, they halted in their tracks and gaped openly.

I'd heard one girl last week call my brother-in-law the sophomore dreamboat, so I guess the girls must've been frozen with awe to find themselves under the dreamboat's attention.

He sent them a knowing smirk. "And his name's Gamble." He gave a dramatic pause, waiting for it to kick in and the girls to gasp with realization before he added, "he's my brother."

Their gazes immediately zipped my way. Everyone at East Ellamore High knew my relationship to Brandt. Faces flushed scarlet, the girls started gushing in unison.

"I'm so sorry, Mrs. Gamble," they started together, speaking over each other. "We didn't mean any disrespect."

I shook my head and waved them silent. "Don't worry about it. I can't help but agree with you." I winked. "He is pretty hot."

As Brandt snorted, the girls laughed out their relief and hurried for the exit, only to nearly collide with the topic of our conversation as he appeared on the doorway.

"Sorry about that, ladies." He stepped aside gracefully and swept out a hand for them to pass through first. They giggled and chorused, "Hi, Mr. Gamble," as they fled.

Brandt and I shared a look, and rolled our eyes in unison.

"I don't think I've ever been called Mr. Gamble by so many people in one day before. It kind of skeeves me out," Noel admitted, oblivious to everything that had just happened.

He reached out and ruffled Brandt's hair as he passed his brother. But his eyes were focused on me.

"Hi." His voice lowered to a husky pitch as he leaned in for a kiss.

"Hi." My toes curled in my flats as his lips lingered on mine. I reached up and clutched the tie he wore, amazed by how permissible it was to kiss him so openly inside a school building. But a lot had changed in the three years we'd been together. As he pulled back, slicking his tongue over his bottom lip as if to relish the lingering taste of me on him, something fluttered deep in my belly.

I was the luckiest woman on earth to be married to this man.

"Noel," Brandt's sharp voice cut into our moment. "Aspen gave me a freaking C on my paper."

Instead of scowling at me in irritation, my husband chuckled. He winked at me before telling his brother, "Well, she gave me two D's, so I don't feel sorry for you."

From the back of the room, what sounded like a pile of books clattered to the floor. The three of us turned to find one student struggling to make her way from the class. As one of the spokes on her wheelchair caught on a desk she was passing, it managed to jerk the pile of books right off her lap.

Noel and I moved to help her, but my sixteen-year-old brother-in-law leapt in front of us.

"Here. Let me get those for you, Sarah." He bent and scooped them up in one graceful swoop.

Sarah pulled back in surprise and ogled him a moment before she ducked her face, letting her dark hair spill forward and cover her scorching red cheeks.

"Thank you," she said in her shy, low voice. She reached out her arms to retrieve her things, her fingers quivering slightly as she did.

But Brandt tucked them under his arm instead of handing them back. "I've got them. You headed to your locker?"

Her head snapped up, eyes wide. "I..." When her

mouth opened and a few garbled sounds came out, she snapped her teeth together and blushed even harder. "Yes," she finally answered.

Brandt sent her a friendly grin. "I'll walk with you. My locker's only a couple down from yours. Oh, here." He quickly reached out and shoved aside the desk that had tripped up her wheelchair, giving her more than plenty of room to pass.

Face lighting up, Sarah beamed at him as she rolled through, once again thanking him for his consideration.

"So how'd you do on your paper?" He continued to smile down at her. Sarah's answer was muffled as they moved into the hall together.

Noel and I shared a glance. His eyebrows lifted. "Is it just me, or did it look like Mason Lowe's little sister has a crush on my brother?"

I laughed. "Well, half the girls in school have a crush on him, so I'd say it's highly possible."

He groaned. "Really? He's *popular* here? That's so not fair." His scowl was adorable.

I leaned up to give him a quick kiss. "He fits in very nicely."

Noel sighed as if disgusted. "I guess it's better than him almost getting jumped into a gang like he'd been at that other place that shall not be named."

All of his siblings had adjusted nicely to Ellamore. They hadn't even seemed upset when their mother had granted Noel guardianship of them without a single protest. Caroline, Colton and Brandt had frankly bloomed under Noel's care, even though it'd taken Colton a good year to warm up to us.

"So how was your first day of teaching, Mr. Gamble?"

I'd been stressed all day that he would regret taking the teaching position here. After he'd broken his collarbone his senior year of college during a football game and lost his chance to play for the NFL,

I'd worried he'd eventually grow to hate the new life he'd had to make. And he'd come to resent me for urging him into changing his major to teaching and coaching.

"It was kind of exhilarating, actually," he said. "When I noticed people paying attention to me when I talked, I almost felt as if I might be able to make a difference in some kid's life."

I could've told him he'd already made a difference in three very important kids' lives. But he looked awed by the realization he'd just reached.

"I'm anxious to start football practice and see what sort of team I'm going to have this season."

Which reminded me of the time. "Doesn't that start in three minutes?" I arched my eyebrow, silently asking him what he was doing in my classroom.

His blue eyes turned smoky. "Yes, it does. But knowing you were in here was too much temptation to resist. Seeing you in your 'professor suits' always reminds me of the days we first met." He ran his fingers lovingly down the lapel of my blazer.

"But now we don't have to hide anything."

"Yeah." He leaned in to kiss me again. "And it still feels too good to be true. I keep expecting someone to blow in here and tell us we can't be together." His arms wrapped possessively around my waist. "This time with you has been the best time of my life. I can't thank you enough for coming back to me, for being my wife."

I rested my head on his heartbeat. "You've given me the best three years of my life too." I patted his abs of steel and kissed his chin. "Now you better get going, Coach, before they decide to replace you on your first day."

"I'll see you at home. Love you, babe." He kissed me again before stepping back. I immediately missed his arms around me.

"I love you too. Don't give Brandt too hard of a

time during practice."

Noel just grinned. "Oh, if he thinks you didn't show him any family favoritism, just wait until he finds out how hard I'm going to ride his ass on the field."

He wiggled his eyebrows and blew me one last kiss before backing from the room.

I let out a pleased sigh and sank into my desk chair. When I'd started working at Ellamore University that fateful semester, I'd had no clue my life would end up here. But I'm thrilled it had. Who knew I'd be insanely happy working at a high school while I was married to the football coach? Or that helping him raise his two younger brothers and sister, a junior in college now, would make me feel so complete? But here I was, more content than I'd ever been, and I wouldn't change my life for anything in the world. All I'd ever wanted was to find love and be loved in return. But this had gone above and beyond. I was completely fulfilled.

***

"What really knocks me out is a book that, when you're all done reading it, you wish the author that wrote it was a terrific friend of yours and you could call him up on the phone whenever you felt like it." - J.D. Salinger, *The Catcher in the Rye.*

~*The End*~

COMING NEXT

PICK & EVA

IN

*A*CKNOWLEDGMENTS

Starting off with my family, thanks a bundle to Kurt and Lydia who have to put up with me day in and day out! I don't know how you guys do it, but I'm so grateful you do! Love you both.

The next acknowledgements goes to Lindsay Brooks. You'll never know how much your friendship and support means to me. Not only do you listen to me rant and rave, but you actually read my stories too! I'm beginning to think of you as my twin on the other side of the world!

On to my beta readers who were willing to look through my story at its very worst and help me iron out the biggest problems. This thank you is for Sandra and Alaina Martinie, Andrea Reed, Ashley Morrison from Book Labyrinth, my awesome author friend Ada Frost, Ami from Romance Readaholic, and Michelle & Pepper from All Romance Reviews.

Stephanie Parent, who agreed to be my editor this time around, deserves a hearty applause for catching so many mistakes! And yet another standing ovation goes to Brynna Curry from Sizzling PR for proofreading!

Some more casual proofreaders I'd like to thank are: Mary Crawford. And then Cindy Alexander, Jamie Hixon, Sandra Martinie, Laina Martinie, Shi Ann Crumpacker, and Katie Cap. Thanks, guys. Best family ever.

And who could forget Lisa Filipe of Tasty Book Tours? Even with a second baby on the way, she fit in the time to set up a cover reveal and book tour for me.

But the grand finale of all thank yous goes to the Good Lord who's given me way more blessings than I deserve.

Thank you, all!

ABOUT THE AUTHOR

Linda grew up on a dairy farm in the Midwest as the youngest of eight children. Now she lives in Kansas with her husband, daughter, and their nine cuckoo clocks. Her life's been blessed with lots of people to learn from and love. Writing's always been a major part her world, and she's so happy to finally share some of her stories with other romance lovers. Please visit her at her website

http://www.lindakage.com

Made in the USA
Las Vegas, NV
30 July 2021